# MURDER ON THE MEDWAY

AMY ROWLINGS: BOOK 4

T. A. BELSHAW

For Holly
Thank you for your support
Best Wishes

SPELLBOUND BOOKS

05/24

First Published by in 2024 by SpellBound Books

*Paul Lautman.*
*Who has an incredible eye for detail.*
*Thank you.*

# CHAPTER ONE

The bubbling, frothing stream glinted silver as it gurgled between the smooth line of stones that ran across the width of the narrow brook. Shallow at this point, the swift running, refreshingly cold water ran the full length of Russell Park before joining the driving currents of the Medway River.

'Silverstream. Isn't that the perfect name for our little brook?' Amy Rowlings said as she watched a family of moorhens paddling downstream. 'It's such a gentle stream now, but years ago, it was a lot deeper and had a lot more of a current. The town's three mill owners-built weirs to allow them to turn the waterwheels that powered the factories, so nowadays it's a mere shadow of its former self. Have you ever been behind the factory I work at? You can still see how they used to power the machinery before the steam engines took over during the industrial revolution.'

Amy lay on her back as she tried to pick out shapes in the few fluffy clouds that meandered overhead. At five o'clock on a Sunday afternoon in the last week of July, it was still hot, perfect weather for the start of the annual factory fortnight holiday. Behind her, down the sharp grassy slope, the shadows of the line of trees were just beginning to lengthen. Amy brushed away a few strands of flaxen hair from her face, then stretched her arms above her head and let out a long sigh.

'I wish we could just lie here for the rest of the summer, Bodkin.'

Inspector Bodkin, of the Spinton police force, grinned as he leaned onto one elbow to look down at her.

'It's all right for those who are on holiday, I suppose. The rest of us are cooped up in offices or driving around in cars that feel like ovens for most of the day.'

Amy smiled as she looked across at him. Shielding her eyes from the sun with one hand, she blew him a kiss.

'It's very nice of you to sneak away from work for a couple of hours. I hope Terry the Tea Leaf or Danny the Dip aren't having a field day while you're skiving here with me.'

'I locked them both up before I came out, so I think the town will be safe until I get back to the station,' Bodkin said with a grin.

'My hero,' Amy replied as she sat up. She turned her face towards the policeman and felt her heart flutter as she took him in. Bodkin was in his late twenties and was handsome in a rugged sort of way. His hair was thick, dark and in need of a good cut. He had two days' worth of stubble on his chin and the bags under his brown eyes told her he hadn't been sleeping well, or at least for long enough. He was wearing a creased, white shirt with a badly starched collar. A pair of wide, striped braces held up baggy, blue trousers that bunched around his ankles, even though he was sitting with his knees raised.

'Bodkin, you really must do something about those trousers,' she said.

'I like them. They're comfortable.'

'My dressing gown is comfortable but I wouldn't go out in public in it,' Amy replied. She sighed again. 'I think it's time we paid another visit to Stan's Emporium. They might have a pair of trousers that actually fit you.'

'I could do with a new suit, I suppose. This one has been ironed one time too many.'

'It hasn't seen enough of the iron. That's the problem,' Amy replied. 'And you could do with at least three inches cutting off the bottom of the legs. I altered your other pair for you. I could have a go at these if you like?'

Amy was a machinist at a local clothing factory nicknamed the Mill, because a hundred years earlier it had been a cotton works, serviced by a huge water wheel.

Bodkin shook his head. 'No, it's all right, thanks, Amy. It's time I got a new suit, or at least a decent second-hand one. These trousers are getting a bit thin in places. I noticed just this morning that I could see my—'

Amy pulled a face and held up her hand to silence the policeman. 'Please don't go into too much detail, Bodkin. I haven't had my tea yet.'

'I was about to say, I could see my hand through the seat when I held it up to the light.'

'Let's go on Saturday,' Amy said. 'We'll find you something nice.'

'As long as it's blue,' Bodkin replied shuffling towards her on his backside.

'You're so predictable,' Amy said as he slipped his arm around her and pulled her towards him.

'People know where they are with predictable policeman,' Bodkin replied. 'They can predict that I'm going to nick them if they step out of line.' He lifted her chin with his fingers and kissed her softly on the lips before pulling away to look into her eyes. 'You're so beautiful,' he added before kissing her again, this time longer and harder.

Amy responded by putting her arms around his neck. She felt his hand rest on her hip before he ran it up and down the side of her ribcage. He pulled his mouth away, then, while making a short rasping noise in his throat, he kissed her again, fiercely this time. His hand moved up from her side and rested on the side of her chest. Shifting his position a little, he slowly moved it across until he was cupping her whole breast.

Amy pulled back and slapped his hand firmly. 'Not here, Bodkin,' she said. 'Not in public.'

Bodkin sat up and looked around. They were sitting on top of a grassy rise that dropped to the stream on one side and towards a small copse of trees on the other. To the left, the empty path ran all the way along the bank until it reached the fenced off edge of the park. To the right, another line of trees shielded them from anyone who might approach from that direction. Beyond the trees, he could hear the high-pitched, excited calls of the town's children as they swung high on swings, slid down the metal slide, or spun until they were dizzy on one of the two wooden roundabouts on the council-built playground that lined the top end of the park.

'No one's about,' he moaned as he pointed down the path that led towards the village of Skelton. 'And you'd need to be carrying a telescope to see us from down there.'

'Not in public, Bodkin. You know the rules.' She brushed some imaginary grass from her dress. 'Anyway. You know what people are like. It's all right for men to be seen groping women in public. They'll just be seen as Jack the lads having a bit of fruity fun, but for women it's different. We'll be classed as being easy.' She wafted her hand in front of her face to fend off a flying insect. 'I don't want to have that sort of reputation.'

Bodkin nodded. 'I know, I'm sorry.' He gave her a lecherous look. 'I just can't help myself sometimes.'

Amy reached across and patted his hand. 'I think you have quite a lot of self-control... for a man, at least. It must be your police training or something.'

'It's nothing to do with the police training, Amy. I respect you too much to try to take advantage.'

Amy smiled softly and leaned across to kiss him. 'I know, Bodkin and I love you for it.' She suddenly looked away shyly. 'There'll be enough time for canoodling when we're...'

'Married?' Bodkin said, dipping his head to look at her face.

'Better acquainted,' Amy replied. She flashed him a quick look, her cheeks burning. 'We can canoodle in private, Bodkin. I love you holding me... it's just that... well, you know... when I walk down the aisle with my dad at my side, I want to wear white without feeling a bit of a fraud. Do you understand?'

'Of course I do. I know what your faith means to you, Amy, and I wouldn't do anything to make you feel bad about yourself.'

Amy put her hand on his thigh. 'You're a good man, Bodkin. I want to do those things with you... all of those things... just not quite yet.' She looked down at her chest. 'Anyway, there are other things we can do... for now...'

'I'll keep my hands to myself in public, I promise,' Bodkin replied. 'But just wait until I get you behind closed doors.'

Amy shook her head. 'And they say romance is dead.'

Before Bodkin could reply, they heard the sound of a screaming girl, followed by the loud shout of an overly excited boy.

Bodkin was on his feet in an instant and leaving his jacket and tie where it lay on the grass, he hurried towards the thin line of trees that screened the bank of the stream from the rest of the park.

Amy got quickly to her feet and followed the policeman towards the sound of the clearly distressed children.

They found a group of four kids, all about seven or eight years old, wearing only their dripping underwear as they stood together by the side of the brook. The rest of their clothes were strewn across the grass. The stream was wider and deeper at this point. A few yards further on, it joined the churning waters of the Medway.

As Amy tried to comfort the girl, Bodkin crouched down in front of a red-haired, freckled-faced lad who was still shouting to someone, possibly his brother, in the playground about thirty yards away.

'Calm down, son,' Bodkin said, quietly but firmly. 'I'm a policeman. What's the matter?'

The boy turned and pointed across the widest part of the stream towards a reed bed on the opposite side. 'There's a lady lying in the reeds. She's dead.'

# CHAPTER TWO

The boy shivered, even though the day was still warm. Bodkin nodded toward the scattered clothing.

'Get yourselves dressed,' he said as he got to his feet. 'Are you sure the lady is dead, son? How could you tell?'

'I saw my grandad when he died in his rocking chair. She looked just like that.' The boy opened his eyes wide and allowed his mouth to gape. 'Like that,' he repeated.

Bodkin patted the lad on the shoulder, then walked slowly towards the water.

'How the hell did they get across there and why would they want to?' he said as he looked down at the fast-flowing, murky stream. The opposite bank was a good twelve feet away.

'We were collecting bulrushes,' the boy answered as he pulled his partly buttoned up shirt over his head.

'Bullrushes?' Bodkin mused.

'They dye or paint them and sell the bundles house to house,' Amy replied.

'Bullrushes?'

Amy nodded. 'They brighten up a room in winter when there are no flowers to pick.'

'Ah,' Bodkin said looking hesitantly down at the stream. 'I wonder how deep it is.'

'How high is that lad's chest?' Amy replied, taking off her shoes.

'You're not going in there, Amy. It will come up to your waist.'

To Bodkin's astonishment, Amy suddenly hitched up her summer dress and tucked it into her beige coloured, French knickers. 'Hurry up, Bodkin, don't be shy,' she said as she stepped into the water.

'Amy, be careful you don't—'

'Oh, Bodkin. Alice and I have waded across here many a time. I think I was only as old as that little girl when I first attempted it.'

Bodkin untied his laces and pulled off his shoes and socks. By the time he had rolled his trouser legs up to his knees, Amy had reached the reed bed on the other side. Concerned about what condition the body might be in, and wanting to protect Amy from anything too nasty, he leapt into the water and waded across. By the time he reached the middle of the stream, the water was sloshing around his crotch.

'Stay there, Amy, don't go any further,' he shouted, but Amy had already stepped further into the tall reeds.

'It's all right, Bodkin. She doesn't seem to have been here too long.' Amy came to a halt as she looked into the flattened area of thick grasses.

Bodkin sloshed up to the side of her and looked down at the woman's body as it moved slowly side to side, as if performing a swaying dance in the weak current.

She was a brown-haired woman in her early-to-mid-twenties. She was wearing a summer print frock, similar in style to Amy's, and black Oxford shoes. Around her neck was a gold locket on a thin chain. Just as the boy had said, her eyes were wide, staring up at the sky, and her mouth was gaping open as though she had just received some shocking news. She wore a thin gold band on her left wrist and a gold, chain-linked watch on her right.

After looking around the area for anything that might have been dropped or discarded, Bodkin squatted down, put his hands under the woman's body and lifted her out of the water.

'Can you feel about under the water, Amy, just in case there's a handbag or something on the bottom?'

As Bodkin headed back to the brook with the body of the young woman in his arms, Amy fished around in the mud at the bottom of the reed bed but could find nothing, so, turning slowly around she looked out towards the Medway where she spotted a gap in the tall reeds. Paddling towards it, she saw a narrow corridor, formed by reeds that had been flattened or broken. Unwilling to move any closer to the river with its unpredictable currents, she turned back and made her way towards Bodkin, who was standing at the right-hand bank of the stream.

'Can you nip back to where we were and get my coat, please, Amy? We'd better cover her face up, at least when we get her across... and get those kids away from the bank. Tell them to wait on the playground. I'll need another word with them when we've got this poor woman covered.'

Bodkin stayed on the far bank with his back to the playground until he heard Amy call his name, then turning smartly he carried the young woman across the stream and laid her down on the grass.

'Cover her face, Amy. I'm just going to get a couple of the older lads to nip up to the telephone box and call 999. Then I want them to get hold of the younger kids' parents. The poor little mites must be terrified.'

'Shall I sit with them, Bodkin? I can pass your message on to the older ones.'

Bodkin coughed. 'Er, no. I was going to ask you a favour, actually.' He rolled down his sopping trouser legs and shuffled about before continuing. 'Could you, erm, take a look up her dress while I'm gone? Make sure she's wearing everything she ought to be wearing, if you get my drift.'

'Of course I will, Bodkin. You want her to keep some sort of dignity. I know I keep saying it, but you really are a very nice man.'

'Oh, I'd have done it if I'd been here on my own,' Bodkin replied. 'But seeing as I've got you handy.'

'Off you go,' Amy said, looking down at the body. 'I'll give her a quick going over. I won't touch anything I don't need to.'

When Bodkin returned, he was full of concern for the children. 'Can you sit with them until the cavalry come, Amy? They are still a bit traumatised. I'll stay here with her.'

Amy nodded. 'She's wearing her knickers, and I've got a few other bits and pieces to report when you're ready to hear them.'

Bodkin smiled. 'Why am I not surprised?' He nodded towards the playground where the four young kids and a few of their friends were sitting mournfully on the floor of the big roundabout. 'Off you go, Amy... and thank you.'

'What for?'

'For whatever you're going to tell me when I see you next.'

'And you moved her body... why on earth did you do that, Bodkin?' Chief Inspector Laws wasn't pleased.

'Two reasons, sir. One, I didn't like to leave the poor girl lying in the water for a minute longer than necessary, and two, I wanted to get a good look at her to see if we could find any sort of clue as to who she is.'

'We?' Laws shot Amy a quick glance as she walked slowly back from the playground. The children were now being looked after by a uniformed policewoman who had been transferred to the Spinton force on a temporary basis a few weeks earlier. 'By we, I take it you mean Miss Rowlings? It never ceases to amaze me how she always seems to be around when a body is discovered.'

'She was with me, sir. We were just having a walk in the p—'

'Hello, my dear.' Law's demeanour suddenly changed as Amy arrived. 'It's so nice to see you again. I haven't had the chance to thank you for the help you gave us with the Nelson Kelly case. You unearthed one or two valuable clues. It might have taken me a little longer than it did to pin down the culprit otherwise.'

Amy looked from Laws to Bodkin and back again, biting her tongue as the inspector imperceptibly shook his head. It had been Amy and Bodkin who had whittled down a long list of suspects to find the murderer, but Laws had taken all the credit for the arrest.

'It's nice to see you too, Chief Inspector.'

'Oh, there's no need to be so formal, my dear.' Bodkin's superior officer laid a soft hand on Amy's arm. 'Mr Laws will do.' He gave her a quick smile, then turned to face Bodkin.

'I'm going back to the station to order up some expert divers from Gillingham. We need to go through that reed bed with a fine-toothed comb.'

'Yes, sir,' Bodkin replied. 'Do you think we could have the use of a uniformed officer and a car to get these kids back to their parents? The four who found the body are still in shock.'

'I'll organise it.' He looked up as they heard the ambulance approach. 'Don't let them take her away until the doctor has had a look. Honestly, Bodkin, you really shouldn't have moved her, you know.'

'I think the doctor might appreciate not having to wade through waist deep water to get to the mud flats, sir,' Bodkin replied. 'You know how grumpy he gets.'

Laws nodded. 'You're probably right, but just in case this goes belly up, remember that the removal of the body had nothing to do with me.'

Amy shook her head as she watched Bodkin's superior officer

walk away. 'Blimey! He was in a good mood today, wasn't he? Has he won the football pools or something?'

Bodkin shook his head. 'No such luck. He might leave the force if he had. No, he's going back to Maidstone in a few days. He's happier down there.'

'Because his wife stays up here,' Amy replied.

'I really couldn't say.' Bodkin winked and knelt down next to the body as two ambulancemen trotted towards them with a stretcher and a thick blanket.

'Could you leave the blanket and wait in the ambulance until the doctor's seen her, lads?' Bodkin pulled the blanket from the stretcher and unfolded it. 'Right, Amy, what have you got to tell me?'

Amy took a deep breath. 'First, she might look like a posh girl, but I doubt that she's a member of one of the richer families around here. She has had a manicure; her fingernails and toenails have been painted recently and her hair is... was professionally cut, but her makeup doesn't look expensive and it hasn't been applied particularly well... as far as I can tell, anyway. She has been in the water for a little while.'

Bodkin stroked his chin as he looked down at the girl. 'Interesting. Go on.'

Amy thought for a moment. 'Okay. Her jewellery is fake... rolled gold. Pretty much costume jewellery. The manufacturers plate a cheaper metal with gold leaf or whatever to give it the appearance of gold, but both her watch and her bracelet have scratch marks, and you can see the base metal underneath. The pendant is worn where it has been opened and closed over the years and has a silver sort of tint to it.' She paused. 'Her dress is interesting. It has a London Connection label... you know, the posh shop I worked in for a while over the summer? Well, this is one of their own label dresses, not one of the London houses. It is mass produced, will have been ordered in quantity, and would only have cost twenty percent of what their exclusive labels cost. Her shoes are from Lilley and Skinner, which, as you know, has branches in every large town in the country. They are hardly exclusive. I have a similar pair at home. Her knickers came from Marks and Spencer, by the way.'

'So, what are your conclusions?' Bodkin asked.

'I'd say she is from a relatively well-off family, at least one step up from me, but nowhere near the upper echelons of society. She's probably local because of the London Connection dress... there's always a chance that she bought it at Brigden's nearly new store. They sell some of LC's second hands there, though I can't remember seeing this one. If I had, I might have beaten her to it.' She smiled at the policeman then went on. 'Because she can afford a decent hairdresser and has professionally manicured nails, it means she isn't from my side of town. She's more likely to hail from the bigger houses down past the Mill or one of the middle-of-the-road Edwardian piles that line the Gillingham Road. She's only a year or two older than me, so if she went to the local school, I'd have almost certainly known her when I was growing up.'

'Well done, Amy. Anything else?' Bodkin looked across the field as the portly shape of the doctor waddled towards them.

'Erm... oh yes. She has the picture of a young man in her locket. He appears to be wearing a university scarf or possibly one connecting him to some club or other. It's hard to say which one as they all look pretty similar in a black-and-white photograph.' She turned to the side and pointed back across the stream towards the reed beds. 'And... there is a patch of reeds growing next to the river that have been flattened. So, she either waded into the reed bed and was killed, or she was killed elsewhere and her body dumped there. Whichever it was, she came via the river.'

'Excellent work,' Bodkin whispered as the doctor dumped his bag on the floor at the side of the body.

# CHAPTER THREE

'I'll just nip in and change my trousers,' Bodkin said as he pulled up outside Bluecoat House, where his flat was situated.

'Well, hurry up about it, Bodkin, I need to get these wet knickers off. They're really uncomfortable.'

Bodkin held the car door open and stuck his head back inside. 'I could lend you a pair of my underpants, just to keep you...' Noticing the look of distaste on Amy's face, he pulled back. 'No, that's probably not a good idea. Hang on, I'll be back in a jiffy.'

The policeman was as good as his word, and he was still fastening the buttons on his fly as he came back out of the front door some three minutes later. 'Sorry about the underpants idea. It sounds silly now, thinking about it.'

Amy wriggled about in her seat. 'It was a kind thought, Bodkin, and don't take this the wrong way, but I'd rather wear nothing under my dress than a pair of your ancient, saggy underpants.' She wriggled again as Bodkin started up the car. 'Which reminds me. We can get you some new ones when we visit Stan's on Saturday.'

'The ones I have are comfortable.' Bodkin shot a sideways glance at her as he pulled the car onto the Gillingham Road.

'You sound just like my dad,' Amy replied. 'Mum has to sneak new underwear into his bedroom drawer and throw the old ones out without telling him.'

'You can't beat a pair of comfy white pants,' Bodkin said.

'Yours were white at one time of day, Bodkin, but if what I saw in your wardrobe the other week is anything to go by, they are a sort of off cream, now.'

'Can we discuss the state of my underwear on another occasion,' Bodkin said as he turned right at the Old Bull pub and onto Long Lane.

Amy eased her bottom up and tugged at the skirt of her wet dress. 'There are a million and one other topics I'd rather be discussing,' she said as the car pulled up outside her house. 'But I need to get these knickers off before I can concentrate on anything.'

Amy opened the white painted gate and shuffled up the path, pulling her wet dress away from her backside. After opening the front door, she hurried up the stairs to her room, leaving Bodkin to close both the gate and the door behind him.

'I'll stick the kettle on,' he called as he walked into the living room.

Five minutes later, Amy walked in wearing a clean, flower print dress. She carried the wet clothes through to the kitchen, turned on the hot tap to kick in the Ascot boiler, and after letting the water run for a couple of minutes, she put the plug in the hole, dropped her knickers into the sink and tipped in a small amount of washing powder.

'I'll leave them to soak until the morning,' she said as Bodkin tipped boiling water into the teapot. 'Heaven knows what's in that stream. We don't want them smelling musty.'

'Perish the thought,' Bodkin replied as he carried the teapot into the living room.

'It feels odd being in here without your mum and dad,' he said as he carefully placed the pot on the wicker coaster on the table. 'Your dad is usually in his chair reading the paper and your mum is in the kitchen or sitting on the sofa with her Woman's Own magazine.'

Amy looked up at the clock on the wall. 'Almost eight o'clock. They'll be on the seafront at Margate, finishing their fish and chips about now.'

'I bet you're missing the seaside. It must be strange for you too; you normally go with them.'

Amy put two mugs on the table and picked up the teapot. 'It's the first time I've been at home on my own. I've been going to Margate with them for the last twenty years.'

'They really must like it there,' Bodkin replied. 'You'd think they'd want to try somewhere else for a change.'

'You're joking, Bodkin. It's all they talk about from Easter onwards. Mrs O'Malley's guest house and buying jellied eels on the seafront. Dad's mad about them. Mum isn't keen; she won't even give him a kiss until he's brushed his teeth after eating them.'

'What about you? Do you take after your dad or your mum?'

'Definitely Mum. Just the smell makes me retch.' Amy poured the tea, then walked back into the kitchen and gave the water in the sink a swish around with her hand. 'I got wet knickers at Margate last year too. I fell over when I was paddling in the sea. I thought a jelly fish was stuck to my foot, but it was just a piece of soggy paper.'

As Bodkin laughed, Amy opened the bread bin. 'What do you fancy on your sandwich? We've got some nice ham on the cold shelf, or you could have cheese and some of Mum's home-made pickle.'

'I love your mum's home-made pickle,' Bodkin replied. 'I could spoon it out of the jar straight into my mouth.'

'I know, that's why Mum made twice as much this time.'

When they were settled at the table, Amy picked up her sandwich and held it in front of her mouth, but instead of biting into it, she put it back on the plate again. 'Are you going back to the station tonight?'

Bodkin nodded. 'Yes, I've got to check in with Laws. He'll still be there because, as we both know; he doesn't like going home to Mrs Laws. We might have a bit more information about the young woman, too. Ferris and Armitage are looking through the missing person reports. I'm not hopeful they'll find her, though. She hadn't been in that reed bed for long.'

'You've got a lot more experience than me when it comes to corpses, but I was thinking the same. What if we'd just missed whoever did it? Those kids were lucky. If they'd have gone looking for bulrushes a few minutes earlier, they might have bumped into the murderer and who knows what would have happened then.' She picked up her sandwich again but didn't bite into it. 'It's definitely a murder, isn't it?'

'For sure,' Bodkin replied. 'If she had wanted to kill herself, she wouldn't have chosen that location. How did she get there? There are only two ways into the reed bed. Via the Silverstream, or the river. No one could have got through those thick briars on the edge of the beds, and she had no scratches on her, anyway. And where is her bag and any other personal effects?' He paused and took a sip of tea. 'No, whoever put her there delivered her by boat. The question we have, apart from who did the deed of course, is, was she killed on the boat or was she killed elsewhere and the boat was used merely to deliver the body to the reed bed?'

Amy finally took a bite of her cheese and pickle sandwich. After chewing a few times, she stared at the ceiling for a few moments, then looked across the table towards Bodkin. 'I wonder what happened to her bag. Women don't let them out of their sight for more than a few minutes. They have all their essentials inside.'

Bodkin nodded. 'The divers will find it if it's there.' He scratched his head. 'What's puzzling me at the moment is how she died and what she died of? There wasn't a drop of blood on her clothes. She hadn't been bashed over the head. There were no marks around her throat, so that would rule out strangulation. She could have drowned, of course, but I can't stop thinking about that look she had on her face. It was as though she had just been surprised by something.'

'She's a bit young to have had a heart attack,' Amy said. 'You can't rule it out I suppose, but again, if it was natural causes, why hide her away like that?'

'We'll know soon. They are holding the postmortem tomorrow.'

Amy picked up her mug of tea and took a sip. 'And hopefully, someone will be missing her by then.'

On Tuesday morning, Amy had a lie in and didn't get up until after eight o'clock. After making breakfast, she emptied the sink and gave the dress and underwear she had worn the previous day, a good hand wash before hanging them out on the line. At nine, she grabbed her bag and the small pile of library books she had to return and caught the bus into town.

In the library she was delighted to at last find a copy of Murder in the Mews, an Agatha Christie short story collection featuring her hero, Hercule Poirot. Amy had requested it a year before, but the library hadn't been able to source a copy.

From the library, she walked back along the High Street and made her way around to her favourite café, where she enjoyed a cup of coffee and a slice of Madeira cake. Thirty minutes later, as she was making her way to the bus stop, she looked across the road to the London Connection fashion shop where she had worked for a few weeks earlier in the summer. After receiving a lightning bolt of inspiration, she hurried across the road and pushed open the thick glass door of the store. Once inside, she waved to Susan, the temporary manageress, who was sitting at a small desk in the far corner studying the order books.

Susan was a petite woman with mousey coloured hair cut in a pageboy style. She had become a good friend over the few weeks she had known her.

'Hello, you,' Susan said as a big smile flashed across her face. 'What are you doing here? I thought Brigden's was more your style.'

'Oh, it is,' Amy replied. 'I can't even afford a hair ribbon from this place.' She looked around, waving her hand in the air. 'I wish I could. There are so many nice things here.'

'I'll send a message to the Mill if we ever have a fire sale,' Susan said with a laugh. 'It is lovely to see you. Have you got time for a cup of tea? It's nearly eleven. I can get one of the young girls to make it.'

'No, it's all right, I just had a coffee over the road. I just thought I'd drop in to see how you are.' Amy looked around with a puzzled look on her face. 'Where's the new girl? Has she got a day off?'

'Ah, her. No, she's not around. Janet, the new girl, has left us in the lurch. She was only here for a few weeks.'

'That's strange. I thought she was looking forward to working here,' Amy replied.

'She was... but she got an offer she couldn't refuse from a shop in Maidstone, so she left. The first thing I knew about it was when I read the note she pushed through the letterbox.'

'Oh dear, that's not good. She could at least have worked her notice to give you a chance to advertise the job again.'

'I had a word with the owner, Josie, about that, Amy. We both decided that we'd like to have you back again, if it is at all possible, even if it's just for the two and a half days a week you worked before.' She smiled at Amy, then continued. 'I know Georgina needs you on your machine at the Mill, and I know you can't... won't, work on Saturdays, but we can get your friend from the factory, Carol Sims to come in then, she always wants the overtime, and she was very good while she was here.'

She paused to pick up a hair clip from the accessories counter. 'Georgina is away for a few days while the factory has its summer deep clean, but I rang her at her niece's house in London, and she said she'd be happy to let you work for us again. She is a partner in the business, after all, and she wants us to do well. She said that you would have to make the final decision, though. You'll still be doing half the week on your machine at the Mill, and your weekly bonus will be averaged out.' She put the hair clip down and took hold of Amy's hand. 'And you get a bit of extra money in your pay packet for the hours you do here.'

Amy thought for a few moments. She had enjoyed working in the shop. She loved anything to do with fashion, but she had found the job was a little slow at times. When she was working on her machine, she was so busy that the hours seemed to fly by.

'When would you need my answer?' she asked. 'Only I'm on the factory fortnight holiday at the moment. I've worked hard all year and I really need the break.'

'Oh, I'm not suggesting you start this week, or next, Amy. If you could let Georgina know when you get back to the Mill after the shutdown, that would be lovely. I'm sure Carol will be delighted too.'

'I will give it some serious thought,' Amy replied. 'It was fun working here, even though it was a little slow at times.'

'I can fix that. I can show you how to do the stock books. You can learn how to order in the items we need. That will give you plenty to do when there are no customers in the shop.'

Amy grinned. 'That sounds great. I hate standing around doing nothing. I feel guilty that I'm being paid for it.'

Susan blew out a sigh of relief. 'You don't know how happy I am about this, Amy.' She put her hand on her wrist. 'You were perfect; our customers loved you.'

'Speaking of customers... and order books... I wonder if you could do me a big favour?' Amy asked.

'If it means you'll take the job, then the answer is yes... unless you're after a free dress or something.'

Amy laughed along with her former manageress. 'No, I'm all right for dresses, thanks.' She paused as she worked out how to phrase the question. 'It's like this, Susan. Do you remember Inspector Bodkin? He came in once to see me and you tried to sell him a couple of pairs of camiknickers.'

'I do remember him as it happens. Good looking chap, very easy on the eye.' She paused. 'Are you and he...?'

Amy pulled a face. 'Sort of... in a way... but that's not important, really. I'm helping him out on a case, and he needs to identify someone. The body of a young woman was found near the Medway yesterday. The police don't have a clue who she is, and no one has been reported missing yet.'

'I'm so sorry to hear that, Amy, but what has it got to do with us?'

'When she was found, she was wearing a London Connection dress. One of your own label items. It was a cotton summer dress, mostly white with a blue poppy pattern on it. I know you had a couple of dozen of them in a variety of colours in the stockroom back in late spring.'

'We did, and we sold every one of them. We even had to put another order in. They went down very well with the younger set. Late teens, early twenties. Pretty much your age. It would have suited you.'

'I'd have loved to buy one, but at a guinea...? I can get something similar at Brigden's for six or seven shillings.'

'Ah, but it won't have our label on it,' Susan said with a smile. 'But go on, how can I help?'

'Well, I was wondering if you could look through your order book to see who bought the blue poppy version of the dress. There can't have been more than half a dozen buyers. It really would narrow the search down to a few names.'

Susan walked across to her desk and picked up her customer order book. 'If I remember correctly, we couldn't get as many of the blue as we had requested, so we probably only sold three or four of them. Hang on a minute, I'll write the details down.'

Susan took a sheet of paper and worked her way through the last few pages of the order book. When she had finished, she had six names on her list.

'Now, dear. I think you can forget Mrs Connolley, because she was buying it for her granddaughter and she lives in the midlands. She was going to have it delivered for her eighteenth birthday.' She ran her pencil down the list. 'I don't suppose you know what size it was?'

'Thirty-four bust,' Amy replied firmly.

'That narrows it down to two then, providing the dress was purchased from here. As you know, we send any seconds we get to Brigden's, so there is a chance it was bought there.'

'It wasn't in Brigden's; I go in there every week on the day the new lines go on show. There were similar ones, I bought one, but it had a Farnley's of Manchester label in it, not a London Connection one.'

'Well then,' Susan said as she crossed out three more of the names. 'It was one of these two.' She put the pen on the table and handed Amy the sheet of paper.

'Thanks so much for this. You've been a really big help,' Amy said, as she read the names on the sheet.

'Just remember that when you make your decision about the job,' Susan said, putting her hand softly on Amy's arm.

'Oh, I think I've already made up my mind,' Amy replied. 'If you speak to Georgina again before the Mill reopens, tell her I've agreed.'

Amy left the shop with the paper clutched in her hand and hurriedly made her way across the High Street. After turning the corner onto Middle Street, she almost ran past the cinema to get to the police station as quickly as she could. At the station, she pushed open the heavy door and, panting slightly, approached the front desk. PC Ferris, Amy's friend, was on duty.

'Hello, Amy. What brings you in here on such a lovely day? You ought to be sitting in the sunshine with a cold drink.'

'Is Bodkin here, Ferris?' Amy asked quickly, waving the sheet of paper at him. 'Only I think I know the identity of the young girl that was found in the water yesterday.'

# CHAPTER FOUR

'Just the person I've been told to look for,' Bodkin said as he came out of the corridor, heading towards the front desk. He opened the side door to let Amy into the non-public area of the station. 'Mr Laws would like a word with you. He asked me to come and pick you up, but as you're already here...'

'Me! What have I done now?'

Bodkin winked at her. 'Follow me, please.'

He led her along the corridor and up a short flight of stairs to the next floor. Ten feet along the passage that led off the stairway, he stopped and knocked on a door.

'Enter.'

Bodkin opened the door and stood aside to allow Amy to walk in first. 'Miss Rowlings, sir.'

Laws stood up as she entered. Walking around his desk, he offered a podgy hand to her. 'It's always a pleasure,' he said.

Amy shot a glance at Bodkin, who looked back with a straight face.

'Sit down, my dear,' Laws said as he stepped back behind the desk.

Amy moved a chair so that it would be facing the chief inspector, then sat down on it and smoothed down her dress.

'You must be wondering why I've asked to see you, Miss Rowlings,' Laws said with a beaming smile. He looked from Amy to Bodkin, then back again. 'Well wonder no longer, because I'm about to tell you.' He paused for a moment as he looked across the desk at her. 'I believe you formed your own private detective agency, which enables you to give limited help to the police in our investigations. Do you have one of your cards with you?'

Amy opened her bag, fished around for a pink card and handed it over to the Chief Inspector. Laws read it, turned it over, read the other side, then opened a draw and dropped the card into it.

'I like the pink colour,' he said. 'Very swish, very feminine.'

'Thank you,' Amy replied. She was just about to explain the only reason she had a pink card was that they had been made out of printer's offcuts to save money, when she felt Bodkin's knee push against the back of her chair. 'I'm very pleased with them,' she added.

'Chief Superintendent Grayson informs me that all the correct forms have been filled in and you are now a police accredited investigator.' He rubbed his hands together. 'Congratulations.'

'Thank you,' Amy said again as she wondered where this was all going.

'Both the chief super and I have been very impressed with the way you have conducted yourself during the last few months. Inspector Bodkin has also been singing your praises, but that may be for different reasons.' He held up his hand to silence Bodkin before he could protest. 'Right, let's get down to brass tacks. We have a staffing problem at the Spinton station, Miss Rowlings. We lost our only female police officer just after the Kelly murder, and her temporary replacement, Miss Blissett, is going back to Sittingbourne tomorrow. I believe you met her yesterday?'

'Briefly,' Amy replied, still none the wiser as to what Laws wanted.

'Well, that leaves us rather shorthanded, Miss Rowlings. We are also about to lose even more temporary assignments. Two police constables who were loaned to us from Maidstone have to go back for further training. It seems they were not up to the rigours of the job.' He took out a handkerchief from his pocket and wiped a few beads of sweat from his brow. 'All this means that for the next few months, or until we can get a few more officers trained up, we will be extremely short staffed. I am myself returning to Maidstone in a few days' time, and sadly, I won't be replaced until Chief Inspector Harding returns from sick leave.' He held out both hands, palms up. 'So you see, my dear, we are looking for all the help we can get, and as you have been invaluable to the force recently, I have been tasked with asking you if you would be prepared to assist Inspector Bodkin for the next few weeks.' He flashed a smile towards her, then went on. 'Because of budget cuts, I'm afraid there will be no renumeration for your services... but... we might be able to fork out for a few incidental expenses... the odd taxi fare, or a gallon of petrol if you drive your own car... Bus fares if not.'

Amy looked over her shoulder at Bodkin, her eyes bright.

'This does not mean you have the power of arrest, nor may you act alone in questioning witnesses, unless you have been given permission by a senior officer. Is that clear because it's very important? We can't have you running around the town dragging people off to the cells, can we?'

Laws laughed so hard at his own joke that it resulted in a coughing fit. When he had recovered, he spoke again.

'You will, however, have access to certain case notes, but you will not be allowed to take them off the premises. Trixie, my secretary, will hunt down anything you need if Inspector Bodkin or Constable Ferris are busy. You will not be allowed into the evidence room, nor the record's office, unless you are accompanied by a serving police officer.'

Amy's eyes narrowed at the mention of Trixie's name. She and the blonde bombshell had started off on the wrong foot and had been hopping around on the same one ever since. The last thing she intended to do was to ask her for help.

'Does this mean I'll have access to the inner workings of the police station?' she asked.

'To a limited degree. You will be allowed into the station whenever Bodkin is on duty. Trixie will show you where the kettle and the ladies' lavatory are.' Laws looked away as he said the word 'lavatory'. 'As I mentioned, you will not be allowed to take any files or evidence away from the premises and you will only have access to files relevant to the cases Bodkin is currently working on, and even then, only when he is present. Is that clear?'

Amy nodded eagerly. The last thing she wanted was to be in the same building as Trixie let alone the same room, but this was an incredible opportunity and she had no intention of picking nits or anything else out of the offer.

'Right, then sign here,' Laws said, pushing a sheet of typed paper over the desk.

Amy pulled out a pen from her bag and quickly signed the bottom of the sheet without reading it.

'Thank you so much,' she said as she slid the paper back over the desk.

In return, Laws passed her a white card with the logo of a crown with the letters GR underneath and Spinton Police printed below that. Further down the card, in smaller print, were the words 'Amy Rowlings. Accredited'.

'Just don't let us down, Miss Rowlings,' Laws said, getting to his feet. 'Head office took a lot of persuading.'

. . .

'Blimey,' Amy said as she followed Bodkin into his office. She looked at his untidy, file strewn desk and wondered if she should offer to tidy them up now that she had been given access to them. 'That's a turn up for the books and no mistake.' She looked across the desk at the inspector before smoothing her skirt and sitting down. 'Did you know about this?'

Bodkin shook his head. 'Not until about an hour ago. Laws called me in. He'd just been involved in a telephone discussion with head office. They really are struggling for manpower... womanpower too. Your friend Superintendent Grayson put your name forward. The bigwigs insisted you join the force and wear the uniform to begin with, but when Grayson told them that you had no intention of becoming a WPC and then handed them the report I'd written on the Kelly murder case, they were soon swayed.' He scratched at his head just above his right ear. 'The fact that you wouldn't receive a wage obviously helped too.'

'They do know I have to go back to work after the factory fortnight holidays and I'll only be able to help out in the evenings and at weekends, don't they?'

'I don't think they particularly care about that, Amy. You aren't costing them anything other than the odd bus ticket, and that makes them happy. You'll be down as an accredited assistant to the CID in the official figures and that will make it look like the Spinton station isn't as shorthanded as it appears to be. It's a win-win situation for them.'

Bodkin picked up the kettle, shook it to check to see if there was any water in it, plugged it in at the wall socket and switched it on before dropping Lipton's tea bags into two clean mugs that were sitting on the top of the filing cabinet.

'Please don't think that you're being offered the position out of mere desperation, although it might look that way... You're here because Grayson wants you here. He rates your input so highly that he'd have you in the CID at the drop of a hat if he was allowed to. You're here purely on merit, Amy. You're the first person I've ever heard of to be offered such a position. I can't tell you how proud of you I am.'

Amy's eyes lit up as he brushed away a few strands of hair from her face. 'Bless you, Bodkin. You mentioned that they read your report on the Kelly case. Does that mean you'll get the recognition you deserve for bringing his killer to justice? Do they know that Laws had little to do with cracking the case and he was merely claiming the credit because of his rank?'

'Oh, they know, Amy. Grayson put his own report in, and your name would have been mentioned prominently. It certainly was in mine.'

Amy clapped her hands together, then looked around the untidy office.

'I think we're going to have to do a bit of a clean-up if I'm going to be spending my holidays in here,' she said.

Bodkin poured boiling water into the mugs and picked up a half full bottle of milk. He sniffed at it suspiciously before pouring it into the brewing tea. 'It should be all right. I only bought it yesterday.'

After taking the mug from Bodkin, Amy slid her spoon under the tea bag and bobbed it up and down in the water for a few seconds. 'Tea bags are the best invention since knicker elastic,' she said as she placed the mug carefully on the desk. Then, sticking her hand into her pocket, she pulled out the piece of paper that Susan had given her.

'You haven't asked me why I came round to see you yet, Bodkin.'

'I did wonder, but my thought processes have been taken up with other matters since then,' the inspector replied. 'I was sort of hoping that you just couldn't wait until tonight to see me.'

'There was a bit of that, actually,' Amy said with a smile. 'But the main reason was this.' She slid the sheet of paper across the desk towards him. 'I nipped into London Connection on my way back from the library. Susan asked me if I'd consider working there again after the holidays.'

'Are you considering it? I'd love it, of course, because I'd get to see you for lunch sometimes,' Bodkin replied.

'I have accepted as it happens, and you can buy me lunch any time you like, but that piece of paper is much more important than any lunch date.' She waited for Bodkin to pick it up before she continued. 'Those are the addresses of the only two people who bought the exact same dress that our unfortunate victim was wearing. They sold six of that pattern, but only two in a thirty-four bust.'

She smiled grimly as Bodkin looked across the table at her. 'You can tell Ferris to stop looking at missing person reports, Bodkin. I think we've found her.'

# CHAPTER FIVE

'Meadow View, Spinton... now where have I heard that name before?' Bodkin asked as he read the information from the sheet for a second time. He looked up at Amy. 'Not to worry, there's a phone number I'll give it—'

'Bodkin, you can't just ring and say have you got a daughter, sorry she's been found dead,' Amy said with a look of horror on her face.

'I wasn't about to ask that,' Bodkin said with a slight shake of his head.

'What were you going to say, then?'

Bodkin shrugged. 'I honestly don't know. I'd have played it by ear... so to speak. I might have asked for Monica.'

Amy sighed. 'Monica?'

'It's as good a name as any. It was just a way into the conversation. I would have said something like, "So you don't have a daughter, I must have the wrong number".'

'I think it would be much fairer on them if we just went around and rang their doorbell, Bodkin. I mean, I wouldn't like to receive that sort of news over the phone.'

Bodkin nodded. 'You're right, of course.' He thought for a moment... 'Meadow View...'

'You recognise it because it's the house next door to the Kelly's at the top end of the High Street. It has a big sign carved in wood at the end of the drive. We parked outside there after questioning Mrs Kelly about her husband's murder, remember?'

Bodkin stuck up a thumb. 'I do now you mention it.' He looked at the sheet of paper again. 'What about Black Gates?'

It was Amy's turn to shrug. 'I have no idea where that might be, Bodkin. It's in Spinton somewhere though. Susan copied the details from her order book.'

The inspector suddenly picked up the phone again.

'Bodkin, you can't...'

'Don't worry,' Bodkin mouthed.... 'Hello, operator, could you put me through to Spinton Post Office please... yes, I'll hold.' He winked at Amy as he waited for the call to be connected. 'Hello, this is Inspector Bodkin from Spinton Police. I wonder if you could help me find the location of an address...'

Two minutes later, Bodkin put the handset down and grinned across the desk at Amy. 'It's off the Gillingham Road before you get to Braithwaite's Hotel.' The inspector pulled a penny coin out of his pocket and motioned to Amy to choose. 'Heads or tails?' he asked.

'Heads,' Amy replied.

'Heads it is,' Bodkin said, 'so it's Meadow View first. Let's go and have a word with...' he picked up Amy's sheet of paper... 'Mrs Gladys Dunwoody.'

Meadow View was a large, Edwardian house set back from the High Street with a wide asphalt drive which was lined by lush-green lawns and manicured flower beds. The entrance to the property lay between two wide brick pillars, one of which held a large, oval shaped wooden sign with the house name carved into it.

'Meadow View?' Bodkin queried as he pulled off the High Street and drove slowly along the drive. 'All you can see is the High Street.'

'It was probably named after the view from the back of the house,' Amy replied. 'The owners would have been able to see all the way across open fields to the Silverstream before the pensioners' bungalows and the children's playground was built about ten years ago.' She paused as a smile appeared on her face. 'I remember the day the playground was officially opened. Every child in the town was there. We had to queue to get onto the slide and swings.'

'It's like having my own personal local history society to hand,' Bodkin said as he pulled up on the forecourt in front of the house. He looked up at the imposing structure as he climbed out of the car. 'I smell money, and lots of it.'

'Now, now, Bodkin, don't let your reverse snobbery get in the way. The people who live here may have worked hard for their money. Not all of them made it off the backs of working people, you know.'

'I'm not going to hold my breath,' Bodkin said as he pressed the cast iron bell push.

It took a full two minutes before the ring was answered. Bodkin took a pace back from the step as the solid oak door opened and the figure of a forty something woman was revealed. She was attractive in an old-fashioned sort of way. Her dark hair was pinned back at the sides and fell onto the nape of her neck. She wore a knee length emerald green dress with a lace collar.

'Yes,' she said curtly.

Bodkin produced his warrant card and held it up in front of him. 'Mrs Dunwoody? I'm Inspector Bodkin from Spinton police and this is Amy Rowlings who is assisting us on this inquiry.' He took a step forward. 'I wonder if we could come inside for a moment. There is something we'd like to discuss and it's quite important.'

'I'm busy. What's it about?' she snapped as she pushed her feet together and lifted her chin, almost looking down her nose at the policeman.

Bodkin shot Amy a glance and gave her an almost imperceptible shake of his head.

'We are investigating a very serious matter, Mrs Dunwoody. Could I ask...? Do you have a daughter?'

'I do have a daughter, not that it's any of your business.' She was silent for a moment as she glared at Amy. 'Why do you want to know about Celia? I can assure you she's the last person who would ever get into any sort of trouble.'

'Is she at home?' Bodkin asked.

'No, as a matter of fact, she isn't. I'm not expecting her back until late this evening. She's out with some of her friends from university.'

'When did you last hear from her?' Amy asked.

'About an hour ago, she called to say she wouldn't be home for dinner.' She turned her attention back to Bodkin. 'What's this about?'

'We're investigating a serious crime, Mrs Dunwoody. You only have one daughter, I take it?'

'Yes, just the one.' She frowned as she took hold of the door handle. 'And if that's it, I'll get back to my novel.'

Mrs Dunwoody closed the door firmly, leaving Bodkin and Amy looking at each other on the doorstep.

'You were saying?' Bodkin muttered.

'She might just be having a bad day, though I do think she was a little rude.'

Bodkin turned on his heel and led her back to the black Morris car. 'Well, that rules her out. I'm glad it wasn't her daughter.

Imagine having to deal with her over an extended investigation. She's the sort that would demand the chief constable take personal charge of the inquiry.'

Amy sighed. 'They aren't all like that, Bodkin, though she did seem a little... what's the word?'

'Entitled. Boorish. Arrogant?'

'I was thinking something like, privileged,' Amy replied. 'Some of them don't know any better. It's how they're brought up. They don't mean anything by it.'

Bodkin shot her a quick glance, but said nothing. After starting the car, he drove along the grass lined drive and pulled out onto the High Street.

'Right, let's see what Mrs Watkins is like. At least she has a common enough surname. I'd put money on her being as nice as pie. It's always the decent ones that get the bad news.'

Black Gates was, as the name suggests, a property hidden away from the main road behind a pair of huge, black, wrought-iron gates set into a ten-foot-high stone wall that ran either side of the entrance as far as the eye could see. The gates were open and Bodkin shook his head in disbelief as he drove between them and the full splendour of the eighteenth century country house was laid out before them.

'Good God,' Bodkin spluttered. 'This place makes Mrs Dunwoody's house look like a terraced cottage.'

'It's a beautiful house, isn't it, Bodkin? But can you imagine how much it costs to run? The coal bill alone must be as much as I earn in a year.'

Bodkin made a quick calculation as he drove slowly towards the huge house. 'Eighteen windows across the front alone. These people weren't bothered about paying the window tax back in the day, were they?'

Amy slapped the back of Bodkin's hand as he let go of the hand brake. 'Don't pre-judge, Bodkin. Wait until you see the evidence. You're a detective, after all.'

Bodkin grunted as he opened the door and stepped out onto the gravel forecourt. On the wall at the side of the wide porch was a brass plaque with the word Reception written across it.

'Blimey, they've even got a receptionist to receive guests.' Bodkin pushed open the heavy door and stepped aside to allow Amy to enter.

Inside, they found themselves in a reception area reminiscent of a hotel. The floor was tiled in a checkerboard pattern; the walls were littered with eighteenth-century portraits. Sitting behind a long desk directly in front of them was a young woman wearing a white blouse and a navy cravat. Her fair hair was pulled back tight and gathered at the back. She looked up from her paperwork as they approached.

'Good afternoon. Welcome to Black Gates. How can I help you?'

Bodkin gave her a quick look at his warrant card. 'I'm Inspector Bodkin and this is Miss Rowlings. We'd like to speak to Mrs Watkins. Is she the owner of this place?'

The girl smiled as she shook her head. 'Good heavens no. Black Gates is owned by a property company. The house was divided into twenty separate apartments just after the Great War. I doubt any individual owner could keep a place like this going in this day and age. I'm Penny Montville, by the way.'

Bodkin nodded. 'Ah, I see.' He looked around the spacious hall. 'Well, Miss Montville, could you point us in the right direction? It's Mrs Miranda Watkins we're looking for.'

Penny checked a list of names on the wall behind her. 'She's in apartment eleven.' She pointed to a door at the far end of the room. 'Through there, up the stairs to the first floor and it's the second door on the right.'

'Thank you,' Bodkin said as he turned away from the desk. He stopped suddenly and turned back to the receptionist. 'Does she have anyone living with her? A husband, perhaps... maybe a daughter?'

Penny shook her head. 'She lives alone. I believe her husband died some time ago.'

Bodkin frowned. 'So, she doesn't have any children?'

'She does, but they don't live with her. A son visits occasionally. I've never seen a daughter, but then I've only been here a few months.'

Bodkin led Amy through a pair of double doors and into a long corridor with five doors running off it. To their right, a wide staircase led upward.

At the top of the stairs, they found themselves in another long corridor. The door to Mrs Watkins' apartment was some thirty feet along it. Bodkin rapped on the door and grimaced towards Amy as they heard the dull sound of footsteps approaching.

The door was opened by a woman of about fifty years of age. She had an oval-shaped face with short, brown hair showing flecks of grey along the central parting. She was wearing a long black skirt, a light blue blouse and a navy, loose knitted cardigan. She tipped her head to the side as she looked at them.

'Yes?' she said with a faint smile.

Bodkin once again fished out his warrant card as he made the introductions.

'Police?' the woman said with an exasperated expression on her face. She gave a quick look up and down the corridor before standing aside to usher them inside. After closing the door, she turned around to face the policeman. 'It's Effie, isn't it? What on earth has she done now?'

# CHAPTER SIX

'Make yourselves comfortable,' Mrs Watkins said as she led them from the hall into a floral papered lounge with two brown leather sofas facing each other across a large square of carpet. Between the sofas was a long, beech coffee table. In the window bay was an oval drop leaf dining table with four chairs tucked underneath.

As Amy sat on the right-hand sofa and smoothed down her dress, Bodkin scratched at the stubble on his chin.

'Do you have a photograph of Effie we could have a look at?' he asked.

'I've got one somewhere.' Mrs Watkins walked to the back of the lounge and began to rummage about in a desk drawer. 'Here you are. This was taken on holiday about six years ago. It's the only adult one I have of her.'

Bodkin had a quick look at the sepia photograph of a teenager looking sullenly at the camera before passing it to Amy.

'I think it might be better if you sat down, Mrs Watkins. We have some bad news for you, I'm afraid.'

Mrs Watkins walked back to the sofas but remained standing. 'It's all right. I'm used to bad news when it comes to Effie.' She wiped the palm of her hand across her forehead. 'Out with it. What's she been up to now?'

Bodkin took a deep breath. 'I'm afraid it's the worst of bad news, Mrs Watkins. Your daughter is dead. She was found in the reeds by the Medway. We don't have the cause of death yet, but we believe she has been murdered.'

Miranda Watkins did sit down then. 'Goodness me, who would want to do such a thing to her? Mind you, when I think of some of the people she hung around with...'

'I'm sorry, Mrs Watkins, but I have to say I wasn't expecting a reaction like this.'

The woman shrugged. 'We weren't that close, to be honest, Inspector. Effie wasn't my daughter... flesh and blood, I mean. She was my stepdaughter.' She got quickly to her feet. 'I see I'm going to have to explain a few things. Shall we have tea while we talk?'

Five minutes later, Miranda came out of the kitchen carrying a tray, which she put carefully down on the coffee table before pouring tea for them all and adding a bourbon biscuit to each saucer.

'Now,' she said as she took a dainty sip from her teacup. 'I'd better explain about Effie.'

Mrs Watkin tipped her head to the side as she worked out in her mind where to begin.

'Effie was almost thirteen when Claude and I were married. He'd lost his first wife to the flu at the end of the war. My husband, John, had died in the battle of the Somme. We had one son, also called John, who was at university when I met Claude. Effie never got over her mother's death. It was almost as though she blamed me for it, although I didn't meet Claude until ten years after she had died. We always had a difficult relationship. She would accept punishment for her bad behaviour from her father, but never from me, no matter what she had done. Effie was surly, disrespectful and spiteful. She used to make up stories about the way I treated her. Once, she got her schoolfriend to hit her in the face and then tried to blame the nasty-looking bruise on me. Thankfully, the event had been witnessed by a teacher, so her plan to drive a wedge between Claude and me failed. She was a bright girl, but also very lazy. She didn't expect to have to work for anything. Her father didn't help with that. He gave in to her every demand. I didn't... not at first, anyway. If she wanted anything from me, she had to earn it, but things got so difficult that by the time she was sixteen I found life much less stressful if I let her get her own way.'

Miranda paused to take another sip of tea. 'Amazingly, she got reasonable results in her exams and Claude managed to find her a place at a female college in Maidstone. That's where we were living back then, but she only stuck it for a year and at the tender age of seventeen, she began to hang around with a crowd of young men from... well, not from our level of society, let's put it that way.'

'Were they getting into trouble?' Amy asked.

'They were never out of it. Drinking, fighting, stealing... she used to come in at all hours, sometimes three sheets to the wind, with her clothes dishevelled. Goodness knows what she got up to with that crowd. I shudder to think about it. At least she didn't get... Well, that was one small mercy.'

Miranda put her cup and saucer on the coffee table and leaned back on the sofa.

'Claude died when she was eighteen and she blamed me for that as well. I had brought a curse on the family, according to her. We had a huge stand-up argument on the night of his funeral, but oddly, that seemed to clear the air a little and we bumped along together for a while after that.'

Miranda leaned forward to pour another cup of tea, then sat

with her hands on her lap as she looked across the table at Amy. 'I sold up and moved up here a few months later. Effie came with me but things soon went awry. She met a new crowd of young men and took to staying out all night. Sometimes I wouldn't see her from one week to the next and to be honest, I wasn't too upset by that, as we had begun to get into some long, heated arguments again. This crowd was better bred than the last lot, but their attitudes to life were very similar. The police brought her home on quite a few occasions after some party or other had turned violent. Eventually, she moved out altogether. She asked me for some money to put down as a deposit on a flat up in Spinton, and I was happy to provide it.

'She got in with yet another new crowd then. They were surprisingly well to do, considering they lived on the outskirts of an industrial town like this. At least one of the lads was at university or had just finished there. Anyway, she used to hang out with them at the Highwater Boat Club. I did hear from her now and again, mainly when she wanted something. The last time was around Easter. She'd seen a dress she liked in a shop in Spinton and she asked me if she could have it. She came to pick it up on the weekend before her twenty-second birthday, and that was the last time I saw her.' Miranda leaned back on the sofa and stared into space. 'We didn't get on, Inspector, we were never close, but I wouldn't have wished this on her.' She hesitated before continuing. 'She wasn't... it wasn't a violent... I mean she wasn't badly hurt, was she?'

'There were no initial signs of any injuries, Mrs Watkins,' Bodkin replied. 'We'll know more soon.' The policeman put his own cup and saucer on the table, then took out his notebook and a pen. 'Can you remember any of the names of the men she was hanging out with up here, and did any of the old crowd follow her up from Maidstone?'

'No to both questions, Inspector. I can't be a hundred percent sure about the second one, of course, but I don't think so. Most of them will be in prison, I imagine.'

'Was she still occupying the flat the last time you saw her?'

'I really can't say. I have the address written down. I'll give it to you before you go.'

'That would be very helpful,' Bodkin replied. 'Do you think I could keep this photograph for a while? I will return it, of course.'

Miranda shrugged. 'Keep it as long as you like. It will only go back in the drawer.'

Amy, who had been listening intently to the conversation, suddenly put her hand on Bodkin's knee as he was about to ask another question.

'You said she was hanging around with members of a boat club? I wouldn't have thought they'd be the type to get into too much trouble with the police.'

'True, this is the first time the police have come to see me in a year or so.'

Amy nodded. 'Did you ever meet any of her friends?'

'Up here? No, not exactly. I did see her coming out of the Milton cocktail bar with a crowd of people. She looked happy that night.'

'This crowd, were they well to do? All men? What sort of age?'

'There were a couple of young women with them, but there must have been about seven or eight men. As to ages, anything from twenty to thirty-five. One of them had a striped university scarf around his neck. I remember that. Some of the older men wore blazers with a pair of crossed oars embroidered on the pocket of their jackets, so I assume they were from the Highwater Boat Club. I could be wrong, of course, there are two other boat or yachting clubs just a bit further along the river.'

Amy nodded again. 'Effie wore a locket that contained the picture of a man with a striped, university-style scarf. Do you know if she had a steady boyfriend? This particular man must have meant something to her.'

'I had no idea she wore a locket, Miss Rowlings.'

'Please, call me Amy.'

'I had no idea about the locket, Amy.'

'What about a watch or a bracelet? The items she was wearing when she was found were only gold plated, costume jewellery. They wouldn't have been expensive. Did she have those when she was living with you?'

'She had a very expensive watch when she lived here. Her father bought it along with a bracelet, a pendant and a pair of matching earrings for her sixteenth birthday, though I can't remember her wearing any of the set after she was eighteen. I assumed she had sold or pawned them.'

'Was she happy with the dress you bought her?'

'I honestly couldn't say. I assume so, as she had asked for that particular dress. I was relieved she hadn't chosen one of the more expensive labels.' Miranda narrowed her eyes slightly as she thought back. 'She never showed much in the way of positive emotion, not around me, at least. She did say thank you, albeit through gritted teeth. I slipped two pound notes into her card as well because the dress only cost a guinea.'

Bodkin's mouth tightened as Amy smiled across the table.

'I know the dress. I used to work at the shop when they were first put on sale. I'd have liked one myself, but I couldn't afford to buy it.'

'Oh, so you're not actually with the police, then?'

Amy opened her bag and pulled out one of her pink cards. 'I'm officially accredited, so I'm allowed to help with their investigations.'

'Can I keep this?' Miranda asked. 'You never know when you're going to need a private detective.'

Amy nodded eagerly, then pulled out the new card that Laws had given her. 'Here's my official proof of identity.'

'I'm impressed, my dear,' Miranda replied. 'It's about time we had female involvement in the boys' clubs.'

Amy grinned happily as Bodkin tapped his notebook with his pen.

'Do you know if Effie had a job? She must have been supporting herself somehow.'

'I don't think so... oh dear, this might sound rather mean, but I honestly can't see Effie working for a living. She always got by off the backs of others. She used men as much as they used her, Inspector. One flash of those eyes and they were smitten. Three or four of them were almost fighting to be the one she linked arms with when they came out of the Milton that night.'

'Would you recognise any of them if you saw them again?' Bodkin asked.

'I don't think so. It was dark, and they were in a bit of a maul. There was a lot of shouting, pushing, and shoving. I stood back to keep well out of the way.'

'What about the girls?' Amy asked. 'You said there were a couple of young women there. Would you recognise them if you saw them again?'

'Again no, I'm sorry.' Mrs Watkins thought for a moment. 'They were young, pretty much the same age as Effie, if not slightly younger. One had dark hair, cut in a bob. She was hanging onto one of the men with the oars badge on his jacket, one of the older men. He was a good-looking chap, as I remember. Dark hair... long on top. He must have been in his thirties. About the right age for a girl in her early twenties.' She looked from Bodkin to Amy. 'They're a little more grown up... more mature, aren't they, dear?'

# CHAPTER SEVEN

A few minutes later, Bodkin and Amy got to their feet as Mrs Watkins picked up the teacups and placed them onto the tray.

'One last thing,' Bodkin said as she was about to carry the crockery into the kitchen. 'How did Effie and your son John get on? Was it a closer relationship than you had with her?'

'John did his best. He tried, but there was no sort of response from her. He was a good few years older, mind you. When she got to sixteen, he offered to take her out to a show and on her seventeenth, for a meal, but she didn't take him up on his offers. He used to buy her nice presents at Christmas, but she didn't buy him anything in return, not that I remember anyway.' She put the tray back onto the coffee table and picked up one of the many pictures of her son from the sideboard. 'This is John. He's a vet. The photograph was taken just after he joined the Fullerton veterinary practice in Sittingbourne. It was a few weeks after he graduated.'

Bodkin took the photo frame from her and studied the image. It showed a tall, thin, bespectacled man in his late twenties, wearing a tweed jacket and plus fours trousers. His hair was thinning prematurely. At his feet were two liver and white spaniels.

After handing the picture to Amy, he smiled at Mrs Watkins. 'A vet. You must be very proud. Does he visit you often?'

'Not as often as I'd like. He has work commitments these days. I last saw him at Easter. He came up for the bank holiday, before then it was Mother's Day.'

Amy placed the photograph back on the sideboard and took a quick look at a couple of the other pictures. 'That's a shame. You must miss him.'

'I'm used to not seeing him, to be honest. John was at Cambridge University for years, then he took up the post in Sittingbourne.' Mrs Watkins picked up the tea tray again. 'He gets up when he can. He was supposed to come up the weekend just passed, but something came up at work... an urgent matter with a flock of sheep, so he had to call it off.'

'I see.' Bodkin smiled at Mrs Watkins and turned towards the door. 'We'll be in touch when we learn anything more.'

As Mrs Watkins reached for the door handle, Amy asked the question that had been nagging at her since they found Effie's body in the reed beds. 'Did Effie have a favourite bag? We women can't live without one, but she didn't have hers with her when she was found.'

'She only had one bag, and she never went anywhere without it.' She pointed to the photograph that Bodkin was still holding. 'It's the one in the picture. She was really proud of it and it was of great sentimental value to her. Her father bought it for her in Italy when we were on holiday. It's an Accardi original. I have to admit, it's a beautiful thing.' She pointed to the picture again. 'Red, soft Italian leather, with glass beads formed to make the shape of a large, white rose on either side. It has a magnetic clasp and a thick, chain-link silver chain. It also has a grip handle, so you could remove the chain strap.' She paused as Bodkin looked again at the photograph. 'It's very distinctive. I doubt there's another one like it in the area. It cost Claude the equivalent of twenty-five pounds back then.' Miranda sighed, 'Effie used to pawn it when she was running low on funds. She never asked much for it, just a few shillings to tide her over. She had to be sure she could afford to reclaim it when she had the money.'

'Twenty-five pounds!' Bodkin was aghast.

'It's a small price to pay for something so beautiful that will probably last you a lifetime, Inspector.' Mrs Watkins picked up her own handbag from a small hall table. 'I've had this for over fifteen years and it looks even better now than the day I bought it. Italian leather ages so well.'

Amy nodded appreciatively. 'I'd love to own something like that. There's one in Brigden's Nearly New Store that I'd give my eyeteeth to own. It's only three pounds, but it's still beyond my means. I can see what you mean about quality, though. I've got through two cheap bags in the last three years. Something like that would see me into my dotage.'

'It's just a bag,' Bodkin muttered as he stepped out into the corridor. 'Twenty-five pounds is three month's wages for some people.'

'Not for Claude, it wasn't,' Mrs Watkins replied as she eased the door closed behind him.

'He spent twenty-five pounds on a handbag.' Bodkin shook his head as they approached the stairs.

'And we are so lucky that he did,' Amy replied thoughtfully. 'It's a very distinctive bag. You wouldn't expect to see it in Spinton. Especially if someone like me was carrying it.'

'I wouldn't notice the bag if you were,' Bodkin replied. 'But I'd notice you in the largest of crowds.'

Amy smiled and slipped her arm through the policeman's as they walked down the stairs. 'You say the nicest things, Bodkin, but you're a typical man, and you really are a bit of a philistine when it comes to fashion. You only ever notice a woman's face, chest and legs.' She shot him a quick glance. 'I'm not having a go at you, because, as I said, it's typically male. A woman would notice a lot more. She'd spot the hair, the makeup, her clothes, shoes and any jewellery she might be wearing. She'd definitely notice a fabulous bag like that one.' Amy let go of Bodkin's arm as they reached the bottom of the stairway and walked through the double doors into the reception area. 'As a detective, you really are missing a trick.'

'I don't need feminine instincts when I've got you with me,' Bodkin said, nodding to the receptionist as they passed by the desk.

'You'll never acquire them either, Bodkin. It was just the same when I tried to explain female body language to you. A man's brain doesn't work the same way as a woman's. It's why so many female criminals evade capture.'

'Do they?' Bodkin replied, scratching his head. 'Maybe it's just that women don't commit as many serious crimes as men.'

Amy shrugged. 'Possibly not, but to say we number half the population, there must be a hell of a lot who aren't being caught.'

'Are you saying that women are more intelligent than men?' Bodkin asked as he opened the door of the black Morris for her.

Amy looked quizzically at him. 'Of course I am,' she said.

# CHAPTER
# EIGHT

'So, what's next?' Amy asked as Bodkin drove the car through the black gates and out onto the open road.

'Lunch?' Bodkin said, flashing a smile at her.

'It's a bit late for lunch,' Amy replied, checking her watch. 'It will be teatime in an hour and a half.' She looked across at Bodkin, studying him for a moment. 'Have you eaten at all today?'

'Not yet,' Bodkin said. 'That's why I mentioned taking you to lunch. I lose track of the time when I'm on a case.'

Amy checked her watch again. 'You'd better have a snack at least, Bodkin. Fasting might be good for Indian mystics, but in the real world, we need to eat to keep the energy flowing. If you want to stop off at mine, I'll make you a quick sandwich. I'll cook for you tonight if you like. How do you fancy egg and chips?'

Bodkin licked his lips. 'Double egg and chips is my favourite meal.'

'Alongside my mum's shepherd's pie and her famous Sunday roast.'

Bodkin grimaced as his stomach rumbled. 'Stop talking about food, please. I think I can hang on for the egg and chips. We ought to drop in to see the kids that found Effie's body yesterday. They should be home from school soon and I'd like to know if they can remember anything more now that they've had time to get over the shock.'

'I think it will take them a while to get over it, Bodkin, but it's probably better to talk to them while the incident is fresh in their minds. Who knows what embellishments a child's mind might add to the story over a period of time. They do have very active imaginations at that age.'

'Danny found her. I didn't actually see her face, but I saw her legs and feet,' Diane Trainor said as she twiddled her fingers, sitting at a greasy-looking kitchen table. Her mother busied herself poking the fire in the range. Although it was another hot day, every house on the street would have a fire in the grate to enable them to cook the evening meal when the men returned home from work.

Bodkin looked around the dirty kitchen. Damp patches formed their own patterns in the wallpaper, and the earthen tiles that had been laid onto a dirt floor were lifting in places. 'That's all right, Diane,' Amy said softly. 'Are you still thinking about it?'

The child shook her head quickly.

'Yes, she is,' her mother said sharply. 'She wanted to come into my bed last night because she said she had seen the dead woman's ghost.'

Amy reached across and took Diane's hand. 'Ghosts don't exist,' she said. 'Honestly, Diane, there are no such things as ghosts.'

'There are,' Diane said quickly. 'Danny O'Toole saw his grandad after he died.'

'Danny O'Toole's mother is Irish,' Mrs Trainor said, as though that explained everything.

'Are you sure you didn't see anyone else in the reeds, Diane? Think very carefully,' Bodkin said.

'I didn't see anyone else. It was just me and Danny in the reeds. Charlie and Ben were still in the Silverstream.'

Amy patted the girl's hand. 'You're very brave, Diane. You were the only girl to cross the stream. It's quite scary when you first do it, isn't it?'

Diane nodded and looked up at her with wide eyes. 'That was the first time I've done it; the water came up to here.' She put the flat of her hand across her chest. 'The boys dared me to do it. I didn't want to, really.'

'I was the same the first time I waded across to get to the bull-rushes. Some boys dared me and my best friend Alice. We were scared too, but we did it. You can't let boys win all the time, can you?'

Diane shook her head.

'Is Danny your best friend?' Amy asked.

Diane grinned. 'He's my boyfriend. Caroline is my best girlfriend.'

'Did you see Danny at school today? Did you talk about what happened?'

'Danny wasn't at school today.'

'Really? You were very brave going yourself, Diane, after the shock you had.'

'Mum said I had to go.'

'Kids take too much time off.' Mrs Trainor grunted as she lifted a heavy pot containing a watery soup onto the hot plate. 'That Danny's hardly ever there. He'll be as thick as two short planks when he leaves school. Who's going to want to employ a lad who can't write his own name?'

'He can write his name. Danny is top of the class,' Diane protested.

Mrs Trainor spat into the flames, then pulled a tin out of her apron pocket and selected a thin, hand-rolled cigarette. Sticking it between her lips, she rolled up a thin strip of newspaper, stuck it into the fire, then held it up to the cigarette to light it. Coughing, she dropped the paper onto the fire and turned to face Bodkin. 'He's as rough as a badger's arse, that one.' She was silent for a moment as she took another draw on her cigarette. 'Takes after his father.'

Bodkin got to his feet. 'Are you sure you can't remember anything else, Diane? Did you see any boats on the water?'

Diane shook her head again. 'The reeds were too high; I couldn't see over them.'

Bodkin nodded. 'Right, Mrs Trainor, we'll let you get on with cooking your tea. I'm sorry to intrude, but these things have to be done.'

Mrs Trainor pursed her lips as she nodded. 'At least it's taught her a lesson. She won't be going collecting bullrushes for a while. It's a shame because we could use the extra money. Sixpence goes a long way when you've got nothing in the pantry.'

The O'Toole family lived five houses along the Victorian terraced street on the other side of a narrow alleyway. Bodkin and Amy found Kathleen, Danny's mother, hanging washing on their side of the cobbled yard. She had just pushed the wooden prop under the line and wedged the bottom of it between two bricks as they pushed the gate open to gain access.

'You'll be the police, I take it,' Kathleen said in a Kentish accent with just a hint of Irish. 'Marty said you'd be around.'

Bodkin pulled out his warrant card and introduced himself and Amy. 'Marty?'

'My other half. Some would say it's the better half, but then they don't know Marty.'

'Marty is your husband, then?'

'Sort of. We're not married. My husband died five years ago, fell under a bus, drunk.'

'I'm sorry to hear that, Mrs O'Toole,' Bodkin replied.

'I'm not. He was an evil bastard, too quick to use his fists. The one I'm lumbered with now is no better, mind you, but at least he works. Eamon never worked an honest day in his life.'

'That must have been hard for you with a young family.'

Kathleen shrugged. 'The boys didn't know him. By the time he rolled home at night, they were fast asleep and when he got up, he'd only find time for a mug of tea before he went out to do whatever it was he did to make his drinking money.'

'Boys? So, there's more than just Danny?'

'I have two boys, lost three more at birth.' Kathleen crossed herself then turned back towards the house. 'You had better come in if you want to talk to Danny.'

The house was in an almost identical state to the Trainor's, except that it was much cleaner. Mrs O'Toole obviously took pride in her home, dilapidated as it was.

'Danny, get yourself in here,' she shouted as she led Bodkin and Amy through the scullery into the kitchen.

A few seconds later, a door opened and a young boy of seven or eight stuck his head around it.

'It's the police,' Kathleen said. 'They want to talk to you again.'

'Marty said I wasn't to talk to them,' the boy said, nervously. 'What if he finds out?'

Mrs O'Toole's voice softened. 'I won't tell him, and I'm sure this lady and gentlemen won't.' She pulled out a chair from under the table and motioned for Amy to sit. Bodkin dragged another one out and the pair sat looking across at the young boy, who was still standing in the doorway shuffling his feet.

'Come in, son. No one's going to hurt you,' Bodin said as gently as he could. He raised a finger and beckoned the boy in with it. 'Come and sit down.'

'Would you be wanting tea?' Kathleen asked, her Irish accent much more pronounced.

Bodkin looked at Amy, who shook her head. 'Not for us thanks, we've not long had one, but don't let that stop you.'

Kathleen shrugged and said nothing.

Danny, meanwhile, had crossed to the table and was standing with his hands behind his back as though he was about to receive a lecture from the headmaster.

'Now, Danny,' Bodkin began. 'I'd like you to take us back to yesterday. Is there anything else you can think of that might help us with our inquiries?'

Amy smiled warmly at the boy. 'Sit down, Danny, you're not in school assembly now.'

The boy's mouth twitched, but the smile didn't appear. 'I can't remember nothing. Just what I said I saw.'

'You didn't see anyone in the reeds, or a boat nearby?'

Danny shook his head. 'I told you. I don't remember nothing else.' He looked quickly at his mother. 'Can I go now?'

'I won't keep you long, Danny,' Bodkin said. 'Just stay where you are for a little longer.'

Danny twisted his body stiffly, then groaned.

'Are you all right, Danny?' Amy asked, getting to her feet.

'It's growing pains. He gets growing pains,' Kathleen said as Amy walked around the table towards the boy.

Amy crouched down next to Danny and put her hand on his shoulder. The boy flinched as though he'd been struck. 'It's all right, Danny,' Amy said softly. 'I'm not going to hurt you.'

Danny groaned again as he straightened his back.

'Growing pains... Don't they usually affect the legs?' Bodkin asked.

'Danny gets them in his back,' Katheen said quickly.

Bodkin got out of his seat and walked around the table to stand next to the boy. 'Turn around, son,' he said. Danny reluctantly did as he was told, and Bodkin tugged the child's shirt from the waistband of his trousers and pulled it up his back to expose the skin.

'Oh, my goodness!' Amy put her hand to her mouth as she saw the black and purple welts that ran across the boy's back.

Bodkin let the shirt fall back, then crouching down himself, he put both hands on the boy's shoulders and gently turned him around.

'It's all right, son... it's all right,' he said quietly.

Danny's chin fell to his chest. 'Don't say you saw; please don't say you saw.'

Bodkin straightened and ruffled the boy's hair. 'I didn't see a thing, Danny, so I can't tell anyone about it, can I?' He walked back to the other side of the table and looked down at the youngster through sad eyes. 'Are you sure you didn't see anyone at all at the river yesterday, son?'

'You won't tell Marty I said anything?'

Bodkin gave the cub's salute. 'Scout's honour.'

'I heard a boat.'

'You heard a boat... you didn't see one?'

'No, I heard it. It was a motorboat. It didn't sound as though it was close by and I didn't see anyone. Honest, mister, it could just have been sailing down the river.'

'We didn't hear one when we came out of the woods,' Bodkin replied. He looked across at Amy. 'I can't remember seeing a motorboat on the river.'

Amy shook her head. 'I didn't see or hear anything either.'

'You're sure it was a motorboat, Danny? Was it a loud noise?'

'It wasn't close by.' Danny looked from Bodkin toward his mother. 'Can I go now?'

Kathleen glanced at Bodkin, then nodded. 'Off you go.'

'You won't say I told you anything... you promise?' Danny begged as he backed off towards the door.

'We didn't even come here, Danny. Don't worry,' Bodkin said with a soft smile.

The inspector stared at the closed door for a full minute after Danny had left the room. Then, turning his attention to Mrs O'Toole, he let out a long sigh. 'I take it that was Marty's doing?'

Kathleen nodded. 'Danny can be a bit of a rascal; he needs the discipline.'

'No child needs disciplining like that, Mrs O'Toole,' Amy said. 'It was hardly a smack on the back of the legs, was it?'

'Marty is... Danny isn't his son, so he doesn't feel any... what's the word, empathy?'

'Does he treat your other son the same way?'

Kathleen nodded. 'Brian wasn't involved with the police yesterday, so he just got a slap around the head for allowing his brother to speak to you.' Kathleen took a deep breath, then reached for her tobacco tin. 'Marty hates the police. He wouldn't say a word to them if he was the only witness to a murder.' She picked up a matchbox from the shelf and lit her cigarette. 'Not that either of the kids have to talk to the police to get a good hiding. Beatings are commonplace here; they get dished out routinely. They only have to look at him to cop a slap.'

'That's disgraceful,' Amy spat.

'Danny wasn't at school today,' Bodkin said. 'Was your Brian?'

'I kept Danny away as he was in a lot of pain this morning. Luckily Marty gets up for work at five, he's at the pit. The kids don't usually get up until after seven.'

'Does he hit you too?' Amy asked.

Kathleen tipped her head back and blew out a long plume of smoke. 'Doesn't every woman in this town cop it now and then?'

'I don't and my mother doesn't,' Amy retorted. 'And you shouldn't have to put up with it, either. Why don't you call the police?'

Kathleen flicked the ash from the end of her cigarette into the fireplace and snorted a laugh. 'You're kidding,' she snorted.

Before Amy could respond again, Bodkin touched her on the shoulder.

'Come on, we have things to do.' He smiled across at Kathleen. 'Thanks for your time. Please assure Danny that we won't say a word about our visit today to anyone. Marty will never know.'

Kathleen blew out her cheeks, then let the air out slowly. 'It doesn't matter whether you say anything or not. The neighbours will be queueing up to tell him.'

Back out on the street, Amy was beside herself with the injustice of it all.

'She just laughed when I mentioned her going to the police, Bodkin. Surely that's what they are there for. Stopping vile men attacking women and children is part of their job description, isn't it?'

Bodkin sighed. 'Left to me, I'd arrest every single one of them, but sadly, the force looks on things like this as domestic incidents, and they don't want to get involved. The system would collapse under the weight of actual bodily harm cases if they did. The courts wouldn't be able to function. Our magistrates wouldn't thank us for all the extra work.

'That doesn't mean these bullies should be allowed to get away with it, Bodkin. What gives men the right to come home drunk and beat their wives because she went to bed without leaving his supper on the table?'

'The law turns a blind eye to it, Amy. There used to be a thing called the rule of thumb, which meant that a husband was allowed to beat his wife with a stick, providing it was no thicker than the circumference of his thumb. Women have had the right to a divorce on the grounds of cruelty since the eighteen sixties, but the vast majority of victims didn't use the law because once they had left the marital home, they found that they had made themselves destitute, and the only place to go was the workhouse.

Amy stopped dead as they approached Bodkin's car. 'So, are you telling me that people like this Marty can happily beat their spouses... and their children, and walk away scot-free?'

'It depends on the magistrate, Amy. A lot will just issue a small fine and tell them not to do it again. Meanwhile, the kids would rather put up with a beating than be taken away from their families and put in a children's home, or even sent abroad to be abused by men on the other side of the world.'

'It's all so unfair, Bodkin,' Amy said as he opened the car door for her. 'You sound so blasé about it.'

'What can one lone copper do about it, Amy? I hate the fact that these men get away with it every bit as much as you do, but you can bet your best boots on this. Somewhere in Kent, a police officer or a magistrate, will go home after work today and dish out exactly the same sort of punishment that little Danny got on the wrong end of. It's the way it is. It will take more than an act of parliament to stop it happening, and anyway, there just isn't the political will.'

'Because all the institutions are run by men, and all they care about is controlling women. This is the twentieth century and boys are still growing up thinking that this is the way a father should treat his family. It's a never-ending cycle because they will grow up, get married and do the same thing. It has to change, Bodkin... doesn't it?'

Bodkin slammed the door of the car, sat back in the driver's seat and closed his eyes. 'Change can't come soon enough for me, Amy. I want to see these men behind bars for what they do, but we'd have to build a prison on every housing estate in the country if we are going to lock them all up. It's attitudes that have to change, and that's going to take another generation or more.' He thought for a moment. 'It looks increasingly likely that this country is about to face another war. The last time, women got the vote at the end of it because they proved they were the equal of men, especially in the workforce. Sadly, the vote was all they got. They didn't get equal pay or equal rights in many other areas, especially marital ones. Soon, women will have to take on the breadwinner role again. There will be millions working on the land and in the factories. This time they have to demand meaningful change at the end of hostilities.' Bodkin half turned to look at Amy. 'You can't take your foot off the accelerator.'

Amy's eyes brimmed with tears as she listened to the policeman. 'Oh, Bodkin. I wish you were the prime minister,' she said.

Bodkin started the engine, but before engaging the gears, he turned back to face her. 'I'd be totally useless as prime minister, Amy. If we are dragged into another war, the vast majority of men will be away fighting and the women will take have to take their places. What the country will need is for articulate, intelligent women like you to put their ideas forward. You have to be brave, be bold, there can be no going back to how it is now when the war ends. There has to be real progress on equality.' He leaned across and patted Amy's hand. 'You can't rely on men to do it, Amy. The women of this country will be looking to people like you to speak up for them. I'll just be one of the more enlightened males, cheering you on in the background.' He put the car into gear and pulled away from the kerb. 'Until then, what we witnessed tonight will remain the norm. You might have lofty ideals, Amy, but down here on the ground, I have to deal with the reality.'

# CHAPTER NINE

'You're very quiet tonight, Bodkin,' Amy said as the couple sat next to each other on the sofa listening to the BBC orchestra on the National radio station's Monday at Seven programme.

Bodkin smiled, stretched out his legs, and rubbed his stomach. 'I'm just feeling rather content after eating such a scrumptious meal.'

Amy rested her head on the policeman's shoulder. 'You're tired, you should get an early night.'

Bodkin put his arm around her and pulled her to him. 'I'm good for a few hours yet. I never drop off when I go to bed early, anyway.'

'What have we got on the agenda tomorrow? Ooh, no, wait, I love this tune. Come on! Get on your feet, man.'

Bodkin got awkwardly to his feet as Amy waited with outstretched arms. 'Do you know this song? It's Glen Miller, Moonlight Serenade. It's the perfect smooching tune.'

After the slow, clinging dance, the BBC orchestra livened things up with The Woodchoppers Ball, so Amy and Bodkin went back to the sofa.

'Where were we?' Amy said as she took hold of Bodkin's arm

and wrapped it around her shoulders. 'Oh yes, what's on the agenda tomorrow?'

Bodkin thought for a moment before replying. 'Well... the postmortem results should be on my desk first thing. I was supposed to get them by five o'clock today, but I had a phone call telling me it had been delayed and won't take place until late this afternoon.'

'At least we'll know how she died,' Amy said softly. 'The poor girl looked like she'd just received some shocking news.'

'It's not often we get a body with no real outward signs of injury. It could be a poisoning, of course. The postmortem might not tell us if that's the case, but the toxicology tests on the blood and organ samples will, although as with the Reverend Villiers case, it might be a few days before we get the results.'

Amy snuggled up closer as another slow tune came from the radio speaker. 'It's such a shame you're banned from my bedroom, Bodkin. This would sound so much nicer coming from the speakers of the radiogram I have upstairs.'

'It's a good job I'm a gentleman and will stick to your parents' house rules,' Bodkin replied, stretching his neck to look at her smiling face.

'I wonder how they're getting on in Margate,' Amy said, more to herself than anything.

'I bet they're wondering how you're getting on by yourself. It's the first time they've left you in charge of the place and you've had a man on the premises two evenings running.'

Amy slapped Bodkin's thigh playfully. 'Well, if we had a telephone, they'd have been able to ring me to see how things are. So, it's their fault if they can't check up on me.' She smiled to herself. 'I reckon I'll get a postcard by Wednesday. "Hello, Amy, mainly sunny skies here and having a lovely time. I hope you're behaving yourself in our absence. PS Dad stinks of jellied eels".'

Bodkin laughed, then stretched his arms above his head. 'Do

you know, I am feeling rather tired. It's far too early for bed, though. Do you fancy a couple of port and lemons at the Old Bull?'

After breakfast the next morning, Amy spent a couple of hours cleaning the house and hand washing her underwear. At eleven she got changed into a green, floral print summer dress and after deliberating for a few moments in the hall, she pulled on a cotton jacket and unhooked her umbrella from the coat rack. Outside it was cloudy and the temperature was some five degrees below what it had been at the weekend. Turning right at the gate, she made her way down to Mollison Farm to have a quick chat with her best friend, Alice, who had taken up the running of the farm after her father had died the year before. Alice, although unmarried, had a one-year-old daughter called Martha. She had been Amy's best friend since their early school days and the pair used to spend every Saturday night together at the local picture palace along with Bodkin and the mellow voiced crooner, Constable Ferris. Alice was an attractive young woman with classic high cheekbones and dark chestnut hair. She so closely resembled the Hollywood starlet Rita Hayworth that the local cinema owner had offered her money to walk up and down outside the theatre when one of her movies was being shown.

Amy found Alice in the yard, feeding scraps to the chickens. She was wearing dirty overalls over a short-sleeved man's shirt. Her dark, wavy hair was tied back with a strip of red material.

'Hi there,' she called as she saw Amy come through the gate. 'I wouldn't get too close. These overalls are ripe. I've only just finished cleaning out the porkers.'

Amy waved her hand in front of her nose as if to waft away the aroma. 'You forget, I'm used to your piggy smell. It's far less pungent than the perfume you wore on Saturday. Where on earth did you get that?'

Alice rolled her eyes. 'I got it from Alf Mistry's market stall, if you must know. He took it from his mother's dressing table when she died. He threw it in as a gift with the box of talc I bought.' She paused for a moment. 'I had a quick sniff when he gave it to me. It didn't smell too bad out in the open air.'

'Promise me you'll never wear it again, dear heart,' Amy said, stifling a giggle. 'Give it to someone you don't like as a Christmas present. Personally, I'd give it to Big Nosed Beryl at work.'

Alice laughed. She knew that Beryl didn't have a particularly big nose. She just couldn't resist sticking it into everyone else's business.

'This is a nice surprise, I must say. I wasn't expecting you to drop in until Wednesday evening... oh, wait... it's factory fortnight, isn't it?'

'It is, and I'm only on my second day off,' Amy replied with a grin. She looked over her shoulder as if to check they couldn't be overheard. 'We've... that is, Bodkin has a new case. I've been given official permission to help him with it.'

Alice tipped the almost empty bowl of scraps upside down, then turned to walk back to the kitchen. 'Well, Detective Inspector Rowlings, you can make yourself useful by putting the kettle on while I have a quick wash and get changed into something less whiffy.'

'I'm not staying long,' Amy replied as Alice walked through the kitchen towards the bathroom that lay on the other side of the parlour door. 'I'll put the kettle on for you, though.' She picked up the big kettle, shook it to gauge how much water was inside, then, after topping it up from the tap, she turned on the gas on the hob and lit it with a match. 'I just came around to remind you that you had offered to teach me to drive.'

'I remember as it happens. Are you sure you want to learn in my old truck, though? It's fifteen years old, it's as temperamental as hell, and you have to start it with a crank handle.'

'I'll let you do the starting, dear heart. I just want to be able to steer it in a straight line and stop it when I need to.'

'On your head be it.' Alice undid the fabric tie and shook her hair loose. 'You'd be much better off learning in one of those little black cars. Bodkin has one. Won't he teach you?'

'He can't. It isn't his car; it belongs to the police, and he'd get into serious trouble if I had an accident in it. I do want to get my driver's licence, though. How long have you had yours now?'

'I got mine when I was eighteen. I actually took my test in the truck.'

Amy sighed. 'Up until four years ago, I wouldn't have needed to take a test. Still, things are what they are. The government know best. When do you think you'll have time to give me my first lesson?'

'Come over on Saturday, about eleven. I'll have Big Brenda's engine warmed up and she'll be out front, raring to go.'

'It's a good job Long Lane is one straight road, isn't it?' Amy replied. 'I won't be ready to take on a bend for a lesson or two.'

'You'll need to build your muscles up for that,' Alice replied. 'You'd better start eating spinach like Popeye the Sailor Man.'

'I was just about to nip around to your house.' Bodkin smiled as Amy entered his newly tidied up office.

'Wow, you have been busy in here, Bodkin. It only needs a mop running over the floor.' She ran her finger across the edge of his desk. 'And a duster on the furniture.'

Bodkin shook his head. 'I had ten minutes to spare while I waited for the post-mortem results. I don't have time to dust and mop. The cleaners used to come every day to do that, but now because of the cutbacks, they only come in at weekends.'

Amy hung her jacket and umbrella on the stand and sat down on the seat in front of the desk. 'You got the post-mortem results? That's great. How did she die, Bodkin?'

'The pathologist doesn't know for sure, but he has an idea. He'll know more when he gets the blood tests back at the end of the week.'

'He doesn't know?'

Bodkin picked up a buff folder from his desk and opened it. 'Thankfully, I get two reports, one in medical speak and one in plain English. He says that there was no sign of injury externally. Effie was a fit, healthy girl who had never so much as broken a bone or had a tooth extracted. Her last meal was made up of sandwiches. Ham and cheese to be precise. There was also some alcohol, but not an excessive amount. There were no sign of any puncture wounds, so at first sight, it appears that she wasn't injected with anything nasty.'

'So how did a healthy young woman like that die all of a sudden?'

'I asked myself the same question when I read this.' Bodkin dropped the folder on the desk. 'Then I telephoned and asked him. He said he couldn't give a definitive answer until he has the blood tests back, then he said something rather interesting.'

'Oh, come on, Bodkin, don't keep me in suspense.'

'He had noticed a slight reddening around the lips and in the back of the throat. When he opened up the stomach lining, a rather sweet smell emerged. To begin with, he couldn't quite work out what it was, then his assistant told him.'

'Bodkin!'

'His assistant had been to the dentist at the weekend so he could clearly remember where he had smelled the substance before. He was sure it was Chloroform. He's going to do further tests, particularly on the lungs, the stomach and the brain because apparently, it will leave tell-tale signs that can still be found quite a time after death.'

'Chloroform? The stuff they use to knock you out while they pull out your teeth?'

'The very same.'

'But surely all that proves is that she went to a dentist to have a... ah, I see, her teeth were in good condition, weren't they? She would have had no need to visit the dentist.' Amy thought for a moment. 'But they only give you a few drops sprinkled on a cloth, don't they? It evaporates in the air; how would any traceable amount get into her stomach?'

'You'll make a detective yet, Amy,' Bodkin said with a grin. 'That was my next question and he couldn't explain it.'

'So, we're assuming she died with an overdose of Chloroform?'

'It's a possibility. He did say there were no obvious puncture marks. It doesn't mean there aren't any hidden away in her scalp or under her nails, and her body had been immersed in water for a time. The toxicology report will help, but even with modern testing techniques, a lot of poisons would be untraceable by the time the post-mortem was carried out. Cyanide included. Though there are some signs they can pick up on.'

'Blimey! What a puzzle. But at the moment, the only thing we have to go on is the Chloroform, so, our early suspect is either a dentist... a doctor... who else has access to it?'

'Anyone working in the field of medicine or at medical research centres... not that there are any around here that I can think of. Then there are the chemical manufacturing plants. We do have one of those in town.'

Amy nodded. 'We really need to find out who she hung around with and who would have had access to that stuff. There can't be too many.' She rubbed her hands together. 'Where do we start?'

Bodkin pulled a folded sheet of notepaper from his pocket. 'We start at her flat. Mrs Watkins provided me with the address yesterday. She lived in an apartment block at the far end of Main Street. Shall we take a walk? I fancy stretching my legs.'

# CHAPTER TEN

Cramley Lodge was a tasteful block of twenty-four apartments built out of yellow brick in a crescent shape. Its balconies were covered in a cream-coloured render. Built in the nineteen twenties, the building stood out in the town as the only example of its type. On the right-hand side of the building was a glass staircase tower that led to all four floors. The main entrance doors were built into the tower structure. On a brick plinth was a metal plate with six rows of brass buttons that would buzz the individual flats. Bodkin pressed the button for flat twelve and waited. After a full minute, he pressed the button again, only to find the door opening. Then the face of a pretty, dark-haired girl appeared.

'Sorry, it takes me a minute or so to get down here,' she said. She looked from Amy to Bodkin and back again. 'What can I do for you?' Her eyelashes fluttered as she looked into Bodkin's face.

'I'm Inspector Bodkin and this,' he held out a hand towards Amy, 'Is Amy Rowlings. We're looking for the owners of flat twelve.'

'I live in flat twelve, but I'm not the owner. I could never afford to buy something like this on my wages.' The young woman rolled her eyes skywards. 'I'm Daphne McAllister, by the way.'

'What about Effie Watkins, Daphne? Does she own the flat?'

'Oh dear, what's Effie done now?' the girl asked.

'Do you think we could speak inside?' Bodkin said. 'The conversation we are about to have would be better held in private.'

Daphne led Amy and Bodkin up the winding staircase to the second-floor corridor. 'We're at the end,' she said pointing to the right. 'We've got a lovely view of the river from our flat.'

The apartment was painted white with a series of red and green flashes littered at random intervals on the walls. The main room was open-plan with a kitchen at the far end. On the left-hand side, four doors led off. In the centre of the room was an oval-shaped carpet on which sat a powder blue sofa with a gun metal framed, glass topped coffee table sitting in front of it.

'You're lucky to catch me, actually. I phoned in sick at work.' She put both hands on her stomach and looked directly at Amy. 'Women's troubles,' she mouthed.

'Where do you work, Miss McAllister?'

'I'm a typist come general dogsbody at Donnelley's Law practice just up the road,' she said. She looked closely at Bodkin. 'What's this about? What has Effie done?'

'We'll come to that in a moment,' Bodkin replied. 'Do you mind if we sit down?'

'Please, be my guest,' Daphne said, holding out her hand towards the sofa. 'Would you like a cup of tea?'

Bodkin shook his head. 'Not for me thanks.' Amy licked her lips at the prospect of a drink but shook her head too.

'When did you last see Effie Watkins, Miss McAllister?'

'Call me Daphne, please. Miss McAllister seems so formal. It's what they call me at work all the time. I've almost forgotten my Christian name.'

Bodkin smiled as the young woman pulled a chair from beneath a round shaped table. After sitting down, she looked directly at Bodkin and slowly crossed her legs. Amy shot Bodkin a glance, but when he didn't respond, she closed her eyes and muttered something under her breath.

'When did you last see her, Daphne?' Bodkin repeated the question.

Daphne blew out her cheeks and placed a slender fingered, beautifully manicured, hand on her throat. 'It would have been a couple of weeks ago, I suppose. She came back for the weekend. She was flashing a new bracelet about. She said she was going to sell it, pawn it... something like that. I didn't see that much of her to tell you the truth.'

'Does she own the flat or do you share the tenancy?'

'It's a bit complicated.'

'I do complicated,' Bodkin replied. 'A big part of my job involves dealing with complicated.'

Daphne fidgeted in her seat. Her eyes looked at the carpet, then back up at Bodkin. 'You won't tell anyone, will you? I mean, you won't report me to the landlord. I risk being thrown out.'

'If there's no need to question the landlord, then he won't hear anything from me.' Bodkin gave her his most reassuring smile.

Daphne ran her hand over her thigh, then slowly crossed her legs again. 'I sublet,' she said. 'It's against the rules and both Effie and I could be thrown out if the agency we rent from finds out.'

'You sublet. How big a share of the rent do you pay, and how long does the tenancy agreement go on for?'

'I pay all of the rent,' Daphne said. 'Well, Dad pays half of it; I just have to find the rest. Effie took out a three-year tenancy. It's up for renewal next summer.' She looked appealingly at Bodkin. 'Please don't tell them. I'll never be able to find another place like this. I don't have the connections and you need good connections for your references.'

Bodkin nodded slowly. 'Effie's mother provided her references, I assume.'

Daphne nodded. 'No one would ever turn her down with a reference coming from that address.'

'We've been there,' Bodkin said. 'It's very impressive.'

'Have you met her? Effie's mother I mean,' Daphne asked.

'We met her yesterday. She's a very nice woman.'

'She doesn't get on with Effie. They hate each other.'

'I don't think hate is the right word,' Amy put in. 'Not on Mrs Watkins' part at least.' She paused for a moment. 'They did have a rather strained relationship, though.'

'Strained? That's putting it mildly, you should hear some of the things Effie says about her.'

'Sadly, we won't be able to do that, Daphne,' Bodkin said. 'That's why we're here. Effie was found dead at the weekend.'

Daphne raised both hands to her mouth. 'Oh my goodness, what a dreadful thing to happen. How did... where... Oh my goodness, this is awful.'

'Can you tell us a bit more about her?' Bodkin asked. 'Who did she hang around with? How often was she here? Did she ever bring anyone back?'

'As to the last part of your question, no. She never brought anyone back here to my knowledge. This was her bolt hole; she only came back when she was having a bit of man trouble or she wanted to get out of a relationship. Not that it happened all that often. When she got her claws into someone, it usually lasted a few months before they became tired of her, or she of them.'

'What was she like, as a person?' Amy asked.

'Oh, she was friendly enough. We got on really well, which is why I'm living here. I met her at one of the Highwater Boat Club evenings. It was her first time there and she didn't know anyone.

She hadn't been invited, she just turned up at the door saying she'd lost her invitation. No one knew her, of course, but there was no shortage of men trying to convince the club secretary that they had invited her in person but had forgotten to put her name down on the guest list. Anyway, to cut a long story short, we ended up sharing a bottle of champagne at one of the tables while half the men in the club were fawning over her. I liked her. She obviously came from good stock. Although I think she could put that clipped accent on at will; she didn't always use it. She was well connected, that was for certain. She knew exactly what names to drop into the conversation.'

Daphne looked up at the ceiling as she gathered her thoughts.

'We became friends very quickly. I rescued her... or at least I thought I had... from a couple of the club members at the end of the night. Both were trying to get her to go back with them. She was very drunk... or seemed to be. She soon sobered up when I got her into the ladies. I asked her where she lived and she gave her mother's address, then she said she couldn't go back there as they had had a blazing row. I was renting a room at the time in a house just past the Mill. It's a clothing factory on the other side of town. Anyway, I sneaked her into my room that night, but when I got up in the morning, she had gone. She had obviously remembered part of the conversation we had engaged in the night before, because on the Monday she turned up in the reception at Donnelley's. We went out to lunch. I paid; I seem to remember. She said she was temporarily financially embarrassed but that when she finally made up with her mother, she'd have funds again. After lunch, we had a walk by the river and we passed this place. There was a sign on the wall advertising an apartment to let. I remember saying what a lovely building it was and how lucky anyone would be to be able to afford to live here. About a week later she turned up at the office again and announced that she had talked her mother into paying the first year's rent on this apartment, and would I like to sublet. Well, I jumped at the opportunity and the following month I moved in with her.'

'Did she continue to visit the Boat Club?'

'Oh yes, she was there all the time. She always got herself a lunch invitation and never missed one of their formals. The Highwater isn't as big as the two clubs down the river towards Chatham, but they must have a couple of hundred members. They compete in a three-way boat race with the other two clubs every summer. They win it sometimes too... the eights, that is. I don't think they've ever won the quads or the sculls.'

'What sort of men did she hang around with?' Bodkin asked.

Daphne laughed. 'As long as they were male, age didn't matter. She has a lot of admirers, shall we put it that way, and not all were single.'

'So, were the women resentful?'

'Some were.' Daphne clasped her hands in her lap. 'A few wives were desperately unhappy, but they were far too refined to make a scene. Her popularity with the men didn't go down well with some of the young female members either. They used to be the centre of attention before Effie showed up. A couple of them made a bit of a fool of themselves at one of the presentation nights. Claire Bottomley threw a glass of champagne all over her, but Effie just laughed and asked the club captain to rub her down with his handkerchief. That got a lot of cheers... from the men, at least.'

'Did she have any real friends amongst the women, apart from you, that is?'

'I can't remember her being particularly close to anyone but then I didn't go all that often. I didn't really feel all that safe, to be honest. Some of the men... well, wandering hands don't come close. The older ones were the worst for that. There was one fellow, always wore a white captain style hat... what was his name? Gerald something... anyway, he had arms like an octopus and he didn't care if anyone slapped him around the face, either.' She paused before continuing. 'There were rumours about Effie and him, but he was over sixty and she was a beautiful young girl with her whole life in front of her, so I put that down to vicious rumour-mongering.'

'How did she support herself financially?' Bodkin asked.

'She lived off the backs of the men she met. That's the honest truth. I have no idea where she stayed, or who with, but she always seemed to have a new dress when she needed one. Her wardrobe is full of them. I know that when she was struggling a bit, she'd come back here for a week or so. She had a lovely handbag; it was worth a lot of money. She also had some nice jewellery that she used to pawn now and then to see her through. She was never without a man for too long, though. The Boat Club wasn't the only place she'd go to meet them. She used to hang out at the Milton Cocktail Bar, and the Braithwaite hotel.'

'The Braithwaite?' Bodkin whistled. 'There's posh, and then there's another level of posh on top. Do you know who she used to meet there?'

Daphne shook her head. 'No, but there was always some business convention or society gathering going on there. Effie could blag her way into anywhere. One flutter of those beautiful eyelashes and men used to be putty in her hands.'

'But she never resorted to... how shall we phrase it... taking money for... favours?'

'Oh, she always took money for favours. That was her life in a nutshell, but if you mean was she a prostitute, the answer is a definite no. She did use the word Courtesan once, but that's just an upper-class prostitute, isn't it? I wouldn't say she was that at all.'

'Have you been in her room lately?'

'Only to open a window to let some air in now and again. There isn't much in there apart from a wardrobe full of dresses.'

'Do you mind if we have a look?'

Daphne pointed to the second door along the wall and Bodkin pushed it open to allow Amy to go in first. She made straight for the double wardrobe that was standing on the wall next to the window.

'My goodness, there are some beautiful clothes in here, Bodkin. They're all labels too, London ones mostly. These men have spent some serious money on her.' Her eyes fell onto the shelves that were stacked with items of silk or satin underwear. 'She had expensive tastes, that's for sure.'

Bodkin grunted in acknowledgment as he opened and closed the set of drawers that were next to the bed. 'Nothing of note in here,' he said. 'Come on, it's time we were getting back.'

'Just a minute, Bodkin, there's a lovely-looking jacket here.' She pushed her hand into the shallow right-hand pocket, then into the one on the left-hand side. Pulling out a folded sheet of high-quality notepaper, she opened it up and turned around into the light so she could read what was written on it.

*My darling Effie. Just a little something to say thank you for a wonderful weekend.*

*Angus*

'I wonder how little a something it was?' Amy mused. 'It might have been a cheque or possibly a nice piece of jewellery.'

'I don't suppose we'll ever know,' Bodkin replied. 'Is there a return address in the letter?'

'No, but there's a date. Bodkin, this was only written a fortnight ago!'

Back in the lounge, Bodkin showed the letter to Daphne. 'Have you any idea who Angus might be?'

Daphne scanned the letter and shook her head. 'Sorry, I have no idea. She only ever talked in general terms about the men she was involved with.'

'She had a locket. It had the picture of a young man wearing a university scarf inside. Have you any idea who that might be?'

'That would be Quentin Foxley-Walton. She was mad about him for a time.'

'How long a time?' Amy asked.

'A long time... he was the one bloke she never tired of. He used to hang around her a lot, sometimes down at the club but more especially at the Milton. He's from very good stock. He was away at uni a lot, but he always made a beeline for her whenever he was in the neighbourhood.'

'Is he still at university? Do you know which one?'

'He is, but he isn't, if you see what I mean. Quentin majored in chemistry. He works in a research lab somewhere now. I'm not sure which one or where it is. It will be somewhere in Kent though. His family live down in Sittingbourne and he's big on family. He wouldn't live too far away.'

As Bodkin stepped towards the door, Daphne turned towards him with a look of concern on her face. 'What shall I do with her things... and what about the flat? Her name is on the tenancy.'

Bodkin shrugged. 'I'll tell her mother about her belongings, and I'll explain your situation to her. As you were her daughter's friend and as she's a very nice lady, I think there's a good chance she will put a word in for you with the agency. I wouldn't worry about it too much; you've got a year left, anyway.'

The policeman reached for the door handle, then stopped and turned back. 'We'll send someone over to itemise the clothes just in case we're able to trace them back to where they were bought, but when this case is over, and assuming that Mrs Watkins doesn't want them, I think you'll be allowed to consider them as yours.'

Amy smiled softly at Daphne. 'They aren't your size to be

honest, but if you pack them up and take them down to Brigden's Nearly New Store, I'm sure they'll give you an excellent price for them.'

Back on the pavement, Bodkin stroked his chin as the pair walked back towards the High Street. As they passed a row of shops, Amy suddenly stopped and grabbed hold of Bodkin's arm.

'Bodkin, have you still got Effie's picture in your pocket?'

Bodkin nodded. 'I was going to drop it into the photographers to get some copies made.'

'Good, we can do that in a few minutes, but let's go in here first.' She pointed to the next shop along the street. Above the door was a sign reading APEX JEWELLERS, but above that were the unmistakable three brass balls that marked the sign of the pawnbroker. 'Remember what Daphne said? Effie had a new bracelet, and she was going to either sell it or pawn it. Now, as this is the closest shop to her apartment, if she was going to pawn something, this is almost certainly the place she'd use.'

## CHAPTER
# ELEVEN

THE SHOP WAS SPLIT NEATLY INTO TWO HALVES, WITH THE JEWELLER'S goods displayed on the right-hand side and the pawnbroker's wares displayed in glass cabinets on the left. At the far end of the shop, an elderly man sat behind a glass fronted counter. He was stick-thin with rheumy eyes and white hair and wore a faded navy suit with a black cravat tied loosely at his neck. He looked up as the doorbell tinkled.

Bodkin pulled out his warrant card and introduced himself and Amy.

The proprietor shook his head sadly. 'Ah, you're after information. I was hoping that you'd come in to buy this lovely lady a gift.'

'Another time, perhaps,' Bodkin replied. 'Mr...?'

'I'm Filbert Brownbear,' the man replied. 'I know what you're thinking. No one could look less like his surname than I do.' He sighed, 'It was ever thus, even when I was young.' He paused, then a twinkle appeared in his watery eyes as he continued. 'It's a Viking name you know? So at least some of my ancestors would have looked the part.' He glanced at Amy, then returned his gaze to Bodkin as he smiled. 'It's not always good to have an unusual name.'

Bodkin suddenly looked uncomfortable. Reaching into his jacket pocket, he pulled out the photograph of Effie Watkins and slid it under the glass screen. 'Do you know this young lady?'

Filbert was about to answer when the bell jingled and a stout woman with thick arms, carrying what looked like a rolled-up piece of cloth, came into the shop. She marched up to the counter, and ignoring Bodkin and Amy, slid the bundle under the screen.

'Excuse me while I deal with this customer,' Filbert said. He reached for his ticket pad and scribbled out a few details on it before sliding it across the counter to the woman. 'Two shillings, Mrs Broadbeam.'

'I got two and six for it last week.'

'I hadn't noticed how worn the seat of the trousers were then,' Filbert replied. 'They have a hole the size of your thumb.'

'It's still good quality though. It's worth two and six just for the jacket.'

'Not to me it isn't, Ruby.'

'Two bob won't last us until he gets paid on Saturday morning,' Ruby complained. 'I need to get bread, tea and something for the pot that will last four days. Come on, Filbert, you know I'm good for it.'

Filbert sighed, took back the ticket and made an alteration to it. 'If your George spent less in the pub and on the nags, you'd have enough money to see you through the week, and you wouldn't have to pawn his suit.' He slid the paper and a half-crown piece across the counter.

'Ah, but if he did that you wouldn't get my business,' Ruby replied. She gave Amy and Bodkin a curt nod and while Filbert dragged the navy suit from the counter, she hurried towards the entrance.

As the door was pulled shut behind the woman, Filbert

turned his attention to Bodkin again. 'Now, where were we? Ah yes, the young lady.' He picked up Effie's photograph, and after adjusting his spectacles a couple of times, he nodded slowly. 'Yes, I know her. She's a frequent customer.'

'What sort of things does she pawn? Do you still have any of her... what do you call them... pledges?'

'No, no pledges. She used to bring that fancy handbag of hers in now and then, but I only ever had hold of it for a few days. She always paid her due within a week.'

'What about jewellery?' Bodkin asked.

'Up until last year, she'd pawn a complete set. Earrings, necklace, bracelet and a watch, but she sold them to me about nine months or so ago. Since then, she's only ever pawned her handbag.'

'Do you still have the items?'

'Sadly not, Mr... Bodmin, was it?'

'Bodkin.'

'Ah yes, that's right. I don't have the items anymore. I sold them as a job lot to a very good customer of mine. He has his own jewellers in Canterbury.' Filbert was silent, as though remembering the transaction. Then he spoke again. 'I bought a bangle off her a couple of weeks ago. I still have that.'

'Could we see it?'

Filbert pulled a bunch of keys from a drawer under the desk and let himself into the shop via a black painted door on the right of the screen.

'I put it in here with the bargain items,' he said, flicking through the keys until he found the one he needed to unlock the cabinet.

'The bargain items?'

'Yes, unfortunately for young Miss Watkins, the bangle wasn't as valuable as she thought it was.' He lifted the glass lid of the cabinet and pulled out a solid-looking, gold-clasp bracelet which was about half an inch wide and had a wavy pattern engraved onto it.

'How much is it worth?'

'I gave her fifteen shillings for it. It was probably worth about thirty shillings new. It's only nine carat gold, you see.'

'Oh dear,' Amy said under her breath. 'Somebody wasn't quite as generous as she thought he was.'

'You said new? Wasn't this new?' Bodkin asked.

'Look at it closely, Mr Botpin. It's quite worn on the inside and it's hallmarked with a square and a Roman X so that tells me the item was stamped in Birmingham in 1922.'

'I see,' Bodkin stroked his chin as he mused. 'Have you anything else of hers at all?'

Filbert shook his head. 'She hasn't been back since she sold me this.'

Filbert replaced the item, locked up the cabinet, and returned to his place behind the counter. After pushing the photograph back under the screen, he looked up at the inspector. 'What has she done? I'm assuming the item isn't stolen, or you'd be asking to take it away with you.'

'Nothing that we know of,' Bodkin replied. 'Thank you for your help, Mr Brownbear.'

'You're very welcome, Mr Butlin. Are you related to the people who opened the holiday camp in Skegness a few years ago? My daughter keeps saying she'd like to go there.'

Bodkin shook his head as he turned towards the door. 'No relation,' he said.

'Are you sure you aren't related to the Butlins of Skegness, Bodkin? Mum and Dad might like to take a break from Margate if you could get them a discount.' Amy grinned at the inspector as he stuffed the photograph back into his pocket.

'I could use a holiday myself,' he said. 'But I wouldn't go there to spend a week being entertained by community singalongs and knobbly knee contests.'

'Don't knock it, Bodkin. I saw your knees when you came out of the Silverstream on Sunday. I think you'd stand a good chance of winning the first prize.'

Bodkin laughed. 'I saw your legs too, right up to your...'

'Bodkin!'

'I was about to say what a pleasant experience it was. I wasn't about to suggest you had knobbly knees.'

'That's all right then,' Amy said, biting her lip. 'Where to now, Mr Botpin?'

'The photographer's shop, then I thought I might buy you lunch.'

The Sunshine Café wasn't too busy for a Tuesday lunchtime and while Amy found a table by the window, Bodkin went to the counter to order a pot of tea and two plates of cheese and pickle sandwiches.

They chatted about the latest Spinton gossip as they ate. Amy had just finished her sandwich when the door to the café opened and the mayor's wife, Shirley McKenzie, walked in. She spotted Amy straight away, and wearing an ear-to-ear smile, she waved to her before walking up to the counter.

Two minutes later, and after a warm hug of a greeting, Shirley sat down and blew out her cheeks.

Shirley was a dark-haired, well-dressed woman with a friendly manner. They had become friends during a murder investigation a couple of months before, when she had helped set up a Mayor's Fund meeting so that all of the chief suspects were gathered in one place. Shirley was now ecstatically five months pregnant. She had received the news during the investigation. She and her husband, Robert, had been trying for a baby for years without success.

'I'm still as excited as I ever was,' she replied. 'Robert has stripped the bedroom we'll use as a nursery and has bought two different sorts of wallpaper. One in blue, one pink. He says he'll decorate the room himself while I'm in hospital with the baby.'

'You're going in then?' Amy asked. 'You don't want to have it at home?'

'At my age, the midwife thinks I'm better off in hospital.' She looked across at Bodkin and smiled. 'I hadn't realised thirty-six was old until she said that.'

Bodkin gave her a quick smile, then got to his feet. 'If you two ladies are going to talk babies, I think I'll get back to the station. There were burglary and car theft reports on my desk this morning and there's no one else around to look into them.' He leaned across the table and Amy kissed him on the cheek. 'I'll catch up with you later, Amy.'

'If you come around at teatime, I'll cook again,' Amy replied.

Bodkin grinned. 'It's a date,' he said, then after a quick nod towards Shirley, he turned around and left the café.

Amy watched through the large plate-glass window as Bodkin walked past on his way to Middle Street. When she turned back to Shirley, she found she was grinning.

'You're a proper bone fide couple now, aren't you?' She reached across the table and took hold of Amy's hand. 'I'm so pleased for you. You're so good together.' She leaned forward and lowered her voice slightly. 'He's madly in love with you, you know that, don't you?'

Amy blushed. 'Is he?' she said quietly.

'It's as plain as a pikestaff. You only have to see the way he looks at you. He's smitten, my girl.' She lifted Amy's hand in the air. 'There'll be a ring on that finger before the year is out, mark my words.'

Amy cleared her throat and lifted her teacup to her mouth, although only the cold dregs remained. 'You sound just like my mum,' she said. 'She hears wedding bells every time she sees us together.'

'She'll be buying a new hat for next spring,' Shirley said, picking up her own cup.

Amy decided to change the subject. 'I was hoping to bump into you, Shirley, as I know you're keen on women's welfare issues.'

Shirley put her cup down on the saucer and tipped her head slightly as she looked at Amy. 'As it happens, I'm trying to set up that single mother and baby unit, but I'm not quite getting the support I expected from local businesses. The subject is taboo with a lot of them. I think they are under the impression that they'd be seen as helping women with loose morals.'

'Men,' Amy scoffed. 'I met a woman with two boys yesterday and all of them are beaten regularly by her live-in partner. I brought the matter up with Bodkin, but he said there's nothing the police can do unless someone gets hospitalised after an attack. They lump all these assaults together and list them as domestic incidents, then they just forget about the poor people who are being abused.'

'I know only too well, Amy. I was at the school the other week, speaking to the children at assembly, then I visited a few of the classrooms to see them in their lessons, and in every class there was at least half a dozen kids with black eyes or bruises on their faces. I had a word with Robert about it and he had a word with Superintendent Grayson. He was very sympathetic but, as you have just said, he doesn't think there is anything the police can do about it. It's endemic in society, it seems.'

'Something has to be done,' Amy replied. 'The poor little boy I met yesterday was covered in bruises. He was terrified of the man that inflicted them.'

'The poor mite. How can anyone treat a child like that?' She paused as she sipped at her tea. 'What do you think we ought to do about it?'

'I was reading in the paper... it was a while ago now, so I can't remember all the details, but it seems there are a few women's refuges dotted around the country. Places where mothers can take their children to get away from an abusive partner. Do you think anything like that could be set up here?'

Shirley pulled a face. 'If we did, it couldn't be for the women of Spinton, Amy. It would have to be for women and families from outside the area. The men would find them far too easily if they were hiding in their own town. It's not an easy thing for women to accept either. When they go into those places, they have to cut off the relationships with the rest of their family. No letters, no phone calls. The husband or partner would find them too easily, you see.'

Amy sighed. 'I just feel so impotent. There has to be something I can do to help that poor woman and her little boys.' Her lips formed a thin line. 'I'll think of something... I know... I'll ask the vicar to see if the church can help in any way. If they can't find it in their hearts to help them, then I don't know why I bother attending church. Suffer the little children and all that?'

Shirley reached across and patted Amy's hand again. 'I can see you're upset, Amy, but don't go questioning your faith if the church can't help. Let's both go home and have a think about it. I'll talk to Robert again. He's the mayor, for pity's sake. Surely, he'll have some influence. We'll pool our thoughts the next time we meet.' She rested both hands on her stomach. 'Please believe me when I say I'm behind you one hundred percent over this.'

'Hello, Bodkin,' Amy said as she opened the front door to let the policeman in. 'Have you caught your car thief?'

'As it happens, I have.'

'Already? Good Heavens. You don't mess about do you. Where did you catch him?'

'He ran out of petrol right outside the police station. He tried to claim he'd found the car abandoned on some waste land and he was bringing it in. He even asked if there was a reward.'

'But how did you know that it was him who stole it in the first place?'

'We had a report that a man fitting his description had tried to sell it at a second-hand car showroom in Gillingham this afternoon. There was also the fact that the owner of the car saw him take it... and he knows him.'

'Oh dear,' Amy said, laughing. 'We don't have the brightest set of criminals in Spinton do we?'

Bodkin took off his jacket and hung it on a peg before following Amy into the living room. 'Throw in the fact that he drove around offering people he found waiting at bus stops a lift into town for threepence a ride all day Saturday.' Bodkin shook his head. 'The stupidity of these people. They may as well stick a badge on their coats, saying I did it.'

Bodkin pulled out a chair from beneath the table and sat down as Amy walked through to the kitchen to get the teapot. 'You know how the newspapers like to give these people nicknames? Well, Ferris beat them to it. He's calling him the Calamity Cabbie.'

Amy burst out laughing. 'Really? Oh, that's so funny. Well done, Ferris. He ought to be a comedian instead of a singer.'

'Don't tell him that, please,' Bodkin said seriously. 'His jokes are usually awful, almost as bad as his impressions. I caught him behind the front desk trying to do James Cagney this afternoon. He sounded more like Jimmy Durante... Ha cha cha cha.'

'That was very good, Bodkin. Maybe you ought to try your luck on the stage.'

Bodkin rolled his eyes heavenwards. 'I would honestly rather spend an hour sticking rusty knitting needles in my...'

'Bodkin!'

'I was going to say, eyes.'

'Oh course you were. I'm sure that's what Harry Tuft meant to say when he used to come out with it at school, only he never did use the word, eyes.'

'Something smells good,' Bodkin said, quickly changing the subject.

'Bangers and mash,' Amy said. 'I've done lots. I hope you're hungry.'

Later, when the couple were once again sitting on the sofa listening to the radio, Amy asked Bodkin whether he had heard anything more about the blood tests.

'No, I'm not expecting anything until the weekend, even though our tests are supposed to be a priority.'

'So, what's on tomorrow?'

'Unfortunately, I'll be in Maidstone all day tomorrow. I've got to drive down for a meeting with the chief super and a few of the big wigs down there. He thinks we might be able to talk them into giving us another police officer or two. One for the front desk would be a start. It would free Ferris up to help me out a bit. I'm going down first thing in the morning.'

'What time will you be back?'

'I'm hoping to be back for eight, maybe nine. I won't disturb you. You've been missing out on your reading time. I'll see you on Thursday at some stage.'

'I have to admit, I haven't picked a book up since last week. I finally managed to get hold of a copy of Agatha's Murder In The Mews from the library. It's a short story collection. Have you read it?'

Bodkin shook his head. 'I haven't had much time to read myself just lately. Let me know if it's any good and I'll see if I can get it out myself when you've done with it.'

'Let you know if it's any good?' Amy was incredulous. 'It's Agatha, for goodness' sake, Bodkin. It will be more than just good. It will be magnificent.'

# CHAPTER TWELVE

After breakfast the next morning, Amy found herself at a loose end. She played a few records from her American music collection on the radiogram she had bought second-hand from her Uncle Maurice's contacts, but she couldn't get the thought out of her head that she was wasting the day, and that she ought to be doing something productive to help Bodkin while he was away. She had just taken If I Didn't Care, by the Ink Spots, off the turntable, when she suddenly had a thought. Hurrying across to her wardrobe, she looked through her dresses until she found the strawberry and cream flower print dress that she had bought from Brigden's in June. After carefully applying a thin layer of makeup and a little mascara, she finished the process with the Max Factor Vermillion lipstick she had bought mail order via an advertisement she had seen in her Photoplay magazine. Happy with the results, she brushed her flaxen hair and pulled on a pair of cream coloured Oxford shoes. Then, after picking up her handbag, she left the house and made her way to the bus stop, across the road from the Old Bull pub.

At the bus station, Amy had to wait for almost fifteen minutes for the bus that would drop her off only a few hundred yards away from the Boat Club.

Highwater had begun life as little more than a hamlet in the seventeenth century, but it had expanded with the industrialisation of Spinton, although it didn't have any of the heavy industry that blighted the skyline of its near neighbour. The town was made up of mostly Edwardian houses that had been erected at the turn of the century, but if a visitor ever stepped away from the elegant main streets, they would find themselves in slightly less salubrious locations, made up of mid-sized, early Victorian houses, built by the tradesmen who had been attracted to the area following the introduction of the ironworks and the increasingly important output produced from the many small coal mines that littered the area.

The terminus for the buses was located on a large, oval shaped green, edged by beech and horse chestnut trees. Running along the northern end of the green was a row of shops that included a grocer, a baker, a haberdashery, a chemist-come-surgery, and a newsagent. The residents would never have need of a pawnshop. On the side of the green where Amy had alighted from the bus, there was a large pub called the Steamboat and thirty yards away from that, set behind railings and a tidily kept graveyard, was the local church.

After asking directions from an elderly man who was throwing a stick for his collie dog, she passed the church and turned right onto a path that led her by the side of the river. Two hundred yards along, she found herself at the open gates of the Highwater Boat Club. After following a sign that pointed to the rear of the building, Amy walked past a row of boat sheds that lined the banks of the river. A couple of the doors were open, and she looked inside one to see three sculls stacked on racks, one above the other. The oars were lying on hooks above each individual craft.

At the end of the row of sheds, Amy walked around the corner of the main building and found a pair of double, half-glass doors with the word Entrance written on a sign above them. She pushed on the right-hand door and it swung open with a loud creak. When no one came to investigate the noise, Amy stepped into a corridor with half a dozen doors leading off it. At the far end she could see a sign reading Ballroom. Calling out, 'hello' she walked along the corridor until she got to the end, then turning right, she passed through another pair of swing doors and found herself standing on a dance floor. There was a long bar on the far side and a stage on the right. Behind the bar was a young woman of about Amy's age. Her brown hair was shoulder length and was gathered at the nape of her neck. A pair of rhinestone decorated hair clips above her ears kept the style in place. Her blue eyes were framed with a pair of round tortoiseshell spectacles.

'Hello,' Amy called across the room. 'I appear to be lost.'

The girl smiled at her and beckoned to her to approach the bar. 'Everyone gets lost in here at one time or another,' she said. 'It's like a rabbit warren.'

Amy looked around the empty dancefloor. 'It seems to be very quiet today.'

'Oh, we've had a few in. Some of the lads are in training for the in-house competitions at the weekend. They're out on the river and won't be back for an hour or so.' She nodded towards a pair of double doors at the opposite end to the stage. 'There's another bar through those doors. The old boys all congregate in there. They're in most days. Most of them are retired or don't have to work.' She held up her hand to her mouth and whispered, 'lucky so and so's.'

Amy nodded her agreement. 'I sometimes wish I could give up work, but that would probably mean I'd be getting married and having to look after a family.' She shuddered genuinely. 'I'm dreading that, if I'm honest. I'm too young to be tied down.'

'A kindred spirit, at last,' the girl said. 'Let's shake on that.' She held her hand over the bar. 'I'm Lesley Philby.'

Amy took her hand and shook it. 'I'm Amy Rowlings.'

'Where are you from, Amy? I haven't seen you around the village?'

'You won't have. I'm from Maidstone originally. We moved up here when my dad became a partner in a law firm in Spinton. Donnelley's, do you know it?'

Lesley shook her head. 'I don't go over that way much. I sometimes tag along if there's a crowd going over to the Milton, but to be honest, I don't like Spinton much. It's a bit rough.'

'Some parts are nice,' Amy said, defensively. 'I have an apartment near the river.'

Lesley put down the glass she had been absent-mindedly wiping and picked up another. 'So, Amy Rowlings, what do you do for a living?'

'I erm, I work in my dad's law firm. I'm not training to be a solicitor or anything, I'm just the general dogsbody, but it pays the rent... or most of it. Dad pays more than half.'

'I'm a bit similar to that. I do bits and bobs around here. I help behind the bar and I help organise a lot of the events we put on. We've got the presentation event on Saturday night for whoever wins the medals in the races. We have a bit of a problem with that, though. The singer we had booked broke her leg in a car crash, so she's taking some time off. It's a bit short notice to get anyone else in, so it looks like we'll have to let old Gerald play the piano and tell a few of his rubbish jokes.'

'I might know someone who can stand in,' Amy said quickly. 'I'd have to ask him if he's busy, though.'

Lesley grabbed Amy's hand over the counter. 'That would be fantastic.' She hesitated. 'Is he any good?'

'He's wonderful. He's got a fabulous voice. He has a regular booking at the Milton. He's called Orlando Ferris.'

'Orlando, is that his real name?'

'I think it's his stage name, to be honest. It does sound a bit exotic, doesn't it?'

'He'll get a fiver at least. We might be able to go to six if he goes down well.'

'Oh, he'll go down well,' Amy replied. 'He gets encore after encore at the Milton. You should hear him sing Old Man River.'

'I'm surprised I haven't seen him,' Lesley mused. 'Has he been working there very long?'

'Not long, just a couple of months. He only has a monthly slot at the moment. He's got other commitments down in Gillingham and Rochester.'

'Wow! A professional. I can't wait to hear him.'

'I'll have to check that he can make it first. Don't count your chickens just yet.'

Lesley put the glass down and picked up another. 'You didn't say why you were here?'

'Oh, sorry. I was thinking of joining, to be honest. I have a friend who's a member here and she told me she's had some great fun since she joined.'

Lesley opened a drawer at the end of the bar, pulled out a form, and handed it to Amy. 'Here's our membership form. It's a fiver a year for the men, but we girls only have to pay a pound. Unless you want to go out on the water, that is, then it's two pounds, ten shillings.' She looked Amy up and down. 'You don't look like a rower. You don't have Pansy Potter muscles.'

Amy lifted her arm and flexed her bicep. 'You wouldn't get very far if I was pulling the oars.' She frowned as she looked at Lesley. 'Pansy who?'

'I can tell you don't have a little brother. Pansy Potter, the strongman's daughter, is a character in the Beano comic.'

'Ah, I see. I don't read comics. I'm a full-on novel girl. Agatha Christie is more my style.'

'Oh, me too,' Lesley replied. 'Have you read that short story collection yet? What's it called... Murder In The Mews? I've only read the title story so far, but it was really good.'

'What a coincidence,' Amy replied. 'I'm reading that too.'

'I love Agatha. Mum met her, you know. It was years ago now. I was only about six or seven. She was launching a new book at one of the big bookshops in London and Mum went in and bought one.'

'How exciting! Imagine meeting her. I'm so jealous.' Amy's eyes were wide.

'She didn't put Mum's name on it, but she doesn't care about that. It just reads, From Agatha Christie.'

'Goodness. I'd have it sealed up in a safe and I'd just get it out to look at every birthday or Christmas if it was mine,' Amy said. She picked up the membership form. 'Do I have to fill this in today? I'd like to check it's okay with Dad, but he's on holiday with Mum at the moment. They've gone to Mar...'thinking Margate might sound a bit common, she quickly changed it to 'Marseilles.'

'Ooh that is posh. We always used to go to Margate when we were kids. Dad still likes it there even though he can well afford to go abroad now. He loves the jellied eels.'

Amy quickly changed the subject back to the form. 'Do I have to be a member before I can join in the fun? My parents won't be back until a week on Saturday.'

'It will be all right if you want to come. You can get your friend to sign you in, but if she's not around, I'm sure one of the male members will oblige. They're like flies around a jam pot when a potential lady member shows up, especially a pretty one like you.'

'What if I want to come to see the races on Saturday?'

'It's the same procedure... oh, hang on a minute, hold on to your underwear.' She looked over Amy's shoulder, then flashed a quick smile as Amy heard heavy footsteps approaching. 'Hello, Admiral.'

Amy half turned to find an elderly man standing uncomfortably close to her. He was wearing a white captain's cap, which made his tanned, weather-beaten face stand out even more than it might have done.

'By Jove, what have we here?' Amy stepped back quickly as the man attempted to put his arm around her waist. 'Don't be shy, my dear. You'll be safe enough with me, won't she, Lovely?'

'It's Lesley, as well you know, Gerald.' She took off her spectacles and began to polish them on her cloth.

'You look so much more attractive without those things on your face,' Gerald said, giving her a leer.

Lesley put her glasses back on, then took them off again. 'Do you know, Gerald? You look much more attractive when I'm not wearing them as well. Isn't that a coincidence?'

Gerald took off his white captain's hat and scratched at his balding pate. 'Be careful, young lady, or I'll put you over my knee.'

Lesley pursed her lips. 'I don't think Joe Lyndsey would like that, Gerald. You know how possessive he can be.'

Gerald suddenly found he had to be somewhere else rather urgently, and after giving Amy a slow once over, he winked, then turned away towards the doors that led to the member's bar.

'That was a great reply to his callous remark,' Amy said. 'Well done, you.' She treated Lesley to a big smile. 'Who's Joe, by the way?'

'Joe Lyndsey is the Boat Club captain. He's in his thirties, built like an Adonis with looks that would put Cary Grant to shame.'

'Is he your boyfriend?'

'I wish... Sadly, no. He doesn't do long-term relationships.'

'Oh, that's a shame. He's a bit of a ladies' man then?'

'To put it mildly. He's taken me out once or twice, but only when we've been in a crowd.'

'I wonder if he's the one my friend was always going on about? There was a man here who she liked a lot.'

'What was her name? You didn't say.'

'Didn't I? Sorry, she's called Effie, Effie Watkins.'

'Effie Watkins.' Lesley shook her head. 'How long have you known her? I can't remember her mentioning you.'

'I went to school with her down in Maidstone, but we lost touch when my family moved away. We lived in Canterbury for a while, then we came up here. I bumped into her again in the Milton a few months ago. She was with a crowd of chaps, but she remembered me.'

'Ah, I see.' Lesley breathed onto a glass then began to rub at it with her cloth. 'She didn't have a lot of female friends. Most of the women here were jealous of her... With good reason.'

'She hasn't changed over the years then. She was the same at school. All the boys loved her. She only had to snap her fingers and they'd come running.'

'That still happens,' Lesley said with the shake of her head.

'Has she been in lately? The last time I saw her, she said she'd introduce me to the club secretary and I might blag a free membership.'

'I can introduce you to him if she doesn't. He's my father.' She was silent for a moment. 'Like all the men in here, he loved Effie. She made a bit of a fool of him, but that didn't stop him fawning all over her.'

'Oh dear, your father?'

'It didn't bother me. Dad split up from my mother years ago. He's a free agent. He deserved what he got, though. He's old enough to know better.'

'I'm nothing like Effie,' Amy said quickly. 'We're like chalk and cheese, really. I only mentioned her because she said it would smooth the way for my membership. We've never been very close, really.'

Lesley tapped on the form. 'Fill it in and I'll give you a temporary membership until your references have been verified.'

'References? How many do I need? Mum and Dad could—'

'Mum and Dad can't refer you,' Lesley said. 'They think they run a posh club here, but it's only a rowing club, really. When it first started up, they had all sorts of boats here. There was a paddle steamer that used to take day trippers up to the estuary, and there were more than a few yachts on the water. It's not like that anymore. It's all rowing now. There are a couple of motor launches in the sheds, but they don't get taken out too often.' She tapped the form again. 'Boat Club sounds very grand and they won't change the name, but it isn't half the place it was in its heyday. Have a look at some of the pictures on the walls or talk to old Gerald about it... no, on second thoughts, that's probably not a good idea. He's got tentacles for arms, that one.'

Amy grimaced. 'The referees then. Who shall I ask to sign the form?'

'Anyone the committee might have heard of? Do you know anyone with a sir or lady as a title?'

'I'm very good friends with Robert and Shirley McKenzie. He's the Mayor of Spinton.'

'They'll do nicely, Amy. They come here now and again.'

'And I know Francis Drake and Helen and Horatio Kelly,' Amy said, dropping a few of the local business hierarchy's names into the conversation. She'd met them during the investigation into the murder of the businessman of the year a couple of months previously.

'You won't have a problem with membership if you're moving in that level of society.'

'I don't actually mix with the business people a lot. I find them a bit boring. But I had tea with Shirley McKenzie only yesterday.'

'Stick her name down here.' Lesley pointed to a section of the form. 'And her husband's too. Dad will phone them to check your credentials, but it's only a matter of a quick chat. Once they admit they know you and you aren't going to run off with the club's funds, you'll be added to the membership. In the meantime, I'll vouch for you. If you want to come to see the racing on Saturday or just sit on the bank sipping Pimm's, ask for me at the door. I'll be around somewhere.' She lifted the polished glass to the light and looked through it. 'Now, what can I get you? The first drink for a new member is always on the house, and I'm feeling a bit thirsty myself.'

Half an hour later and feeling very relaxed after sipping a large bowl of Pimm's, Amy began to feel a little bit safer about her cover story. She and Lesley were getting on well. She had just finished telling Amy a hilarious story involving two of the rowing team who had collided with a pleasure boat full of women on the river, and had had to be rescued by them, when the doors to the members' bar flew open and a handsome, muscular, dark-haired man rushed into the ballroom clutching a folded newspaper. Ignoring Amy, he thrust the paper into Lesley's hands.

'Look at the headline,' he ordered.

Lesley opened up the folded paper and read the headline and first paragraph of the front page, then after staring open-mouthed at the man, she turned her attention to Amy.

'It's your friend, Effie... She's been murdered.'

# CHAPTER THIRTEEN

'You were her friend? You don't seem to be too upset by the news.'

'We weren't that close. I was just explaining to Lesley that I was hoping Effie would put me up for membership.'

The man's face became softer. 'I'm sorry; I didn't mean anything by that statement. It was just the shock of the news. Most women were only acquaintances of hers. She didn't have a lot of girlfriends, I know that.' He held out his hand. 'I'm Joe, Joe Lyndsey, the club captain.'

Amy took his hand and shook it. 'What terrible news! Do they know how she died? Oh, I'm Amy Rowlings, by the way.'

'It just says she was found by some schoolchildren in the reeds by the Silverstream. It's a bit light on detail, though the reporter does speculate a bit. He says the Post is waiting for the police to comment. There's been no official announcement yet.'

'All that Sandy Miles does is speculate,' Amy said bitterly. 'If he can't find a real fact, he'll make one up.'

'Have you ever met the man?' Joe asked. 'He did a feature on the club once. He made us sound like a bunch of Hooray Henrys.'

'I've met him, but if I never bumped into him again, it would be too soon,' Amy replied.

'How long have you known Effie?' Joe asked.

'Amy grew up with her down south, then came across her again in the Milton. She lives in Spinton now, don't you, Amy?' Lesley said, eager to stay part of the conversation.

'Really? Whereabouts.'

'Cramley Lodge. On Main Street, it's that art deco style apartment block.'

'Ah, so you're the girl from Donnelley's. Effie mentioned you once or twice, but never by name. Aren't you subletting from her? What are you going to do now?'

'I haven't had time to think about it, to be honest.'

'No, I'm sorry, of course you haven't. This will probably affect you more than any of us.'

Amy shrugged. 'Daddy will look after me, I'm sure.' She studied her empty glass for a moment and considered buying a second Pimm's, but she didn't want to pay a fortune for it and was afraid to ask the price in case they became suspicious of her supposedly well-to-do background.

'Ah well, I'd better be getting back. It's been lovely to meet you both.'

Lesley got to her feet and picked up the empty glasses from the table. 'Don't forget to ask for me on Saturday afternoon. I'll set up your membership for you as soon as Dad contacts your referees.'

'I'll sign you in if the references don't come through in time,' Joe said. 'It's one of the perks of being the club captain. I can invite who I like.' He gave Amy his best smile. 'Are you coming for the presentation ball in the evening too?'

'I hope to. Is it all right if I bring a friend? Alice loves a dance, and she's a good friend of Ferris too.'

Joe grinned. 'You can bring half a dozen girls if they're as pretty as you.'

'She's far better looking than me,' Amy said. 'Dark hair, high cheekbones and a figure to die for.'

Joe rubbed his hands together. 'I'm looking forward to Saturday already.' He smiled at Amy again, then gave her a puzzled look. 'Who's Ferris?'

Lesley took the opportunity to get involved. 'Orlando Ferris. I'm hoping Amy can persuade him to sing for us. He performs at the Milton now and again, so he must be good.'

Joe tipped his head to the side as he thought. 'Issy Palmer was telling me about a new singer they'd found. She said he's a bit of a crooner and very handsome too.' He stuck up a thumb to Amy. 'Here's the deal, Amy. You get this chap to come and sing for us and I'll give both you and your friend Alice a pass for the dance. How does that sound?'

Amy grinned. 'That would be perfect. Could you give me your phone number please, Lesley? I'll check with Ferris but I'm sure he'll be pleased to sing for you. I know he isn't at the Milton this week. I'll ring to confirm later on today.'

Lesley scribbled the club's telephone number on the white margin of the newspaper, then tore off the strip and handed it to Amy. 'I'm here until ten tonight.'

Amy folded the sliver of paper and put it into her bag. 'I'll get a copy of the Post at the newsagents. I can read it on the bus.'

'The bus? I can't allow a new member to catch the bus,' Joe said, springing to his feet. 'Come on, my car's outside. I'll give you a lift.'

Joe led Amy around the side of the building to an area of wasteland that served as a car park. In the middle of a row of three cars was a beautiful, red, open top, Riley Lynx.

'Hop in,' Joe said, climbing over the driver's side door.

When Amy was seated, Joe charged the system, then hit the starter button on the dash. 'Hang on to your hat,' he said, revving the engine for all it was worth.

'It doesn't have a lid,' Amy said, looking over her shoulder into the plush leather seats at the back. 'Don't you get wet when it rains?'

'The 'lid' is hidden under that flap at the back,' Joe replied. 'It's a bit of a faff getting it up, but it keeps the rain out well.'

Over the next fifteen minutes, Joe went into car salesman speak. Ninety percent of it went straight over Amy's head, especially the bits about brake horsepower, cylinders and litres. By the time he'd got around to boasting about the four-speed gearbox and the top speed of ninety miles an hour, they had reached the outskirts of Spinton.

'We'll take the back road in,' Joe said. 'It will lead us straight to your apartment building.'

Worried that he might want to be invited in for a cup of tea, Amy asked if she might be dropped off on Long Lane instead, as she wanted to warn her best friend Alice about the change of plans for Saturday night.

Joe stuck up a thumb and Amy gave him directions as he steered the beautiful car through the streets of Spinton.

As they pulled up outside the farmhouse, Amy gave Joe her best smile and thanked him for the lift. 'It was very kind of you,' she said as she pulled the lever to open the car door.

Joe leapt over the driver's side door without opening it, and by the time she had walked around to the front of the car, he was waiting for her.

'I'm looking forward to meeting your friend Alice,' he said. 'If she's as beautiful as you say she is, I'd like to get on first-name terms before any of the other chaps get the chance.'

'Oh, I'm sorry, Joe, she'll be furious if I take you into the farmhouse. She won't want you to see her in her overalls. She'll just about have finished cleaning out the pig pens and she'll be covered in slurry.'

'Ah,' Joe looked down at his immaculately clean white shirt and fawn trousers. 'Better not bother, then. I'd like to see her at her best. First impressions and all that.'

'I'm sure Alice will be pleased. She believes in first impressions too.'

'So, if a cup of tea is out of the question, what else can I have as a reward?'

'You have already had my thanks,' Amy said, stepping to the side to get around him.

'Thanks are ten-a-penny,' Joe said, grabbing her by the waist and pulling her towards him. Amy twisted her face to the side as he tried to force his lips onto hers. With her bag sliding halfway up her forearm, she put both hands on his chest and tried to push him away.

'I don't know what gave you the impression that I would welcome this sort of attention, but I don't like it. I'm not that sort of girl.'

'You're all that sort of girl, some of you just don't know it yet,' Joe grinned and pushed his face towards hers again.

'Are you all right there, Amy?'

Amy breathed a sigh of relief as Joe released her and turned with a fixed smile on his face to see Barney, Alice's large framed foreman, step onto the road from the track that ran alongside the house.

'I'm fine, thank you, Barney,' Amy said as she stepped around Joe and walked towards the farmhand.

'I'll, er, see you on Saturday then,' Joe said turning back towards his car. 'Are you coming to see the races in the afternoon?'

'I'll be there, though Alice won't. She'll be busy on the farm until teatime.'

'Shall I pick you up? My first race isn't until one o'clock.'

'No, I'll make my own way over, but thanks for the offer. I've got things to do on Saturday morning and I don't know what time I'll be ready.'

Joe jumped back into the car, started it up, and revved the engine mercilessly before pulling a skidding three-point turn. 'See you on Saturday,' he yelled, raising his hand in the air as he screeched away.

Barny fell in step with Amy as she walked towards the back gate. 'He seemed to be quite a self-obsessed young man,' he said as he pushed the gate open to allow Amy to step through.

'He's full of himself,' Amy replied, turning towards the kitchen steps. 'So full he could burst.'

# CHAPTER FOURTEEN

'Who on earth was that?' Alice asked as Amy walked into the kitchen. 'I heard you coming a long time before you got here.'

'That,' Amy replied, sticking her thumb over her shoulder and pointing it towards the lane, 'was Joe Lyndsey, the captain of the Highwater Boat Club and serial womaniser.'

Alice shook her head slowly. 'He looked the part. I had a quick peep through the front window when he pulled up. He's a handsome chap, I'll give him that. Nice clothes, nice car, nice smile...'

'More arms than an octopus,' Amy added.

'There's always a downside,' Alice said sadly. 'Where did you find him?'

'At the Boat Club. I went over there earlier.'

Alice put tea leaves in the teapot and filled it from the kettle. 'That's not the sort of place you'd usually go. Did you give them a quick rendition of Jolly Boating Weather while you were there?'

Amy laughed. 'Not on this occasion. I went because the girl we found dead in the reeds on Sunday was a member. Her killer might well be a member too, so I thought I'd nip over and take a look at the place.'

Alice put the teapot on the table, then rinsed out two large cups. 'Is it as posh as it sounds?'

'The people are, I suppose, and the ballroom looked very swish.'

'They have a ballroom?' Alice pursed her lips. 'Well, that sounds rather posh.' She poured the tea, added milk, and passed a cup to Amy.

'Ooh, thanks, I'm ready for this,' Amy said, blowing into the steaming brew before taking a sip.

'Did you spot the murderer while you were there?'

'No... Well, I might have, if the killer was Joe, the club steward's daughter or a sleazy old codger called Gerald, who you'd be well advised not to get within groping distance of.' Amy sipped her tea. 'He wears a captain's hat, though I'm not sure if he ever was one.'

'Is Groping Gerald related to Captain Joe?'

'I don't think so, though you wouldn't bet against either of them in a bottom pinching competition.'

'Oh dear.' Alice shook her head again. 'Why do men think they can get away with that sort of behaviour?'

'In Joe's case, it's almost certainly because he has a sense of entitlement. He's typical of his kind. Public school, good breeding... whatever that means. Oh, and I'll bet his father encouraged him to sow his wild oats before settling down and providing an heir to the family fortune.'

'That bad is he?'

Amy frowned as she thought. 'No... not really. He's pleasant enough. He'd probably be good company on a night out. The problem would be, getting rid of him when you wanted to go home.'

'Fancy a bit of cake?' Alice walked to the pantry and picked up a cake tin from the second shelf. 'It's a seed cake. Miriam made it at the weekend.'

Miriam was Alice's friend and live in housekeeper.

She took the lid off the tin and inhaled deeply. 'Ooh, I've been looking forward to this. Miriam said it has to stand for a week but it smells ready to me.' She grinned as she picked up two small plates and a bread knife from the draining board. 'It's her own fault for leaving it in plain view. If she'd really wanted me to leave it alone she'd have hidden it in her room. She knows I can't resist her baking.'

Alice cut two thick triangles from the cake and slid them onto the plates. After taking a bite, she closed her eyes and began to chew. 'Heaven,' she said.

'Did you have to give me such a big slice? I'll be going up a dress size if I visit you too often.' Amy bit into her cake, chewed quickly, then took another large bite.

'What does Bodkin think about you gallivanting around the country lanes with a rich, handsome young rower?'

Amy pulled a face. 'I erm... he doesn't know yet.'

'About the handsome young man or the visit to the Boat Club?'

Amy grimaced. 'Neither. I went over there on a whim. He's down south all day trying to browbeat his superiors into letting him have a couple of new recruits.' She took another bite of cake, then pushed the crumbs into a pile on the edge of her plate. Picking it up, she tipped her head back and poured them into her mouth before returning the plate to the table.

'It's a good job Jaunty Joe didn't see that,' Alice said with a grin. 'You're not fit for polite society. They'd never let you join their little club if they saw your table manners.'

Amy smacked her lips. 'Too late,' she replied. 'I've already joined.' She paused. 'On a temporary basis at least. Just while my credentials are checked.'

'Your credentials? You didn't show them your shiny new police accreditation card then?'

Amy pulled a face. ‘They, erm… they don’t know who I really am… that is… they know I’m Amy Rowlings but they think I’m someone else.’

Alice put her hand to her forehead and shook her head again. ‘Who do they think you are, then?’

‘They think I’m Effie’s… that’s the girl who died… they think I’m her flatmate, Daphne. They also think I work at a lawyer’s office in town… they know my name is Amy, though. I was honest about that. I thought I’d better give them my real name in case you let anything slip on Saturday night.’

‘ME! Why would I…’ She looked suspiciously at Amy. ‘Out with it. What have you got me into now?’

‘I’m sort of going to the presentation ball on Saturday night, and you, Cinderella, are coming with me.’

Alice held up both hands towards her best friend. ‘I’m going to a posh ball? Wha… no, wait…’ she picked up the teapot and emptied the still warm contents into the sink. ‘This discussion will require a fresh pot.’ She put the kettle on the hob again and lit the gas with a match. ‘I think you’d better tell me the whole story so that I know which version of you I’m going to the ball with. I mean, you wouldn’t want me to ask you what stuff you’re knocking out on your machine at the Mill when you’re supposed to be pushing a pen on a desk at a posh lawyer’s office, would you?’

Amy sighed. ‘I suppose not… but it’s quite simple really. You see, my dad isn’t an engineer at a factory in Gillingham and he and my mum aren’t on holiday in Margate at the moment.’

Alice put fresh tea leaves in the pot. ‘No? Where are they then?’

‘Marseilles.’

Alice’s chin almost hit her chest. ‘Marseilles? You mean the MarSEILLES in France as opposed to the MarGATE on the coast of Kent?’

'Yes.' Amy said firmly. 'I had to make out I was lot posher than I am.'

'So, what does your dad do in Amy's new world?'

'He's a lawyer at Donnelley's.'

'A lawyer?'

'A rich one. He doesn't live in a cottage on Long Lane either, and... oh yes, he owns a few hundred acres around here... around this place, actually... and I wasn't born in Spinton. We moved up here a few years ago from Maidstone.'

Alice scratched her head. 'Anything else I should know?'

'Well, as I said, I work in Daddy's law firm but I live in a rather nice apartment at the end of Main Street... you know that gorgeous art deco building...? I sublet from Effie, that's the girl who—'

'Died. Yes, I remember that bit.'

'I'll go over it all with you again before we go.' She looked at the big clock on the wall above the fireplace. 'But now I have to pad out my backstory with the McKenzies and I also have to let Ferris know he's got a paid singing job at the ball on Saturday.' She blew out her cheeks. 'Do you think I could use your phone for a few minutes?'

Alice nodded dumbly as she stared into space.

'The McKenzies, as in the mayor and his wife?'

Amy grinned as she got to her feet. 'I gave their names for references. The Steward is going to ring them soon, so I'd better prepare them. Then I have to ring Ferris. He'll be on the desk at the police station.'

'What if he can't do Saturday night?' Alice asked.

'They're paying a fiver, six if he goes down well. Of course he'll do it.'

'Thanks so much, Shirley, I really appreciate it.'

'It all sounds so exciting. I'd love to come and help out, but we're going to London on Saturday. Robert wrangled us some theatre tickets. We're going to see, Me and My Girl.'

'How wonderful! I'm so jealous. Don't forget to join in singing The Lambeth Walk.'

'I've been practicing in the lounge. I can even do the dance, but I'd better not get up and do that.'

Amy laughed. 'I'd be tempted. Alice and I did it last Christmas in her kitchen, after we'd had a few glasses of port and lemon. There was only Miriam to witness the event, thank goodness.'

'I'd love to have seen that,' Shirley said.

'You missed a treat,' Amy said with a giggle. 'Right. I'd better leave you to get on with your day. I don't want to tie the line up in case the steward from the Boat Club calls. Say hello to Robert for me and I hope you enjoy the performance.'

'A fiver? Of course I'll do it. I'm free anyway, I'm not at the Milton until next week.' Ferris seemed delighted at the prospect of singing at the ball.

'You might get six if you go down well,' Amy said encouragingly. 'And I'm absolutely sure they're going to love you.'

'Thanks for the ego boost, Amy. One quick question, though. How are we getting there? I know you told them you know me, but will it be all right if we share a taxi between the four of us?'

'Four? There's only three of us, Ferris. Me, you and Alice.'

'What about Bodkin?'

'I, erm... haven't had the chance to talk to him about it yet. You know Bodkin, he'd want to start questioning witnesses, and I think that a subtler approach is required. Especially at a ball. You know what he's like when he mixes with the upper class. He'd have their backs up as soon as he set foot in the place. I think I can get them to open up a bit to me. They'd all be on the defensive if Bodkin planted his size tens on the stage and demanded they all come up one at a time for questioning.'

Ferris laughed. 'You know him so well.' He paused for a moment. 'You are going to tell him, aren't you? It is a murder investigation, after all. I can broach the subject with him when he gets back from Maidstone if you like. I'm on until ten.'

'No, it's better coming from me, Ferris. I'll come up to the station tomorrow to tell him all about it. Keep it to yourself until then, please.'

'Okie dokie. I'd better get some practice in over the next couple of days, then. I've got some new songs I'd like to try out... new to me, that is. They're not bang up to date.'

'Ooh, that sounds interesting. What are you adding to you repertoire?'

'Forty-Second Street, from that film and Cheek to Cheek... you know the one... from the Fred Astaire, Top Hat musical?'

'Excellent, Ferris. Forty-Second Street is lively, that will get them dancing and Cheek to Cheek will do the same.' She hummed the melody. 'I'm really looking forward to hearing you sing them.'

'What about the band? Do you think they'll know the songs?'

'I'm sure they will, but you can check with Leslie Philby at the club. I'm going to give you her number in a minute. I'm not sure which set of musicians they use for their functions, but you can rest assured they'll know all the classics.'

Amy read the Boat Club number out to Ferris, then listened as he read it back to her. 'Don't forget, Ferris. You only know me from the Milton. You know my dad has money and that I work at Donnelley's, but that's all you need to mention, really. We're only acquaintances. Oh, I wouldn't give them the police station telephone number in case they want to contact you. Give them Alice's.'

'You can rely on me, Amy.... Now, how are we going to get there?'

'Me and Alice will meet you outside the Town Hall at seven. We'll get a taxi from there. I can ring for one from the club to bring us back. We can't book it in advance, as I have no idea what time the dance finishes.'

'That sounds good. I'll see you tomorrow. You can fill me in with all the details of who you and Alice are supposed to be, then.'

'Thanks again for doing this, Ferris and... please; don't say anything to Bodkin until I've had the chance to prepare him.'

'I have no idea what I'm going to wear,' Alice said when Amy came back into the kitchen. 'I'll have to dip into my mum's wardrobe again, I suppose. She had something for every occasion.'

Alice's mother had died a couple of years previously, following a long illness. Her father died of a broken heart a year later.

'You could wear that sparkly green mermaid dress,' Amy said, her eyes bright. 'I bet you'd look stunning in that.'

'Not likely,' Alice replied. 'It's such a faff to get on and it's so tight around the hips and thighs I'd have major problems if I needed the lavvy.'

Amy laughed. 'You have tried it on, then?'

'I've tried them all on at one time or another. Just to see what fits. That one took me twenty minutes to get off. I had to shout for Miriam to give me a hand.' She shuddered at the memory as Amy burst into a fit of laughter. 'What are you going to wear?'

'I honestly don't know. I have that blue bias cut dress I wore for the awards at the Town Hall, but I might nip up to Brigden's on Saturday morning to see if they have anything that might suit.'

Brigden's was a dress shop in the town that sold nearly new clothes. Many of the items boasted designer labels and Amy could pick up good quality dresses for a fraction of what they sold for when they were new.

'An evening dress will set you back a bit, even a second-hand one,' Alice warned.

'I'll raid my post office savings account,' Amy replied. 'Although, I've got a couple of dresses I bought a year or so back which I've only worn once. I might take them in to see what they'll give me for them. I might be able to push my budget a bit further that way.'

'Good thinking,' Alice said... 'Hang on. Wasn't I supposed to be giving you a driving lesson in the truck on Saturday?'

'That will have to wait for a while, my dear. It's very kind of you to offer, though. I'm going to be a bit tied up with this investigation, so I might not get another chance over the factory fortnight. I still want to take you up on the offer at some stage. I'm really looking forward to getting behind the wheel.'

'Just give me a shout and I'll find the time,' Alice replied. 'What are you doing later tonight? Anything nice?'

'Catching up on my reading,' Amy replied. 'And trying to work out how to explain everything to Bodkin tomorrow.'

# CHAPTER FIFTEEN

At ten o'clock the next morning, Amy walked into the police station to find PC Ferris in his usual position behind the counter.

'Morning, Ferris. Are you working twenty-four-hour shifts behind the desk now?'

'It feels like it,' Ferris moaned. 'Things are looking up, though. Your friend and mine, Inspector Bodkin, struck a deal with the high ups. We're getting a permanent desk officer. He can't start until tomorrow as he's getting married today. He's seventy-two.'

'Seventy-two? He's coming out of retirement, then?'

Ferris nodded. 'You don't need to be too active to work behind here.' He looked around with a sour expression on his face. 'I'll be glad to see the back of it. Pounding the beat looks like a step up from where I'm standing.'

'Assisting Bodkin in running the likes of the Calamity Cabbie to earth?'

Ferris grinned. 'He told you, did he? I was quite proud of that nickname. It was all my own work and it actually made it into the newspaper last night.'

Amy laughed. 'I bet the Post's ace reporter wasn't too pleased.

He likes to dream up silly nicknames for the town's criminals himself.'

'Hey, less of the silly,' Ferris said with a wink. 'Even Bodkin was impressed.'

'Speaking of His Nibs. Is he in?'

'He'll be back in about half an hour, Amy. He's had to go out on an urgent call.'

'Ooh, what's happened? Anything exciting?'

'An anonymous caller rang in from a telephone box. Old Mrs Pendlebury's got her husband trapped in her outside lavatory again. She chased him down the yard, hitting him with her big iron skillet, so he's locked himself in and won't open the door until she promises not to hit him anymore, and she won't.'

'Nellie Pendlebury from Albion Street? She must be all of eighty.'

'Eighty-three,' Ferris replied. 'I know because I've just been looking at her charge sheet. It's three pages long.'

'Good grief! I know she got into trouble for throwing her husband's dinner at him in the Dragon when he was late home one Sunday lunchtime, but I didn't know she was a regular offender.'

'Twenty-seven offences, the vast majority of them for assaulting her old man.'

'He must be six feet tall and eighteen stones in weight,' Amy said in astonishment.

Ferris nodded. 'She's five foot two and as skinny as a rake. In one report, it states that she had to stand on a chair to clobber him on the bonce with a saucepan.'

Amy shook her head in disbelief. 'Twenty-seven offences. You'd think he'd have cleared off after he realised it was going to be a regular thing. It's usually the men who dish out the punishment in this town.'

'It only ever happens when they get on the drink. She likes a bottle or two of nut brown ale, but it doesn't like her. He gets a bit mouthy when he's had a few pints of porter and it's not a good mix.' Ferris picked up the three charge sheets and placed them on the desk behind him. 'The thing is, when they're sober, they're like a pair of newlyweds.'

'Will Bodkin arrest her?' Amy asked.

'I doubt it. Once Bodkin gets there, she'll start to simper and pat at her hair. She fancies the pants of him. Walter will come out and they'll both try to claim that the bolt on the door got stuck. They can't afford a fine, they live on their pensions and what Nellie can make from reading tea leaves.'

'Tea leaves?'

'Oh yes, people come from streets away to have their fortunes told.' Ferris paused. 'You'd think old Walter would get her to read his tea leaves. He might get an idea when the next attack was coming.'

Amy laughed. 'Oh my goodness. That's hilarious. Ferris, you really ought to include a joke or two in your act. You're a natural comedian.'

'Try telling Bodkin that,' Ferris grumbled.

'He doesn't like your impression of Groucho Marx, does he? But I think it's pretty good.' She quickly qualified her statement. 'I've seen worse, at least.'

'I might do it on Saturday night. Or do you think the crowd will be a bit too posh to appreciate it?'

'I might leave it out on Saturday,' Amy said thoughtfully, 'but I'd definitely keep it in your armoury if you ever do places like the Bell again. It would go down a storm in there.' She suddenly became more serious. 'Now, about Saturday night...'

For the next fifteen minutes, Amy filled Ferris in on the plans for her spying mission. She had just finished when the front door opened and Bodkin walked in.

Amy greeted the inspector with a smile. 'Hello, Bodkin,' Amy said. 'Did you rescue Walter?'

Bodkin sighed. 'The offending skillet is back in its rightful place on the stove and Mr and Mrs Pendlebury are now sharing a cuddle and a cup of tea on the sofa.'

'How did you calm her down?' Amy asked.

'I just did the same as I always do when I visit them. Mention the five-pound fine she can expect if it goes to court. That's an awful lot of tea leaf reading.'

Amy grinned. 'You're a nice man, Bodkin. Any other copper... Ferris aside, would have arrested her to get the solved crime numbers up.'

'I'd have demanded a free reading,' Ferris said.

Bodkin snorted.

'Hey, don't knock it,' Ferris replied. He winked at Amy. 'A gypsy once read my tea leaves and told me that I should be wary of a tall, dark, stranger, and the following day, Sergeant Bodkin, as was, turned up at the station.'

Amy stuck her thumb up to Ferris. 'You haven't lost it,' she said.

Bodkin looked puzzled.

'It's an in joke,' Amy said. 'Now, shall we go to your office? I've got something to tell you and I think it will be best if you heard the news over a strong cup of tea.'

# CHAPTER SIXTEEN

Bodkin led Amy along the corridor to his office and stood to one side to allow her to enter first. Then, after closing the door, he walked behind the desk and picked up the kettle from the top of the filing cabinet. After shaking it to judge the contents, he plugged it into the wall and switched it on.

'I'm out of tea bags so it will have to be loose tea today. The shop I get them from forgot to put the order in. I'm the only one that buys them, it seems.'

'I'm okay with tea leaves,' Amy replied. 'Providing you read them for me when I've finished drinking.'

'I'll get old Nellie to drop by later. She owes me a favour.' Bodkin reached into the filing cabinet and pulled out a tea caddy and a metal strainer. 'Though she'll have to tip them out of the strainer to do it and I'm not sure that works as well.' He took the lid off a small brown teapot and sniffed at it before tipping in three spoons of tea. 'It must be harder trying to tell a fortune from a pile of soggy leaves dumped onto a saucer. I mean, the tall, dark handsome stranger, bearing good luck, might really be great grandad Isiah, who has a dire warning message to impart from the other side.'

Amy laughed, then was suddenly serious. 'I know we had a laugh about Nellie and Walter's antics, but it's not that funny, really. Physical abuse shouldn't happen inside a family, whether it's a child, a wife or a husband that's on the wrong end of it.' She thought for a moment. 'They must have been on the sauce very early if drink was the cause of the argument.'

'They both had serious hangovers this morning, so they treated themselves to what is commonly known as the hair of the dog. They keep a bottle of gin put by for occasions such as this and they started on it as soon as the sun came up.' Bodkin shook his head. 'As to arresting her, Walter wouldn't press charges anyway. She doesn't hit him very hard with the skillet. She's hardly got the strength to swing it these days. Anyway, I've heard some of the things he says to her when he's in drink, and to be honest, he deserves all he gets.' He poured boiling water into the pot and replaced the lid. 'I can't see what good locking her up would do. I think it would probably be the end of her. Not because of the harsh regime, but because she'd miss him so much she'd die of a broken heart. Those two are so close, one couldn't survive without the other.'

'You're such a softie, Bodkin,' Amy said with a smile.

'Don't let on,' Bodkin replied. 'My reputation as an old cynic would be at risk.'

Amy closed her eyes and thought about how to approach the subject of the Boat Club, but before she could say anything, Bodkin lifted a folder from his desk and waved it at her.

'Effie's test results are back. She died of chloroform poisoning. Apart from the signs of burning in her mouth and throat, they found traces in her blood, her liver and in her adrenal glands. They say she must have taken in a lot of the stuff for them to find residue in places like that.'

'Poor Effie,' Amy said quietly. 'How on earth did that happen? Dentists only give you a quick sniff of it.'

Bodkin nodded as he poured their tea through the strainer. 'I wonder if she'd been exposed to a spill at a chemical plant or something like that?' He pulled out a bottle of milk from the filing cabinet, sniffed at it, then poured some into each of the cups. 'Remind me to get some fresh. This will be on the turn by tomorrow.'

He passed a cup and saucer across the desk to Amy. She sniffed at it suspiciously before taking a sip.

'Is that the first port of call, then? The chemical factory, I mean?'

'We need to find out if they make the stuff there first. I'll have a chat with the chemist to see what it can be used for, and where she sources her stuff from.'

'I hadn't thought of that, Bodkin. It must have other uses as well as being used as an anaesthetic. Most chemicals do.' She sipped at her tea as Bodkin failed to suppress a yawn. 'Are you tired, or just bored?' she asked.

'Just tired. I had a really bad night. I hardly slept. I think it was the two long drives yesterday. My eyes were on stalks by the time I got home last night. I'll admit to being more than a little grumpy today.'

'More than usual then?' Amy bit her lip to keep herself from laughing.

'Nellie Pendlebury reckons I'm like a bear with a sore head today.'

'Nellie said that? Blimey, talk about pots and kettles.'

Bodkin yawned again. 'I might have to have a bit of a nap in the back of the car.'

'You might as well go home and get a proper nap. You only live over the road.'

The inspector scratched the back of his head. 'I'll try for an early night. My brain will kick in when there's something to stimulate it.'

'Meaning my presence doesn't?'

'Your presence is all that's keeping me on my feet.'

Just then, there was a knock on the door.

'YES!' Bodkin shouted.

Ferris opened the door and stuck his head into the gap. 'There's a lady asking for you at the counter, sir. She seems a bit flustered. It seems that her best underwear has been stolen from her clothesline overnight.'

Bodkin sighed. 'Can't you deal with it, Ferris?'

'I offered to, sir, but I'm not far enough up the ladder to deal with it, apparently. She asked for the chief constable at first.'

'Christ on a... Sorry, Amy,' he added quickly as he stormed from behind the desk. 'Come on, Ferris, let's see if she has any idea of who the notorious night time knickers nicker might be.'

'That's very good, Bodkin,' Amy said as he hurried through the doorway. 'Even better than the Calamity Cabbie, I'd say.'

~

Fifteen minutes later, Bodkin returned to find Amy reading the report from the laboratory.

'Do you understand all these big words, Bodkin?' she said, looking up from the file.

'No, but I am now an expert on women's undergarments,' he replied, dropping a sheet of paper containing a long list of stolen items onto the desk. 'She must have a blooming big clothesline, that's all I can say... I mean... how many pairs of knickers can one woman own? Surely one pair a day is enough for anyone. She must have enough silk in her drawers to make a parachute.' He paused. 'I mean drawers, as in the kind found in an item of furniture, not the amount of silk it took to make her knickers.'

Amy snorted. 'Oh, Bodkin, you do make me laugh.'

Bodkin slumped into his chair and held his head in his hands for a full minute. Then, after picking up his cup of cold tea, he took a sip, pulled a face, then put it back on the saucer. 'I'll send Ferris for fresh milk,' he said. 'And a large tin of Nescafe instant coffee. I think I'm going to need it.'

'They opened up a factory in Manchester last year so you can buy it by the bucket load if you like,' Amy said.

'I doubt Alf Newton's little shop sells it by the bucket load, tempting as it would be.' Bodkin rubbed at his eyes, then squinted as he refocused on Amy. 'Now then, what was your news? You said you had something to tell me.'

Amy swallowed hard. 'I joined the Highwater Boat Club while you were away,' she said.

Bodkin's eyes opened wide. 'You did what?'

'I was at a loose end, Bodkin. I was restless. I couldn't find anything to occupy myself, so I took the bus over to Highwater to have a look at the place. I, erm, ended up joining the club.'

If Amy thought the news would please the policeman, she was to be disappointed. He sat, stoney-faced as Amy gathered her thoughts.

'It's all right. They think I'm Daphne McAllister, well, that's not exactly true, they know I'm Amy Rowlings but though they've heard that Daphne sublets Effie's flat and although she's been to the Boat Club herself, no one associates Effie's flatmate with Daphne, if you see what I mean, so I told them I shared the flat. I told them I worked at Donnelley's too... oh and they don't think my mum and dad live on Long Lane. They think he and mum live in a big house and own a few hundred acres of land down by Alice's farm... and they are on holiday in Marseille, not Margate.'

Bodkin placed his head in his hands again. 'Anything else?' he asked, quietly.

'Oh yes, there's lots more,' Amy said eagerly, and went on to describe in detail, all the events of the previous day.

'And you let this man... Joe, a total stranger, drive you home in his sports car?'

'Yes, but... well, I couldn't really say no to his offer. I got home safely, though. I got him to drop me at the farm, not our cottage.' Amy decided to skip the fact that he had tried to kiss her.

'You got home safely.' Bodkin sighed. 'Amy, you've just told me that this man was close to Effie. He spent time with her, he took her out... he... Well, goodness knows what else he got up to with her. You do realise you could have been in a car with her killer?'

'Yes, of course, but... Look, you weren't there, Bodkin. He was extremely friendly and was obviously upset when he read the news about Effie's murder in the Post.'

'He might be a good actor. Have you thought of that?'

'Of course that crossed my mind, Bodkin.' She looked into his stern face, then looked away quickly. 'I thought you'd be pleased.'

'Pleased? Good God, Amy. Anything could have happened to you. What on earth were you thinking?'

'I was thinking that I could be of some help,' Amy replied with a defiant note in her voice. 'I'm on the inside now, Bodkin. Can't you see the advantage of that?'

'It would take just a few minutes to check your story and find out who you really are. That's what I can see.'

'They won't find out, Bodkin. I gave Robert and Shirley McKenzies' names as my referees. I've already spoken to Shirley about it and—'

'You dragged the town's mayor and his wife into your devious little scheme? For pity's sake, Amy, this gets worse by the minute.'

'She was happy to become part of it.'

Bodkin shook his head again. 'I'm not sure Robert would agree.'

'Oh, I see. So you think because she's a woman, she's impetuous and can't think clearly herself? You think she needs a man to do her thinking for her?' Amy leaned forwards in her chair and glowered at Bodkin. 'I thought you were better than that.'

'I don't mean that at all, and you know it. But Robert is the mayor, and if it got out that he was helping you impersonate someone else, then I don't think it would go down well with the voting public.'

'It's not like I'm impersonating a police officer or committing a fraud for monetary gain, is it?'

'I sometimes wonder if you forget you're not a police officer, Amy.'

'BODKIN!' Amy sprang to her feet.

'I'm sorry. I didn't mean it to come out that way. Just calm down.'

'Don't you DARE tell me to calm down. I hate being patronised,' she snapped.

Bodkin rubbed at his temples with his fingers. 'Amy... you know me. I wouldn't—'

'I thought I knew you,' she said, looking down at her feet.

Bodkin took a deep breath. 'Sit down, Amy. Let's talk about this sensibly.'

'What do you think I've been doing, Bodkin. You're the one who's blowing it out of proportion.'

He put his hands to his head again. 'I don't seem to be getting through to you, Amy. Our killer could easily be a member of that posh club. In fact, the odds are that he...or she... is. You can't put yourself in danger by going in on your own like that.' He paused for a moment, then went on, his voice a little less stern. 'Your mum and dad would never forgive me if I let anything happen to you. I'd never forgive myself, either.'

'Nothing is going to happen to me, Bodkin. I'm not a silly teenager who falls head over heels for the first handsome man she sees. I'm an independent woman and I make my own grown up decisions.'

Bodkin rolled his eyes heavenwards. 'Do you think a murderer cares about whether you're an independent woman or not?'

'I think a murderer would have to think a lot harder about trying to convince an independently minded, intelligent woman to go somewhere she didn't want to go.'

'But you got into a car with a stranger and let him drive you into the back of beyond, where there would be no help forthcoming if you needed it.'

'Yes, but I made that decision, Bodkin. I thought about it and considered his offer carefully. I didn't just swoon at his good looks and fall under his spell. Besides which, the steward's daughter knew he was going to give me a lift home. Don't you think she'd have found it a tad suspicious if I'd suddenly gone missing?' She softened her gaze as she looked at him again. 'Bodkin. I'm on the inside. I've already met three of the club's members and I can easily get to meet so many more of them. I don't look like a threat. One of them might let something important slip while we're chatting. I'm sure we stand more chance of getting a few snippets of information this way than you would, turning up on their turf and forcing them into being questioned as suspects. That would really get their backs up.'

Bodkin was silent for a moment. When he spoke, his voice was soft, but firm. 'I can't let you do that, Amy. You're not to go there again. Do I make myself clear? I'm in control of this inquiry and what I say goes.'

Amy's lips became a thin line. 'You're ordering me about as if I was your lackey. You have no right to stop me from going there. I'm doing nothing illegal.'

'It's too dangerous on your own, Amy.'

'I'm going there on Saturday, as it happens. Oh, and don't be concerned about me. I won't be on my own. Alice is coming with me, and so is Ferris. The club is holding a presentation ball on Saturday night, and Ferris has been booked to sing.'

Bodkin's mouth opened and closed like a goldfish. 'Ferris... booked... What on earth has been happening? I was only away for a few hours and you seem to have taken control of the station.'

Amy shrugged. 'He's being well paid for it. He's an entertainer as well as a policeman, Bodkin. You don't really have a lot of say as to what he gets up to in his free time.' She waited to see if he would reply. When he didn't, she continued. 'I thought you'd be pleased to hear that a man... Ferris, in fact, would be on hand to look after me and Alice if things went awry.'

'Leave Ferris out of this, Amy. You're not going to this ball. I forbid it.'

'You... FORBID IT? Who do you think you are, my father?' Amy stuck out her neck and glared at Bodkin. Then she turned on her heel and stomped out of the room.

# CHAPTER SEVENTEEN

'Watch out, Ferris, he's really in a strop,' Amy said when she stepped into the foyer.

'I know,' Ferris replied. 'He almost bit my head off earlier on. Mind you, I probably deserved it. My impression of Oliver Hardy wasn't that great.'

'He's not happy about Saturday night. He might have a go at you because you're appearing on stage without his say so. It's my fault, Ferris, don't take the blame yourself.'

'I don't care what he thinks about it. It's up to me what I do in my free time and I'm not turning down the chance of a fiver and possibly a repeat booking, no matter what he says.'

'I've never seen him like this before,' Amy said. 'I know he's exhausted, but he's been tired plenty of times before. The poor man hardly sleeps.'

'Don't worry about me,' Ferris winked. 'You should have heard some of the tickings off I got when I first started here. Inspector Laws was in charge back then. I couldn't do anything right according to him.' He grinned as Bodkin's raised voice echoed around the corridor.

'FERRIS. MY OFFICE. NOW!'

'Sorry,' Amy whispered as she opened the front door and stepped outside.

~

Amy stood on the pavement for a few moments, unsure of what to do next. She didn't fancy an afternoon sitting alone at home reliving the argument with Bodkin over and over again, so she decided to take a walk along the riverbank to try to clear her head.

She had just turned the corner onto Main Street when she spotted Kathleen O'Toole stuffing a ticket into her purse as she came out of the pawnbrokers.

'Hello again,' Amy said as she approached. 'How's Danny?'

Kathleen tugged the brim of her hat down and tipped her head to the side as she spoke, but Amy had already spotted the purple bruise around her eye. 'He's back at school.'

'How's his poor back? I hope it's not hurting quite as much as it did.'

'He's got a black eye now to take his mind off the pain in his back,' Kathleen said. 'No little thanks to you.'

'ME? What have I done?'

Kathleen sighed. 'It's not really down to you, but that nosy old so and so, Mickey Holder recognised Inspector Bodkin as you left the house the other day. He couldn't wait to tell Marty all about it.'

'So he hit Danny just because he was helping the police try to solve a murder?'

'He's been hit for a lot less than that,' Kathleen said.

'What about Brian?'

'He got it this time too, even though he wasn't even there.'

'That man is despicable,' Amy snapped. 'He should be locked up.'

'We aren't that lucky,' Kathleen said. 'Anyway, we couldn't survive without his wages. At least he's not workshy.'

Amy put her hand gently on Kathleen's arm. 'You have to leave him. You have to get the kids out of there. They aren't safe with a violent man like him.'

Kathleen raised her eyes to the heavens. 'And where would we go? How would we get by? It's all right saying we'd be better off out of it, but we probably wouldn't be. I'd end up just like Sharon Tatler. She finally plucked up the courage to go, but she was back with her tail between her legs inside a week. She had no one to help her. She couldn't go to her mother's because he would have only found her there. She couldn't get any help from the church and the only charity refuge she could find was in Gillingham, and that would have been the second place he looked.'

'What if I helped you find somewhere safe?' Amy pleaded. 'Would you leave him if you had somewhere safe to go?'

'I'd think about it,' Kathleen said. 'But it would have to be at least a hundred miles away from here.'

As Kathleen made her way towards the food shops to spend the pittance, she had just acquired from the pawnbrokers, Amy decided to walk around to Shirley McKenzie's house to see if she had found the time to talk to her husband about setting up a family charity. She knew that Kathleen and her children wouldn't be safe anywhere near the town, but she felt that with Shirley alongside, they might be able to come up with a solution between them.

Unfortunately, Shirley wasn't at home, so Amy, frustrated and still angry about her argument with Bodkin, walked back to Middle Street and caught the bus to Long Lane.

That evening, after a meal of scrambled eggs on toast, Amy sat on the sofa with her Agatha Christie book of short stories but found that she couldn't concentrate on what was usually a gripping narrative. Realising that she had read the same paragraph three times, she closed the book, laid it carefully on the arm of the sofa, then stood, crossed the room and turned on the radio. She swayed to the rhythm of the BBC Light Orchestra as they played their version of the old Hoagy Carmichael hit, Georgia on my Mind. Smiling to herself, she picked up her mother's holiday postcard from the dining table. It was the second one she had received, even though her parents had only been away for five days. She knew she'd get at least two more before they returned home.

*Hello Amy, The weather is lovely. Dad has a sunburned nose. The jellied eels are going down so well that I've had to buy a new tin of toothpaste for him. We're going to have a walk down the pier again tonight. We miss you terribly and hope you are safe and well at home on your own, but then I expect Bodkin is looking out for you. He really is such a lovely man. Wish you were here.*

*Love*
*Mum and Dad*
*XXXX*

Amy read the last line twice and began to think that maybe she had been a little hard on Bodkin, but then she remembered the anger in his voice as he demanded that she did as she was told.

'Hard luck, Mr Policeman,' she said aloud. 'I'm a big girl now. I make my own decisions.'

She walked through to the kitchen and put the kettle on the hob before preparing the teapot. She had just finished spooning the tea leaves into it when she heard a knock at the front door.

Thinking it might be Alice, she hurried through the lounge, into the passage and pulled open the door, fully expecting to see her best friend standing on the porch. Instead, she saw an exhausted-looking Inspector Bodkin.

# CHAPTER
# EIGHTEEN

Amy looked directly into Bodkin's face before turning away and retracing her steps to the living room. Bodkin stepped inside the hall and quietly closed the door behind him. As he entered the room, he found her standing by the dining table with her arms folded and a serious look on her face.

'Amy, I'm sorry. I should have phrased my objections much better than I did. I was tired and rather confused by your news. I should have thought about things a little more before responding.'

'And have you thought things through now?' Amy asked.

'I have. But I still think I was right. It was the manner in which I spoke to you that was wrong. I'm truly sorry about that. The last thing I meant to do was sound patronising. You deserve better than that.'

'So much better than that,' Amy replied. 'You've never spoken to me like that before. It's like I'm seeing a different side of you, and I don't like that side very much at all.'

Bodkin looked down at his feet, then his eyes returned to look into hers. 'There is no other side to me, Amy. I'm just the same as I've always been. I am sorry for the way I spoke and I've come over here to see if there's a chance that you'll forgive me. My only excuse was that I was utterly exhausted.'

'It takes more than a quick sorry to be forgiven for that, Bodkin. Your attitude was really condescending.'

'I know, I know. It's just that... well, I worry about you, Amy. I hate the thought of you being put in a dangerous situation.'

Amy turned away and looked at the wall. 'I've told you, Bodkin. I'm a big girl now. I don't need a chaperone when I go out on my own.'

'But this is different, Amy. It's a murder investigation. Surely you can see that? What would the bigwigs at headquarters say if they found out you were investigating the case on your own, with no supervision or back up? They'd take that accreditation card off you without a second thought.'

Amy shrugged. 'Well, I'm not going to tell them.' She turned around to face him again. 'Are you?'

Bodkin sighed. 'Of course not. But I am responsible for your welfare when we're working on a case. I'd never forgive myself if anything happened to you.'

Amy's face softened a little. 'I know, Bodkin. But honestly, nothing is going to happen to me. I'll be with Alice and Ferris... at the ball at least. In the afternoon, when the rowing is on, there will be scores of people around me.' She looked at him earnestly. 'It's a wonderful chance to do a bit of digging around, you must see that. At the very least, I should be able to get a few bits of gossip about who she used to hang around with. Who she was really close to. Group tittle-tattle, Bodkin. None of the members know I'm not who I say I am. They'll let their guard down. They'll be relaxed as they sip their drinks and enjoy the day. I'm sure I can pick up some interesting facts as I mingle amongst them.'

'I can see the logic, Amy. Believe me, I can. I know people will be more willing to discuss things in an informal setting, and as it happens, I've been racking my brains trying to think of a way to get in there myself. These people tend to keep things back when they're under official scrutiny and they're much more likely to open up to someone they think belongs to their little clique, especially if that someone is a young, attractive woman. I just don't like the idea of what might happen if you ask the wrong question of the wrong person. I'd much rather be close by if that happened.'

'But haven't we agreed, you would almost certainly be recognised? There's bound to be someone there who knows you're a copper.'

'That might well be true, Amy, but there's a good chance there'll be someone there who has seen you around town, too. Especially after those evenings we spent in the Milton, and you've crossed paths with a good many of the town's elite as we've been going about our investigations.'

'How many knew I was a machinist at the Mill, though, Bodkin? One or two at the most. No one in the Milton has a clue about my background. And I've got the McKenzies' good name behind me now. Who's going to ask too many in-depth questions about me? I'm no one to them, just another silly young girl out for a bit of fun.'

'That's the other thing that worries me. Some of the female members might be jealous of you, especially if you are getting a lot of attention from the men in the room, and being as attractive as you are, that's bound to happen. We already know that Effie had problems because of that.'

'I can look after myself, Bodkin. I've had men come on to me before, so I know exactly what to expect.' She smiled suddenly. 'And as for the women. If I can handle Big Nose Beryl and her cronies at work, I can definitely handle any jealous women I might come across amongst the membership.'

'I'd still prefer to be with you, so I can keep an eye on things.

What happens if a brawl breaks out and you're stuck in the middle of it?'

'Now you're just being silly,' Amy tutted. 'Anyway, as I've said at least three times, Ferris and Alice will be there.' She paused as she looked sternly at him. 'You didn't give Ferris a hard time, did you? I got him into this.'

'We discussed the issue,' Bodkin said, unable to hold Amy's eye.

She sighed. 'I can imagine.'

'I haven't ordered him to stay away from the event. You're right, what he does in his free time is his own affair.'

'And what I do in my free time is mine.'

'Ferris isn't likely to end up with a horde of chinless wonders pawing at him all night,' Bodkin replied somewhat unconvincingly.

'Nor will I, Bodkin. Believe me. How do you think Alice and I went on before we had you to stand guard over us?'

'Amy...'

'We managed to look after ourselves just fine. Sure, there were a few hairy moments, but we always got home safely. Despite her starlet looks, Alice is as tough as old boots. She has to be working on that farm. Have you forgotten that she orders a dozen men around all day every day and not one of them even thinks about giving her a bit of back chat. Her right hook is the match of most of the men in this town, especially those of the chinless wonder variety.'

'You're not going to let me talk you out of it, are you?' Bodkin said quietly.

'Did you honestly think you'd be able to?'

'I hoped to.'

'Then you ought to have known better, Bodkin. I was just saying I might not know you as well as I thought I did, but it's patently obvious that you don't really know me that well either.'

'I know you better than you think I do, and I think you know the real me, too.' He paused, then went on. 'I'm not that man, Amy. Please believe me. I worry about you because I lo...' Bodkin suddenly looked flustered. His eyes flicked up at the ceiling as he scratched the back of his head. 'Oh, it doesn't matter how I feel about things. You'll just do what you like, anyway. We're going around in circles. Let's talk about something else.' He looked past her into the kitchen. 'What else have you been up to today?'

Amy shrugged. 'Not a lot. I bumped into Kathleen O'Toole in town. Danny has a black eye now to go with his set of bruises. She's got one too. It's a beauty.'

'Poor kid.'

'Poor woman, too. She gets it just as regularly as he does.'

Bodkin nodded. 'That's usually the case.'

'You still seem to be very blasé about all this, Bodkin.'

'I'm not blasé at all. I think it's disgusting. There's just not a lot I can do about it.'

'Well, it's a good job one of us is going to try to help.'

Bodkin's shoulders sagged. 'Amy, don't tell me you've been trying to talk her into leaving again? Where would she go? A single woman and two kids? Where would she get the money for food? They'd need somewhere decent to stay. She can't just take off like that.'

'I'm going to help her, Bodkin, I don't care what you say. Those kids deserve so much better.'

'Amy, please be careful. You'll end up making it worse for them.'

Amy's nostrils flared, and her eyes narrowed. 'How can I make it worse? How can it possibly be worse?'

Bodkin's mouth became a thin line. 'Believe me, it can get much worse.'

'How would you know, Bodkin? You never get yourself involved. You just sweep it under the carpet and pretend it's not happening.' Amy glared at the policeman. 'Well, I am involved and I'm going to remain involved until I find a way to help them. There has to be someone she can turn to.'

Bodkin opened his mouth to reply, then thought better of it. 'I think I'd better go,' he said quietly.

'I think that's the best idea you've had all day,' Amy replied. She gave him a scornful look. 'Shut the door on your way out.'

'Amy, please—'

'The discussion is over, Bodkin. I really don't know what's got into you. There's a poor kid being beaten half to death and all you can say is, don't make it worse than it is.' She swung away from him and stared at the cross on the wall next to her father's chair. 'Goodbye, Bodkin. I'll see you around.'

Bodkin walked slowly out of the room, but when he had almost reached the front door, he suddenly stopped and retraced his steps. Reaching into his inside pocket, he pulled out a battered address book. Opening it, he flicked through the first few pages until he found what he was looking for. Then, taking out his pen, he turned to a blank page at the back of the book and jotted down an address and a telephone number. He tore out the page and handed it to Amy.

'Ring this number. She'll help you if she can.'

Amy looked at the crumpled sheet of paper, then back to Bodkin. 'Who is it? How can she help?'

'It's my sister, Sal,' Bodkin said. 'She's still living in Dover. She helps run a homeless and family charity. They ought to be safe enough at that distance.'

Amy's face softened as she looked at the inspector. 'Bodkin, I'm sorry about what I just said. I didn't mean it to come out like that.'

Bodkin shrugged. 'I deserved it after this morning.'

Amy sat on the sofa and patted the seat next to her. 'Sit down for a minute.'

Bodkin shook his head. 'No, it's all right. I have to go. There's something I need to do before bed and I'm going to have an early night.'

'Just give me a minute then,' Amy said. She read the address on the piece of paper again. 'You never mentioned a sister. Are you close?'

'We used to be.'

'What happened?'

'We had a disagreement. I tried to... well, it doesn't matter now. Let's just say we're estranged.'

'You don't keep in touch at all? That's so sad, Bodkin. I'd have loved to have had a sister to talk to, or even a brother.'

'We exchange a card at Christmas, just so we know where to find each other in an emergency.'

'Oh dear, Bodkin, I'm so sorry. It must have been something really serious for you both to have let it go this far.'

'Something and nothing,' Bodkin replied.

'You're not going to spill the beans are you? It's like I said, there's a big part of you I know nothing about. You're a very private man, you keep so much locked away inside. I'm not sure that's good for you.'

'Some things are better left buried, Amy.'

'Okay, I can't force it out of you.' She folded the paper, then picked up her bag and dropped it inside. 'Thanks for this. I really appreciate it. Is it Sal or Sally? Is she married? Is that address close to where you grew up?'

'Sal, it's not short for Sally. No, she's not married and the house she lives in is the one we grew up in. She wanted to keep it on after my father died, so I agreed. Both our names are on the deeds, but I have no intention of ever calling in my half of it. It's all hers, as far as I'm concerned.'

'I hope you'll explain it all to me one day, Bodkin. I think it's so sad. You're family. You should be able to talk it through, no matter what the problem.'

Bodkin shook his head. 'Naa, it's been too long now. We're better off as we are.'

'How long is too long?'

'Five years. I left the same year my dad died.'

'That's four years wasted then, Bodkin. It's high time you sorted out your differences. She's the only person you've got left in your life.'

Bodkin smiled faintly at Amy. 'Not the only one I hope.' He turned away and let himself out, leaving Amy sitting teary eyed on the sofa.

# CHAPTER NINETEEN

AMY SLEPT BADLY. SHE SPENT THE WAKING HOURS GOING OVER HER angsty conversations with Bodkin and wondering how the two of them could make it right. Would their relationship ever be the same again? She thought there might be a chance. Bodkin was a deep one, that was for certain. He was a very private person and played his cards very close to his chest. He hadn't even told her his first name, for goodness' sake. She knew he cared for her. He had almost told her he loved her. What a time to do it, though. Slap bang in the middle of an argument. Bodkin's timing was impeccable.

The next morning, she had a strip wash in the bathroom, then made herself a plate of bacon and eggs before getting dressed and taking the short walk down the lane to Alice's farm. In her bag was the scrap of paper that Bodkin had given her the night before. She had decided to ask Alice if she could use her phone to call Dover. It would work out a lot cheaper than calling from the telephone kiosk at the top of the lane. She didn't have much in the way of change in her purse, anyway. Alice would let her owe her for the call. She'd give her a shilling in payment at the ball on Saturday night.

She found Alice in the kitchen. She had just finished cleaning out the pigs.

'Hello, you. I wasn't expecting a visit today.'

'I admit to having an ulterior motive,' Amy replied. 'I need to make a phone call to Dover and it would be much less of a faff if I rang from your front room. I'll pay for the call when I get some change. My purse is as empty as the Devil's heart.'

Alice picked up the kettle and filled it at the tap. 'Who do you know in Dover?'

'No one, yet. But I'm hoping to speak to Bodkin's sister, Sal.'

Alice put the kettle on the hob and lit the gas with a match. 'I didn't know Bodkin had a sister. He kept that quiet.'

'They had a bit of a bust up, apparently. Whatever it was, created a bit of a gulf between them. They haven't spoken for years.'

'That's sad, isn't it? She must be his only living relative, although he doesn't talk about his past much. There might be others out there somewhere.'

'I don't think there is. He is a very private man. No one could say he wears his heart on his sleeve, but I admit, it came as a bit of a shock to find he has a sister. She runs a family oriented charity and I'm hoping she can find a place for Kathleen O'Toole and her boys.'

Alice put the blue striped teapot on the large wicker coaster in the middle of the table and washed two large mugs that were decorated with a scene from the coronation of King George the sixth. Amy sat down on a chair at the right-hand side of the huge, old oak table as Alice pulled out the chair next to her.

'If you don't mind me saying. You don't look too full of the joys of spring this morning? You look like you've lost a florin and found a sixpence.'

Amy sighed. 'I've had a bit of a row with Bodkin. We're not really speaking at the moment.'

'Blimey! I thought you two were joined at the hip. Miriam says she can hear wedding bells.'

'My mum hears them too,' Amy said with a sigh.

'What did you argue about?'

'The ball on Saturday night and me taking a trip to the Boat Club on my own the other day. He thinks I'm putting myself in danger. Oh, and he's not keen on me trying to help Kathleen O'Toole and the kids, either. So, quite a few things, really.'

'Okay, I sort of get the bit about the Boat Club, but offering to help an abused mother? I can't see what he'd see wrong in that.'

Amy shook her head. 'He thinks I'll make the situation worse by getting involved.'

'Someone has to help them,' Alice replied, patting Amy's hand. 'It ought to be the police's job really, but I know firsthand that they won't get involved in anything that might come under the general heading of a domestic incident.'

Amy blew out her cheeks. 'I know. It doesn't make sense. The law willingly turns a blind eye to it and so, it seems, does Bodkin. I thought he was better than that. He's usually so sympathetic to the idea of women's emancipation.'

Alice poured tea, added milk, then passed one of the mugs to Amy. 'How bad was the row about the Boat Club?'

'Bad... Really bad. He said some things I thought I'd never hear come out of his mouth. He was so patronising, Alice. As I just said, I honestly thought he was better than that, but... it seems he's just like ninety-nine percent of the men in Spinton.' She paused to sip her tea. 'This happened in his office at the police station. He came around to apologise last night, but we ended up having another row about the O'Toole family and I said a few things I wish I hadn't.' She looked at her best friend through misty eyes. 'I'm not sure things can be put back to how they were before, Alice. It might all be over between us.'

Alice patted Amy's hand again. 'There's not a snowball in

Hell's chance of that. We've all seen the way he looks at you. The way he can't take his eyes off you when you're together. Most of the women I know would kill to get one of those looks from their men. He's in love with you, Amy, there's no two ways about that.' She smiled encouragingly at her best friend. 'This will all blow over. It's just a storm in a teacup.' She drained her mug, picked up the teapot and waved it towards Amy. 'Speaking of teacups.'

~

'Hello, Sal Bodkin speaking.'

'Hello. You don't know me; my name is Amy Rowlings and I live in Spinton in the north of Kent. I was given your number in the hope that you might be able to offer some advice regarding a family suffering regular domestic abuse.'

'Is it your family that is suffering the abuse, Amy?'

'No, it's a family that lives nearby. A woman and two young boys. The man of the house beats the boys on a regular basis and the woman gets her fair share too.'

When Sal didn't reply, Amy spoke again.

'It's just that. Well, one of the boys, Danny, is covered head to foot in bruises. He was punished just for talking to the police about the body of a young woman he'd come across while out playing. You would think the police would be grateful to him, but they don't want to know anything about the abuse.'

'Sadly, that attitude is commonplace, not just amongst the magistrates and the police, but it's also prevalent amongst the public in general,' Sal said. 'Kids need discipline or they'll grow up with no sense of right or wrong and because the parents themselves have been brought up that way, they can't see what's wrong in dishing it out to their own offspring.'

'Women have a terrible time of it up here,' Amy said. 'It's

unusual when you see a woman without a black eye on a Sunday morning.'

'It's nice to find someone else has the same feelings about this as I do,' Sal replied. 'Just give me a moment. I'll grab a pen and take down a few details.'

Amy gave Sal as much information as she could about the O'Toole family's situation, then she asked if she thought she'd be able to help them.

'You're a little out of our catchment area, to be honest. We have a refuge in Sittingbourne, which is a lot closer to you. They might be able to help.'

'Kathleen is reluctant to leave without being certain that this Marty character won't be able to find her. Sittingbourne might be a fair way from Spinton, but it's only a short train ride, really. I think if she's going to make the leap, they'll have to go as far away from here as possible and Dover is twice the distance.'

'She does know that she won't be able to stay in touch with her friends and relatives? The kids won't be able to write to school friends, not for a good while at least. It has to be a clean break. You'd be amazed at how cunning the abusers can be. They pick up snippets of information here and there and follow the trail until they find their quarry.'

'I haven't really spoken that much about the procedure because I've not been able to find anyone until now who can tell me how it might work,' Amy said. 'Do you have some leaflets you could post to me so I can pass the details on to her?'

'That wouldn't be a good idea. If the abuser found one of our pamphlets lying around, he'd know that she was planning to make a run for it. People in these situations tend to think it can't get any worse than it already is, but believe me when I say it can get much worse.'

'Someone said the same thing to me only last night,' Amy said.

'Someone knew what they were talking about then. Have they had experience of abuse?'

'No, it was...' Amy hesitated, then decided to reveal everything to Sal. 'It was your brother.'

'My brother!'

'Inspector Bodkin of the Spinton police.'

'And he gave you my telephone number? Did he say anything else about me?'

'Not really. He said that you've been estranged for a few years and you haven't spoken at all during that time but that you send each other a Christmas card every year.'

'And that was all he said? Is he a friend of yours?'

'He's my best friend. Apart from Alice, that is. I've known her all my life.'

'Boyfriend?'

'Sort of... He's... well, he's Bodkin. He's a one off. I care about him very much. He's under so much stress at work at the moment. He's virtually running the town's police station on his own and it's taking its toll on him.'

'He hasn't changed a lot by the sounds of it. You called him Bodkin just then. Hasn't he told you his Christian name yet or is it just that he's brainwashed you into using his surname all the time?'

'I have no idea what his first name is. He flatly refuses to tell me.'

Sal laughed. 'That's Gee for you.'

'Gee?'

'That's what even I have to call him. He really hates his given name. Mind you. I'm not a big fan of my name, which is why I've shortened it to Sal.'

'Isn't it short for Sally then?'

'It's short for Salome, but I'll bite the head off anyone who calls me that. It's a biblical name... it's—'

'The woman who danced for Herod Antipas, and demanded the head of John the Baptist,' Amy cut in.

'You know your bible then. Are you religious?'

'I go to church every week with my parents, but they are both far more religious than I am. My dad writes the sermons for the local vicar.'

'Dad was a big believer. He's the one who chose my stupid name.'

'I don't think it's stupid,' Amy replied. 'Unusual maybe.'

'It's definitely that. I've never worked out why he chose that particular name when there are so many in that blooming book to choose from. Why couldn't I have just been called Ruth or something?'

'What about your mum? Didn't she have a say?'

'He dominated in our house. Mum didn't have a say in anything. She turned to the bottle in the end. He was a big drinker too, but it took Mum early. Dad's liver was made of stronger stuff.'

'He never talks about his past... Bodkin I mean. He obviously thought a lot of your dad, though. He's still got his old armchair in his flat. He won't part with it. It's nice to have something that will bring back memories, isn't it?'

'It depends on the memory, I suppose,' Sal said. 'Gee has always kept things bottled up inside, even when we were kids. No one ever really got to know him.'

'Tell me about it. I had no idea he had a sister until last night.'

'How long have you known him?'

'We met just after the New Year. I stumbled across him when he was working on a murder case at the factory I work at. Because he was new to the area and I've lived here all my life, I was able to help get people to talk to him. Folk around here tend to clam up when the police start asking questions. Anyway, I've helped him on a couple of investigations since then. We work well together.'

'You work with him? I thought you said you worked in a factory.' Sal sounded puzzled.

'I do. I'm on the factory fortnight holiday at the moment. Bodkin wrangled me a police accreditation card, so I'm allowed to help him in a limited sort of way when I have the time.'

'I'm glad he's found someone who understands him at last, Amy. You sound really nice. I'd love to meet you. I could explain a few things about what happened between Gee and me.'

'Was it a big row? Only we've just had one... sort of, and I'd hate it if he didn't speak to me for the next five years.'

'He thought he was helping me, but he wasn't. I needed to stand on my own two feet. He thought he was doing the right thing, but I didn't. I felt he was interfering in my life. He thought he was protecting me. That's it in a nutshell.'

'Oh dear,' Amy said quietly.

'He's doing the same thing again, isn't he?' Sal said. 'He'll never learn.'

'I know he means well,' Amy said. 'And it might turn out that he was right, but I need to learn from my own mistakes. I'm an independent woman and proud of it. I don't like to be told what to do. Even my father knows he can't get away with that.'

'In my case, he was right. Not that I'd ever admit that to his face. As you said, Amy, if men are allowed to make mistakes, then women should be allowed to make them as well. We're not living in Victorian times now. Women are capable of making their own decisions and, as you said, we need to learn from our own mistakes.'

'Have you forgiven him, then?' Amy asked.

'Oh yes, a long time ago, but I'm just as stubborn as he is, and I'm not going to be the one to make the first move. He has to lose at least once in his life.'

Amy heard the sound of laughter in the earpiece.

'I could be the middle man... woman... if you like,' Amy said. 'I think it's so sad that you two still aren't speaking after all this time.'

'It is sad, and I really should have done something about it before now. I'm pretty sure that if we ever do meet, our dispute would be a thing of the past within seconds.'

'I'll do everything I can to get you back together,' Amy said. 'Just name it.' She was silent for a moment. 'I mean, I could take him a note telling him to stop being so silly and get in touch. I'd talk to him about it, but we're not in the best of places as things stand.'

'I know a way it might work,' Sal mused. 'Look, Amy, I have a meeting at the Sittingbourne refuge on Sunday. I'm driving up, so I'm getting an early start. What about I come up to Spinton to see you after my meeting? It's only a few miles further on. We could kill two birds with one stone. If you can get Mrs O'Toole to meet with me, I'll explain how things work. I can definitely find her and the kids a place down here. It will be in the refuge to begin with, but only for a few weeks. We ought to find them a flat, or even a small house in the area before too long. The charity will help with the rent, food, etc. until she can find some paid work and the kids have settled into a new school.'

'That sounds wonderful,' Amy said happily. 'But you said killing two birds with one stone?'

'We have to find a way to get Gee to pay you a visit. If you can find somewhere quiet, we can spring our little surprise on him.'

'I'll get him around to my house. My parents are away until next week. What time do you think you'll get here?'

'I can be in Spinton for twelvish if you think you can get Mrs O'Toole on board. It won't take me long to explain what we can do for her. Do you think you can sweet talk Gee into coming round to yours for about one o'clock?'

'I don't know if he'll even be talking to me after I go to the

Boat Club ball on Saturday night... but I'll make sure he gets there, one way or another.'

'Fabulous. Thank you, Amy, I'm so looking forward to meeting you. I think the two of us are about to become very good friends.'

After they had said their goodbyes, Amy put the handset back in its cradle and walked through to the kitchen where she found Alice, standing in her underwear as she towelled herself dry from the strip wash she'd just had.

'What was she like? Did she sound like Bodkin?'

'I think she's a heck of a lot like him. She certainly has the same stubborn streak and the same sense of humour.' Amy stood by the table as she watched Alice dry her legs. 'You might get to meet her soon. She's coming up on Sunday, but it's all hush hush. Bodkin can't know anything about it.'

'Do you think he'll scarper if he gets wind of it?'

'I don't know what he'll do if I'm honest, but I don't want him to think I'm interfering in things that are nothing to do with me, again.'

'Of course it's something to do with you. She could be your future sister-in-law.' Alice winked.

'That's looking a lot less likely than it might have been a week or so ago,' Amy replied.

'Oh, you two will sort it out soon enough. I'll be amazed if Bodkin isn't knocking on your door before the day is out.'

'I do hope so,' Amy said quietly. 'Oh, I did find something out. Bodkin's first name begins with the letter G. His sister calls him Gee because even she isn't allowed to use his Christian name.'

'You'll find out what it is without him even telling you,' Alice said. 'The vicar will have to let it slip when you take your wedding vows.' She opened the door to the parlour and tossed the damp towel into a wicker basket. 'Now, come and help me choose something from Mum's wardrobe. I seem to remember there's a shimmering red, calf-length dress in there somewhere. I think it will be perfect for a Boat Club ball.'

# CHAPTER TWENTY

Amy stayed at the farm for a lunch of thick cut ham sandwiches, a slice of Miriam's seed cake and two more cups of tea. Miriam had arrived back at the farm after taking Alice's daughter, Martha, to pay a visit to Bessie, the shire horse who had just been returned to her paddock after helping to move the trunk of a fallen tree.

After bouncing Martha on her knee while Alice filled the housekeeper in with news of the Boat Club ball, Amy returned home and worked through the short list of domestic chores that her mother had placed on the dining table before she left to go on holiday.

Two hours later, with the carpet sweeping and dusting done, and with a few garments washed and hung out to dry on the line, Amy switched on the radio, turned the volume down low and sat on the sofa as she once again tried to concentrate on her book. After ten minutes of going over the same two paragraphs, Amy gave up and stretched out on the sofa with her head resting on a pair of soft cushions. Was Alice right? Would Bodkin bite the bullet and pay her a visit after work? If he didn't, would it be because he was too busy, too tired, or would he stay away by choice? She wasn't nearly as convinced as her best friend was that he would suddenly turn up with a bunch of flowers and an apology on his lips. Bodkin could be stubborn. His long running stand-off with his sister proved that. She considered catching the bus to the police station to attempt to clear the air with him once and for all, but after thinking it through, she decided to leave it until the morning. She could call in at Bluecoat House, where Bodkin lived, on her way back from Brigden's. If he wasn't there, she'd look in at the station, as he often worked on a Saturday morning.

She stared up at the ceiling as she worked through a couple of imaginary conversations with him, all the while listening for the click of the front gate. At nine-thirty she gave up hoping, and after turning off the radio and the lights and checking the doors were locked, she picked up the latest edition of her Photoplay magazine and went up the stairs to bed.

~

At nine o'clock, on Saturday morning, Amy caught the bus from the stop at the end of Long Lane and got off at the Flag pub on the High Street. Just around the corner was her favourite shop, Brigden's Nearly New Store.

The shop had been set up to resemble one of the London designer stores, and carried a stock of labelled items, many of which had hardly ever been worn. Amy loved walking around the store, even though many of the items on offer were beyond her means. Some of the more expensive items were displayed in small, well-lit niches. Others were shown off on the bodies of faceless porcelain mannequins.

The usual focus of Amy's interest were the two, long, bargain rails at the rear of the shop, but today, to Sharon the assistant's surprise, Amy walked straight to the top end of the shop where she stood in front of a line of mannequins.

'Have you come into some money, Amy? You don't usually waste your time at this end of the shop.'

'I'm looking for a reasonably priced ball gown... no, evening gown would be nearer the mark.'

'We've got a few in, but you'd need to take out a mortgage to be able to afford any of them,' Sharon replied. 'None of them are what I would call reasonable.'

Amy walked along the line of mannequins, then took a few minutes to look in the well-lit niches that lined the right-hand side of the shop. Retracing her steps, she stopped in front of a steel-coloured, faceless figure, adorned with a full length, mint green, sleeveless, backless evening dress.

'Wow!' Amy said, as she walked around the mannequin, taking in every detail of the dress. The label boasted that it had been made in London by the Maison Flambert Company, a designer brand Amy had never seen before. The garment had a wrap over front, pinned at the waist, which would reveal quite a lot of cleavage. The back was laced across and again there would be a lot of flesh on show.

'You definitely have the figure for it, but do you have the money?' Sharon asked, taking hold of a lower part of the dress and pulling it towards her. 'It's slashed right up to the thigh. You won't be able to wear your winter bloomers with this one and you wouldn't want the wind to whip up while you're out and about either. You'd show off everything you've got.'

Amy looked dreamily at the dress and said nothing.

'It is rather revealing,' Sharon added.

'I can add a stitch here and there to hold it together,' Amy said eventually. She ran her hand across the silk fabric. 'It's beautiful,' she whispered.

'And I think you could carry it off, if anyone could,' Sharon replied.

'How... how much is it?' Amy asked as she walked around the figure again, inspecting every detail of the dress. None of the more expensive dresses in the shop had a price tag pinned to them. Eileen, the manageress, had always said that, if you needed to see the price of an item, then you couldn't afford to buy it.

'Twenty pounds,' Sharon said.

Amy whistled. 'Blimey!'

'It's a fifty-pound dress,' Sharon explained. 'You couldn't buy anything like this in Spinton. Not even at that posh dress shop you used to work at.'

'I'm going to be working there again soon,' Amy said. She looked around for the manageress. She spotted her at the counter and made her way across the shop towards her.

'Hello, Eileen, about that evening dr—'

'Seventeen pounds, ten shillings. There's a mark on the bottom seam, which I'm sure you've already spotted.'

'It's too much,' Amy replied. 'I do love it though.' She placed the Brigden's bag she had brought with her on the counter. 'How much will you give me for these? I bought them last autumn and I've only worn them once. I had to make a repair on the blue one and it's as good as new now.'

Eileen took the dresses out of the bag and examined them, minutely. 'I'll give you five bob each for them.'

'Five shillings? They cost me ten and I've only worn them once.'

'I'm not a charity, Amy, I have to turn a profit.'

Amy pouted. 'Even so, five shillings.'

'What did you want the evening gown for, anyway? Are you off to a palace garden party?'

'I'm going to a ball tonight at the Highwater Boat Club.' She paused. 'They call it a ball, but it's probably just a posh dance. I'm going with Alice, but she'll find something appropriate in her mum's wardrobe.'

Eileen nodded. 'Alice's mother had a wonderful dress sense. She had the right outfit for every occasion. Her sister used to take her down Oxford Street on her birthdays. I met her once... the sister, that is. She married well, didn't she?'

'Yep, she lives in Kensington. She's rolling in it.'

Eileen smiled at some memory or other, then turned her full attention to Amy. 'Highwater, eh? You're mixing with the toffs, are you?'

Amy shrugged. 'They're only the same as us, really, and a lot of them aren't that much better off financially. They just live under a veneer of respectability.'

'You wouldn't want to buy that dress, my dear. It's too expensive for just for one night.'

Amy sighed. 'I know, but it was a nice dream, even if it did only last for a few seconds.'

Eileen laid the two dresses on the glass counter, then walked around to the other side to stand next to her. She slipped her arm through Amy's and led her back across the shop towards the mannequins.

'Unless our government gets its act together and does some sort of deal with that maniac, Adolph Hitler, I can see us being at war again before the year is out. If we are, there's going to be an awful lot of belt tightening around here. Even nearly new shops selling quality items like this one are going to suffer. With the men away fighting, people are going to be feeling the pinch, even the better off in society.' She paused for a moment. 'The rich will stay rich of course, I doubt anything will ever affect them, but the middle classes, the well to do's who frequent places like this won't have it as easy. Women will think twice before buying a twenty-pound dress, even for a family wedding. No, I think there'll be a return to make do and mend, much like we had the last time we got dragged into a stupid war.'

'What will happen to all your lovely stock?' Amy asked.

'It will probably just sit here gathering dust,' Eileen said. 'Which is why I've come up with a rescue plan.'

'Rescue plan?'

'I'm going to start hiring out dresses as well as selling them. People might not want to pay twenty quid for a dress, but they might consider paying fifteen shillings to a pound for the privilege of wearing something nice to a posh do.'

'That's a great idea,' Amy said enthusiastically, 'but on a personal note, I couldn't really run to a pound just to wear something for three or four hours, much as I'd like to.'

Eileen stopped as she and Amy reached the lime green dress that Amy had lusted after. 'Oh, I wouldn't charge you a pound, dear. You'd look after it, make good any damage and send it back in better shape than it left the shop.' She ran her fingers down the silk dress. 'No, as this is a special occasion and you're one of my regular customers... and, as you'd be my first dress hire client, I think I could let you have it over the weekend for... ooh, let me think... fifteen shillings.'

Amy blew out her cheeks. 'Fifteen shillings... It's so tempting, but I've got the blue bias cut dress at home. That will do at a pinch.'

'Is it as beautiful as this one, though?' She stood back to take Amy in, then turned her eyes to the dress again. 'You would be the belle of the ball in this.'

'Oh...' Amy shuffled her feet as she looked heavenwards. 'Get thee behind me, Satan.'

'Let me think now,' Eileen said with a mischievous look on her face. 'I could run to seven and six each for the two dresses you brought in; as you said, you've only worn them once, and one of them has been professionally mended.'

'You'd do that for me?' Amy asked, her eyes suddenly misting over.

'You'd need a shawl, too. A jacket would spoil the look and it can get very nippy on the riverbank, even at this time of year.'

Amy threw her arms around the manageress and gave her a hug. 'Thank you, thank you,' she said, her voice breaking with emotion. She looked towards the changing room at the back of the shop. 'Can I try it on?'

~

Clutching her precious bag containing the dress and shawl which had been wrapped carefully in tissue paper, Amy left the store and walked around to the Sunshine café where she enjoyed a coffee and a slice of Madeira cake. From there, she took a right turn onto Middle Street and walked down the hill until she got to the police station on the corner of the Gillingham Road. As she pushed the door open, she was greeted from behind the counter by a broad faced, white-haired man, wearing a police uniform that was at least one size too small for him.

'Good morning, miss. How may I be of assistance?'

'You must be the new recruit,' Amy said, smiling at the officer. 'Ferris said you'd be starting soon. I'm Amy Rowlings. I'm a friend of PC Ferris and Inspector Bodkin. I was hoping to have a word with the inspector. Is he in?'

'I'm sorry, Miss Rowlings but they're both out at the moment. PC Dutton is in though.' He leaned over the counter and looked at Amy conspiratorially. 'He's new too. We came two for the price of one.'

'It's Bodkin I wanted to see,' Amy said. 'Has he gone home? I know where he lives. I could catch him there.'

'He and Ferris are both on the trail of...' he picked up a sheet of paper and read from it... 'the notorious, night time, knickers nicker. A lady from one of the really posh houses down the Gillingham Road called in. Someone has a bit of a thing for silk, it seems.' As he smiled at Amy, he suddenly looked ten years younger. 'I thought you might have come in to report that some of your... ahem... delicates had been stolen too.'

'No, my knickers are all accounted for, thank you.'

The constable picked up his pen. 'Can I take a message for the inspector?'

Amy shook her head. 'No, it's all right. I'll catch him another time.'

# CHAPTER TWENTY-ONE

At ten fifty-five, after arriving home and hanging up the hired dress to remove any creases that might have formed while it was in the bag, Amy caught the bus back into town and after alighting at the terminus, just managed to catch the eleven twenty-five bus to Highwater.

She was wearing a light blue summer dress with a red rose print and carried a cream knitted cardigan over her arm. The sky looked clear, and the sun was warm but, as Eileen had warned, it could get a little nippy at the side of the river.

From the Highwater town square, Amy made her way past the church and joined a short queue of people as they had their names checked against a list at the gates of the Boat Club.

'Rowlings... Rowlings... no, sorry I can't find a Rowlings.' The security man showed page six of his eight-page list to Amy. 'The names are in alphabetical order and there's no Rowlings on it. I've got a Ribble and a Robson, but no Rowlings.'

Amy felt her shoulders droop. Maybe her little scheme had somehow gone awry, and they'd seen through her feeble story. Bodkin had suggested that they might. 'I would only have been added to the list last Wednesday. Maybe there's an updated one?'

'This is the only list, madam.' The man flipped through the pages one at a time. 'There's no... hang on. Here you are. You've been added right at the end, along with a Mr Orlando Ferris and a Miss Alice Mollison.' He looked over Amy's shoulder and back up the narrow track that led to the town. 'Are they coming separately? Your names are all grouped together inside a pair of big brackets.'

'My friends won't be coming until tonight,' Amy said as she took her pass from the man and stepped past him. Turning to the right, she walked across the car park and made her way around to the back of the building. Most of the boathouses were now empty. The last of the racing craft was just being lowered into the river by its crew on the wooden jetty.

Amy showed her pass to the two female club members who were checking them at the back door and walked along the narrow passage until she came to the members' room. She found Lesley Philby standing near the bar with Joe, the club captain, and another man who looked to be in his late forties. Joe was wearing shorts and a rowing singlet that bore the club's crest. He pulled in his stomach and stuck out his chest as he saw Amy approach.

'They let you in, then?' he said with a grin.

'The man on the gate found my name added to the bottom of the list,' Amy replied, turning towards Lesley and treating her to a big smile. 'Thanks so much for sorting my membership out.'

'I wasn't about to type the whole list out again. It took me hours,' Lesley said, pulling a face. 'No problem about the membership. Dad telephoned the McKenzies and he was really impressed with what they had to say. You are very highly regarded.' She looked up at the middle-aged man as she spoke. 'This is my father, by the way.'

The man was tall, with a thin frame, an angular shaped face and narrow blue eyes. He raised his thick brown eyebrows, then bowed his head towards Amy. He was wearing navy blue trousers with a white shirt that was open at the neck. 'Welcome to the Highwater Boat Club,' he said, as he offered his hand to her. 'I'm Timothy Philby, the steward of the club.' He ran his eyes over Amy's body as he raised his head again. 'It's an absolute pleasure to make your acquaintance. If there's ever anything you need, my office is just down that corridor.' He pointed a long finger to the right, but his eyes never left Amy's chest.

Amy wondered whether Effie had ever spent time in Timothy's office, but she kept her thoughts to herself and instead thanked the steward for fast-tracking her membership.

'Are you coming out to watch my races?' Joe asked, leaning around the thin frame of Timothy.

'Races? Are you in more than one, then?'

Joe gave her a look full of false modesty. 'I'm in three, actually. The singles, the fours and the eights.'

'Gosh,' Amy replied. 'You'll be ready for bed tonight, then. How long a distance are the races over?'

'A mile. We row slowly up the river and around the bend to the start line. Then we come back. Hell for leather with the current. The finishing line is by the jetty.' He paused and stuck out his chest again. 'I've got an hour between races, so I've got plenty of time to recover.'

'He'll win all three,' Lesley said, looking at him dreamily. 'He always does.' She forced her eyes away from the club captain and focussed them on Amy. 'Would you like a drink to take outside? We've set up a temporary bar on the riverbank, but they've already run out of ice.' She led Amy across to the club bar, where they found Gerald perched on a stool. He regarded Amy with interest as they approached.

'Hello, hello, what do we have here then?' He looked Amy up and down. 'What's your name, my pretty?'

'Amy,' Amy said, giving him a wide berth as she stepped up to the bar. 'We met the other day.'

'Did we... are you sure? I never forget a pretty face.' He tipped his head to one side as he thought. 'No, can't remember.' He looked towards Lesley. 'The sun must have been way over the yardarm.'

'You were a little bit groggy,' Lesley replied sticking to the nautical theme.

Gerald got off his stool and took a step towards Amy. She took a step back and watched him nervously as he reached out a hand towards her. Turning away from him, she fished about in her purse as Lesley placed a glass of Pimm's on the bar.

'I've put lots of ice in, so you can take your time with it,' she said.

Amy handed her a half crown and slipped the loose change back into her purse. Then she picked up the drink and backed away from the leering Gerald. 'Nice to meet you again, I'll just... erm... go and find a spot to watch the races.'

There was quite a crowd of people on the river bank, many of them sitting on blankets on the grass watching some teenage rowers take part in a one hundred yard contest. Behind and to the right of the picnickers were rows of seats, most of which were occupied. Across the strip of land between the clubhouse and the seated audience was a row of three trestle tables. One was selling shirts, caps and miniature wooden oars, emblazoned with the Boat Club logo. Another sold miniature union jacks, assorted nautical flags and small black triangular pieces of cotton bearing a skull and crossbones. The third trestle had a canopy over the top and was selling gin or rum based cocktails, along with tall glasses of lemonade. At the end of the table sat a woman in a pale pink, button down dress. She waved a book of raffle tickets at Amy.

'Sixpence a sheet. You could win a pair of day passes to the Henley Regatta.'

'I'm not sure I want to go to the Henley Regatta,' Amy replied.

'There are plenty of other prizes... You could win. Dinner for two at Hoskin's.'

Hoskin's was a restaurant in Highwater. It was well known for its influential clientele.

She handed over a sixpence and received a strip of five numbered tickets, which she folded carefully and dropped into her purse. *It would be a lovely surprise for Mum and Dad. I wonder if they serve jellied eels?*

Amy found a place to the right of the trestles and looked about her. Everyone seemed to be enjoying themselves. Families shared picnics, teenage girls chatted in small groups while the adolescent boys ran about shouting at the tops of their voices. Every so often, a mother would call out, warning some young lad or other, that they were getting dangerously close to the river.

A middle-aged woman, standing with a man who Amy assumed to be her husband, looked Amy up and down, then after realising that she had been caught out, she stepped towards her, carefully carrying a bowl of punch. A thin cocktail stick with a pierced cherry on the end of it, rattled on the side of the glass.

'I haven't seen you around here before. Are you the friend of Effie that everyone has been talking about today?'

'I was a friend of Effie,' Amy said with a nod. 'I'm not sure why everyone is talking about me, though.'

'She didn't have many friends... not of our sex, at least,' the woman replied. 'She had plenty of admirers amongst the men, though.' The woman shot a quick glance at the man behind and caught him giving Amy an appreciative look.

Amy decided to play innocent. 'She was always lucky in love,' she said.

'She wasn't that lucky though, was she? Not in the end, at least. Look where it got her.' She took another quick glance behind and then gave Amy a stern look, as if warning her off.

'I'm not sure I understand what you mean.'

The woman took Amy's arm and led her up the bank. 'Young girls like you need to be careful,' she said, looking Amy up and down. 'We all had a figure like yours at one time, but it doesn't last. Children and gravity soon make short work of it.'

Amy gave her a puzzled look. 'I'm still not sure why you're telling me this.'

The woman sighed. 'I'm just saying. I know what it's like to be admired by men. It's flattering, especially when the men are, how shall I put it, more mature?'

'It depends what you mean by mature,' Amy said, looking about. 'For someone my age, I'd say anyone up to about thirty is fair game. Any older than that and it's getting into father or uncle territory.'

This news seemed to cheer the woman up considerably. She took a sip from her drink, then held out her free hand. Amy took it. 'I'm Francoise Slowcombe, but my friends call me Franny.' She coughed and put her hand to her throat as she said it.

'Fanny?' Amy asked.

'Franny,' Mrs Slowcombe swiftly corrected her, putting a big emphasis on the r.

'Ah,' Amy said.

'Correct,' Franny replied, treating her to a narrow smile. She nodded down the slight incline to where the man she had been standing with was in conversation with Joe, the club captain. She sighed and placed her hand on her chest. 'He's such a handsome chap, isn't he?' Amy assumed she meant Joe, because her husband was anything but. He was on the short side, with a round face and a pair of sunken eyes that made him look years older than he probably was. His blue shirt was stretched tight across a rounded paunch. When Joe leaned in and whispered something to him, he laughed and his entire body, including his double chin and his paunch, wobbled like a jelly that had just been tipped from its mould.

'Oliver used to look just like him when he was younger,' Franny said wistfully.

'Really?' Amy replied. 'Is that your husband? What does he do?'

'He's in property,' she said. 'He buys land and sells it on to developers at a profit.' She preened. 'He does very well out of it, too.'

Amy stepped to the side as a woman of about fifty walked purposely up the bank towards them, but instead of passing by, she came to a sudden halt next to Franny. She was a grey-haired woman with narrow suspicious eyes, a beak for a nose and a slit where her mouth ought to be. Her clothes seemed to hang on her stick thin frame. Her collar bones jutted out through her blouse, the top two buttons of which were undone, showing the wrinkled beginnings of a turkey neck. After taking a quick look at Amy, she turned her attention to Mrs Slowcombe.

'Hello, Franny. Have you seen Theo about?'

'He was with James and Alphonse Noseworthy about forty minutes ago. They were over by the jetty, lining up the posts to mark the finish line. I think they were going to set up a book for when the proper races start.' She nodded towards Joe, who was just making his way down towards the river. 'Oliver wanted to put a few pounds on Joe winning all three of his races, but the odds they gave him weren't worth having.'

The thin woman scowled. 'Gambling is the work of the Devil. It will serve them right if they got caught.' She turned to the crowd as if looking for someone. 'It wouldn't surprise me if the police didn't have a presence here today. They're bound to want to question us all at some stage. That murdered girl was a member, after all.'

Amy took a deep breath but said nothing.

'Have the police questioned you yet? You were a friend of hers, weren't you?'

'Friend might be pushing it,' Amy replied. 'She was an acquaintance of mine.' She waved her arm out towards the crowd of picnickers. 'Everyone seems to know me, but I hardly know anyone. Word certainly gets around quickly.'

'You're the talk of the town, or the talk of the club, at least. It's hardly surprising when you show up asking questions about the poor creature, even before the news had got out that her body had been found.' She looked at Amy through narrowed eyes. 'Some people might think that's very suspicious.'

Amy sighed. 'I can't see why, Mrs...?'

'Lampton. Jessie Lampton.' She turned to look back down the slope as she heard her name being called. 'Ah, here he is,' she said as the figure of a tall man walked towards them. He was almost as birdlike as Jessie. When he came to a halt, he ignored his wife and looked directly at Amy.

'Hello,' he said breezily. 'I'm Theo Lampton. It's a pleasure to meet you.' He lifted his chin and beamed a smile.

'She's a friend of that flooz... the girl who was found murdered,' Jessie said, as if her words ought to be enough to make her husband's interest flag.

'Ah, you're the girl, are you? There's been a lot of speculation around here today. I heard you were a pretty young thing, but none of the descriptions did you justice.' He smiled at Amy again. 'Can I buy you a drink, my dear?'

Amy shook her head. 'I've got one, thanks. I have to pace myself or I won't feel like drinking tonight.' She looked at her half-drunk Pimm's. 'I'm switching to lemonade after this one.'

As a small group of middle-aged women walked up the hill, waving and calling to Franny, Amy sidestepped to make room for them before making her way down the hill towards the river to watch the climax of the first serious race of the afternoon. She found a space on the grassy bank and sat down as Joe and four other rowers began to make their way slowly upstream to the start line. She held up her hand to shield her eyes from the glare of the sun on the river and wished she had bought a brimmed hat with her. Squinting at the water, she watched a pair of swans make their elegant way downstream. They changed direction and swam to the near bank as three young children threw the leftover crusts from their sandwiches into the river.

Twenty minutes later, she heard the crowd stir, and the members began to get to their feet. Cries of 'Come on Joe' and 'Well done skipper,' filled the air. Amy stood up with the rest and from her vantage point, saw Joe cross the finish line in his small single scull, some twenty yards ahead of his nearest competitor.

Amy continued to applaud with the crowd as Joe steered his boat towards the bank. Then, as two club members held the boat steady, he tossed his oars onto the grass and clambered out of the craft. Raising his hands above his head, he clasped his fingers together and took the salute of the crowd. Spotting Amy he made a bee-line for her, shaking the hands of members as he walked.

'That's the first one out of the way,' he said, wiping a hand across his perspiring brow.

'Well done!' Amy replied trying to match his excitement.

'I've got an hour to recover for the next one,' Joe said, treating her to his best smile. He rubbed his biceps, then flexed them twice. 'I'd better find my sweater. I don't want to risk my muscles getting cold.'

'Heaven forbid,' Amy said, taking a sip of her Pimm's. 'I don't know much about regatta racing. Which events are you in again?'

Joe stuck up a thumb to a fellow member as he walked towards them, carrying an armful of white woollen sweaters. He sorted through them until he found the one with Joe's initials on the front and passed it to him.

'Good start, skipper,' he said before making his way down to the river to hand over sweaters to the other racers.

'I've got the fours and the eights to come,' he said, before giving Amy a lengthy explanation about the events and equipment, most of which went straight over her head. Joe went into great detail about his sport, tossing words like, sculls, shells, coxes, coxless, stroke, sculler and sweep at her. Amy nodded now and then, as if taking it all in, but soon found her concentration waning.

'Where did you keep your cox in the race you've just finished?' she asked when he'd finished speaking. 'There doesn't look like there's room for any extra equipment in that little boat.'

Joe looked at her with a puzzled look on his face. 'Singles are all coxless.'

'It's probably a good job,' Amy replied. 'Goodness knows what might happen if they got loose and started thrashing around in the bottom of the boat.'

Joe placed his palm on his forehead. 'I don't think you quite understood.' He paused for a moment. 'It's like this—'

'Well done, Joe.'

Amy breathed a sigh of relief as a man of about forty, wearing a blue and yellow striped blazer, made his way towards them. He was a good-looking man with a pleasant smile and sparkling blue eyes. He took off his straw hat to reveal a head of neatly parted dark brown hair, with just the beginnings of grey at his temples. He slapped the club captain on the back, then turned to Amy and smiled.

'Hello, my dear. We haven't been introduced. I'm Ronald Parkin. If you ever need a tooth pulling, I'm your man. I own the dental surgery in Highwater.'

As Amy smiled at the man, he ducked his head to look into her mouth. 'Not that you'll need my services by the looks of it. Your teeth seem to be in perfect condition.'

Just then, a dark-haired woman appeared at Ronald's side. Her hair had obviously been dyed and was in need of a touch up around the roots. She was dressed in a candy striped summer dress and white sandals. She gave Amy a wide, friendly smile as she introduced herself.

'You're Effie's friend, aren't you? I was so sorry to hear the sad news about her. She was such a lovely young woman.' She looked sideways towards the man, then back to Amy as she held out a white gloved hand. 'I'm Annette Parkin by the way, but my friends call me Nan.'

Amy shook Nan's hand and returned the smile.

'Joe's just been explaining all the rowing terminology to me, but most of it went right over my head. There's so much to learn. I know nothing about it, I'm afraid.'

'It can get confusing,' Nan said, patting Amy's arm. 'Oh, that reminds me, Joe, Timothy is looking for you. Something about the race order.'

Joe stepped back to pull on his sweater, then he excused himself and hurried off to find the steward.

Nan watched him go; her face etched with appreciation.

'He's a lovely man, isn't he? He represents the club so well.' She turned back to Amy. 'He's one of the few really good rowers we have left now. The regatta was very competitive in days gone by.'

'Is the membership dwindling then?' Amy asked.

'Amongst the more athletic types, it is,' she said sadly. 'We can't seem to attract the right young men anymore. Everyone seems to want to play cricket or rugby these days. The two bigger clubs down river seem to snap up all the best talent.' She paused as she reflected. 'We enter the challenge cup against the other two clubs every year, but we haven't actually won it since nineteen thirty-five. Mind you, we had some real athletes amongst our ranks back then. One was in the Cambridge team. He raced against Oxford on the Thames that year. They won too.'

'Is he still a member?'

'Yes, but he doesn't live around here anymore and the nature of his work means he doesn't get a lot of free time to visit us.' She looked out over the river with a wistful look on her face. 'We've become a bit of a backwater now.'

'Cheer up, Nan, don't go putting the young girl off. She's only just joined. We need some new blood about the place.' Ronald put his arm affectionally around his wife's shoulders. 'We're both on the committee, so if there's anything you're not sure of, or if there's anything we can help you with, just give us a shout.'

'Thank you, I will,' Amy replied, taking the last sip of Pimm's.

Ronald held up his own empty glass. 'Who's for a refill?' he asked.

'Just a lemonade for me, Ronald,' Nan said.

'Lemonade for me too, if that's all right?' Amy passed Ronald her glass.

'What a pair,' Ronald said. 'You're no fun at all.'

'I'm saving myself for tonight,' Amy replied. 'Alice and I will probably hit the port and lemons at the ball.'

'Alice?' Nan cocked her head to the side as she looked quizzically at Amy. 'Is she a new member, too?'

'No,' Amy replied. 'Alice is coming as my guest. She's my best friend. We've known each other for years.'

'Well, she'll be very popular if she looks anything like you,' Ronald said as he gripped the stems of the glasses.

'Oh, she's much prettier than me. She's a dead ringer for Rita Hayworth... you know... the Hollywood starlet.'

Ronald whooped. 'Jolly good show. I like her.' He leaned across to whisper something into his wife's ear. She smiled and gave him a peck on the cheek.

'I should think so too.' She looked at him affectionally as he pursed his lips and blew her a kiss.

'He's an old romantic,' she said to Amy as they watched him walk towards the temporary bar.

Nan reached into her bag and pulled out a fan. She wafted it in front of her face and blew out her cheeks. 'It's getting rather hot. It will be a little cooler under the shade of the trees.' She took Amy's arm and walked her across the grass to a small copse of elder trees. 'Ronald will find us.'

As they walked, they passed a group of young men, all dressed in similar white shirts and dark trousers. Nan nodded and smiled at them as they passed. One of the men, stopped dead, then whistled at Amy.

'Please tell me you're not married,' he said.

'Get away with you, Sam Smedley,' Nan said. 'Leave the poor girl alone.'

Another of the men pushed his way past Sam and presented himself in front of Amy. He bowed formally. 'Are you at the ball tonight? Please tell me that you are. I'd be honoured to have the first dance.' He lowered his head again. 'Tom Brannigan.'

Sam dragged his friend out of the way. 'I saw her first. Get in the queue.'

Nan took a deep breath and shooed the young men away. 'Honestly, I thought your mothers had brought you up better than this. You especially, Sam Smedley. You just wait until I see her at the W.I.'

The young men backed away, waving and calling to Amy as they went.

'The sap is rising,' Nan said as she opened the clasp on her leather bag and pulled out a cotton tablecloth. She offered one end to Amy, and they spread it out under the shade of the elder trees. Motioning at Amy to sit, she smoothed down her floral print dress and sat down, facing the river. 'That lot are incorrigible. They were the same with that poor girl, Effie. What's that saying? Like flies swarming around a jam pot.'

Amy wasn't sure she liked being compared to a jam pot, but she bit her lip and smiled at the dentist's wife. 'Did you get on with her? From what I've heard, she seemed to polarise opinion.

Mind you, she's always managed to do that. People either loved her or hated her, there didn't seem to be an in between position.'

'I could take her or leave her,' Nan said. 'She wasn't really my cup of tea. Not many of the women liked her, not that she cared. The men used to follow her around like little lost sheep. Even the ones old enough to know better.'

'There you are. I thought I'd lost you.' Ronald walked into the shade carrying three tall glasses of lemonade. 'No Ice, sorry. They have kept the pitcher in the shade, so it shouldn't be too warm.' He handed a glass each to Amy and Nan before sitting down and taking a sip from his own drink. 'Come on then. Let's have the juicy gossip. What have you been chatting about in my absence?'

'We were just discussing Effie Watkins,' Nan said. 'Amy knew her before she came to Highwater.'

'Ah, her. Everyone is shocked at the news of her demise. Some will miss her more than others.'

'He's one that will,' Nan said, nodding towards a broad-chested man wearing a navy blazer and a straw hat who was walking towards them with a smartly dressed woman who looked to be at least ten years younger than him. He waved to Nan when he spotted her, then after pointing her out to his companion, he stepped towards them, calling out a greeting.

Nan turned to Amy and lowered her voice. 'This is Granville Cresswell of Creswell Chemicals. He is one of those who should have known better.'

# CHAPTER TWENTY-TWO

'Don't get up, please,' Granville said as he ducked beneath a low branch. He ran his eyes over Amy, making her feel very self-conscious. As his gaze lingered over her legs, she tucked them beneath her and tugged the hem of her dress over her knees. He crouched down and held out a hand. 'I'm Granville Cresswell, I'm delighted to meet you.' He twisted his head towards the woman. 'And this is my, erm, friend, Katherine Downey.'

The woman gave a curt nod to Amy, then sat down on the tablecloth after Ronald got to his feet to make room for her. Amy smiled, then wafted her hand to shoo off a wasp that was taking more than a casual interest in her drink.

Granville eased down onto his backside and grinned at Amy. He was a handsome man who obviously liked to look his best. His dark moustache was trimmed neatly, his hair was an identical colour, parted sharply on the left and held in place with a thick coat of Brilliantine. He had a square jaw and thick, almost feminine lips. His brown, almond-shaped eyes looked at her from beneath a pair of recently trimmed brows. 'Whom do I have the absolute pleasure of addressing?' he asked.

'I'm Amy Rowlings,' Amy said.

'Ah, you're the mystery woman everyone is talking about,' Granville said with a wink.

'I'm not the slightest bit mysterious,' Amy replied, wafting her hand again at the persistent wasp.

'All women are mysterious. That's what makes them so appealing to us,' Ronald said, smiling down at his wife.

'Amy was a friend of Effie's,' Nan said, looking from Granville to Katherine. 'She works at Donnelley's, you know, the Spinton law firm?'

Katherine was a fair-haired woman with an oval-shaped face, high cheekbones and generous lips that were coloured a deep shade of red. She made an O shape with her mouth. 'Really? I know someone who works there. You must know her. She's called Daphne McAllister?'

'Of course I know her,' Amy said. 'She knew Effie too.'

'Effie was a lovely girl,' Granville said sadly. 'Who on earth could do something like that to such a fascinating creature?'

Amy fidgeted with her glass. She could feel Katherine's eyes on her.

'You're from Spinton, I assume? I haven't seen you in Highwater before today.'

Amy nodded, then quickly tried to draw the attention away from herself. 'What do you do, Granville?'

Granville preened. 'I own the chemical works in Spinton.'

'What sort of chemicals do you make there? Are they mainly insecticides?'

'We manufacture a lot of chemicals, arsenic and strychnine for pest control, but we produce a lot of solvents too, depending on what the market is looking for.'

Amy bit her lip to stop herself asking about chloroform. 'That must be dangerous, working with all those poisons. Do you produce a lot? I live in Spinton, but I don't know much about your chemical plant. I don't think I know anyone who works there.'

'We're the biggest chemicals manufacturer in the South East,' Granville said proudly. 'We take adequate measures, of course. We have to adhere to the strictest safety standards.'

'Oh, stop all this boring business talk,' Katherine said. 'I'd like to know more about you, Amy.'

'There isn't much to know,' Amy said wafting at the wasp again but this time deliberately spilling her drink over the table-cloth. 'Oh, dear,' she cried, getting quickly to her feet. 'I'm so sorry, Nan. That was very clumsy of me.'

'It will wash out,' Nan said, waving away Amy's apology.

As Katherine opened her mouth to ask another question, Amy got on her tiptoes and looked across to the riverbank where the crowd were once again getting to their feet. A commentator's excited voice boomed out of the Tannoy system. 'As they come around the turn, it's the blue team skippered by Joe Lyndsay, a length ahead of the reds with the greens a distant third.'

'Oh, this sounds exciting.' Amy left the shade of the trees and hurried across the grass so that she could get a view of the finish line. Ninety seconds later, Joe's crew, wearing blue sashes, crossed the line that was marked by a wooden post, with the red sashed team just two boat lengths behind. Amy cheered along with the crowd as the crew steered their scull to the bank. Joe climbed out immediately and left the rest of the team to secure the boat.

'Two down, one to go,' he said as he trotted up the bank towards where Amy was standing.

'Oh, well done!' Amy cried as she clasped her hands together.

'I'd love to stay to chat, but I've got to meet that damned reporter from the Post. He's doing a piece on me for the centre page sports spread on Monday.'

'How exciting,' Amy replied. 'I'll look forward to reading it.'

'I'll find you again after my last race. It will be about forty-five minutes. They've had to reschedule a couple of events.' He turned to leave but stopped when Amy put her hand on his arm.

'I'm sorry, Joe, but I won't be here to see that one. I've really got to go. I have to get a bath and something to eat before I get ready for tonight. Alice is coming over to my place at five.'

'But you'll miss my big moment of glory. No one's ever won all three events before.'

'I'm sure they'll have a photo or two in the Post.' She smiled sweetly at him. 'I'll see you tonight. You can tell me all about it then.'

'Don't be late. I want the first dance.' Joe reached towards her, but when Amy didn't respond, he shook a puzzled look off his face, then went in search of the reporter.

'You've got them fawning all over you, just like little Effie.'

Amy turned to see Katherine standing behind her. 'I'm nothing like Effie,' Amy said firmly. 'Now, if you'll excuse me, I have to go.'

'There's no need to rush,' Katherine said. 'I'll give you a lift.' She pulled her car keys from her purse and waved them in front of Amy.

'Don't put yourself out, Katherine. I'm fine, thanks. You don't want to miss Joe's last race.'

'To tell you the truth, I'm bored to tears,' Katherine said. She took hold of Amy's arm and led her across the grassy bank. 'And I'm sure what you have to tell me will be far more interesting than watching some egotist splash about on the water. To be brutally honest, I hope he sinks.' She paused, then stopped and turned to look at Amy. 'You see. I know you're not who you say you are. You don't work at Donnelley's and you're definitely not a friend of Daphne's. I saw you working in the London Connection when I went in with Daphne a few weeks ago.' She set off again, still holding Amy's arm. 'So, Amy Rowlings. I'll give you a lift home to wherever it is you really live, and you can tell me who you really are.'

## CHAPTER
# TWENTY-THREE

KATHERINE LED AMY INTO THE CAR PARK AND STOPPED WHEN SHE CAME alongside a sleek, red Aston Martin convertible. The hood was down, so the sun had been at work on the leather seats for the best part of the afternoon.

'You'd better sit on your cardigan unless you want to toast your behind,' Katherine said as she draped her jacket over the seat before climbing into the car.

'It's a beautiful car. Is it yours?' Amy said as she laid her cream cardigan over the passenger seat.

'I get the use of it, but it belongs to Granville,' Katherine said as she worked through the starting routine. 'Do you drive?'

'I'm going to learn this summer,' Amy said. 'My best friend, Alice, is going to teach me.' She almost told her about the ancient farm truck she was going to learn in but managed to bite her tongue before she mentioned it.

On closer inspection, Amy found that Katherine looked to be a fair bit younger than she had first thought her to be. Liberally applied lipstick aside, she wore very little makeup and yet there were no discernible lines around her eyes or mouth. Her forehead, or what she could see of it beneath her fair-haired fringe, was smooth. She wore a white dress with a lemon and green floral print. She had kicked off her white, heeled shoes before she started the car.

'So... Amy Rowlings, tell me about the real you,' Katherine said as she steered the car past the security guard at the gates.

'There's not a lot to tell, really,' Amy replied hesitantly. 'What would you like to know?'

'How about this, for starters. Is Amy Rowlings your real name?'

Amy nodded as Katherine turned left and drove past the old church and on towards the row of shops that lined the oval shaped green.

'Yes, that's my real name.' Her mind raced as she attempted to find a plausible explanation as to why she claimed to work at Donnelley's law practice. In the end she decided to be as truthful as she could, without giving too much away about her relationship with the Spinton police.

'I said I worked at Donnelley's because I didn't think they'd allow me to join if they found out I worked at the dress shop,' she said, hoping against hope that Katherine didn't know that she was actually a trained machinist at the Mill, a garments factory that produced mainly women's clothes for the lower end of the market.

'There is a bit of a clique,' Katherine admitted. 'But then they let Effie Watkins join.'

'Effie's from good stock,' Amy said. 'Have you seen where her mother lives?'

'I've heard she has a nice apartment.'

'It's huge,' Amy said. 'You can't get any posher than that, really.'

'I heard that you knew her growing up. Or was that a lie too?'

'Yes and no,' Amy said. 'I know all about her past. I know she mixed with the wrong crowd in Maidstone and got into a lot of trouble. She left most of that lifestyle behind when she came up here.'

'So, you only recently became friends then?'

'Again, yes and no. We met a few times when our respective groups came into contact with each other, but we never became good friends.'

'Do you know her mother?'

'Yes, we've met. She had a hard time of it with Effie.'

'I've never met her. What's she like?'

'She's about fifty. She's still got her looks. I like her, she's a very friendly woman. She did a lot for Effie, but she had most of it thrown back in her face.'

'Did you ever meet her step brother?'

'John, the vet? No. I never met him.'

Katherine slowed the car and made the sharp left-hand turn that would take them onto Spinton Lane.

'All right, you obviously know the family, so I believe that you knew Effie too.'

Amy turned her head to look at Katherine as she put her foot on the accelerator and worked through the gears. 'Did you and Effie get on well?'

'To begin with. I thought she was a lot of fun, even though she was nine years younger than me. She wormed her way into the affections of a lot of the club's members. Pretty much all of them men. I didn't really care. I could see that she was on the make. She used her assets to their fullest advantage. Age didn't bother her, providing the men in question had money. That's all that mattered.'

Amy looked thoughtful. 'She knew how to get what she wanted from the older men. But wasn't there someone who didn't fit that category? Wasn't she infatuated with that young researcher? He was always wearing a Cambridge university scarf whenever I saw him.'

'That would have been Quentin Foxley-Walton,' Katherine said as she slowed, then accelerated hard to pass a man on a bicycle. 'He was the one for her, but it was never going to work. He'll marry someone with a little less of a past than Effie when the time comes.' She flashed a sideways glance at Amy. 'Do you have a boyfriend?'

'Yes and no,' Amy replied, not really wanting to get onto that topic.

'All your replies start with yes or no,' Katherine said with a little laugh. 'Which is it?'

'I was seeing someone, but we had a few words the other night and I'm not sure how we are as things stand.'

'He'd be mad to drop you,' Katherine said. 'Anyway, I wouldn't worry too much about it. There are plenty more fish in the sea and with what you have for bait, you won't go hungry for long. The fish will be fighting to get on the end of your hook.'

'I'm not really interested in being tied down. There's plenty of time for that. I want to have a bit of fun before I have to submit to a lifetime of domestic drudgery.'

'Never submit to it,' Katherine replied as she turned onto Main Street. She pulled up outside Cramley Lodge and looked up at the beautiful art deco building. 'Right, I know you don't want dropping off here, so where do you want me to take you?'

'Do you know the Old Bull, pub?' Amy asked. 'It's at the end of Long Lane. I can walk from there and you'll find it easier to turn around at the telephone box.'

'I know it,' Katherine said. 'I've never been inside, though. It's a little bit... agricultural for my tastes. I prefer pink gins to draught porter.'

Katherine drove the car onto High Street, past the Town Hall and then onto Middle Street. 'Where do you like to go for a night out?' she asked.

'Oh, I like the Milton but I don't' go as often as I'd like to. I can't really afford the prices unless my friend Ferris, is singing. Alice and I get cheap drinks when he's performing.'

'Who's Alice?'

'Alice is my best friend. She's beautiful. She's coming with me tonight. She owns her own farm, although she's younger than me.'

'How beautiful, on what scale?'

'Any scale you care to measure beauty on,' Amy replied. 'Do you know who Rita Hayworth is?'

'The actress, of course. Who doesn't?'

'You'll spot Alice straight away, then. She's her doppelgänger. She'll be the one with the crowd of men fussing around, begging her to dance.'

Katherine sighed. 'And I thought I had enough competition with you.'

'I'm not in competition with you.' Amy shot a glance towards the police station as Katherine came to a halt at the junction with the Gillingham Road.

Katherine looked right before turning left. She gave Amy another quick look. 'We're all in competition, my dear. I only realised this recently. I thought my place in Granville's affections was secure until Effie stepped in.'

'He threw you over for Effie? And you're happy to take him back?' Amy pulled a face. 'I don't think I'd be so generous.'

Katherine pulled up just outside the Old Bull but left the engine idling as Amy opened the car door to climb out.

'He has something most men don't have, Amy Rowlings,' she said firmly. 'He has money, and lots of it. Now, believe me when I say that I have no intention of allowing someone younger and prettier to get their hands on it. Effie thought she could take him away from me and it looked for a while as though she had got her way.' She paused for a moment as her eyes became narrow. 'She was wrong. And you would be wrong if you think you can take my place.' She patted her hair into place, then revved the engine. 'I like you, Amy, but I still don't think you've told me the whole truth.' Her eyes narrowed, and she glared at her. 'You really don't want to get on the wrong side of me. It's not the safest place to be.'

Amy leaned into the car to retrieve her cardigan, then, after slamming the door shut, she stepped back as Katherine shot forward and with wheels screeching, turned the car around at the telephone box, then with a quick glance and a raised hand, she roared away down the Gillingham Road.

## CHAPTER
# TWENTY-FOUR

When Amy got home, she made herself a pot of tea and drank a cup while she ran her bath. After tipping in a generous amount of her favourite, rose scented bath salts, she had a twenty-minute soak, washed her hair and after wrapping her head in a towel, she pulled on her floral dressing gown and walked back to the lounge to dry off properly.

At five o'clock, she had a quick meal of sardines on toast, then she went up to her room where she brushed her hair and applied her makeup while listening to Bing Crosby, Louis Armstrong and The Ink Spots records on the radiogram that her Uncle Maurice had found at such a reasonable price for her. At six, her face made up and with her emerald green clips holding her hair away from her ears, Amy slid her beautiful mint green dress from its hanger and carefully slipped it on. After checking herself in the mirror for over ten minutes, moving this way and that, she decided to err on the side of caution and after taking off the dress; she put a few stitches in the fold over front and a few more where the split in the dress showed just that bit too much of the top of her thigh. Sharon was right, the dress had been made for someone with slightly longer legs than Amy, and even wearing the skimpiest knickers in her drawer, she found they were visible when she stuck out a leg in front of the mirror. The stitches could easily be removed and by the time she had finished with it, Eileen, the manageress, would never know that she had made the alterations.

At six, Amy slipped on a pair of silver-coloured sandals that she had bought from Brigden's some months earlier to go with her best, going out dress, and after hearing a knock on the front door, she walked to the top of the stairs and shouted. 'It's open!' A few seconds later, Alice stepped into the hall.

She was wearing a red, mid-calf, figure hugging, low cut dress that sparkled as the light caught it. Her shoulder length chestnut curls were swept back over her ears and held in place with a pair of crimson hair clips. She had chosen a pair of deep red two-inch heels and the outfit was finished off with a cream jacket that she was holding over her arm, along with her best black handbag.

'WOW!' Amy exclaimed. 'You look like you've just stepped off a Hollywood red carpet. Your mum has done you proud again, hasn't she?'

'She never got to wear this, you know. Her sister bought it for her thirty-eighth birthday, but she died without ever being able to show it off in public.' A pained look came across her face. 'Poor Mum,' she said softly.

Amy looked down the stairs and gave her a sad smile. 'I still miss her,' she said.

Alice clapped her hands together. 'Okay, enough of the sad talk. Tonight's the night for partying. Come on, let's have a proper look at you.'

Amy took off her shawl, revealing the deep cut of the dress, she turned around on the landing so that Alice could see the back, at least what there was of it, then she began to walk slowly down the stairs, her leg protruding through the long split in the dress on every other step.

'My Goodness!' Alice exclaimed. 'You'll be fighting them off all night, Amy. I haven't seen so much of your skin since we shared a bath together when we were kids.'

Amy suddenly became serious. 'Do you think it's too much?'

'It's perfect,' Alice replied, getting her to do a twirl again. 'It's a good job that split stops where it does, though, or you might be arrested for indecency.'

'I had to put a couple of stitches in it,' Amy replied. 'Indecent is the word. When I stuck my leg out you could see my—'

'Yes, well, it's a good job you sorted that little wardrobe malfunction.' Alice beamed at her friend. 'You look absolutely stunning. It's such a shame Bodkin won't be there to see you.'

'He'd faint, I think. He's not used to seeing women with so much flesh on show.' She thought for a moment. 'Mind you, he has seen my wet knickers.'

Alice threw up her hands. 'Spare me the sordid details,' she said in mock horror. Standing in front of Amy's long hallway mirror, she reached into her bag and pulled out a large ruby coloured pendant on a gold chain. Slipping it on and fiddling with the jewel as it sat at the top of her cleavage, she turned to face Amy. 'So, what do you think? This one...' she unclasped the chain, handed the pendant to Amy, reached into her bag again and pulled out a jewelled choker. 'Or this one?'

'Ooh, they're both lovely, but I think with that dress, the pendant would be the best match.'

'I thought so too, but I just thought I'd ask your expert opinion.' Alice undid the clasp of the choker, handed it to Amy, and fastened the pendant around her neck again. After checking herself in the mirror, she nodded to herself, then stepped away. 'You can wear the choker.'

'Alice, I couldn't. It was your mum's favourite. She wore it the night she and your dad retook their vows at their anniversary party in the church hall.'

'It will be perfect with that dress, and anyway, it's only a loan. Mum would have suggested it herself if she were here.'

'It looks so expensive. I hope I don't lose it,' Amy said as she hooked the clasp together at the back of her neck.

'It's fake, dear heart. A good fake, but a fake nonetheless.' She put her finger under the large red jewel that sat above her breasts. 'So is this one. If either of them were real, I wouldn't be cleaning out pigs for a living. I'd be living in a villa in Tuscany.' She grinned at Amy. 'Still, these bits of paste might fool the Spinton aristocracy into thinking we're better off than we really are.' She looked Amy up and down, then turned and studied her reflection in the mirror. 'We look the part, at least.'

Amy led Alice into the living room, where she picked up her bag from the dining room table. 'I just hope you've got your tin knickers on under that skin tight dress because I've got a feeling that some of the men up there won't be able to keep their hands to themselves.'

'I'm sure we've fought off worse than them in our time,' Alice replied. 'Do you want to give me a last-minute run through to remind me who you are, who I am and who we're related to before we go?'

'Ah,' Amy said. 'I'm glad you said that. There's been a bit of a hiccup on that front.'

# CHAPTER TWENTY-FIVE

THE DRIVER OF THE BUS DID A DOUBLE TAKE AS AMY AND ALICE CLIMBED aboard. They took the front seat and paid the conductor for their tickets, Amy self-consciously pulling the two seams of the split dress together as three men got on behind them. The driver took a long, last, lingering, look before pulling away from the stop and then spent the next five minutes turning in his seat and craning his neck to get a better view. He was concentrating so hard on Amy's thigh that he almost missed the turn onto Middle Street and had to make a panicked last minute manoeuvre which caused the back end of the bus to skid across the road leaving a good bit of tyre tread on the surface.

Alice wagged a finger at him as they got off the bus outside the Town Hall. Amy just rolled her eyes and ignored him as he attempted to wish them a good evening.

They found Ferris leaning against a lamppost wearing black trousers, a white tuxedo jacket, and a black bowtie at the neck of a crisp white shirt.

'Well done, Ferris, you really look the part. Where did you get the tux?'

'I borrowed it from one of the Milton jazz band crew. I just hope I don't spill anything on it.' He took a step back to take in the full picture of Amy and Alice. Amy stuck out her leg provocatively as she posed. 'I'd keep that tucked away if I were you, Amy,' he said with wide eyes. 'You don't half scrub up well, the pair of you.'

Stepping towards the kerb, Ferris hailed a taxi and held the back door open as Amy and Alice climbed in, then after taking his own seat at the front, he asked the taxi driver to take them to the Highwater Boat Club.

'Have you seen Bodkin today?' Amy asked as the taxi pulled out onto High Street.

Ferris put his elbow on the back of his seat and turned around, his head towards her. 'I saw him just after lunch. He's hot on the trail of the knickers nicker.' The taxi drive shot him a quick glance, then turned back to face the road.

'Have there been more knickers nicked then?'

'We've had two more reports. Both from the same area. This time the items were stolen in broad daylight.'

'He's getting cocky, isn't he? Has Bodkin any idea who the culprit might be?' She twisted to face Alice. 'Someone is going around stealing silk knickers from clotheslines. Bodkin's trying to get to the bottom of it... so to speak.'

Alice laughed at the pun. 'Very good. My drawers should be safe. I can't afford silk bloomers. I buy my cotton pants from Ada and Frank's market stall.'

'I get mine from them too,' Ferris said. 'Underpants, not knickers,' he added quickly. 'It comes to something when women can't hang their unmentionables out.'

'It would be a long walk just to get hold of a pair of my pants and I'm not sure it would be worth the effort,' Alice said. 'Though I caught one of my younger farmhands, Alfie Reynolds, with a pair of my winter woollies in his pocket one day. They'd blown off the line and into the field behind the dairy. He was going to use them to wipe down our old truck's windscreen.'

Amy put her hand over her mouth as she laughed. 'Are you sure that's what he wanted them for? Alfie's tastes might have moved on from wool to silk.'

'Men don't seem to have a problem with underwear thefts,' Ferris said. 'Mind you, having seen Bodkin's underpants on his line the other day, it's not a major surprise. They were so full of holes you'd think someone had used them for target practice.'

'I've actually had words with Bodkin about the state of his underpants,' Amy said, then quickly added. 'I was looking through his drawers... his wardrobe...' she tailed off as Alice laughed. Ferris turned away, biting his cheeks to stop himself from joining in.

The taxi pulled up at the gates of the Boat Club and Ferris wound down his window to give their names to the two security guards, one of whom was checking a list while the other was handing out paper passes. After driving into the car park, Ferris sorted out the fare while Alice and Amy slid from the back seat of the taxi, Amy taking care not to snag her shoes on the hem of her dress.

Ferris refused the offer of paying their share of the fare, telling Amy that he owed her for getting him the booking.

'We'll pay for the trip home, then,' Amy said, giving Ferris a peck on the cheek.

The three friends walked around the side of the building and across the wooden staging in front of the boathouses. As they reached the end of the boardwalk, they heard a cheer coming from their right, so they followed a path lined with hedges until they came to the banks of the river, where what looked like a couple of hundred people, all dressed in their best attire, were applauding two young men wearing beige coloured overalls as they clambered into a pair of speedboats at the water's edge.

After walking to the far side of the crowd to get a vantage point, Amy tugged Alice's sleeve and pointed to a dark-haired man in the nearest of the boats as he started up the engine. 'That's Joe Lyndsay, the bloke who gave me a lift home in the sports car,' she hissed.

'Who's the other one?' Alice asked, raising her voice so that she could be heard above the roar of the engines. She watched as the two boats sped upstream towards the start line that had been used for the races earlier in the day.

'Bertrand Cresswell,' Amy replied. 'He's the nephew of the chemical factory owner.' She looked around to check that she couldn't be overheard. 'He was one of Effie's suitors... the plant owner, Granville, that is.' She looked around until she spotted Katherine. 'That's his girlfriend. She's the one who got the boot when Effie turned up, but she's back in favour again now. Watch her, Alice, she's very protective of him and she knows that I haven't been telling anything like the whole truth.'

Alice's gaze stayed on Katherine for a few moments, then she turned back to Amy. 'It's a bit like an Agatha story, isn't it?'

Amy grinned. 'And we're right in the middle of it.'

Five minutes later, they heard the roar of engines and the two motor boats shot past, bouncing along the surface of the water, throwing spray up in their wake and sending mini waves across the river to wash up on the bank.

'Who was in the lead?' Ferris asked. 'There wasn't much in it.' He gave Amy a quick glance, then concentrated hard as he looked downstream, awaiting the return of the racers. He didn't have to wait long.

Just three minutes later, the motorboats came roaring back upstream again, the far boat crossing the finish line a full two lengths ahead of the other.

The three friends applauded along with the rest of the membership as the drivers brought their boats to the bank. A couple of the younger members tied the craft off to a pair of mooring rings that had been set into the bank and the drivers clambered out onto the grass.

Joe was the first to alight. He stormed up the bank towards where Amy was standing, shaking his head in anger.

'He cheated,' he said as he came to a sudden halt. 'He bloody well cheated.' Joe tore open the neck of his overalls and stormed off towards the clubhouse.

'He's not a happy bunny, is he?'

Amy turned away from the angry club captain as he stomped up the slope, ignoring the calls of 'hard luck Joe,' and focussed on the young man who was standing alongside her. He was a good-looking chap of about twenty-three years of age. His mop of thick brown hair flopped over his forehead. His eyes were a dull blue, and he had faint acne scars across his cheeks. He began to unbutton his own overalls as he waited for Amy to respond.

'He's not happy at all,' Amy said. 'He thinks you cheated.' She held out her hand towards him. 'We haven't met. I'm Amy Rowlings and these two are my best friends, Alice and Ferris.'

'I'm Bertrand Cresswell,' the young man said. 'And I didn't cheat. I used my knowledge of the river to my advantage, that's all.' He nodded to Ferris, then let his eyes linger over Alice for a little longer than he ought to have done.

'I wouldn't have thought anyone knew the river better than Joe,' Amy said with a puzzled look on her face. 'Was it something to do with the current? He was in the lead on the way downstream.'

'Not the current, no.' He leaned in towards her. 'Do you know the river at all?'

Amy nodded. 'A little.'

'Do you know the stretch where the river passes Russell Park?'

Amy nodded. 'Yes, it runs along the back of the children's playground. The Silverstream feeds into it at that point.'

'Exactly, and that's where the Medway widens. Joe went

straight on to the widest point behind the playground before he made his turn, but I started mine at the point where the Silverstream meets the Medway. I'd already completed my turn by the time he started to make his.'

'Well done, you,' Amy said enthusiastically. 'Was it just inspiration or did you know you could make the manoeuvre at that point?'

'Oh, I knew all right. I practiced the turn half a dozen times last Sunday morning, while Joe was still tucked up in bed.'

'Last Sunday?' Amy said thoughtfully.

'Yep, I spent a good two hours running up and down the river, practicing the turn at different speeds until I nailed it.'

Bertrand smiled at her and, after nodding to Ferris and taking one last lingering look at Alice, he turned away and walked towards a group of young people who were standing about twenty feet away, chanting his name.

'Did you hear that, Alice?' Amy said as they followed Bertrand and his friends towards the clubhouse. 'He was at the Silverstream on Sunday morning. One of the kids said they'd heard a speedboat. It must have been him.' She stopped for a moment to watch the young man walk past the two female members who were checking passes at the double doors. 'The thing is, was he just practicing as he claims, or did he use that speedboat to transfer Effie's body to the reed beds?'

# CHAPTER TWENTY-SIX

After showing their passes at the door, Amy led Alice and Ferris along the wide corridor until they came to the ballroom. The tables had been set out across the top half of the room, leaving the bottom half free for dancing. Ferris was about to walk down to the stage to introduce himself to the band, who were just setting up their instruments, when Lesley walked up to them wearing a big smile on her face.

'You must be Orlando Ferris,' she said. 'I can't thank you enough for coming to our rescue.'

'It's a pleasure,' Ferris replied with a slight Spanish inflection in his voice.

Amy dug him in the back with her elbow and Ferris's next sentence came out in his usual regional accent. 'Do you think I could have a quick word with the band? I just want to make sure they know everything I'm planning to sing.'

'I'll introduce you to them in a moment,' Lesley replied. She looked Amy up and down appreciatively, then turned to Alice. 'Wow! Amy said you were beautiful, but she didn't give you half the credit you deserve.' She stared at Alice, her eyes wide. 'If I didn't know better, I'd swear that Rita Hayworth was paying us a visit.' She turned back to Amy. 'You look absolutely stunning. Where did you get that dress?' She looked down at her own evening gown, which was silver coloured with a high neck and tight, short sleeves. 'You've certainly put me to shame. Then again. I don't think I have the figure to carry either of your dresses off. You look like a pair of Hollywood starlets. I hope you have a lot of fun tonight. The bar is open, but there's waiter service too. Not that you'll have much time for drinking. I doubt you'll spend more than ten minutes away from the dancefloor.' She turned to Ferris. 'And you look good enough to eat, too, Orlando... is that your real name, or just your stage name?' she asked as she led him away.

Alice fanned her face with the back of her hand. 'Phew, it's warm in here. Where's the cloakroom? I want to lose this jacket.'

Amy looked towards an open door to the right of the dancefloor. Two chatting women emerged as she pointed.

'Come on then, Amy, time to ditch that shawl,' Alice said.

Just inside the doorway, they found a counter where a young girl of about eighteen was checking in coats. Amy handed over her shawl and received a pink ticket with a number on it. Alice got a similar one in exchange for her jacket. After a quick trip to the powder room to check their makeup, the two friends walked slowly across the dancefloor, Amy holding her bag in front of her with one hand whilst attempting to hold the two sides of the split together with the other. Alice, having noticed Amy's struggle, suddenly slapped the back of her hand.

'Let it go, Amy.'

'But everyone's staring,' she replied.

Alice lifted her chin and turned her face from one side to the other, watching the men watching them as they crossed the dancefloor. Some of the women scowled, others nudged each other and passed hushed comments among themselves. She took a quick look at Amy, who had given up trying to hold the dress together and seemed to be almost floating across the floor, her bare thigh pushing through the dress as she walked. 'What was it Mae West said in that film we saw a few months ago? It's better to be looked over than overlooked?'

Amy shot Alice a quick look, grinned at her, then, smiling at a young man who was watching her with barely concealed interest, she made her way to the bar.

'What can I get you, ladies?' The white jacketed barman asked as Amy and Alice looked over the counter.

'OOH!' Alice exclaimed, turning around quickly as she put a hand on her backside. 'Who did that?'

The only person standing within six feet turned to face her with a puzzled expression on his face. Gerald, wearing a black two-piece suit and his captain's hat, held out his palms towards her and then looked down at the floor as if to emphasise the distance between them. Alice scowled, then turned back to the bar.

'Keep your eye on him,' Amy said.

'I wish you'd warned me earlier,' Alice replied rubbing at her bottom again. 'It felt like a dog bite.'

Amy was just about to order their drinks when she saw Joe walking towards them with Francoise Slowcombe, Jessie Lampton and Nan Parkin, following on behind. They formed a little huddle around Amy and Alice when they reached the bar.

'I doubt you'll be paying for any drinks yourselves tonight, ladies,' Joe said as he looked at them appreciatively. 'What can I get you?'

'We'll both have a port and lemon, thank you,' Amy said, treating Joe to her best smile. Joe put in the order along with a club soda for himself and three gin based cocktails for the women. When the drinks had been served and the total had been added to Joe's bar bill, he focussed his attention on the two friends.

'You look absolutely beautiful, Amy,' he said, then he turned to Alice. 'I heard you were a stunner, but I didn't expect Hollywood royalty.' He bowed his head and kissed Alice's hand.

Alice smiled back sweetly. 'Flattery will get you everywhere.'

'Is it true you spend all day mucking out pigs?' Jessie Lampton asked.

'Not all day,' Alice replied. 'I muck out the cows as well.'

Joe laughed as Amy bit her lip. 'Whatever it is you do, it works wonders,' he said.

'That pig muck must be good for the skin by the looks of her complexion,' Francoise muttered, more loudly than she had intended. Jessie Lampton giggled.

'I'm sure Alice will sell you a bucket or two if you ask her nicely,' Amy said.

Nan Parkin choked on her drink, then turned away, screwing up her face as she tried not to laugh.

'That told her.' Nan took Amy's arm and led her to the edge of the dance floor.

'I didn't mean to be rude,' Amy said. 'It just sort of came out. I hope she wasn't too offended.'

'I hope she was,' Nan replied with a grin. She deserved everything she got. 'That was a really catty remark.'

At that moment, Lesley walked over to the microphone. 'I'd like everyone to put their hands together to welcome our star guest, Mr Orlando Ferris!'

There was a smattering of applause around the room. Amy put her glass on a nearby table and clapped along with Nan, Alice and Joe, as she fought back the urge to shout out, 'knock 'em dead, Ferris.'

Ferris walked up to the microphone, full of confidence. Turning halfway towards the band, he lifted his arm then dropped it as a signal for the musicians to play the Turner Layton song, These Foolish Things (Remind Me Of You.) As soon as Ferris started singing, a flurry of young girls rushed forward towards the stage while a dozen slightly older couples stepped out onto the floor.

'He's good, isn't he?' Joe said as he tapped his foot in time to the song.

'He's the best. Ferris will be in the movies one day. Someone famous will spot him,' Amy replied.

'That's providing we aren't at war before he gets the chance to impress,' Jessie said.

'Oh, for goodness' sake, cheer up,' Nan said with a sigh. 'We're supposed to be having fun.' She picked up her drink and drained half the glass. 'Now, where's that husband of mine? I need a refill.'

Over the next hour, Amy and Alice both accepted offers to dance from a group of five eager young men. The row of port and lemons that were lined up on a table on the edge of the dancefloor was added to regularly, and there were far more full glasses waiting to be drunk than empty ones. After three particularly energetic dances including one where Ferris sang, All God's Children Got Rhythm, to a Lindy Hop beat, he slowed things down with his rendition of I'm In The Mood For Love and Amy and Alice walked back to their table, both fanning their faces with the backs of their hands as they waved away a plethora of men standing on the edge of the dancefloor, almost begging them for a slow dance. Amy passed a glass to Alice, then drank half a port and lemon in one go before dipping into her bag to pull out a colourful paper fan.

As they were chatting, Katherine, Granville's reestablished girlfriend, walked up behind Amy and tapped her on the shoulder. 'I love the dress. You're obviously out to impress.'

'You don't look so bad yourself,' Amy said as she ran her eye over Katherine. She was wearing an emerald green, full-length gown, with a deep plunge front. Unlike Alice's fake pendant, the stone that hung between her breasts was worth more than Alice and Amy's bank accounts combined.

'Granville bought me the dress as a 'begging forgiveness' present.' She lifted the pendant with her little finger. 'This is a family heirloom. I think it was his grandmothers.' She winked at Amy. 'But if things work out the way I'm hoping they work out, it will be mine before Christmas.'

'Good luck with your master plan,' Amy said, almost as though she meant it. She held out her hand towards Alice. 'This is Alice, my best friend. I told you about her earlier.'

Alice held out her hand but quickly dropped it to her side when Katherine didn't reciprocate.

Katherine narrowed her eyes and directed her words towards Amy, although her eyes never left Alice. 'She does know the rules? Keep away from Granville.'

'Alice is a businesswoman in her own right. She has a family of her own. She isn't interested in older men. Don't worry.'

Alice blinked at the news. She had been having an affair with a married lawyer called Godfrey Wilson for over a year, and he was twenty years older than her.

'I don't need the money,' Alice said as Katherine's eyes burned into hers.

Just then, Bertrand turned up and, after offering Katherine a quick greeting, he took hold of Alice's hand. 'Dance with me, please. My friends will be so jealous. They've been watching you all evening, but none of them have managed to summon up the nerve to ask you.'

Alice winked at Amy, then allowed Bertrand to lead her onto the floor as the band struck up Woody Herman's Woodchopper's Ball.

'She'll wear those shoes out,' Amy said, almost to herself.

Katherine watched Alice and Bertrand as they moved about the dancefloor. 'They make a nice couple,' she said.

Amy shrugged. 'It will take more than a handsome face and a bit of money to snare Alice.'

'Then she's a fool. I know plenty of happy rich women but very few poor ones.'

Amy watched Alice disappear into the crowd of dancers, then declined yet another offer to dance from a young lad who looked to be no more than sixteen. He had been standing a few yards away for almost ten minutes, trying to pluck up the courage to ask her. 'I'm just having a breather,' she said to him. 'Come and find me later.' She took another long drink from her glass.

'You remind me so much of Effie,' Katherine said. 'She had males of all ages fawning all over her. She only had to click her fingers, and they'd come running.' She turned her face towards Amy. 'I bet you can, too. Go on... she pointed to a group of four twenty something men who were watching them with interest... I dare you, click your fingers, let's see if anyone comes running.'

'I wouldn't demean either myself or them by doing that,' Amy replied. She put her empty glass down and picked up a fresh one. 'Could I ask you a question? Something I'm intrigued about.'

'Go ahead,' Katherine said. 'I've got something to say to you, too.'

'Why... I mean, what was it that ended the relationship between Effie and Granville?'

'Oh, that's easy enough to answer. He was besotted with her for a few months, but she was only ever a trinket, something for him to show off to his peers. She made him look a fool one time too many. He put up with her dalliances with men of Joe's age. Young women need the company of people their own age. He understood that. But he drew a line when he found out she was also seeing someone older than him.'

'That annoyed him?' Amy asked.

'He was furious.'

'How much older was this other man? I mean, Granville is in his fifties, isn't he?'

'Fifty-six,' Katherine replied. 'This man was in his mid-seventies.'

'Good grief, she was only twenty-three. What on earth did she see in someone that old?' She paused as she thought. 'Don't tell me it was fidgety fingers, Gerald.'

Katherine laughed. 'No, not him, although I wouldn't have put it past her.'

Amy bit her lip as she waited to see if Katherine would disclose the name of the other man.

Katherine smirked. 'You're dying to know, aren't you?'

'You have piqued my interest,' Amy replied. 'Is he here tonight?'

'Oh, yes, he's here.' She pointed across the room to the corridor where the steward's office was situated. 'He's in there with Granville, Timothy Philby, and one or two others. Timothy likes to give them a little treat to help keep them on their feet all night.' She laughed as Amy gave her a puzzled look, then she put a single finger to one of her nostrils and sniffed.

'Ah,' Amy said. 'I thought that was a younger man's thing.'

'It is, in the main. Granville just has a sniff to keep him going if it looks like being a long night. Too much booze makes him sleepy.'

'I thought cocaine was a regulated drug,' Amy said

'It is, but not if it's issued by a doctor... or dentist,' she added with a wink.

'You said Effie liked to hang around with people her own age. Did she have flings with any of them?'

'All of them, probably... if they had money, at least. Effie and Joe were very close right up until the end, and she had an on off thing with Quentin Foxley-Walton. Mostly, though, she went for the men whose egos could be easily massaged.'

'Wasn't there any jealousy?'

'Oh yes, the green-eyed monster was running rampant. It wasn't just the men who were jealous of each other, either. A few knew they were putting their marriages at risk. Our honourable steward, Timothy Philby, made a proper fool of himself. Mind you, he wasn't alone in that. Effie certainly put herself about. I'm actually amazed that there wasn't anything nasty being passed around, if you catch my drift.'

Amy pulled a face, then took another sip of her drink to take away the bad taste that had suddenly attached itself to her taste buds. 'And you think I'm like Effie?'

Katherine looked hard at her, then her expression softened. 'No, there was only ever one Effie. Anyway, I know the reason you've taken such an interest in our club.'

'You do?' Amy put on a puzzled look and crossed the fingers of her left hand.

Before Katherine could say any more, Alice returned with Bertrand. 'You're next up,' he said to Amy. 'But I just need to...' he stuck his thumb over his shoulder and flicked his head towards the corridor where the toilets were situated.

'He's an excellent dancer,' Alice said, picking up her drink. 'OOH!' she turned on her heel, her eyes like hot coals as she glared at the crowd of men behind. They looked back at her with confused looks on their faces. Then Gerald turned around and winked. He was at least eight feet away, but there was no doubt that he had been the culprit.

'How the Hell does he manage that?' she said, turning back to Amy and Katherine. 'He strikes as fast as an angry King Cobra.' She moved her hand towards her backside before deciding she wasn't going to give him the satisfaction of letting him watch her rub it. 'Third time pays for all,' she muttered under her breath.

'Ah, here comes the cavalry,' Katherine said as a group of mostly elderly men strolled across the floor towards them.

'There you are, my dear,' Granville said, beaming at Katherine. Noticing Amy, he bowed his head to her before settling his gaze on Alice. 'What have we here?' He turned quickly to Katherine. 'Aren't you going to introduce me to your friend?'

'She's Amy's friend, not mine,' Katherine said coldly as she flashed Amy an angry look.

A tubby man in his mid-seventies, wearing a black suit with a bow tie wrapped around an old-fashioned winged collar, nudged Granville aside as he moved forward with a speed that belied his body shape. His head was covered in a mass of tangled, steel grey hair. His thick moustache was an exact colour match. After taking a long leisurely look at Alice, he turned his rheumy grey eyes on Amy. 'I haven't had the pleasure,' he said.

'Not yet at least,' a thin man behind him said. Then he roared with laughter at his own joke.

The portly man flashed him a look of distaste before reaching out to take Amy's hand. Putting it to his lips, he fixed his eyes on hers. 'Delighted, my dear. I'm Angus McIntosh. Who might you be?'

Alice turned away from Angus and took a firm hold of Amy's arm. 'Excuse us,' she said, leading her in the direction of the ladies' powder room.

'Did you see that moustache?' she said, slowing her pace when they were out of earshot. 'It was covered in white powder.'

Amy nodded. 'I did notice. Granville has it stuck to his nostril hairs too.' She stopped to allow Alice to walk into the corridor before following her into the ladies' room. 'Did you catch the old guy's name? That's Angus, the man who wrote the note we found in Effie's pocket.'

A few minutes later, as the friends were standing in front of the mirrors in the powder room, the door opened and Katherine stepped inside. Standing next to Amy, she checked her hair, then pulled a lipstick from her bag and gave her lips a generous coating. After checking her appearance again, she looked at Amy's reflection, then spoke. 'I told you I had a couple more things to say to you, but I really don't know if I can be bothered now. I will give you a word of warning, however.'

Amy and Alice exchanged glances.

'I saw the way Granville looked at the pair of you just now, and I didn't like it one bit. You have no idea how hard I've had to work to get him back and if you think I'm going to step aside to allow one of you floozies to take my place, you've got another think coming.' She glared at Amy and pointed a warning finger at her. 'If you know what's good for you, you'll keep well away from Granville.'

'Is that a threat?' Alice said, lowering her eyelids as she stared back at Katherine.

'It's a promise,' Katherine replied. 'I never make idle threats. Just ask Effie.' She turned towards the door, then looked back. 'Oh, you can't, can you?' She held her hand to her mouth, tittered, and then left.

# CHAPTER TWENTY-SEVEN

When Amy and Alice returned to the ballroom, they found Angus waiting for them with two full glasses of a gin-based cocktail.

'I wasn't sure what you were drinking, so I took a punt on these.'

'Thank you,' said Amy, taking a glass from him. She turned to Alice and whispered. 'I'll get blotto at this rate.'

'I love that word.' Alice grinned.

Amy took a sip of the drink and smiled appreciatively at Angus as she waited for him to strike up a conversation, but his attention was firmly fixed on her chest. On the stage, Ferris announced his last song before the band took a break to allow the medals presentation and raffle draw to take place.

'I didn't know there was a raffle,' Alice said. 'What's the first prize, a day out in a dinghy?'

'Close enough,' Amy said, turning her body away from the ogling Angus. 'I bought a strip of tickets this afternoon. I always seem to win something on the tombola on Spinton Sports Day, so I might fall lucky again.'

'You won a second hand pot,' Alice reminded her.

'It was a very nice pot.'

'It had a crack all the way through it.'

Amy took a sip of her drink and almost spat it out as a memory came back. 'Mum was going to use it as a vase, but it fell in half the first time she put water in it. Her feet got soaked.'

Just as Ferris started singing It's A Sin To Tell A Lie, Ronald the dentist sauntered towards them looking slightly the worse for wear.

'My turn for a dansh,' he said, grabbing Alice by the wrist. Alice looked at Amy, shrugged, then passed her the cocktail. Grinning all over his face, Ronald ushered her onto the dancefloor, pulled her in close and led her into a poorly performed foxtrot. 'That'sh a very tight dress you have on,' he grunted into her ear.

Angus, having finally realised he was now staring at Amy's back, tapped her on the shoulder. 'I've been hearing things about you,' he said.

'Nothing too ghastly, I hope,' Amy replied with a look of fake shock on her face.

'Fear not. Nothing that would harm your reputation.' He took a long swallow of his whisky. 'I'm led to believe that you were a friend of poor Effie.'

'I knew her, yes.'

Angus looked into the distance as he thought. 'She was a lovely girl. An absolute stunner.'

'She was very pretty. I was horrified when I heard the news.' Amy sipped her drink and looked up into his fleshy face. 'Did you know her well?'

'She was more than an acquaintance. I'll leave it at that,' Angus replied. 'She was a sweet thing, always eager to please. She made me feel young when I was in her company.'

Amy shuddered as she thought about the connotations of his statement. 'I wouldn't have thought you'd have much in common, what with your age difference.'

'Oh, we got on like a house on fire. We spent a lot of time together. She had quite expensive tastes, but it was worth it to have someone with so much vigour on my arm.'

Amy averted her eyes as he looked into her face. 'You're shocked?'

'No, not at all,' Amy said quickly. 'Age is no barrier to love. You can never be sure who will capture your heart.'

Angus put his hand softly on her wrist. 'You are a very enlightened young lady, Amy Rowlings. We might find we have plenty in common, too.' He winked at her, then looked her up and down again.

Amy took a gulp of her cocktail and swallowed it quickly.

'Would you allow me to take you to dinner one night soon?'

Amy blew out her cheeks. 'I'm not sure that's a good idea, Mr McIntosh.'

Angus produced a business card and passed it to her. 'Think about it for a while. There's no rush. Just give me a call if you decide you'd like to come.' He leaned towards her and lowered his voice. 'I'd be extremely grateful and, as anyone will tell you. I can be the most generous of men.'

Amy took the card and pretended to read it, but before she could decline his offer, Lesley Philby's voice came out from the loudspeaker.

'Would Angus McIntosh please come to the stage? The awards ceremony is about to begin.'

An annoyed look spread across Angus's face. 'Damn. Just when things were getting interesting.' He half turned away, then snapped his head back. 'I have to go, my dear,' he said, as though he thought Amy might be disappointed. 'I'm presenting the awards. I'll find you again later. Think about what I said. I *can* be extremely generous.' He winked again, then walked across the emptying dance floor towards the stage, passing an angry-looking Alice as he went.

'Oh dear,' Amy said, spotting the look on her friend's face. 'Isn't he a very good dancer?'

Alice stopped about four feet away, then turned her back and patted her behind. 'Has someone pinned a target on this or something?'

'Not that I can see,' Amy replied. She craned her neck to look around Alice to where Ronald and Nan were standing. Ronald still staring towards Alice, Nan was concentrating on the stage.

'I thought, with him being a dentist, he'd be interested in my mouth, but he was far more interested in my backside. He was like a blooming octopus. As soon as I dragged one hand off my bum, the other one took its place.' She picked up her cocktail and took a long glug. 'What is it about men? They can't just admire a woman's figure. They think they have the God given right to manhandle it.'

'I take it you told him he was wrong about that? It's a good job his wife didn't see what he was up to.'

'That's the strange thing about it. Every time I turned to face her, she was watching. She must have seen everything that happened. Including me eventually pushing the randy old goat away.'

Sensing a movement behind her, Alice raised her hand and in one movement, spun around and landed a slap so hard on Gerald's face that it left a red imprint.

'OW! What did you do that for?'

'For not keeping your hands to yourself,' Alice spat.

'But, but I didn't touch you.'

'No, you didn't, but that was payment for the times when you did.' Alice gave him the sort of look that would curdle fresh milk before turning back to Amy.

'Filthy swine. The better bred people are, the more they think they can take advantage.'

Amy held the business card up to show Alice. 'That one thinks he can buy his way into my affections.' She flicked her head towards the stage where Angus was presenting Joe with the first of his awards. 'He just asked me out to dinner.'

Alice shook her head in disbelief. 'He's old enough to be your grandad.'

Amy opened her bag and dropped the card inside.

'You aren't thinking of taking him up on his offer, are you?' Alice asked, mouth agape.

'Not on your Nellie,' Amy replied. 'But it's nice to know that I can get in touch with him if I want to.'

'Be careful, Amy. I don't know what Bodkin would say if he knew.'

Amy shrugged. 'I think he'd understand why I took the card. It's a way in if we ever want to catch him on the hop.' She drained her glass, then fanned herself with her hand. 'I'm feeling a bit squiffy. What on earth was in that cocktail?'

Twenty minutes later, the awards had been handed out and Lesley was on stage holding a tin bucket as Angus dipped in his hand to pull out the winners of the raffle draw. There was a squeal from two young women near the stage when they realised that the fairer haired of the two had won the Henley Regatta tickets. The next prize, a magnum of good quality champagne, went to Franny. Amy stood at the back of the crowd as number 252 was called out. When no one claimed the posh dinner for two prize, Lesley called out the number again.

'Have you checked your tickets?' Alice asked. 'No one's claiming it.'

Amy fumbled in her bag and pulled out the folded strip of tickets. She opened them out and blinked twice as she focussed on them. 'It's mine! I've got it,' she yelled as if she had just marked down the winning number in a game of Housey Housey.

Blushing after her outburst, Amy made her way to the stage where Angus presented her with an envelope containing a colourful card, inviting two people for dinner at Hoskin's restaurant. She waved her prize in the air as she stepped down from the stage with Angus. Taking her arm, he led her through the applauding crowd to where Alice was waiting. He bent his head as they walked. 'I'll take you to Hoskin's any time you feel like it,' he said in a stage whisper. 'You have my number.'

As Amy waved her prize towards Alice, Angus, having spotted Timothy Philby beckoning him from the corridor near his office, excused himself, and left the two friends alone.

Amy showed the ticket to Alice, then stuffed it into her bag.

'That's Mum and Dad's anniversary present sorted for his year,' she said happily.

'How lovely,' Alice said. 'They'll get such a shock when they see it.'

'Don't you dare say a word, Alice Mollison,' Amy said, wagging a finger.

'As If I would.'

'Alice, you're the worst secret keeper I've ever met. You're almost as bad as Big Nose Beryl from work.'

Beryl was the worst gossip in Spinton. If she didn't have a real fact to share with anyone who might be interested, she'd just make one up.

'Blimey!' Alice replied. 'I know I haven't got a great track record, but to compare me with Beryl...'

Amy snorted and reached for another glass from the rapidly shortening line of port and lemons, but before she could pick one up, Joe arrived, his neck adorned with three different coloured ribbons, each one connected to a silver medal. He was carrying a tray of cocktails.

'Celebration time,' he said, placing the tray on the table. He picked up one of the four glasses and handed it to Amy, then passed another to Alice.

'Down the hatch,' he said.

Amy blew out her cheeks, then took a long swig of the gin based drink. 'Bottoms up,' she said.

'Stop talking about bottoms,' Alice said, causing Joe to look at them both with a puzzled look on his face as the two friends burst into a fit of giggles.

'Sorry, Amy, my presence is required elsewhere,' Joe said as he acknowledged Timothy Philby's waving hand. 'Don't forget, I've booked the last dance.'

'Have you?' Amy asked. 'I can't remember that.'

'Okay, have it your way,' Joe said with a cheeky grin. 'But you're booked now. I've had a word with the singer. It's going to be a slow one.'

'That's probably a good thing,' Amy said to Joe's back as he walked away. She giggled. 'I don't think I'd manage to stay on my feet for a quickstep.'

'They're a funny lot, aren't they?' Alice said, seriously. 'But they don't seem to get my jokes.'

Amy looked at her quizzically.

'Well, one of those young lads I was dancing with was going on and on about how good he was getting with his sculling. He was rambling on about scull this, scull that, so I asked him if he was an archaeologist. He just looked at me like I'd gone mad and started to explain it all over again.'

Amy chuckled. 'Joe was the same this afternoon. Once he gets on a topic, you're stuck with it for an hour. Today it was regatta stuff, last time it was cars. Honestly, if only they knew how boring it all is.'

The friends stood chatting for a while until they were once again asked to dance. Alice fell lucky and ended up with a thirty something man with a well-kempt moustache, who led her around the dancefloor with some panache. Amy, however, wasn't so lucky. She was lumbered with a very drunk, Timothy Philby, who spent the entire dance, telling Amy how welcome she would be if she felt like spending half an hour alone with him in his office.

'If ever you're at a loose end, you'll find me down there,' he said, pointing vaguely in the direction of the office corridor. 'Effie used to come to see me,' he said wistfully.

'I'm not Effie,' Amy reminded him, wincing as he caught the top of her foot with his heel.

'No, you wouldn't be as nasty as her.' He pulled his head back so that he could look into her face. 'She led me on, you know?' His lip trembled. 'I proposed to her, and she laughed at me.' A tear rolled down his cheek. 'I got down on one knee. I was sure she was going to accept me.'

'Oh dear,' Amy replied. 'She shouldn't have led you on. It's not right.'

'Well she got what she deserved in the end.' He stopped dancing and looked at her seriously. 'Do you know what karma is?'

Amy nodded.

'Well, it came back to bite her with a vengeance. I hope she realised in her last few moments, just what she had done.'

Amy pulled her hands away from Philby's. She staggered a little as she stepped back. 'I think that's more than harsh, Mr Philby. She was only a young woman, just like me. We all make mistakes. She didn't get the chance to learn from hers.'

Turning away from him, Amy eased her way through the dancing couples and made her way back to her table, where she pulled out a chair and plonked herself down on it.

Alice stayed on the floor for the next two dances, returning to the table when she began to feel the effects of the cocktails herself.

'Are you okay?' she asked as she squatted down in front of Amy.

'I'm fine, just a bit woozy,' Amy replied. 'I've had one too many, I think.'

'I'm feeling it a bit myself now,' Alice said. 'Don't go anywhere. I'll pick up a couple of glasses of water from the bar.'

For the next forty minutes, Alice and Amy sat watching the dancing as they chatted quietly. By the time Ferris announced that the last dance would be the Al Bowlly classic, Blue Moon, Amy had begun to feel a little better. Her head wasn't spinning anything like as much, so when Joe hurried over to ask her to dance, she felt she'd be able to get through five minutes on her feet. It was a slow dance, after all.

Blue Moon was one of Ferris's best songs and as he crooned into the microphone, the couples on the dance floor pulled their partner close and shuffled their feet as they clung onto each other. Alice was partnered up with Archie, the man she had been dancing with earlier. She laughed as he whispered something into her ear before looking over her shoulder to see how Amy was doing.

Amy was feeling a little woozy again and had rested her head on Joe's shoulder as they swayed, barely moving their feet at all. As the band played the last few slow notes of the song, Amy pulled her head back to look up at him. Joe's head moved towards hers and before Amy realised what was happening, he was kissing her, deeply and urgently. His hand moved up from her waist to the underside of her breast. Amy shook her head and put both hands on his chest in an attempt to push him away. After a couple of feeble, futile attempts, Joe finally got the message and, after letting her go, stood stock still as he stared at her with a big grin on his face.

'You wanted it,' he said.

Amy swayed and almost fell, waving her hands impotently in the air. She blinked twice and tried to focus. A few seconds later, she found Alice at her side. Ferris jumped down from the stage to see if he could help.

'I've got her, Ferris,' Alice said as she led her slowly from the dancefloor. She took Amy back to the table and sat her down while she fanned her with a handkerchief.

'I'm all right,' Amy said, waving her away. 'I'm all right, Alice, I just need a bit of air.'

Alice handed Amy her bag, then picked up her own from the table. 'This way,' she said, leading Amy towards the cloakroom. A line of club members tutted and whispered amongst each other as they passed.

The door at the end of the short corridor was open and Amy breathed in deeply as she felt the cool night air on her face. 'I'll wait by the door,' she said as she fumbled in her bag for her cloakroom ticket. Alice took it from her and waited at the counter for the young girl to come back from wherever it was she had disappeared to.

Amy walked slowly down the corridor and leaned against the doorframe as she breathed in deeply. Behind her, she could hear Alice calling for the attendant.

'I'll see you outside. I just need to walk for a bit,' Amy called over her shoulder.

Alice nodded quickly. 'I'll be two minutes,' she called.

The night air was chilly after the heat of the dancefloor and Amy tipped back her head, feeling the cool breeze on her neck and chest as she walked. As she approached the corner of the building, she passed another open door. A few seconds later, she heard a voice behind her.

'Are you all right, Amy? You looked a bit peaky back there.'

'You shouldn't have done that,' Amy said, not looking back. 'You took advantage.'

'I honestly thought you wanted me to kiss you,' Joe said. 'I'm sorry if you're offended.'

Amy blew out her cheeks and shook her head.

'Oh, forget about it. A drunken kiss doesn't mean anything.'

Joe increased the length of his stride and caught up with Amy before she reached the corner. As she swayed again, he put his arm around her shoulders and turned towards the car park alongside her. 'Come on, you need to sit down,' he said as he walked her down the side of the club.

His Riley Kestrel sat alone in the third row of parking spaces. 'It's got its lid on,' he said, making Amy laugh.

Joe fiddled in his pocket for his key and opened the passenger side door. 'Have a seat, old girl,' he said as he tried to ease Amy through the gap. Amy shook her head again and tried to pull away, but Joe had his hand in the middle of her back. 'Don't be silly now. Get in.'

'I don't want to get in,' Amy said. 'Where's Alice? I want to go home.'

'I'll take you home,' Joe said. 'Don't worry about that... although, you might feel better with some coffee inside you. If you come back to my place, I'll make a nice strong one for you. I'll take you home later.'

He put pressure on Amy's back again as he tried to ease her into the car. When she resisted, he put his hand on her shoulders and pushed her forwards. Amy fell into the car, throwing out her arms to stop her face from hitting the seat.

'Get off me!' Amy kicked out, forcing Joe to step back. As he reached down to get hold of her flailing legs, a pair of headlights pierced the dark night. Joe was temporarily blinded. He put his hand over his eyes as he stared into the dazzling beam.

'Private hire for Rowlings, Mollison and Ferris,' a voice called out from behind the lights.

Amy pushed herself up on her hands, then, bottom first, she backed out of the car.

As she straightened, she heard Alice's voice. She looked across the car park to see her hurrying from the side of the building. 'Amy, I'm here.'

Amy took a few stumbling steps towards the car, shielding her eyes from the glaring light. Joe cursed, jumped into his own car, and quickly started the engine. Shouting something Amy didn't quite catch, he put his foot to the pedal and roared through the gates of the car park.

Alice ran to Amy's side and, after wrapping the shawl around her shoulders, she pulled her into a tight hug. The headlight beam suddenly dimmed and a car engine revved loudly.

'Are you going to stand there all night?' the driver shouted.

'I'm coming, Bodkin,' Amy said quietly.

# CHAPTER TWENTY-EIGHT

'Where the heck is Ferris?' Bodkin asked as he turned to look at the two women in the back seat of his little black Morris.

'Don't blame him, Bodkin, please. I told him I was looking after Amy, so he went to find Lesley to get his singer's fee.' Alice pulled the shawl together around Amy's shoulders. She was shivering, although it was a warm night.

Bodkin slipped off his jacket and passed it between the gap in the two front seats. 'Cover yourself up,' he said, nodding at Amy's bare leg. She tugged the two sides of the split together, then covered her knees with his coat.

Bodkin turned back to the front, shaking his head, then, spotting Ferris walk into the car park, he flashed his headlights to get his attention. Ferris trotted over to the car, pulled open the passenger side door, and slid onto the seat.

'I got the full six quid,' he announced. 'And they've booked me for a wedding party next month.'

'Well done, Ferris,' Alice clapped her hands as she grinned at the crooner.

'Never mind weddings, Ferris, what in God's name happened tonight?'

Ferris looked puzzled. 'Nothing. At least I don't think anything untoward happened. Mind you, I was on stage most of the night. I jumped down to see if Amy was all right at the end. She looked a bit wobbly on her pins.'

Bodkin put the car in gear and eased out of the car park as some of the club members walked towards their cars.

'We had lots of cocktails,' Alice said. 'We didn't have to pay for anything ourselves. I think they were giving us double measures. Amy felt really woozy at the end.'

'You look to be all right, Alice,' Bodkin said.

'I spent a lot more time on the dance floor than Amy did, so I didn't get to drink quite as much, but even I was feeling it during the last hour.'

'That's typical of men like that,' Bodkin muttered. 'They make out they're so refined, but underneath, they're worse than any of the working-class men in the town. They always try to take advantage.'

'Most men I know would try to take advantage,' Alice said. 'But as for tonight, you're right.' She lifted herself up in her seat and rubbed her bottom. 'My backside is going to be black and blue tomorrow.'

Bodkin took the sharp left onto Spinton Lane a little too aggressively, forcing Alice and Amy to grab hold of the front seats to steady themselves.

'What about you, Amy?' Bodkin asked, twisting his neck to look into the rear of the vehicle. 'How's your bottom?'

'My bottom is unmolested, thank you,' Amy said rather coldly. She pulled the shawl aside and studied the deep cut of her dress. 'Those extra stitches I put in have been pulled loose though. I hope the dress hasn't been damaged.' She tugged the two sides a little closer together as Bodkin shot another glance over his shoulder.

'Are you feeling a little better now?' he asked. 'You were

roughed up a bit back there.'

'I'm fine,' Amy said, turning to the side to look out of the window. 'I'm tougher than I look.'

'I'm not saying—'

'The other good news is, I've got a date,' Ferris said, turning around in his seat to face the girls in the back.

'Who with?' Amy and Alice shouted together.

'Lesley Philby, the club secretary.' Ferris grinned. 'She's nice, isn't she?'

'She's lovely, Ferris,' Amy replied. 'Where are you going to take her?'

'I'm not sure yet. I thought about the pictures, but I don't know if she's a movie buff. I could take her to dinner, but I reckon she'd know a lot more about food than I do and I don't want to make myself look like an idiot when I'm choosing the wine.' He paused for a moment. 'I'd probably order beer, anyway.'

Bodkin looked sideways at Ferris and sighed. 'I hope you'll be very happy together,' he said.

'BODKIN!' Amy said sharply. 'Can't you just be happy for him?' She turned her attention to Ferris. 'If you're a bit unsure of yourself, why don't you invite her to lunch? That's much easier. Order a pot of tea and let her make her own choice from the cake trolley. You could maybe take her for a walk along the river afterwards... not the canal. There are too many awful things floating in it.'

'That's a great idea,' Ferris said enthusiastically. 'Thank you, Amy.'

Bodkin rolled his eyes and blew out his cheeks. 'Just don't let her know you're a copper, Ferris. Can you put her off until this case is over?'

'You're such a romantic, Bodkin,' Amy said, shaking her head.

'It's a valid point,' Bodkin replied.

'Ferris isn't going to leak information to her about the investigation,' Amy argued.

'I'm not saying he will. I'd just rather he kept quiet about it until we've questioned the people who run that boat club.' Bodkin turned left onto Middle Street, drove down the hill, and came to a stop outside the police station. Ferris lived above in the rooms allocated to members of the force.

'Thanks for keeping us entertained, Ferris. You were on top form tonight,' Alice said as the constable climbed out of the car.

'Why do you always have to be so grumpy, Bodkin?' Amy said as the inspector pulled away from the kerb and turned left onto the Gillingham Road.

'I'm not grumpy,' Bodkin replied, moving up a gear. 'Someone has to keep their feet on the ground. We're in the middle of a murder investigation.'

'And you're tired and grumpy,' Amy said, turning her head to look out of the window again.

Bodkin took a right turn onto Long Lane, passed Amy's cottage, and drove the half mile down to Alice's farmhouse. He parked up, leaving the engine running, as Alice gave Amy a hug and a kiss before opening the back door of the car.

'Could I have a quick word, Bodkin?' she said as she climbed out.

Bodkin wound down his window, but Alice had already stepped away from the car, so he clambered out after her.

'Firstly,' Alice said, looking around the inspector's broad frame towards the car. 'Thank you for not saying 'I told you so' to Amy when she got herself into a bit of bother. She knows she made a mistake.'

'I couldn't see what it would achieve,' Bodkin said. 'She told me she has to make her own mistakes, and she's right. It's just that... I can't stop myself from trying to protect her.' He held out his palms towards Alice. 'I worry about her.'

'I know you do, Bodkin, and she knows it too.' She stepped closer, stretched onto her tiptoes and planted a kiss on his cheek. 'Thank you for being our knight in shining armour. Now... go and make up with her. She's feeling a bit flat at the moment.'

Alice blew him a kiss, then turned away to walk around to the back of the farmhouse. 'If you haven't sorted it out by tomorrow, I'll be having words with you both.'

'Goodnight, Alice,' Bodkin said as he turned towards the car. He found Amy staring blankly at the windscreen when he climbed back in. 'Right, let's get you home.'

Amy put her hand in front of her mouth to stifle a yawn. 'What did Alice want?' she asked.

'That's for me to know and you to find out,' Bodkin said as he performed a three-point turn in the lane. 'I'm sure she'll tell you the next time you see her. You two don't have any secrets.'

Bodkin drove back up the lane until he came to Amy's cottage. Then, after shutting down the engine, he opened the driver's door and walked around the back of the car to find that Amy had already opened the rear door. She passed him his jacket, then slammed the door shut behind her. Giving him a quick look from under her eyelids, she walked slowly up to the gate, slipped the latch, and stepped through onto the short path that led to the front door. Leaving the gate open, she walked up to the porch before turning to see if he had followed. He hadn't.

Amy sighed. 'A gentleman would see a lady right up to the front door,' she said.

Bodkin stepped through the gate and walked slowly up to the porch. Amy had let the shawl fall loose over her shoulders and her dress gaped open where the stitches had come away. Her bare thigh jutted out from the split in the skirt as she looked up into his face.

Bodkin dropped his head, looked down at his feet, and let out a long sigh. 'You look like...'

Amy's eyes narrowed and her chin lifted as she stared at him. 'What... what do I look like, Bodkin?'

'A princess,' he said softly. 'A beautiful fairy tale, princess.'

Amy's eyes misted over. She reached out a hand and placed it softly on his cheek. 'Oh, Bodkin,' she whispered. 'I hate it when we argue. Let's be friends again.' Bodkin lowered his head and kissed her softly on the lips. She put her arms around his back and pulled him close before kissing him again, this time longer and deeper, as Bodkin slipped one hand behind her shoulders and placed the other on her waist.

'I never want to argue with you like that again. I'm truly, truly sorry, Amy.'

'So am I, Bodkin. I'm just as much to blame. We're too stubborn, that's our problem.'

'The making up bit is all right though,' Bodkin said as he kissed her again.

Amy took hold of his hand and slipped it inside her dress before taking her own hand away. Bodkin squeezed her breast gently and kissed her deeply. 'Christ,' he whispered.

'That's enough of that talk,' Amy said, pulling his hand away and slapping it. 'That's all you're getting, Bodkin. Don't let your hopes get too high.'

The policeman grinned. 'Me and my big mouth.'

Amy laughed. 'I love your big mouth.'

They kissed again, then Amy pulled away, opened her bag and fished about for her keys.

'What's that?' Bodkin asked, when he spotted the envelope with the Hoskin's logo printed on the front. 'It looks expensive.'

'It's a surprise for Mum and Dad on their wedding anniversary. I won it on the raffle.'

'You had a good time, then? Honestly, Amy, I'm so glad you enjoyed yourself.'

'It could only have been bettered if you had been there.'

He grinned. 'Next time I won't be so bloody silly,' he said.

Amy put the key in the lock as Bodkin walked back to the gate. 'Will I see you after church tomorrow?' he asked.

'I can't, Bodkin, I'm sorry. There's something I have to do, but I've got so much to tell you about what I discovered tonight. Can you come around about one-ish? I'll make lunch.'

'It's a date,' Bodkin said, as she pushed open the front door. He watched her into the house before turning away.

'Thank you for rescuing me again, Bodkin.'

He looked back. She blew him a kiss, then slowly closed the door.

# CHAPTER TWENTY-NINE

WHETHER IT WAS DOWN TO THE DRINK SHE HAD CONSUMED OR THE FACT that she had been reconciled with Bodkin, Amy found that she had slept like a log and didn't as much as turn over in her sleep until the alarm went off at seven-thirty. After a strip wash and a breakfast of eggs and bacon, Amy got dressed and made her way up to the church, where she answered the same question about her parents at least half a dozen times.

'They're having a lovely time, thank you. I got a postcard from them only yesterday.'

At ten-thirty, Amy walked around the back of the church and across to the west wall where Alice's parents' grave lay in the shade of a two-hundred-year-old oak. After saying a quick prayer, Amy tidied away the dead flowers that lay on the grave and replaced them with the bunch of hand-picked ones she had taken from her garden.

'Did you see Alice, last night wearing that beautiful red dress of yours? I'm so sorry you never got the chance to wear it yourself, but Alice did you proud. Thank you for the loan of that lovely choker. It really made my outfit come alive.' She paused for a moment before addressing Alice's father. 'She's looking after the farm just as well as you knew she would. All the yields are up in the fields and she's thinking of adding a couple more Friesians to the herd....'

At ten forty-five, Amy left the churchyard and made her way home. After brewing a pot of tea, she set to making two plates of sandwiches for the Bodkins' family lunch. She knew Bodkin was a big fan of her mother's homemade pickle, so she made up two rounds of cheese and pickle and two rounds of ham. After slicing up the quarter of seed cake that Miriam had given her, she covered the plates with a sheet of muslin and rinsed out the teapot in readiness for a fresh brew. If things went as she hoped, she'd have her own lunch with Alice, Miriam and Martha down at the farm, leaving the siblings to finally sort out their differences in Amy's front room.

At a quarter to twelve, Amy left home and walked up to the top of the lane, where she stood by the telephone box and waited for Sal to arrive. She had only been standing there for a few minutes when she saw a sleek, black, Ford model A Tudor Sedan heading towards her, as it slowed at the Old Bull, the driver's window was lowered and a pretty, dark-haired woman stuck her hand out to wave at her.

'Hello,' the woman called with a big smile on her face. 'Are you Amy?'

Amy rushed across the road to greet the new arrival. 'Hello, Sal. You look so much like him,' she said as she crouched down to look into the car.

Sal nodded. 'I know. People thought we were twins when we were kids, even though he was a foot taller and three years older.' She patted the passenger seat. 'Hop in, let's go and find Kathleen and the kids.'

Amy climbed into the car and after turning around at the telephone kiosk, Amy directed her through the town, past the station and into the old Victorian slum estate that lay like a scab between the pretty town centre and the dirty industrial landscape beyond.

At the O'Tooles' house, Amy knocked on the door and stood nervously with her fingers crossed, desperately hoping that Marty had gone to the pub. As it turned out, she needn't have worried. Kathleen and the boys were inside, waiting for them to arrive.

When the door was opened, Sal crouched down as the two badly bruised faces of the boys looked from behind the safety of their mother. Amy made the introductions and Sal reached into her pocket to pull out a bag of striped humbugs. The boys forgot their nervousness immediately as they stuck their hands into the bag, each transferring a huge minty sweet to their mouths.

As Sal straightened, Amy smiled at the children, then took her leave. 'I'll wait by the car. You have a lot to discuss and I don't want to get in the way.'

Amy walked back to the shiny Ford and sat in the passenger seat with the door open as she watched several small groups of children playing further up the street. The boys won or lost marbles as they rolled them into a ring that had been drawn in chalk in the middle of the road. Further along, five girls chanted the words to a skipping game as two of them turned the rope while the other three waited their turn to join in as the rhyme progressed.

*I had a little puppy*
*His name was Tiny Tim*
*I put him in the bathtub to see if he could swim*
*He drank all the water, he ate a bar of soap*
*The next thing you know, he had a bubble in his throat.*
*In came the doctor (a girl jumped in)*
*In came the nurse (a second girl jumped in)*
*In came the lady with the alligator purse (a third girl jumped in)*
*Out went the doctor (first girl jumped out)*
*Out went the nurse (second girl jumped out)*

*Out went the lady with the alligator purse (third girl jumped out)*

Amy laughed to herself as she chanted the rhyme she knew so well from her own childhood. She was so engrossed in the game that she didn't notice that Sal had returned to the car.

'Takes you back, doesn't it?' she said.

'They were happy days, though just like now there was a lot of poverty about. You don't have to own expensive toys, do you? All you need is a bit of rope and you can have hours of fun.'

Sal smiled as she got into the car. 'We used to chant that exact rhyme in the playground.'

'We used to skip outside our cottage, but it was only me, Alice and our friend Nora from the top end of the lane.'

Sal sighed. 'We weren't allowed to play games on the street. My dad thought it was common.'

'That's so sad,' Amy said, twisting in her seat and pulling the door shut.

'Oh, we used to do it if we knew he was going to be out for any length of time.'

'Good for you,' Amy said. 'Now, how did you get on with Mrs O'Toole?'

Sal's mouth became a thin line. 'They've had a really bad week. He's been even more violent than normal. Kathleen isn't sure what brought it on, but she's had enough of it. She wants to get out before one or both of the boys ends up in hospital.'

'Or herself.'

'Like most abused mothers, she doesn't think about herself. She just accepts it as a normal part of a relationship.'

Amy banged her hand down hard on the dashboard. 'Oops, sorry, it's just that I get so angry when a woman just accepts things as the norm when it should be the last thing she ever experiences.'

'Well, she'll be out of it soon. I was going to suggest I pick her and the kids up on Saturday, but she says it would be best if they left in the week when she knows for certain that he'll be at work. So, I'm going to make a quick trip up on Wednesday morning. I'll organise a room for them at the shelter. We'll find them something permanent a little later.'

Amy grabbed hold of Sal's hand. 'Thank you so much for doing this.'

Sal smiled softly at Amy. 'Thank you for bringing them to my attention. After Wednesday, they'll have a future to look forward to.' She started up the car and drove to the end of Nelson Street before turning right and driving past the Dragon pub. As they passed the police station at the bottom of Middle Street, Sal took a quick look to her right before turning left onto the Gillingham Road. She took a deep breath and let the air out slowly. 'Now for the difficult bit,' she said.

At one on the dot, Amy got up from the sofa and walked through the hall to let Bodkin in. On hearing the knock, Sal slipped into the kitchen and hid behind the door. 'Let's give him a surprise,' she said.

Bodkin followed Amy through to the living room, and at her invitation, sat down on the sofa.

'Do you fancy a cuppa?' she asked.

'My throat's as dry as a Skegness donkey's hoof,' he said.

As Amy stepped into the kitchen, Sal came out. Bodkin had been tying a loose shoelace. 'That was qui...' His voice tailed off as he looked up at the woman standing in front of him. He slowly got to his feet, then hesitantly held out his arms towards her. 'Sal...' he whispered. 'Is it really you?'

The siblings fell together and tears rolled down Amy's cheeks as she watched the scene progress. Sal, with her arms around her brother's neck, blurted out incoherent words as she sobbed onto his shoulder. Bodkin's arms were around her back, his eyes were closed, tight.

Amy turned away and wiped her eyes on her sleeve before lighting the gas and putting the kettle on the hob. After loading up a tray with cups, saucers and the plate of sandwiches she had made earlier, she tapped on the door and carried it through to the living room. Bodkin and Sal were sitting side by side on the sofa as they held hands. Sal's mascara had run onto Bodkin's collar.

'I made a few sandwiches for you,' Amy said as she placed the tray on the table. 'I'm going to leave you alone to catch up now. I'll be at the farm for the next hour. I'll come back at two-ish, if that's all right?' Her eyes went to the sofa where Sal was dabbing at her face with a white handkerchief. Bodkin's face was turned towards Amy. His lips moved, but no words came out.

'Please don't say I've been interfering again, Bodkin,' Amy pleaded. 'You belong together, you're family.'

When Bodkin spoke, his voice was husky and cracked. 'I was trying to say thank you.'

Amy took a couple of steps towards him and planted a kiss on his upturned face. 'I'll leave you to it,' she said softly.

At the farm, Amy found Alice and Miriam sitting in the two big armchairs at either side of the fireplace. Miriam was cradling Alice's daughter, Martha in her arms.

'Hello, everyone,' Amy said breezily as she closed the kitchen door.

'How did it go?' Alice asked, getting to her feet and walking across the kitchen to the put the kettle on the hob.

'Really well, they're sitting on my sofa holding hands like two little lovebirds. Bodkin won't let go of her.'

Miriam's eyes opened wide as Alice's mouth gaped.

'I was talking about you and Bodkin last night,' Alice said, still looking confused. 'What are you talking about? Whose hand is Bodkin holding, why is he holding it and what is he doing holding it on your sofa?'

Amy pulled out a chair and sat down at the well-scrubbed oak table. 'His sister's up from Dover... I did tell you, Alice. They've been estranged for—'

'Of course. I'd forgotten all about that. So... have they kissed and made up?'

Amy grinned. 'Oh, Alice, it was so lovely to see. I left them to it. They've got a few years of catching up to do.'

Alice spooned tea into the pot and stared at the kettle, willing it to boil.

'There's a saying about that,' Amy said noticing her friend tapping her foot as she stared at the steaming kettle.

Alice turned around to face her. 'As to my initial question. How did it go last night? Are you friends again?'

Amy nodded. 'All is forgiven and forgotten.'

'Phew!' Alice exclaimed. 'I thought I was going to have to knock your heads together.' She looked at the kettle again before turning quickly back. 'Have you had lunch? We had ours at twelve, but there's some cut bread and a couple of slices of ham left over if you're hungry.'

'I'd love a sandwich, thanks, Alice. I made lunch for Bodkin and Sal before I left, but I haven't had anything myself.'

Miriam rose to put the sleeping Martha down in her cot in the parlour, then walked to the sink to rinse her hands. 'She's teething. She's been dribbling all over me for the last half hour.'

When the kettle finally boiled, Alice poured water into the pot and sat it in the middle of the table on a wicker mat, then picked up two coronation themed mugs from the draining board. She winced as she sat down at the table, then lifted her backside off the seat before sitting down again. 'My bottom's still sore from last night. I think all the little bruises are combining to make one huge, big purple mess.'

'It's your fault for having such a pinchable bottom,' Amy said as Miriam put a platter on the table containing the leftover ham, some cut bread and a butter dish. 'That dress of yours left very little to the imagination. I was almost tempted to pat it myself.'

Alice laughed. 'You might have ended up with a face as red as Gerald's,' she said. 'I've been feeling a bit guilty about that this morning. I didn't half catch him.'

'Joe Louis would have been proud of that slap,' Amy said. 'He deserved all he got, the letch.'

'I shouldn't have done it, but I was fed up with having my backside slapped. I felt like Milkshake, our prize Friesian, when the lads try to coax her into the milking parlour. I'm sure they're gentler too.'

'Rub a bit of butter on it,' Amy said. 'That's what Mum used to say to me if I had a lump on my forehead or a graze on my knee.'

'My knickers will stick to me,' Alice said, seriously. 'I've got to muck out the dairy yet.' She paused for a moment. 'It's not bath night, but I think I might have another soak later.' She turned to Miriam. 'I know it's your day for the bathroom, but I'm sure the Ascot will run to two, just this once.'

'You get in when you feel like it, Lovely. I can wait until tonight for my bath. I haven't had men fondling me all night.'

'You sound quite disappointed about that, Miriam,' Amy said, winking at her. 'Your John had better up his game.'

'There's no game to up,' Miriam said, handing Amy a plate holding a thick cut sandwich. 'He thinks his dead wife is watching him like a hawk, so he daren't take the risk.'

'Poor Miriam,' Amy said. 'Maybe Alice ought to have a word with him about it. She was quite willing to help me and Bodkin with our difficulties.'

'Leave me out of it,' Alice said as she squirmed in her seat again. 'I've got enough on my mind dealing with this.'

When Amy had finished her sandwich, she asked Alice if she could have a sheet of paper and a pen. Then, when Alice had furnished her with a notebook and her best fountain pen, she started to write down a list of the people she now knew to have been in some sort of relationship with Effie.

'You're a proper little Hercule Poirot,' Miriam said as she took her seat by the fireplace and picked up her copy of Agatha Christie's The ABC Murders.

'That,' said Amy, 'is a seriously good mystery. It had me thinking hard.'

'Did you guess who the killer was?'

'Nope, I was in the dark right up to the end. She really had me going with that one. It's a beautifully disguised denouement.'

Amy concentrated on her list again as she thought about the four motives that her fictional detective hero, Poirot, used when solving many of his cases. Revenge, Gain, Jealousy, Fear.

1. Granville Cresswell. Motive, Jealousy. Effie had injured his oversized ego. Owns a chemical plant that produces chloroform.
2. Timothy Philby. Revenge. Effie had humiliated him in front of club members.
3. Katherine Downey. Gain. She thought she had lost everything when Effie took her place.
4. Joe Lyndsay. Unknown Motive. But he was very close to her just before her death.
5. Angus McIntosh. Unknown Motive. Elderly gentleman with more money than sense. Effie may have made one demand too many of him.
6. Assorted Female Club Members. Motive, Jealousy. Many were angry because Effie flirted with their

husbands. (Maybe it went further than flirting in some cases.)

7. Assorted Male Club Members. Motive, Jealousy. Some of the men might have been jealous when others formed a relationship with her, however briefly.
8. Bertram Cresswell. Motive, Fear. He is very close to Granville and might have murdered Effie on his uncle's orders for fear of being ousted from the family business. (No evidence at all of this.)
9. Ronald Parkin. Motive, Unknown. Dentist who has access to chloroform.

People on the margins.

1. John Watkins. No Motive that I can see, but he is a vet, so has access to chloroform. Has yet to be questioned.
2. Quentin Foxley-Walton. Unknown Motive, but he was very close to Effie for quite a time and she seemed to have a fixation on him. Is a university trained research chemist and must have access to a range of chemicals. Maybe she was pressurising him into a deeper relationship that his parents wouldn't have accepted. Has yet to be questioned.

When she had finished her list, Amy screwed the top back onto the pen and laid it down on the table, then, after a quick look at the big clock on the wall, she folded the sheet of paper in half and got to her feet.

'I think Bodkin and Sal have had enough time to become reacquainted by now.' She waved the sheet of paper at Alice. 'And I'd like to go through this list with Bodkin to get him up to speed on the probable suspects.'

# CHAPTER THIRTY

When Amy returned home, she found Sal washing the lunch plates. Bodkin was nowhere in sight.

Amy hurried into the kitchen with a worried look on her face. 'Is everything all right? Where's Bodkin?'

Sal put a washed plate on the draining board and smiled. 'Everything is fine. He's got to call in at the station. Something about an underwear thief? A lady was due to give a statement to the constable on duty this morning and he just wants to give it the once over before he gets back on the case tomorrow.' She paused as she hung up the tea towel. 'Then he's nipping round to his flat to dig out the stack of letters he's written to me over the years, but never posted. I've just given him the pile I wrote to him.'

'Phew!' Amy said. 'I'm so glad you're back together again. Five years is too long for siblings to be parted. If you don't mind me asking, what caused the breakup?'

'Let's sit down and I'll tell you all about it, but, basically, it came about because Gee was trying to protect me from myself.'

Amy led Sal into the lounge and they sat on the sofa, Amy turning sideways on with her legs underneath her.

'Has Gee told you anything about his past?'

'Nothing, I know his dad died, and he carries his old armchair around everywhere he goes, but apart from that, nothing, really.'

'He didn't mention the beatings?'

Amy's jaw dropped. 'No... nothing like that.'

Sal uncrossed her legs and placed her hands on her lap. 'I'll go right back to the start with a bit of family history.' She stared at the cross on the wall on the other side of the room, then, having gathered her thoughts, she went on. 'Gee was born in nineteen eleven. Mum and Dad were living in Ashford at the time, but then Dad's brother died. He was quite a well-to-do man who had never married. He left Dad a small, terraced house in Dover. I came along three years later, just a few months before the war began. Dad was called up in nineteen-fifteen and the loneliness really hit Mum hard. She had never really settled in Dover and hadn't made any friends at all. She began to drink to try to put her anxieties aside and by the time the war ended, she was pretty much an alcoholic.

'Dad somehow managed to get through the war, but he was a changed man. I didn't know him anyway as I was still a toddler when he left for France, but Gee still had vague memories of him. He'd always been very religious. That's why Gee and I got our ridiculous names. He never explained why he chose those two instead of the thousands of more appropriate ones he might have picked. He never missed church on Sundays, even before the war, but when he came back, he was almost fanatical. I know a lot of men turned against God after what they'd witnessed on the front, but his experiences had reinvigorated his faith. He went back to his old job at the tannery, but he wasn't well liked there. God, Jesus and the Holy Ghost were the only things that meant anything to him. He was forever preaching to his workmates. He even stood in the town on a Saturday berating people for their sins as he read out Bible verses on the market square.

'Our day started early. He'd get us up to pray before he went to work and we'd have to learn parables or short passages from the Bible by the next morning. If we didn't get it right, word for word, we got no breakfast. Gee had a better memory than me, so he'd get fed when I didn't. He always saved me exactly half of whatever he'd been given though. It wasn't much, half a slice of bread and beef dripping, but it was better than nothing.

'Mum died when Gee was twelve and then things took a turn for the worse. Her liver gave out on her. Dad was devastated and he turned to drink himself. He always felt guilty about his sinful ways and started to attend both Sunday services to say sorry to God for his weakness. He dragged us along to the morning service, but we were always spared the evening one. Instead, he gave us extra Bible passages to learn while he was out. It was about that time that the beatings started. Gee was in charge at home when Dad was either at work or in the pub. It was his job to find food on the market and to prepare it for our tea or supper, depending on what time Dad got home. He gave Gee a pittance to buy the scraps of whatever the traders had left over at the end of the day. He was only a kid, but he did his best. Sometimes he'd bring me home a bruised apple that had been left under the stall, other times he'd steal an extra potato and we'd eat it in secret before Dad got home.

'I can't remember the exact reason for that first beating, but I know it was something to do with the blessing that Gee had to recite before we ate. I don't know if he stumbled over the words or not, but I remember Dad throwing his bowl of stew at the wall and telling Gee to bend over the armchair. That first time, he used his leather-soled slipper. Gee was so shocked by the experience, he went to our bedroom and cried himself to sleep. I saw his back and buttocks as he pulled off his nightshirt the next day when he got dressed. He was covered in bruises.

'It was like the dam had burst after that and Gee was bent

over the chair most nights and at least once every weekend, usually after Dad got back from evensong. By the Christmas of that year, he was using his thick leather belt on him. Gee refused to cry out. I think that made him angrier.'

Amy wiped away a tear as she listened to Sal's dreadful recollections. 'What... did he ever do anything to you?'

'Not sexually. He wasn't that sort of man, but my turn came when I was ten. The weather had been awful and although I'd washed him a clean shirt for church, I couldn't get it dry. He always said a coal fire was a luxury and would only allow it to be lit on really cold days. Anyway, his shirt was still wet on the Sunday morning so it was my turn on the chair. It didn't last as long as the beatings he dished out to Gee, but he left a lot of bruises. Gee came in from an errand he'd been sent on just as Dad let me get up. He had fire in his eyes and I'm sure he would have thrown himself at Dad if I hadn't begged him not to.

'After that, I was beaten once or twice a week and always for some incredibly slight misdemeanour. Gee wasn't aware of it at all. Dad made sure he was out of the house when it happened. I think he felt guilty and didn't want any witnesses. Not that his shame stopped him from hitting me.

'Once, after Gee had received a particularly brutal beating, he spoke to the vicar at Sunday School but instead of instructing Dad to spare the rod, he just reported what Gee had said, so the poor kid got an even worse beating for airing the family's dirty laundry in public. That taught him a tough lesson and when a teacher remarked on his injuries, he'd just say he'd been in a fight or had fallen from a wall or something. He once said to me. 'Never think things can't get any worse, because they can.'

Amy lifted her hand to her mouth. 'So that's why he said that. Poor Bodkin. I thought he was just toeing the company line on domestic violence when he came out with it. Oh dear, Sal, I'm so sorry you had to go through all that.'

'It also explains his distrust of religion, Amy. He used to be a big believer when he was younger, but Dad, and the vicar's reaction to his pleading, knocked that out of him. He's the world's biggest cynic when it comes to the Almighty now. I have to say, I share that cynicism. If God, who sees everything, can allow something like that to be done in His name, then He isn't worth knowing.'

'I struggle with it myself at times. Mum and Dad are devout, but I question my faith regularly. Especially when I see the conditions a lot of children have to grow up in.' Amy put her hands together and lowered her head, almost as though she was about to pray.

'The beatings went on as usual, but when Gee became aware that I was being punished too, he got it into his head that he had let me down. He was my big brother, and it was his job to protect me from harm, so the next time he was told to go on an errand, he didn't go. He waited in the kitchen and when he heard Dad yell out my name and instruct me to bend over the chair, he came into the room and told Dad he wasn't going to deliver the message he was supposed to take to his drinking partner who lived next door.

'Dad was furious. He dragged me to one side, got hold of Gee by the scruff of his neck, threw him onto the chair and delivered the worst thrashing Gee had ever received. I tried to make him stop; I begged him not to hit him anymore but to no avail. After that, every time I was called in to receive my lesson in humility, Gee would say or do something to bring out the worst in Dad and he'd take my punishment on top of his own.

'By the time he was sixteen, Gee's body had filled out, despite the poor rations he was getting. Dad was older by then and he was nowhere near as fit as he had been in his younger days. The drink was taking its toll, too. One Sunday after church, Dad came back in a foul temper. I'd seen him in plenty of bad moods, but that night he was raging on about driving out the Devil. He caught me by my hair and dragged me across to the chair. Gee heard my screams and came running. Before Dad could land his first lash, Gee was on him. Dad called him the son of Satan and raised his belt to hit him, but Gee snatched it from his hand, spun him around, forced him onto the chair, then let him have it with the buckle end of the belt. I managed to pull him off a couple of minutes later, but he had left his mark both physically and mentally.

'We didn't get hit again after that. Oh, he used to sit in that bloody chair of his, hurling abuse at us, calling us the spawn of the Devil, but we both knew he'd never try to hurt us again.

'By then, Gee had two jobs. He was working on the market in the mornings and at the coal yard in the afternoons. Dad still had money coming in from his brother's estate, but we never saw much of it. I started working at the big house when I was fourteen, but only at weekends; Gee insisted I kept going to school until I got my national certificate. He used to go to the Working Men's College in the evenings to build on his education. I worried about him, but he insisted he could manage. He saw it as his job to look after me. I'd often find him sitting at the kitchen table at one o'clock in the morning, poring over some book or writing out an essay.

'When he was eighteen, he gave up his work in the markets and the coal yard and joined the police force. They didn't ask for educated men, particularly, but Gee impressed the board so much that they gave him an exam to sit, and when he passed that, they told him they'd pay for him to continue at college and he used to attend one day a week.

'Dad was getting worse by the time I sat my national certificate. He couldn't manage to walk to the pub every night, so he used to buy bottles of cheap alcohol from the off sales three doors away. In the end, he didn't even have to fetch it himself. They'd leave him a bottle a day on the windowsill and he'd pay at the end of the week.

'He died just before my eighteenth birthday. There was only me and Gee at the funeral. His drinking partners and even his friend the vicar had given up on him by then. There was a will. His money, not that there was a large amount left, and the house, went to Gee, but he always told me that half of whatever he had, was mine and he had the deeds to the property changed to include both of our names.

'He still thought he had to protect me, especially from the men I encountered, and that's what eventually led to us falling out on an epic scale.

'I'd had a couple of boyfriends, but none were really serious. They couldn't get too serious with Gee waiting for us when we came out of the tea shop or the pictures. I doubt he'd have thought any man good enough for me. Anyway, I met a rather handsome man called Harry Fisher. He was charming and funny, and I was soon besotted by him. He claimed that he worked in an import-export warehouse at the docks. I was twenty-one by then, so I thought I was old enough to make my own decisions when it came to who I wanted to share my life with. Gee took against him straight away. He didn't like him at all, but after I insisted on seeing him, he reluctantly took a step back. All was fine for a few months. I used to see Harry a couple of times a week. I even had him back to the house when Gee was working late, not that he knew that, of course.

'It came to a head one morning at the end of March. The clocks were supposed to have been put forward, but I had forgotten to do it before Harry and I went to bed. Gee was working on the night shift and as I'd set the alarm for six-thirty, I thought I'd have plenty of time to get Harry out of the way before he got home. I was wrong, of course. He walked in the door just as Harry was pulling his trousers on.

'Gee was furious. We had a stand up row, a beauty. All the pent-up frustrations that had built up over the previous year came out. He told me that not only was Harry lying about his job at the warehouse; he was, in fact, unemployed and made his living on the black market selling stuff he'd stolen from the place he'd claimed to work at. He said he was only one more trip to court away from a lengthy prison sentence. Harry didn't want to hear all this, of course, and slipped away quietly while we were arguing like cats and dogs. When I told him that I didn't believe him, Gee went on to tell me about the females he'd seen Harry with while he'd been out patrolling the town. Some of the women he hung around with had been arrested for prostitution. He even claimed that Harry was pimping a few of them.

'I called him a liar, amongst other things. He told me I wasn't capable of looking after myself, so he had to keep an eye on me. I told him I was sick of him protecting me; I felt I was being smothered, and I needed to make my own way in life. I said I didn't need him in it anymore.

'We continued to argue, both of us saying things that would have been better left unsaid. Anyway, the upshot of it all was, he decided to take up a job in Gillingham where he'd have the chance to work with the CID with all the promotion prospects that offered. I basically said good riddance, and off he went.

'We stewed in our own juices for six months. Then he turned up on the doorstep one Saturday morning. Harry was inside with his feet up, reading the racing pages. So, it all kicked off again. I'd been unlucky in that Harry only ever stayed over on Friday nights. He was up to other things the rest of the week.

'We both really dug our heels in this time. Harry had told me he had a new job working nights from Saturday to Thursday and I like a fool, believed him. I was working at the homeless charity by then and I was pretty much running the show. Gee had given me half of Dad's money before he left and as we owned the house, I had no rent to pay, so I was doing pretty well financially. I had to lend Harry a few quid here and there to see him through until payday, and I didn't mind that, even though he never once paid me back. He was still the handsome, funny, plausible man he'd always been.

'So, we fell out again and this time there was to be no reconciliation. After Gee dragged Harry to the front door and threw him down the steps, I told him to get out and never come back. So he did.

'At Christmas he sent a card just signed, Gee, no other message apart from his new address, so I sent him one back signed, Sal and we've been doing that ever since. We've both had misgivings over the years and, as I said, we both wrote long letters to each other that were never posted. We were too stubborn, too utterly alike, to want to be the one to make the first move. So, Amy, I can't thank you enough for making it possible for us to meet on neutral ground. Things are back to how they should be at last.'

'What happened with you and Harry?' Amy asked.

'Oh, Gee was right about him, of course. I found him in the arms of another woman about three months later. He was kissing her goodbye on her doorstep while I was out early on my charity work. He ended up being sent to prison for two years not long after. The sad thing is, even though I suspected there might be some truth in what Gee told me, I still felt I had to trust my own instincts. I needed the freedom to make mistakes. I was a grown woman and I couldn't go through the rest of my life relying on Gee to stop me from making a fool of myself. He didn't see it that way, of course. He just hated the thought of me being hurt. He stopped that happening when we were kids and he felt it was his duty to continue to keep me safe. I can see all that now. I probably could back then and I'll always be grateful to my big brother for what he saved me from at his own expense, but I wanted to be my own woman.' She reached out her hand and took hold of Amy's. 'You can see that, can't you?'

Amy nodded. 'I can see where it all comes from now. Poor Bodkin. It's ingrained in him, isn't it? He has to protect the people he loves most from harm.'

'He's a sweetheart,' Sal said, releasing Amy's hand. 'A real pain in the backside, but a sweetheart nonetheless.'

Amy got to her feet when she heard a knock on the front door. When she opened it, she found Bodkin clutching a bundle of letters and a few old sepia photographs. 'Hello again,' he said, waving the bundle. 'I just nipped home to get these for Sal. She's got to be on her way soon.'

Amy stepped back to allow Bodkin into the hallway, but as he turned towards her after closing the door, she threw her arms around his neck and kissed him softly on the lips.

Bodkin grinned. 'What have I done to deserve that?' he asked.

'You deserve it just for being you,' Amy replied, then she kissed him again.

# CHAPTER THIRTY-ONE

A few minutes later, with Sal sitting with the pile of letters on her lap and with Bodkin out in the lavatory, Amy picked up a couple of the photographs that the policeman had brought with him. One showed a young constable Bodkin on his first day in uniform, another showed him and Sal standing at the front door of their house. They were both smiling.

'He thinks the absolute world of you, Amy,' Sal said in a hushed tone. 'I'm so glad you found each other.' She paused and shot a quick glance into the kitchen. The bathroom was just beyond it. 'Mind you, from what I hear, you've got a bit of competition.'

'Competition? It's the first I've heard about it, if you mean that strumpet, Trixie, who lives in the flat below him then—'

Sal laughed. 'I meant your mother.'

Amy laughed. 'Oh, I see. The way to a man's heart and all that. He loves her cooking. He'd be as fat as Oliver Hardy if he lived here. As far as Mum goes, she thinks Bodkin has son-in-law tattooed on his forehead. Alice keeps telling me that Mum has her eye on a new hat for the wedding.'

'A wedding? He kept that quiet.'

Amy put on a shocked face. 'There is no wedding. It's just wishful thinking on Mum's part and mischievous nonsense on Alice's. I'm not ready for domesticity yet and I honestly suspect neither is Bodkin. For the record, he hasn't asked me, so I haven't had to turn him down.'

'Do you think you'll ever be ready?' Sal asked. 'I'd hate to see a relationship like you have go to waste.'

'One day maybe. I treasure my independence, and Bodkin is in no hurry. He knows our relationship is worth more than just a ring on a finger. We'll know when the time is right. Until then, we're fine as we are.'

Bodkin came back in, wiping his still damp hands on the seat of his trousers. Amy sighed as she looked at the wrinkles and creases that ran from the waistband to the turn ups.

'Has he always looked as dishevelled as he does now?' Amy asked Sal.

'Always. I was in charge of the iron and I made sure everything was nice and smooth. You could cut cake with the crease I pressed into the front of his trousers, but within five minutes they looked like he'd just slept in them.'

'Do you mind not discussing the state of my trousers? They might be a little creased but I feel very close to them.'

Amy shook her head. 'And you've been close to them for far too long, Bodkin. What happened to the new pair we got you from Stan's?'

Bodkin looked away. 'They're awaiting the iron,' he said.

'One day someone will invent a material that holds a crease and never needs ironing,' Amy said. 'They should hire you as a test pilot, Bodkin. If they can withstand you, they'll withstand anything.'

'I got some new underpants on Friday as I promised,' Bodkin said.

Sal's eyebrows raised as she looked at Amy.

'It's a long story and probably best told over a drink,' Amy replied.

Ten minutes later, Sal got to her feet and, clutching the pile of letters in her hands, she gave Amy a hug. 'It's been so nice to meet you, Amy. I can't wait to come back so we can have a proper womanly chat. Thanks again for making today possible.'

'I'll see you on Wednesday, won't I?' Amy said.

'If you like, I'll pick you up before I go over to Kathleen's. I won't be hanging around, though. I want to get those kids to a safe place as quickly as I can.' She turned to Bodkin. 'I'll come up again next weekend. I'll give you a call at home one evening to let you know what time. It will most likely be Saturday. I could stay over.'

'Mum and Dad are back on Saturday evening,' Amy said. 'I know they'd love to meet you. Mum has no idea you exist. She'll be made up when she finds out.'

Bodkin and Sal left the room and walked down the hall to the front door. A few tears ran down Amy's cheeks as she watched them embrace. Then, after wiping her eyes on her handkerchief, she walked into the kitchen and filled the kettle. She was still dabbing at her face when Bodkin came in.

'Sal says thank you again. She reckons she'll be saying that every time she meets up with you.'

Amy sniffed as she tried hard to control her emotions. Eventually she gave up, turned around and, after wrapping herself in Bodkin's arms, she burst into tears.

'Hey, what's brought this on?' Bodkin said, as he folded his arms tightly around her.

'It's... it's... everything,' Amy sobbed. 'I feel terrible about the things I said. I had no idea, Bodkin.'

'About what?' Bodkin gently lifted her head from his chest and wiped away a fresh line of tears from her cheek.

'About... Sal told me about your dad. About how you always

tried to protect her from him. About the pain you suffered for all those years... and there was me... accusing you of having no feelings when I wanted to help the O'Toole boys... Oh, Bodkin, you knew better than anyone what they were going through.' She dropped her head to his chest, and the sobbing began again. 'I'm so sorry you had to suffer that.'

'Shhh,' Bodkin whispered soothingly. 'You didn't know, and that's my fault for not telling you about it when you questioned my attitude. I should have come clean and I'm sorry.'

'Come clean?' Amy looked up at him, her eyes still flowing. 'You make it sound like it was something you're ashamed of.' She put a hand softly on his cheek. 'You have nothing to be ashamed of, Bodkin. None of what happened was your fault.'

Bodkin nodded. 'I know, but... well, it's hard for me to talk about. I'd much rather forget any of it happened.'

'You have to talk about it, Bodkin. It's the only way you're going to get any closure... I don't mean closure... Oh, I can't think of the word, but you have to get it out. I know that much. It will just fester away inside until you do.'

Bodkin sighed. 'I know. I've given that advice out myself to victims of violent crime but it's a lot harder when the secret belongs to you.'

'We can talk about it any time you want to, Bodkin,' Amy said. 'I'll always be there for you.'

Bodkin kissed the top of her head. 'I know, and you don't know how grateful I am for that. Could we do it another time, though? It's a bit raw at the moment, what with seeing Sal after all this time.'

Amy nodded and pulled away from him. After wiping her eyes on her sleeve, she put the kettle on the hob and lit it. 'I really like, Sal. I think we're going to be very good friends.'

'She loves you already.' He chuckled. 'I'm a bit concerned

about what else might come up when you have this womanly chat thing of yours.'

'HA! You should be concerned too, Bodkin.' Amy looked at him through red, narrowed eyes. 'What other secrets might come out? Do you want to fess up before she reveals them?'

'I'll take my chances,' Bodkin said as he picked up the biscuit tin. 'She, erm, didn't give anything else away today, did she?'

'Like?'

Bodkin scratched his stubble, his eyes fixed on the biscuit tin. 'Something personal, maybe. Something I've kept hidden all these years?'

'Like your Christian name? No, she said that's something you'll tell me when you're ready to tell me.'

Bodkin nodded, then was silent for a while. 'I think you ought to know. I mean, you know pretty much everything else about me now.'

Amy put her hand on his arm. 'You don't have to tell me, Bodkin. I know you're embarrassed by it for some reason. I've sometimes thought, come on man, it can't be that bad. But if you want to keep it to yourself, it's fine by me.'

'Goliath,' Bodkin blurted out. 'It's Goliath. Dad crippled me with it at birth. He must have known how hard my life was going to be, harnessed to a name like that. It's not even one of the nicer characters in the Bible. Please don't tell your father. He'll insist on using it, seeing as it's my given name.'

'I'm sorry, Bodkin. Trust me, I won't say anything to Mum or Dad. I can understand why you wanted to keep it hidden.'

'I had a terrible time at school. I couldn't hide it there. My name was read out at assembly every morning and every morning the rest of the class used to wet themselves laughing.'

Amy shook her head sadly. 'It wasn't right. He shouldn't have done that to you.'

'Kids used to threaten me with their home made slings and

catapults. "I'm David and I'm going to kill Goliath".' He paused for a moment. 'In Bible studies, we had that story more than any other. I used to come out of the lesson dreading walking home with the other lads in my class walking behind, taunting me.'

'Oh, Bodkin.'

'It's fine. It's just something I had to get used to. I couldn't change it. One good thing happened, though. It toughened me up. I learned how to look after myself... and Sal, she had a rough time with her name, too. The girls used to ask if she wanted to bake John the Baptist's head on a platter in cookery class.'

Amy shook her head again. 'I honestly don't know how you both got through all that, Bodkin.'

He shrugged. 'It's karma time now. I went through the bad times, so I get to go through the good times now.' He put the biscuit tin down, reached out and pulled Amy towards him. 'And you are the icing on the cake, Amy Rowlings. You're the best thing that's ever happened to me.'

'And I'm going to look after you a little better from now on,' Amy said. 'You might be my knight in shining armour, but even big, brave knights need someone to wipe their fevered brow now and again. You'll have to let me in, Bodkin. Your secrets are safe with me.'

Later, as they finished eating a dinner of double egg and chips, Bodkin sat back, rubbed his stomach, and sighed contentedly. 'You're a chip off the old block, so to speak. Your egg and chips are just as good as your mum's.'

'There's a compliment a girl doesn't hear every day,' Amy said. 'Oh, I've got something for you. Last night might have ended badly, but the object of the exercise was achieved.' She picked up her bag and pulled out the sheet of paper she had worked on at the farm. 'Voila,' she cried. 'A list of possible suspects. There might be more to add to the list as the investigation goes on, but we have a start at least.'

She handed the folded sheet of paper to Bodkin. He opened it up and smoothed it out on the table.

'Excellent work,' he said, looking up at her. 'Now, can we go through each of these people in detail? Tell me exactly who said what to who, about whom.'

'Will I see you at the station in the morning? I've got to return my dress to Brigden's, so I can pop in after that. I might be able to help you track down the phantom knickers nicker.'

'I have to do a bit of work on that case, but I'm hoping my new sergeant might be able to help me out with it. After that I'd like to track down the two names on your list that didn't attend the ball on Saturday, plus I want to set up meetings with a few of those that did attend, and Skipper Joe is the first name on my list.'

'New sergeant? A CID sergeant? Don't tell me you're finally going to get a bit of help?'

'It's even better than that. I had a telephone call from Superintendent Grayson yesterday. Not only am I getting a permanent sergeant, I'm getting the two trainees back. You remember the ones that weren't quite up to scratch? Well, they've been licked into shape, it seems, so that will mean with the new recruits we've had recently, our staffing levels will be almost back to where we were a few months ago. Superintendent Grayson is coming back for good, so I'll have a senior officer to report to, and... here's the news that will make you smile. Ferris is to be co-opted to plain clothes. He'll be Ferris of the CID from tomorrow on. He doesn't know yet. I'll give him the good news in the morning.'

'That's wonderful news, Bodkin. You might be able to take it a little easier now.' She looked at him, then frowned. 'But, knowing you, it won't stop you working all the hours God sends.' She poked him in the chest with her finger and smiled at him. 'I'm delighted for Ferris too, but why did Grayson have a change of heart. It's not that long ago he said he wasn't ready for his sergeant stripes.'

'Firstly, he's still a constable. He's not getting a promotion in rank, as such. Secondly, they were scared they would lose him to his singing career. This way they're hoping he'll stay on and just keep the entertaining side as a secondary interest.'

'Do you think he'll go for it? He is getting more bookings now, and he earns as much in a night as the police pay him for a fortnight's work.'

Bodkin winked at her. 'He'll go for it. He's told me a few times about his dream of getting into the CID. His father was a plain-clothes copper, you see. He'll be proud of our Orlando.'

'I wish I could be there to see his face when you tell him to go home and put a suit on,' Amy said.

'It's probably best if you're not, Amy. There may be manly tears shed.'

'All right, have it your own way. I'll pop in after I've been to Brigden's.'

They kissed at the front door, then Bodkin let himself out. He turned to look back when he reached the gate to see Amy still standing in the doorway.

'Goodnight,' Bodkin said. 'Thanks again for today.'

'I wouldn't have missed it for the world,' Amy replied.

# CHAPTER THIRTY-TWO

At nine-fifteen on Monday morning, Amy got off the bus outside the Town Hall and walked around the corner to the Brigden's store where she carefully placed the bag containing her hired dress on the counter for Eileen to check. The manageress took her time, examining every inch of the dress and shawl before calling to her assistant, Sharon, to re-dress the mannequin with it.

'I'm sorry about that, Amy. I knew you'd look after it, but I have to make sure it's perfect for the next time it's hired out.'

'I understand completely,' Amy said as she folded up the Brigden's bag she had carried the dress in.

'I'm glad you came in today, Amy. I'd like to have a word with you about something.' She called to Sharon as she walked towards her. 'Look after the shop. I'm just going in the back with Amy for five minutes.'

Eileen led Amy through a door at the back of the shop, and into a small stockroom where two rails of as yet unpriced dresses, skirts, blouses and coats were lined up ready to be taken into the store. Against one wall was a long table on which sat two sewing machines. Piled on one end of the table was a small stack of clothing.

Eileen picked up an item from the top of the pile and held it up. The blue and green silk dress had a badly damaged hem. 'I've got a few like these, Amy. Full length dresses that I picked up for a song, but all require some expert mending. They are all evening dresses. The hems have been caught up in car doors, trodden on or tripped over. I'm pretty good on a machine when it comes to repairing the odd seam, but this work is beyond me. I was wondering if you'd help me out. She looked back at the pile. There are four dresses here and I'll pay you five bob a dress. That's a pound's worth of work. I think it would take you an hour at most per dress, so that's five bob an hour. I'd guess that's about half a week's wages for four hours on the machine.'

'Would I have to come here to do the work? The pay is great, Eileen, but it's fitting it in somehow. I have a machine at home, as you know, so I could maybe do them in the evenings after tea.'

'That would be fine by me, Amy. The machines are here though if you need them.'

'When would you like to have them back? I'm on factory fortnight holidays at the moment, but I'm tied up with one or two important things that I can't really put aside.'

'If I could have them back sometime next week, that would be great.'

'I think I can manage that,' Amy replied thoughtfully. 'I'm working at London Connection again in the week. I can drop them in on my lunch break.'

'Fabulous,' Eileen said as she gathered up the garments to carry them through to the shop. 'I'll send you more work as and when I buy more damaged stock. I'm hoping to build up my hire business with these frocks.'

Back in the shop, Amy handed over the bag she had brought her hire dress back in and Eileen carefully folded the damaged garments, wrapped them in tissue paper and placed them carefully in the brown paper bag. 'Will we see you on Saturday, as usual?'

'I'll be here,' Amy said. 'I've spotted one or two dresses on the rail in your stockroom. I'd like to get a closer look at them.'

From Brigden's, Amy took a leisurely walk down Middle Street until she came to the police station, where she found a new face looking at her across the counter.

'Can I help you, miss?' the man asked.

He was a slender man with a long neck and stick out ears. His blue jacket fitted where it touched. He gave Amy a friendly smile as he waited for her response.

Amy fished around in her bag until she found the white accreditation card that Chief Inspector Laws had given her. She handed it to the constable, who took a quick look before handing it back.

'I'm Amy Rowlings and I'd like to see Inspector Bodkin if he's in.' She took the pass back and held it up. 'This gives me access to certain parts of the police station when the inspector or constable Ferris is on the premises.'

'I'll just let him know you're here, miss,' the man said as he picked up the phone. After a short delay he spoke to Bodkin, put the phone back down, then walked around from behind the counter to open the door for her.

'He says you know where to go,' the constable said, touching his forelock.

Amy slipped the card into her pocket. 'Thank you, Constable... I'm sorry, I don't know your name. Are you one of the new intake?'

'Yes, miss. This is my first day. I'm Parlour, by the way. Stephen Parlour. I'm on permanent transfer from Rochester.'

Amy smiled at him. 'I hope you'll be very happy here, Constable Parlour. I know you'll be kept busy.'

'Just how I like it, miss,' Parlour said as he returned to his position behind the desk.

~

Bodkin was speaking on the phone when Amy tapped on his partly open door and stepped into his office. Noticing her, Bodkin pulled the handset away from his ear as he mouthed, Good Morning. Amy walked up to his desk and was about to sit down when Bodkin asked the recipient of his call to 'hang on for a moment' then, half turning in his chair, he covered up the mouthpiece with his hand and pointed to a yellow tinged bottle of milk that sat on top of his filing cabinet. 'Could you do me a favour and nip into the staff office? Ferris has been out to get a couple of bottles of fresh milk, but he hasn't dropped mine off yet. I suspect he's been buttonholed by Trixie. He'll be sharing the office with her from now on and she'll have so much to gossip about, after being stuck there on her own for the past few months.'

Amy stuck up a thumb and while Bodkin returned to his telephone call, Amy went back out into the passage and followed it to the end, where she heard the unmistakable whiny voice of Trixie, the station secretary, as it wafted out through the open door. Trixie was a blonde bombshell who styled herself on Mae West. She was immensely proud of her shapely hourglass figure and took every opportunity to show it off. She was particularly proud of her bosom, which she tended to use as a weapon of intimidation when she was in the company of other women. Amy and Trixie had got off on the wrong foot from the first time they met, when Amy had rung the doorbell to Bodkin's flat, only to see him emerge from the door of Trixie's ground-floor apartment.

When she stepped inside, she found Trixie sitting on the edge of Ferris's desk, her foot swinging idly as she waffled on, dropping hints about having no fixed plans for the weekend.

'Bodkin sent me in for the milk, Ferris.' Amy looked around the large office, which had half a dozen desks all furnished with a typewriter and a large blotting pad. 'I hear congratulations are in order.'

Ferris leapt to his feet. 'Damn. Apologise for me please, Amy, I meant to take a bottle in but I got... waylaid.' He flicked his head towards Trixie as he finished the sentence. After crossing the office floor, he picked up one of three bottles of milk that were sitting on an unused desk. 'Here you go and thank you for the kind words. I was really taken aback by the news. I honestly wasn't expecting it.'

'Is that your best suit?' Amy asked. 'I thought you saved that for the stage?'

'You've got to look the part. My other one is so shiny you can see your face in it.'

'No more ironing uniforms now,' Amy said. 'Will you have to get a new suit for your stage work?'

'Stan's on the job,' Ferris said. 'He's on the lookout for a second hand tux.' Stan was the owner of Stan's Emporium, a second-hand shop in the town.

'You'd better pick up another suit from him as well, because if you wear that one day in, day out, it will end up looking like Bodkin's.'

'Good thinking,' Ferris stuck up a thumb. 'I'll nip in at lunchtime.'

'Should you really be talking about Inspector Bodkin like that behind his back?' Trixie asked, turning up her nose as she looked Amy up and down. 'Did I see that dress on Lenny Steadman's market stall last week?'

'No, it's from Brigden's where I get all my clothes,' Amy replied. 'I don't buy clothes from market stalls, but I hope you found something nice.'

Trixie leapt to her feet as she scowled across the room at Amy.

'You've always got a clever answer, haven't you?' she spat. 'What are you doing in here, anyway? This place is out of bounds to the public.'

Amy pulled her accreditation card out of her pocket and flashed it at Trixie. 'I can go pretty much anywhere I like with this,' she said sweetly. 'But well done for checking my security clearance.'

Ferris put his hand over his mouth to suppress a laugh but couldn't disguise the sound that crept out. Trixie pouted as though she expected something better of him as Amy turned towards the door, carrying the milk bottle in her hands.

'Good luck on your first date, Ferris,' she said over her shoulder.

Trixie looked from Ferris to Amy, then back again. It was obviously unwelcome news to her. Amy stopped, then turned around to look at her crestfallen face. 'Didn't you know? He's got a new girlfriend. It's Lesley Philby from the Highwater Boat Club. She's very pretty. I thought everyone would have heard by now.' Smiling smugly to herself, Amy left the room and walked jauntily down the corridor to Bodkin's office. He had just finished his telephone conversation as she stepped back into the room. She waved the milk bottle at him.

'Is the kettle on?'

Bodkin got to his feet, shook the kettle, then poured water into it from the half full quart bottle that he had filled up at the tap, earlier.

'It is now,' he said.

Over their drinks, Bodkin told Amy about the purpose of his telephone call.

'I've just talked to the people at the Fullerton Veterinary Practice down in Sittingbourne. It seems we can rule out John Watkins as a suspect. They confirmed that he did pay a visit to a local farm to look at a couple of sick sheep on the evening in question. They've just billed the farmer for the treatment he carried out.'

'One off the list then,' Amy said. 'Have you ruled anyone else out?'

'No, everyone is a suspect until they aren't,' Bodkin replied.

'It's a good saying, Bodkin,' Amy replied. 'I reckon you'll have it chiselled onto your headstone.'

Bodkin looked up at the ceiling as if considering it.

'I was joking, Bodkin,' Amy said with a little laugh.

'It's better than what I had planned,' Bodkin replied. 'I was going to have, you're nicked, son.'

Amy almost choked on her tea. 'Oh, please keep that one,' she said. 'It's perfect.'

The policeman grinned.

'Talking about nicked, have you made any progress on the knickers nicker case?'

Bodkin nodded as he sipped at his tea. 'We have a description of him at last, if you could call it that. A lady came into the station yesterday to make a statement. She had observed the said knickers nicker in action on Saturday night.' He sorted through a pile of papers on his desk until he found the one he wanted, then he began to read.

*I had just finished washing the dinner plates in the scullery when I heard a noise outside. I looked out of the window to see a man at the bottom of my garden wearing nothing but a shirt. He was facing away from me, so I could see his bare backside. He then proceeded to pull on a pair of my silk knickers before then putting his trousers back on. I was annoyed about this because they were my best pair. I'd only worn them once, and that was to my niece's wedding. The man was about five foot eight tall with brown hair. I didn't see his face, but his bottom will stay with me for the rest of my life.*

*Irene Potts. Mrs.*

Amy snorted with laughter and held her hand in front of her

mouth. 'Oh my goodness, Bodkin,' she said through a fit of giggles.

'So, we're about to put out a wanted poster. Have you seen this arse?'

Amy doubled over, laughing. 'Oh, stop it! My stomach is hurting.'

When they had recovered their composure, Bodkin dropped the statement on top of the pile, then clasped his hands together. 'Right, back to the murder case. I made a few phone calls before you arrived and I've set up an interview with Joe Lyndsay later on today. I'm not sure if you want to be part of that one or not. I can understand if you'd rather sit that one out.'

'I so want to be in on that one, Bodkin,' Amy said, her mouth becoming a thin line.

'Okay, you're in. I'm also hoping to bump into the steward. He said he'd be around for most of the day. At some stage I'd like you to set up a meeting with old Angus. Don't tell him it's police related. Let him think you've succumbed to his charms. I want to catch him unprepared. In a few minutes, I'm going to make a call to the chemical plant to arrange a meeting with Granville Cresswell. I'll also demand that his nephew be around for a quick word too.' He unclasped his hands and folded his arms as he leaned back in his chair. 'What have you got on today? Do you have anything important to do?'

'Nothing at all,' Amy replied. 'I've been given some dresses that need repairing by Eileen at Brigden's but there's no hurry on those.'

'Excellent,' Bodkin said as he reached for the telephone. 'Because we're going to have a ride out to Rochester to have a chat with this Quentin... thingy-thingy... whatever his posh name is. He works at a laboratory down there.'

## CHAPTER
# THIRTY-THREE

Bodkin gave Amy a lift home to drop off the Brigden's dresses, then turned around, drove back up the lane and headed out of town towards Brompton. From there, they followed the river until they hit the outskirts of the historic city of Rochester. After taking a look at his hastily written notes, Bodkin continued following the river until they came to a collection of newly built industrial units. At the far end of a row of offices, they found Manners and Shelly Research Ltd. At the front of the large red brick building was a sign declaring the company's affiliation with the University of Cambridge.

Inside, they found a reception area where Bodkin presented his credentials. The young woman behind the desk picked up the phone, dialled an internal number, then, after a short conversation she put the phone down and smiled up at the inspector.

'Mr Foxley-Walton will be with you shortly.' She held out her hand, directing them to a row of soft-looking chairs. Amy sat down, but Bodkin remained on his feet, leaning against the wall.

Ten minutes later, a door opposite the desk opened and Foxley-Walton stepped into the room. It was obvious from his face that he resented the intrusion.

'Look, this really is inconvenient,' he said as he held the door open with his back and pointed through the gap to the corridor beyond. 'Step this way, there's a meeting room just along the corridor. It's empty, I checked.'

The meeting room was small and contained a pair of desks that had been pushed together with six chairs tucked underneath. On the wall at the far end of the room was a blackboard that looked like it had been recently wiped down.

Foxley-Walton held out his hand, first to Amy, then to the policeman. 'I'm sorry if I appear to be a little agitated but I'm in the middle of an experiment and it is time critical.'

'We won't keep you long, Mr Walton,' Bodkin said.

'Foxley-Walton,' Quentin corrected him.

'Ah, of course,' Bodkin said without apologising for his error. 'Shall we sit down?'

Quentin took a quick look at his watch. 'I'll stand, if you don't mind. Look, I'm aware your inquiries are important, but I do have an animal on the table in the lab and it won't stay anaesthetised for long.'

'You run animal experiments?' Amy looked at Quentin with distaste.

'It's important work, Miss... Rowlings, was it? Where do you think all the progress that has been made in modern medicine comes from? Our work is vital to the health of the nation. I know some don't like it, but they'll thank us when they're in hospital dying from a condition that we found a cure for.'

Amy grimaced, shook her head and bit her lip, not wanting to let the subject get in the way of Bodkin's questioning.

'I believe that you knew Effie Watkins,' Bodkin began.

'Poor Effie. Yes, I knew her quite well. I saw her at times when I visited the Milton Hotel in Spinton or the Highwater club.'

'At times? We've been led to believe you were a good friend of hers. You spent a lot of time together. Some people thought you were an item.'

'That's just plain wrong,' Quentin replied. 'We were just friends. We used to dance a bit at the Milton, but we were always in a crowd. We never spent much time alone.'

'I see. So you'd be surprised to learn that Effie saw you as a future husband then?'

Quentin coughed suddenly. 'No, she didn't. She knew I wasn't interested in her that way. She was always good fun, but I didn't want to get into a relationship with her.'

'So, you led her on... You allowed her to believe that there might be something there?'

'I never once hinted at it.'

'Well, I'm sorry to say the message didn't get through because she told her friends, many of them in the group you used to hang around with, that there was something between you, that the only barrier between the two of you and wedded bliss, was your parents, who expected you to land someone with a baronet or something similar in the family tree.'

'That's utter nonsense. I didn't mention Effie to them. They certainly never met her.'

'When did you see her last, Mr Walton?'

'Foxley!' Quentin hissed.

'When did you see her last, Mr Foxley.'

Quentin sighed. 'It was a couple of weeks ago. On the Friday. We met at the Milton in Spinton.'

'And was the gang there too... the rest of the bunch?'

'One or two.'

'Did you stay for long?'

'Until elevenish.'

'Where did you go then?'

'I went to bed. I had to get back early on Saturday. There was a progress meeting, and I had a report to hand in.'

'Was it really worth going all the way to Spinton after work on Friday evening then? Did you have something urgent to attend to up there?'

'No, I just wanted to unwind and listen to a bit of music. They have a good jazz band on at the Milton.'

'And there are no jazz bands in Rochester?'

'Yes, of course there are... Look, I like the atmosphere at the Milton, all right?'

'Perfectly all right,' Bodkin replied. 'So, what happened at eleven? That place is just warming up by then.'

'I was tired, I told you. I had an important meeting the following day, and I needed to get some sleep.'

'Where did you get that sleep?'

'I'm sorry?'

'It's a simple question. Where did you stay?'

Quentin pulled out a small bunch of keys from his pocket and began to fiddle about with them. 'The George Hotel. It's just down the road from the Milton.'

'You didn't stay at the Milton, then? Surely that would have been much easier.'

'The George is cheaper.'

Bodkin shrugged. 'Fair enough. Did Effie spend the night with you at the George?'

'No!'

Bodkin ran his hand across the stubble on his chin. 'You're sure about that. We can check?'

'You have no right to delve into my personal life,' Quentin wailed.

'I have every right, Mr Wa... Foxley. I'm conducting a murder inquiry.'

Quentin nodded his head. 'Okay, I understand. But the answer to your question is no. Effie did not spend the night with me. I left her at the Milton.'

'Who with?'

'Bertrand Cresswell and Joe Lyndsay... oh and a girl called, Jilly something'

'Were they in good spirits when you left? There hadn't been any arguments?'

'Everyone was in good spirits.'

'Thank you. Now, let's jump forward to the Saturday morning. What time did you leave?'

'I left the George at around eight o'clock. I skipped breakfast. As I said, I had an important meeting to attend.'

'Quite. And what time was that meeting?'

'Nine-thirty.'

'How many people attended?'

Quentin shrugged. 'I can't remember. There were a couple of heads of department. A girl taking notes... Finley Robertson... he's a member of my team. There were one or two others, but I can't remember exactly who they were.'

'Don't worry about that. I'll find out from reception,' Bodkin said with a quick smile. 'Now,' he rubbed his hands together. 'What did you get up to after the meeting?'

'For Christ's sake, what is this?' Quentin asked in an exasperated voice.

'I told you. It's a murder inquiry,' Bodkin said evenly.

Quentin dropped his bunch of keys, then bent down to pick them up again. 'I can't... oh yes, I do remember. I was tired, so I went back to my flat and caught up on a couple of hours' sleep. Then I drove over to Sittingbourne to see my parents. They were having a bit of a bash for my brother's degree celebrations.'

'How come you were so tired? Aren't the beds very comfortable at the George?'

'The beds are fine. I just didn't sleep well. I told you, the meeting was important and I couldn't clear my mind, so I had trouble sleeping.'

'Saturday night... did you stay over at your parents' house or did you drive back to Rochester... or even Highwater?'

'I drove back to my flat.'

'What time did you get back?'

'I'm not sure... about eleven.'

'You like to be in bed for eleven, don't you, Mr Fox?'

'For God's sake, man, it's Foxley-Walton. How difficult is it?'

Bodkin ignored the jibe. 'Any witnesses?'

'To what?' Quentin looked confused.

'As to what time you got home. Did anyone see you? Come on, Quentin. How difficult is it?'

Amy bit her cheeks and looked at her feet, trying hard not to laugh.

'No one saw me.' His defiance subsided.

'Did anyone see you on Sunday morning?'

'Sunday... no. I had a lie in. I caught up on some sleep.'

'Worrying about another urgent meeting?'

Quentin blew out his cheeks. 'No. I just like a few hours' extra sleep when I get the chance. I work long hours, Inspector.'

'So, did you see anyone at all on Sunday who can vouch for you?'

'There were plenty of regular drinkers at the Riverboat Inn. I got in there about one o'clock.'

'And when they chucked you out at two o'clock when they closed? Oh, don't tell me, you went home for a nap?'

Quentin nodded, then looked nervously down at his watch. 'Look, I really do have to go. That dog will be waking up soon.'

'DOG!' Amy exclaimed. 'What on earth are you doing to the poor creature?'

Bodkin gave Amy a quick shake of his head, then stepped towards the door. 'One last question. Do you use chloroform in your laboratory?'

Quentin nodded. 'Of course. We also use ether.'

. . .

Bodkin smiled. 'Thank you for your time, Mr Foxley-Walton. We'll be in touch if we need to speak to you again.'

'I don't trust him at all, Bodkin,' Amy said when they were back in the car. 'He was as nervous as a kitten.'

'I'd be a nervous kitten if I was anywhere near his laboratory,' Bodkin replied.

'It's not something to joke about, Bodkin,' Amy said, looking down at her clasped hands.

'No, you're right, I'm sorry, Amy.'

'He's lying. I'm not sure what about, but you could almost smell the fear coming off him. He's worried that we'll find something out when we dig into his alibi.'

'I agree,' Bodkin replied as he started up the Morris and pulled away from the kerb. 'And if he is hiding something, I'll find out what it is. Make no mistake about that.'

'Where to now?' Amy asked as Bodkin pulled onto the main road and headed back along the river towards Brompton.

Bodkin checked his watch. 'First, we're going to find somewhere to have a spot of lunch, then we're going to meet up with Joking Joe at the Boat Club.'

# CHAPTER THIRTY-FOUR

On arriving at the Boat Club, they found Joe Lyndsay and Timothy Philby sitting at the bar, drinking whisky. Neither bothered to get off their seats when Bodkin and Amy stepped into the room, although Joe's jaw dropped when he noticed Amy.

Bodkin introduced himself, then said. 'I believe you have already met Miss Rowlings.'

'Have you reported me to the police?' Joe snapped, glaring at Amy.

'Miss Rowlings is assisting the police with our inquiries, but not the same way that you are,' Bodkin replied coldly. He turned to Amy. 'Show them your accreditation.'

Amy pulled her white card out of her bag and handed it to Joe. He took a long look, turned it over and looked at the back carefully before handing it to Timothy.

'So, you were here to spy on us,' Joe said with a note of distaste in his voice.

'I was here to enjoy the ball, as was my friend Alice,' Amy replied with a smile. 'Although I made some notes when I got home.'

'Is there somewhere we can go that's a little more private?' Bodkin asked as Gerald walked into the bar carrying an empty glass.

Timothy handed Amy's card back. 'We could use the ladies' cloakroom, there's no one in at the moment.'

'Why don't we use your office?' Bodkin suggested. 'The one you used when you entertained Effie Watkins.'

Timothy's face reddened. 'I don't see what's wrong with the—'

'I prefer an office to a cloakroom,' Bodkin said. 'It's cosier, don't you think?' He looked at Philby through narrowed eyes.

'If you insist,' Philby said, lifting his backside off the stool.

'We'll speak to Mr Lyndsay first, if you don't mind,' Bodkin said. 'Don't get up, Mr Philby. I'm sure the skipper knows where it is.' He turned his attention to Joe, who downed what was left of his drink and slid off his seat.

They followed Joe towards a narrow corridor a little further down from the bar. Just before he entered it, Bodkin turned back to the bar. 'Don't go anywhere, Mr Philby. I'll give you a shout when we want you.'

'Do you want me too?' Gerald asked.

'Do you have anything you want to tell me that might be relevant to my inquiry?' Bodkin asked.

Gerald shook his head. 'Probably not,' he said.

Joe opened the door to Philby's office and stepped inside. Bodkin hung back to allow Amy to enter before him, then, once inside himself, he closed the door and walked around the desk. Philby's comfortable chair had been pushed underneath. Pulling a second chair from a set of three which lined one of the walls, Bodkin slid it across the floor to Joe. 'Sit down please, Mr Lyndsay.'

Joe remained on his feet as Bodkin dragged another chair

across the floor to use himself. 'You have the comfy one,' he said to Amy. He pointed to the white smears that ran across the edge of the desk in front of her. 'But I'd keep your hands well away from that stuff.'

Bodkin nodded to the chair on the far side of the desk and once again instructed the club captain to sit. This time he did, albeit reluctantly.

Joe turned his angry face towards Amy. 'So, let's have it. What have you been accusing me of doing?'

Before Amy could reply, Bodkin spoke. 'Miss Rowlings hasn't accused you of anything, Mr Lyndsay, but what happened late on Saturday night might come up in the conversation we are about to have.'

'I offered her a lift home. She was drunk. I don't care what she says, that's all it was. An offer to help a young woman who might have found herself in a spot of bother if I hadn't stepped in.'

'I said we might come to that at some stage, Mr Lyndsay. For now, how well did you know Effie Watkins?'

'We had mutual friends, so I used to see her about a bit.'

'A bit? It was more than that, wasn't it? Quite a few people thought you were an item.'

'That's just not true. We were friends, no more than that.'

'You weren't lovers, then?'

'Lovers!' Joe spluttered. 'Look, Inspector, I'm a gentleman. I don't discuss that sort of thing with anyone.'

'I'll take that as a yes, then,' Bodkin said.

'Take it any way you like.'

'Are you denying she stayed over at your house?'

Joe thought about it. He looked away from Bodkin's piercing gaze as he considered his response.

'It's quite a simple question,' Bodkin said.

'I don't know who's been talking behind my back, but I'm

rather uncomfortable answering these questions while she's in the room.' He turned his face towards Amy. 'She's not a policewoman. She has no right to be here.' He checked his watch. 'I'm pushed for time. I'll have to leave soon. I have a meeting at three o'clock.'

'Miss Rowlings has police accreditation which you've seen, Mr Lyndsay but, if you insist on her leaving the room, I'll agree to your demands.' He looked towards Amy, then back to Joe, who sat with a smirk on his face. 'However. As Miss Rowlings has an insight into some of the questions I intend to ask, I can assure you that things would move along much more smoothly if she was in the room with us. Otherwise, if I need to clarify a point, I'd have to go out into the corridor, confer with her, then come back and ask you a secondary question. That might lead to another one, and another.' Bodkin looked at his own watch. 'We could be here all afternoon, and you have an important meeting to attend in what... an hour's time?'

Joe blew out his cheek, then snapped his fingers. 'Oh, have it your way, but if she repeats a word of anything she hears in this room, she'll have my lawyer to answer to.' He glared at Amy, then at Bodkin. 'In fact, it might be a good idea to have him here as I answer these questions.'

'If you want him here, just pick up the telephone. But people a little further up the chain of command than me might wonder what you have to hide. You aren't being questioned as a murder suspect, Mr Lyndsay. This is just a chat, to clear one or two things up.'

Joe looked at his watch. 'Look, I really do have to be elsewhere this afternoon. Let's get it over with.'

'I think that's for the best, Joe. You don't mind me calling you Joe?'

He shrugged and said nothing.

'Okay, now that we're all friends again, let's get back to the matter at hand. When did you last see Effie?'

'A couple of weeks back, I can't really remember the exact date and time.'

'How about the Friday before she was murdered?'

Joe shrugged again. 'I don't think so… Look, I honestly can't remember. I see a lot of people. I have a lot of friends.'

'But you don't sleep with them all, do you, Joe?'

'No, of course I don't.' He pulled his head back and looked at the ceiling. 'I believe I was out on that Friday and I could have seen her. It's all rather vague.'

'It was ten days ago, Mr Lyndsay. Surely your memory isn't that poor.'

'I'd had… we all had rather a lot to drink that night. It's a bit hazy.'

'I might be able to help you a bit with that,' Bodkin said. 'But let's see what you can remember first. Who were you with?'

Joe rubbed his chin. 'Bertrand Cresswell. He was there.'

'And…'

'Jilly Partington. I think she was there.'

'And Quentin Foxley-Walton?'

'Ah, yes, he was with us.'

Bodkin applauded. 'Wonderful, it's all coming back. You see, it wasn't that hard, was it?'

Joe looked at his hands and said nothing.

'The person missing from your list is Effie.'

'All right. She was there, sponging off us all as usual.'

'Sponging? You didn't offer to buy her drinks, then? You didn't include her in the rounds. She had to beg you for drinks?'

'No. Perhaps sponging was a little strong.'

'Where did you go that night, Mr Lyndsay?'

'The George first, then the Milton.'

'How did you get there?'

'I drove.'

'Were you alone in the car? Where did you meet up with your friends?'

'I was alone in the car. I met up with Jilly and Effie in the George. Then we walked around to the Milton.'

'What time did you meet up with Quentin?'

'I honestly can't remember... probably nine, nine-fifteen.'

'And Bertrand, when did he arrive?'

'He was already there, with Quentin.'

'Right, and then you all got rather plastered. What else happened? Was there a band on? Did you dance?'

'There was a band. I danced with Jilly.'

'Not with Effie?'

'No, she was all over Quentin. She had a thing for him. A big thing,'

'Were her feelings reciprocated? Did he have a thing for her?'

'I've no idea but she always used to throw herself at him. It was embarrassing, really.'

'For whom?'

'Oh, you know... her, him... it's just a saying.'

'So, as the night wore on, did you continue buying drinks for Effie?'

'Probably. I just ordered up refills as they were required.'

'What about Quentin and Bertrand? Didn't they put their hands in their pockets?'

'The odd time. I've got an account there, so I just run up a bar bill and pay it at the end of the night.'

'How much was it on this occasion?'

'I honestly can't remember. I mean it. I just handed over a fiver at the end of the night. It covered my share of the drinks and a decent tip.'

'A fiver? You must have really put some away.'

Joe shrugged again.

'What time did it all break up?'

'I don't know... late.'

'What time do you call late?'

'About midnight.'

'And you were all together still, drinking and dancing?'

Joe nodded.

'When it all broke up, what happened then? Who left with whom?'

'I left alone. Jilly got a taxi as she lives down the Gillingham Road.'

'And Effie, Quentin and Bertrand?'

'No idea. I assume they stayed for a while longer. Quentin always books a room at the George when he comes up. Effie may have spent the night with him.'

Bodkin rubbed at the stubble on his chin. 'I'm going to ask you that question one more time, Joe, and if you lie to me again, I think you will have to call your lawyer because I'll arrest you for obstructing the police during a murder inquiry.'

Joe gulped. His eyes shot towards Amy. He stared hard at her as he tried to work out what she had learned about him at the ball. Finally, he held up his hands. 'All right. Effie came home with me.'

'In your car. You didn't get a taxi?'

'No. I drove.'

'Despite the fact that you were under the influence of alcohol?'

'I could see well enough to drive.'

'Mr Lyndsay. Are you aware that under the Road Traffic Act of nineteen-thirty, it is illegal to drive, attempt to drive or be in charge of a motor vehicle on a road or public place while being under the influence of drink or a drug to such an extent as to be incapable of having proper control of the vehicle?'

'I wasn't under... I was quite lucid.'

'It's irrelevant now as I can't prove one way or the other that you drove your car whilst drunk.'

'So why quote the law to me?'

'For future reference, Mr Lyndsay. Try to remember next time you're out and about. Get a taxi, or a bus if you're a bit short of cash.'

Joe pulled a face but said nothing.

'Right then, back to that Friday evening. What happened to Effie? She was in your car?'

'Yes.'

'How did she get in, Joe? Did she climb in herself or did you bundle her forcibly into the car, the same way you tried to force Miss Rowlings on Saturday night?'

'Listen. I did nothing wrong on Saturday night. I've already told you she was drunk. I was trying to help her.' He glared across the table at Amy. 'If she says anything different, she's lying.'

Bodkin shook his head, 'Joe... Joe... There was a witness to your attack on Miss Rowlings... ME!'

'What? Where...'

'I was the private hire driver, Joe. I saw it all. As for accusing Miss Rowlings of lying. You ought to think yourself lucky she isn't pressing charges against you for assault.'

Joe sighed, then ran his hand through his hair. 'I'm sorry,' he said.

'Don't apologise to me. I wasn't the one you tried to manhandle into your car.'

Joe looked at his knees, then raised his head to look across the desk at Amy. 'I'm sorry. I was out of order.'

'You were,' Amy replied curtly.

Bodkin clapped his hands. 'I bet you feel so much better for getting that off your chest, Joe. Now, let's get back to Effie. Did you drop her off or take her to your flat?'

Joe hung his head, defeated. 'My flat.'

'Did she stay the night with you?'

'Yes,' Joe mumbled, not looking up.

'What time did she leave the next day, or did you make a day of it in bed?'

'She left about ten-ish.'

'To go where?'

'The Boat Club, I think.'

'You didn't go to the club yourself?'

Joe shook his head. 'No. I had to go over something with my dad. Business... you know?'

'What is it you do, Joe?'

'I'm a consultant for my dad's firm. We manage share accounts.'

'But you're not based in London?'

'Dad is. I don't go into the city that often. I just study the financial pages and give advice to our local clients. Dad does all the work, really. I'll take over when he retires.'

'So you don't really have a regular job, that's what you're telling me.'

'I get a lot of free time. But I do my bit.'

'Did you see Effie again after you said goodbye at ten o'clock on the Saturday morning?' Bodkin asked.

'No, I never saw her again after that.'

'Did you come to the club on the Saturday night?'

'Yes.'

'But Effie wasn't here?'

'No. She didn't turn up. She said she'd be in, but she wasn't.'

'Right,' Bodkin looked at his watch. 'A couple more questions, then you can go. You'll still be in time for your meeting.'

Joe checked his own watch and nodded. 'Fire away.'

'Did you come to the club on Sunday?'

'No.'

'So you wouldn't know if anyone took a speedboat out that day?'

'No, I can't help you. I wasn't here at all on the Sunday.'

Bodkin got to his feet and opened the office door. 'Thank you, Mr Lyndsay. That will be all for now. Could you ask Mr Philby to come in?'

# CHAPTER THIRTY-FIVE

Timothy Philby slunk into his own office like a man expecting to hear bad news. Seeing Amy in his chair, he shuffled across to the other side of the desk, tugging nervously at his stiff collar. Then, after taking a quick glance at the desk in front of where Amy was sitting, turned his attention to Bodkin.

'So, what's this all about?' His voice cracked as he spoke, beads of sweat appeared on his brow.

'You're looking rather nervous, Mr Philby,' Bodkin said. 'But there's no need. This is just a friendly chat.'

Philby pulled out a handkerchief and dabbed at his brow. 'Sorry, I feel a little hot. I might be coming down with something.'

'Let's hope it's nothing serious,' Bodkin replied. 'Let's get down to it. Then you can take an aspirin or something.'

Philby ran the side of his finger back and forth under his nose. 'What do you want to know?'

'Tell us something about yourself, for starters,' Bodkin said. 'What is it you do? How do you make a living?'

'I own a number of properties in the area. I get good rents from them as some of them are business premises. I have a few hundred acres of arable land that are managed for me, and I own half of this place.' He waved his hand to the side.

'And you're the steward? I find that a bit odd. Wouldn't you just employ someone to perform that role? You say your farms are managed, why not this place too?' Bodkin looked a little puzzled.

'I enjoy running the club.'

'Isn't being seen as merely a steward a little demeaning though, especially as you're really the joint owner? Do you take a wage?'

Philby nodded. 'Every little helps. Anyway. It gives me something to do with my free time and I have a lot of it. As for the title, everyone knows I'm the owner... or one of them, at least.'

'Who is your partner in the enterprise?'

'Angus McIntosh.'

'Does the club make a profit?'

Philby nodded again. 'It makes a good profit. Especially the bar sales. We hold a lot of events here, including non-member weddings, birthday parties and the like. Then there's the annual membership. We have over three hundred members. Not all of them are active, but they pay their dues every year. That brings in a tidy sum. We also rent out boats and provide training in river craft.'

'I suppose there's an added bonus to being the steward. You get to vet the new members. Especially the young female ones.'

'I don't know what you're implying?'

'Just that you get to run your expert eye over every potential female member when she applies.'

'I don't always. Lesley does a lot of that.'

'But you have the final say. Like when Amy applied for membership?'

'I ran a quick background check regarding her references.' He turned to Amy and wagged his finger as he tutted. 'You really shouldn't go around deceiving people like the McKenzies. They are pillars of our community.'

'I didn't deceive anyone, Mr Philby,' Amy replied. 'The McKenzies really are acquaintances of mine. Good friends, in fact. Shirley and I have tea together regularly and Robert has been very helpful whenever I've asked for his help with anything.' She paused and tilted her head to the side as she thought. 'I probably know them much better than you do.'

'It was underhand. You were sent here to spy. I'm sure the mayor wouldn't condone that.'

'I wanted to join the club, Mr Philby. It was as simple as that.' Amy smiled sweetly at him. 'Were Effie's references as good as mine?'

'I can't remember,' Philby sniffed. 'As I said, Lesley deals with the new applicants if they show up at the club.'

'Did Effie just turn up? Was she recommended by anyone? Who were her referees? You must have some idea if you checked them.' Bodkin stared intently at the steward.

Philby rubbed his aquiline nose between his finger and thumb. 'I honestly can't—'

'I'll ask Lesley then. She'll know. I'm determined to get answers to these questions.'

'I don't think she provided references, now I think about it,' Philby said. 'Ah, I remember. I was in the bar when she came through the door. She was a nice, friendly girl. Obviously well brought up, so I signed her application straight away.'

'Did anyone else witness this?'

Philby thought about it. 'No, I was the only one in the bar at the time. As I said, she was a very personable young lady... or so I believed at the time.'

'Indeed. When did you find out she wasn't as personable as you first thought?'

'It took a while. She was a very good actress.'

'Did you bring her here after you signed her application?' Bodkin opened up his arms. 'To your little love nest.'

Philby choked as he tried to reply. 'Once again, I don't know what you're implying?'

'I'm suggesting that you invited young Effie into your office and locked the door, to check her credentials a little more thoroughly.'

Philby got to his feet. 'I don't have to sit here and listen to this nonsense.'

'You don't,' Bodkin agreed. 'We can have a chat in my office at the police station, if that's what you prefer.'

Philby slumped back into his chair. 'I still don't like what you're inferring. I don't invite young women into my office... not alone, anyway.'

'Really! Yet you spent quite a bit of time last Saturday evening trying to tempt Miss Rowlings into spending fifteen minutes alone with you? Didn't you try to persuade her that she'd quite enjoy the experience?'

'If I did, then I apologise,' Philby said, looking directly at Amy. 'I was a bit the worse for wear, as were you, if I remember correctly.'

'Yes, but I wasn't the one making sordid proposals,' Amy said, narrowing her eyes at Philby.

'We know you had Effie alone in your office on more than one occasion, Mr. Philby. We have a witness.' Bodkin leant towards Philby, then eased back in his chair.

'That doesn't mean anything untoward went on.'

'I don't suppose there is any proof. We can't ask Effie. She's dead.'

'That is a shame,' Philby said quietly.

'One thing I'm curious about,' Bodkin rubbed at the stubble on his chin, 'did Effie get to sample your... what shall we call it... medication when she was here?'

A puzzled look came over Philby's face. 'I have no idea what you are talking about?'

Bodkin pointed to the desk. 'The medication you like to share with your friends behind a locked door. An illegal substance that a group of the older members had stuck to their nasal hairs when they left this office on Saturday night.' Bodkin nodded towards the desk again. 'The evidence is still smeared all over the surface.'

'It's not illegal if a doctor prescribes it.'

'Are your friends all listed on the prescription?' Bodkin pulled out his notebook and pen. 'Who is this doctor? I'd like to have a word with him.'

'A dentist can prescribe too, and you have no proof that anyone other than me took the medication.'

'The cocaine,' Bodin corrected him.

'Whatever.'

'You're right, Mr Philby. We don't have the evidence, but we do know you use the substance on a regular basis. I can take a sample and send it off to our labs if you like. They'll be able to tell you if you're getting a good quality product.' He paused and tapped the notebook with his pen. 'Who prescribes cocaine for your personal use? Would it be Ronald Parkin, by any chance?'

Philby shook his head. 'I'm not going to go into that without having a lawyer present.'

Bodkin put his notebook away and began to twist the pen in his fingers. 'That's very loyal. He must be a very good friend of yours.'

'I'm not saying it was him. I'm just saying I won't talk about it without advice.'

'I'll give you some advice, Timothy,' Bodkin said, pointing his finger at the sweating man. 'Answer my questions honestly and truthfully without the slightest attempt at evasion, and you might walk out of this office without being charged with obstruction.'

Philby leaned over his knees and rubbed his sweating palms together. 'All right. Let's get on with it.'

'How often did you and Effie get together privately?'

Philby squirmed in his seat. 'Once a week. Sometimes twice.'

'And you didn't mind sharing her with your mates?'

'I didn't know about what she was up to... not at first, anyway.'

'And when you found out. Were you angry? Did you pull her up about it?'

Philby's head dropped to his chest. 'To begin with, she said that Angus and Granville were just friends who used to take her out for dinner. Then I found out they had been buying her clothes, giving her money. You don't do that for someone who is just a friend.'

'So, were you angry with her?'

'Of course I was angry but, Inspector, believe me, you couldn't stay angry at her for long. One look from those big blue eyes of hers and you'd forgive her anything.'

'And you forgave her a lot by the sounds of it.'

'She said she had to do what she did to survive. She said she didn't like doing it but had no choice.'

'Was she seeing Joe at the time?'

'No, Joe came later. That was very recent. It was all over between Effie and me by that time.'

'You still classed Angus McIntosh and Granville Cresswell as friends, even after doing that behind your back. Weren't you angry with them? I know I couldn't have continued a relationship knowing what was going on.'

Philby looked almost pleadingly at Bodkin. 'I loved her. I wanted to be with her all the time.'

'She was twenty-odd years younger than you, Timothy. She was a reckless girl, a free spirit. It was never going to work out.'

'I know that now, but I was besotted with her and she did encourage me. She led me to believe that she felt the same way.'

'So you asked her to marry you?'

'Yes. It was a bloody stupid thing to do, especially the way I went about it.'

'She turned you down in public. That must have hurt.' Bodkin looked sadly at Philby.

'She humiliated me in the ballroom. They were all there, Granville, Angus, the Parkins... I've never been so embarrassed in my life.'

'Why the Hell did you do it? I mean, you left yourself wide open to ridicule.'

'She had convinced me that the only reason she saw other men was that she had nothing of her own and she used them to survive. She hated the thought of having to work for a living, the lazy little... I offered her a job in the bar here and she looked at me as though I'd asked her to lick the floor clean with her tongue. I thought that if I offered to marry her, to give her all the things she wanted, she'd leave all that behind her. What I didn't know was that's what she lived for. She loved doing what she did, leading men on, then dumping them when she'd had her fill.' He paused as he dropped his head again. 'She made Angus and Granville look foolish, but not in public. She didn't hurt them the way she hurt me.'

'Tell me about the night you proposed, Timothy,' Bodkin leaned back in his chair and clasped his hands in front of him. Amy hid a smile. Bodkin sounded like a psychiatrist helping a patient get to the bottom of their problem.

'I had been building up to it for a while. I almost asked her when I took her for dinner at Hoskin's one night, but Angus came in and sat at our table without being invited, so that put the kibosh on that. I took her into Spinton one afternoon and got her to look at some rings in a jeweller's window. I was dropping hints, pointing at the engagement rings. Some of them were bloody expensive too, but she didn't latch on to what I was getting at… or she did and just ignored it. I finally broached the subject when we were lying in bed one night.' He flashed a quick look at Amy, then looked away again. 'I asked her if she was ready to settle down and she said that she might be if the right man came along. So I asked her if she thought I might be a candidate. She leaned over, kissed me and said, why not? Then she went on to say she'd always dreamed of a rich, handsome man going down on one knee to ask for her hand.'

He was silent for a moment, then went on. 'I took that to mean that she would marry me if I asked. Over the next week, I worked out exactly how I'd do it. I really thought she'd be both pleased and excited about what I had planned. She'd be the centre of attention where she always liked to be, and she'd get the romantic proposal she'd always dreamed of. Not that I considered myself to be handsome, and I'm nowhere near as wealthy as Granville and Angus, but I'm hardly poverty-stricken either. We could have lived comfortably on my income.'

Bodkin continued to sit quietly as he listened to Philby.

'So, I chose the Saturday night when everyone would be there. In my mind's eye, I could picture the scene. A tearful Effie saying, 'of course I'll marry you,' while the jealous Granville, Angus and the rest of the men, looked on. I bought the ring I'd spotted at the jewellers; I didn't know if it was her size or not but the jeweller promised he'd resize it for me if required. She was going to be dolled up to the nines in the new outfit I'd bought her during the week. Everything was set up perfectly. I'd even got a magnum or two of Bollinger on ice.'

'Oh, Timothy,' Amy said sadly.

Tears filled Philby's eyes as he went on. 'I waited until everyone had taken a drink or two, then I walked down to the stage and asked everyone to join me. When they were all congregated on the dance floor, I invited Effie on to the stage. She gave me the sweetest smile as she climbed the steps. I thought to myself, she knows what's coming, and she's happy about it.' He paused and shook his head. 'How wrong could I have been? I motioned her to stand next to me, then I pulled out the ring box, got down on one knee and took hold of her hand. 'Effie, would you do me the greatest honour and agree to be my wife?' There were a few gasps and even a couple of ahs from the crowd, and I could hardly breathe as I awaited her response. She didn't say yes, as she had so many times in my dreams. She just sort of snorted, 'Marry you?' Then dissolved into a fit of laughter, which, sad to say, many of the audience joined in with.'

Philby leaned back in his chair and stared into space. 'I was beyond devastated. It wasn't just the humiliation although that was bad enough. It was the fact that I'd got it so wrong. I stood there, dumfounded, while Effie took the ring box, had a look at the contents, then shoved it back into my hand with a look of distaste, as though I'd given her a brass curtain ring or something. I walked down from the stage in a sort of trance and made my way here. People were sniggering as I passed. All my daughter could say was, 'Oh, Dad'. I locked myself in for the rest of the night with the bottle of scotch I keep in the drawer and my... prescription.'

'That's a very sad story, Mr Philby,' Bodkin said eventually. 'You must have wanted to get revenge pretty badly after that.'

Philby shook his head. 'No, not really. I'd have forgiven her if she'd climbed into my bed again. I did ask her, you know? A couple of months later, but she just gave me a peck on the cheek and called me an old softie. She was seeing Joe by then.'

'When was the last time you saw her?' Bodkin asked.

'It would have been the Saturday before they found her body. She was in the bar at lunchtime until about four-thirty, maybe five o'clock. She made a telephone call from the wall phone in the cloakroom and then left. I thought she'd booked a taxi.'

'You could see her in the cloakroom?'

'Oh yes. The door was still propped open from when the cleaners had been in earlier in the day.'

'How many other people were in the club at the time? Did you see anyone follow her out?'

'She didn't leave straight away. She finished her drink and left about fifteen minutes later. There were only a handful of people in. No one followed her out as far as I can remember.'

'One thing puzzles me,' Amy said thoughtfully. 'Why on earth didn't you just bar her from the club? I'm sure people would have understood.'

'She was a money spinner, Miss Rowlings. Angus wouldn't hear of it, and he's my partner in the club. A lot of men spent a lot of money in the bar when she was in. She was an asset really and anyway, as I said, I still hoped to get close to her again one day. Even if it was just the odd night here and there. I missed her in my bed.'

'Did Angus or Granville ever talk about her to you?' Bodkin asked.

'No, despite everything, they are good friends of mine. They wouldn't want to rub the salt into my gaping wounds. Anyway, the pair of them suffered similar fates themselves. They were both disposed of like a tatty dish cloth. Not quite as publicly, though.'

'And your daughter? How did she deal with it all? She must have felt almost as humiliated as you did.'

'Lesley? She was humiliated by our relationship long before the catastrophe of that night. She'd been calling me a silly old fool for weeks. She knew how it would end. She just told me that I'd got everything I deserved. She didn't stop talking to Effie, though I think a certain frostiness developed. Especially when she got her claws into Joe. Lesley clung onto Joe's every word, though he was never the slightest bit interested in her.'

'Can you think of anyone else who might have had a reason to exact revenge on her?' Bodkin asked.

'Half the members of the club for one reason or another,' Philby said. 'Most of the wives and girlfriends, I imagine. Some of them were made to look very foolish too.'

Bodkin got to his feet. 'Right, that's it for now, Mr Philby. We'll probably want to talk to you again, but we know where to find you.'

'About the, erm...' Philby pointed to the smeared area of the desk.

'I have no proof that it was you who left those marks, Timothy, but I'd make sure your drawers are empty and the cleaners have been in the next time I turn up. It might not be Miss Rowlings accompanying me then. It might be a senior officer who you can bet won't be as easy-going as I am.'

Bodkin and Amy left Philby standing by the door of his office and walked back through the bar to the entrance. Outside, they had just begun to traverse the boardwalk when they heard a voice from behind. Bodkin turned to find Gerald puffing along towards them.

Amy turned around to face him, carefully watching his hands.

'I was thinking there's something you ought to know,' he began. 'I just heard Joe using the telephone behind the bar. I don't know who he was talking to but whoever it was, he was telling them about the interview he'd just had with you and he went into great detail about it.'

Bodkin smiled at the old man. 'Thank you for that... Gerald, is it?'

'Gerald, yes... but that's not the thing I want to tell you. You see, when he was on the telephone, Joe told whoever it was that he had denied being at the club on the Sunday. It was as if he was setting up an alibi. My point is, he was here on the Sunday. I saw him in the boat sheds tinkering with one of the motorboats.'

# CHAPTER THIRTY-SIX

Spinton Lane was a wide, mostly uncared for road that lay between the small, well-to-do town of Highwater and the mostly industrial, much larger town of Spinton. Lined by a pair of deep ditches, backed with thick hedgerows, the lane was wide enough to easily allow two cars or even a car and a lorry to pass each other safely.

After leaving the Boat Club, Bodkin drove past the church and the green with its line of small shops and businesses, then turned left onto the lane. A hundred yards further along, he stopped, pulled on the handbrake, switched off the engine, and got out of the car. After walking around to the passenger door, he opened it and held out a hand to Amy. 'Come on then,' he said. 'Let's have you in the driver's seat.'

Amy gasped. 'Do you mean it? I thought you couldn't... I mean, I thought they wouldn't... Oh, never mind what I thought.' She slid off the seat and almost ran around the front of the car to get to the other side. Slipping hurriedly on to the driver's seat, she grabbed hold of the steering wheel and stared fixedly over the bonnet.

Bodkin grinned as he pulled the passenger door shut and

dropped a hand onto the brake lever, which was situated between the two front seats. 'Okay, here's a quick run through. This,' he patted the lever, 'is the handbrake. You pull this up to stop the car rolling down a hill after you've parked.'

'Got it,' Amy said, before turning away to look along the lane again.

'These,' Bodkin said, reaching across to tap the gear lever which was attached to the steering column, 'are your gears. There are three of them. You pull away in first, then, when you're moving nicely, you slip it into second,' Bodkin pushed down on the stick. 'Then, when you're really rolling along, you move it into third gear like this,' he manoeuvred the stick into the required position, 'and the car can tootle along at top speed.' He slipped the stick into the neutral position. 'Shift the stick to this position before you start the car and when you pull up.' Bodkin held his hand out to Amy. 'You have a go.'

Amy stuck up her thumb confidently, then began to manoeuvre the gearshift between the positions. Bodkin's mouth dropped open. 'My Go... sorry... You did that like you've been driving for years.'

'I don't just sit looking out of the window when I'm in the car with you. I watch you closely to see what you're doing. I even watch your knees go up and down when you're fiddling with your thingy... Gear stick,' she added.

Bodkin shook his head slowly. 'All I can say is you pick things up very quickly.'

'Oh, I forgot to tell you that I used to practise in my Uncle Maurice's car. He's got a Ford, and it's the same, really.'

'So you know which pedals do what? Or do I need to explain them to you?'

'Accelerator on the right, clutch on the left, and brake in the middle,' Amy said confidently. 'I push my foot down on the left pedal whenever I fiddle with the stick.'

'Correct,' Bodkin said. 'Did you ever actually get the car rolling when you were in with your uncle?'

'Only up and down his street, and only when there were no kids playing on it.'

Bodkin nodded again. 'Okay, Amy, this might be a little easier than I thought it might be. I'm going to start the engine now. Put your foot gently on the right-hand pedal until the engine revs a bit, but don't touch the gear stick yet.'

Amy did as she was asked, then gently put more pressure on the pedal until the engine became louder.

'Very good,' Bodkin said. 'Now, I'm going to take off the hand-brake, so I'd like you to keep your foot where it is now on the right pedal. Then, with your other foot, push the left pedal right down to the floor.'

Amy did as she was asked.

'Okay, now for the tricky bit. While the left pedal is pushed down, move the gear stick into the first gear position then slowly ease...'

Before he could finish the sentence, Amy slipped the car into gear and slowly raised her foot on the clutch until the car began to roll forward.

'Well done, Uncle Maurice,' Bodkin muttered as Amy, her face locked in concentration, drove the car down the lane at a speed of around three miles per hour.

'Concentrate on keeping the car in a straight line, Amy. Don't change up gear, we'll do that another time. For now, just keep it steady as we go.'

Amy shot a look to her left. 'What happens if something comes the other way?'

'In that case, I'd like you to steer gradually towards the verge until the two left hand tyres are on the grass, then dip your clutch, take your foot off the accelerator and slip the stick into neutral. I'll apply the hand brake, that ought to stop us at this speed.'

'Righto, Bodkin.' Amy leaned forward and stared over the top of the steering wheel, her foot gradually applying more pressure on the accelerator. The speed picked up to five miles an hour as she steered a dead straight line down the centre of the lane.

'Don't get too carried away,' Bodkin said. 'We're not the Keystone Cops chasing Buster Keaton, remember?'

After another two hundred yards, Bodkin asked Amy to steer slowly towards the grass verge, then as the wheels ran up it, she did as she had been instructed. Bodkin stuck up a thumb as he applied the handbrake.

'Very well done, Amy. I'm impressed.'

'Can we do it some more? Please, Bodkin, let me have another go. If you turn it around, I'll drive back up the other way. It's on the flat, so I should be able to do pretty much the same thing.' She looked at him, her eyes wide with excitement.

Bodkin smiled at her enthusiasm. 'Get out then, stand on the verge and I'll turn it around.'

Three minutes later, Amy was happily steering the car back towards Highwater, and Bodkin was becoming increasingly confident in her abilities. After two hundred yards, he called out, 'Okay, time for second gear. Ease off the pressure with the right foot as you change up.'

Amy clutched the steering wheel tighter with one hand, then after giving Bodkin a big, excited grin, she slipped the gearstick into second. The car lurched a little, but she soon had the correct pressure on the pedal, and their speed increased to ten miles an hour. Amy screamed with delight. 'I'm doing it, Bodkin, I'm driving!'

Back at the cottage on Long Lane, Amy picked up the third postcard from her mum from the doormat and carried it into the living room, reading it aloud.

*Dear Amy.*

*The weather continues to be good. It was a bit cloudy on Friday, so we went to have a look at the Margate caves. In the evening we played Bingo at the Ship Inn, and I won five shillings. Dad spent some of it on a cone of cockles that a local man brought into the pub. He soon wished he hadn't. He was up all night. I won't go into the sordid details.*

*Tomorrow we're taking a coach trip to Herne Bay and if we have time, we might get to see Whitstable again.*

*I hope this card finds you well, my dear. Say hello to Bodkin for us.*

*Mum and Dad.*

*xxx*

Amy put the card on the dining table, then walked through to the kitchen to put the kettle on.

'You've had a mention in all three postcards, Bodkin,' Amy said as she lit the hob. 'I don't know if she thinks I'm going to forget all about you while they're away, but she's not taking any chances.'

Bodkin laughed. 'What time are they due back on Saturday?'

'They'll leave mid-afternoon. They have to be out of the guest house for twelve, so they'll have a long lunch before they take a last walk down the promenade and get the train around three-ish. The train only takes an hour and a bit to get to Gillingham and it's only twenty minutes from there to Spinton once they pick up the connection. They'll be home for about half-past five.'

'Shall we surprise them and pick them up at the station? Save them catching a bus,' Bodkin said.

'That's a very kind thought, Bodkin. Are we still going out on Saturday night? Sal is coming over, don't forget.'

'I wouldn't miss a Saturday night out, but do you mind if we give the pictures a miss? Ferris will be out with his new date and I'd like to show Sal around the place.' He paused. 'When I say around the place, I mean the pubs. She's quite partial to the odd half, is our Sal.'

'I'll tell Alice,' Amy said. 'The film's an old one, anyway. A Marx Brother's comedy, A Day At The Races. We've seen it twice.'

'Thank goodness there won't be a third time. Can you imagine Ferris doing his Groucho impressions all night?'

After a meal of sandwiches, Bodkin and Amy sat on the sofa discussing the case as the BBC orchestra played classical music in the background.

'I have to give Angus a call tomorrow, Bodkin. When do you want me to say I'll meet him?'

'Wednesday afternoon, I think, Amy. I'm tied up briefing the new sergeant and chief superintendent Grayson in the morning and you'll be spending some time with Sal. I've booked us an appointment at Cresswell Chemicals tomorrow at twelve, so we'll get to see what Granville and Bertrand have to say for themselves. I'm hoping that Katherine is hanging about, too. I have a feeling she will be a key part of this investigation.'

'Do you think she could have done it, Bodkin?'

Bodkin thought about it. 'She had the motive and she may have had the means with Granville owning a chemical plant where they make the stuff that killed her. I can't quite see her being able to offload a dead body from a boat, but I could be wrong about that. Effie didn't weigh that much.'

'Katherine doesn't have a large frame, so I think she might struggle with that part,' Amy said. 'But then one of the men might have been with her.'

'It's a possibility,' Bodkin said as he slipped his arm around her shoulders and pulled her towards him. 'I'll pick you up about eleven.'

# CHAPTER THIRTY-SEVEN

'How was your meeting with Mr Grayson and the new sergeant?' Amy asked as she picked up her cardigan and walked towards the front door.

'It went well. I filled them in on the progress in this case, such as it is. Sergeant Conway is an experienced CID officer. He's going to look after the knicker's nicker case, and all the common or garden break-ins and assaults until we've got this one in the bag. He may have nicked the knickers nicker by then, of course, but I don't fancy his chances of getting to the bottom of it unless the culprit trips over a pair of newly acquired bloomers as he's trying to escape.'

Bodkin led Amy down the path towards the black Morris 8, but instead of climbing in himself, he got into the passenger side. 'In you get, we'll have a quick run up and down Long Lane before we set off.'

Amy skipped with delight and hurried around the front of the car.

'Do you know how to start it up?' Bodkin asked as Amy shut the door behind her.

Bodkin had left the car pointing down the lane towards Alice's farm, which meant Amy had a good half mile of straight road to drive along. After taking her through the starting procedure, Bodkin settled back in the passenger seat as Amy steered the car in an arrow straight line down the lane. When they reached Alice's farm, Bodkin took over and turned the car around before letting Amy take control again.

'Where do you want me to pull over?' Amy said as they passed her cottage on the way back.

'Your confidence is building up nicely,' Bodkin replied. 'I think you're ready to attempt a corner now. Keep it in second gear but ease right off the accelerator as we get close to the phone box. Take the left turn very slowly and don't get upset if you stall the engine.'

Amy's face became a mask of concentration as she approached the T junction outside the Old Bull pub. When she reached the telephone kiosk just before the corner, she eased her foot off the accelerator and steered the car effortlessly around the bend.

'How was that, Bodkin?' Amy said excitedly, looking sideways at him.

In response, Bodkin leaned across, took hold of the steering wheel with his right hand and eased the car across to the left-hand side of the road as a large, green bus approached them on the right.

Amy screamed and hit the brakes. The car came to a juddering halt.

'Good first attempt,' Bodkin said, 'but remember, you have to look at what's coming around the bend as you take the turn.'

'Sorry, Bodkin,' Amy said. 'Can I drive it for a little longer? It's a straight road until we get to Middle Street.'

'Better not,' Bodkin replied. 'We have to turn right and the police station is on the corner. I'd rather no one sees you driving at the moment. Once you've passed your driving test, I'll have a word with the chief super to see what he has to say about it.'

'I'd better apply for my licence then,' Amy said brightly.

Cresswell Chemicals was a large industrial plant built on two acres of land on the outskirts of Spinton. The group of buildings comprised eight two-storey production units, a long low-level warehouse and an office block with a metal staircase that ran up the side. Granville Cresswell was waiting for them in his own plush office. He was wearing dark-coloured trousers and a white, open-necked shirt. He got up from his chair to greet them as they entered the room. After holding out his hand to Bodkin, he gave Amy a puzzled look before returning to his chair behind the desk. He pointed to two folding wooden chairs that had been set out on the other side of his desk and asked them to sit.

'Can I get you some refreshment... tea, coffee?'

'Later, perhaps,' Bodkin said.

Granville rubbed his hands together. 'Right, let's get down to brass tacks. What can I do for you?'

'As I said on the telephone, Mr Cresswell, I'm investigating the death of Effie Watkins and it has come to our attention that you were, for a time at least, in a close relationship with her.'

'What does she have to do with the investigation?' Granville said, looking directly at Amy. 'Doesn't she work in a lawyer's office?' He looked quickly back to Bodkin as he reached towards the black telephone on his desk. 'Do I need to get my own solicitor?'

Amy produced her accreditation card and handed it over the desk. Granville studied it for a moment, then handed it back. 'I'm still not sure why you're here.'

'Miss Rowlings is officially assisting us on this inquiry,' Bodkin replied. 'As to your own lawyer, feel free to make that call, but if the interview then becomes formal, we might be better off holding it at the police station.'

Granville's fingers hovered over the telephone. Then, after thinking about it for a few seconds, he pulled his hand away and clasped both of them together on his desk.

'Effie and I were very close, but it was just a bit of fun, nothing serious.'

'You ended your relationship with Katherine Downey to embark on it,' Bodkin said.

Granville shrugged. 'These things happen. It was all over in a few weeks. Katherine and I have reignited our romance since then.'

'So I heard,' Bodkin replied, 'How did she take it when you dumped her for a younger model?'

'She wasn't over the moon about it. She gave me a piece of her mind... several pieces, in fact, but she accepted it in the end.'

'You didn't think Effie was a bit on the young side? I mean, you're old enough to have kids her age.'

If Granville was insulted, he didn't show it. 'I'm not quite over the hill yet, Inspector. Young women often find men of my age quite attractive, especially if those men have a bit of money. They soon see past the grey hair and the wrinkles if a sleek, shiny sports car and a guaranteed table at a flash restaurant comes with the package.' He leaned forward in his chair and tapped the side of his nose. 'You see, Inspector, I'm well aware which part of the package is more attractive to young women. I'm not conceited enough to fool myself into thinking they want me for my manly charms.' He turned to Amy and winked at her. 'What do you say, my dear? Would you turn down a ride in a Rolls Royce Phantom?'

'It depends what the owner was expecting to get out of the trip,' Amy said. 'The model of the car doesn't really impress me that much. As far as I'm concerned they're a convenient way of getting from A to B. Apart from that, it doesn't bother me if the car is a Ford or a Daimler.'

'But you would like to be seen at a well-heeled gathering, wearing a nice frock and a few shiny rocks around your neck. Every girl does.'

'I'm not averse to a pleasant night out,' Amy replied. 'I enjoyed myself at the ball the other night... mostly.'

'And you looked delightful, my dear. You must have someone of substance behind you to be able to afford the dress you were wearing. You really were the belle of the ball.'

'I hired it for fifteen shillings,' Amy said with a smile.

Granville was undeterred by her honesty. 'Someone like you should be on the arm of a more mature man. Think of all the fun you could be having.'

'I have lots of fun, thank you,' Amy replied.

Bodkin, having sat quietly while the exchange between Amy and Granville took place, decided it was time to step in. 'How long did your relationship last?'

'A few months, no longer than that.'

'How did it end?'

'I don't really think that has any relevance,' Granville said, with an edge to his voice.

'I'll decide what's relevant, Mr Cresswell.'

'All right, if you must know. She got what she obviously thought was a better offer.'

'From?'

'I'm not going into detail about that. I'm sure you can find out easily enough.'

'Angus McIntosh?'

'There, you already knew, so there was no need to ask.'

'Was Effie seeing you and Angus at the same time? She was seeing both you and Timothy Philby, after all.'

'She used Philby to get to me,' Granville said. 'She used everyone she came into contact with. It's the way she was.'

'Did you get angry when you realised you had been used?' Bodkin asked.

'I wasn't over the moon about it. I was more than a little peeved, let's put it like that. No one likes to be laughed at behind their backs, Inspector.'

'Quite.' Bodkin leaned forwards in his seat. 'So what did you do about it?'

'What could I do? I denied most of the rumours and laughed the rest off. People soon stopped gossiping when Katherine and I became an item again. She won't have any of that nonsense. She's the protector of my reputation, Inspector. She sees any slight on me as a slight on herself.'

'Was the break up acrimonious?'

'To be honest, I didn't know we had broken up until I came home from the office one day to find she'd moved out.'

'So you didn't confront her about it?'

'We had a few words after I'd seen her in Angus's car. I think Katherine had more to say than I did, but that would have been to ensure that she didn't try to come crawling back when she'd done with the old duffer.'

'You think that meeting might have been vitriolic?'

'Katherine doesn't take any prisoners, Inspector, as I remember to my own cost.'

'Katherine swallowed her pride and came back to you. Did she make any demands?'

Granville shrugged. 'She knows when she's onto a good thing, and I was made to promise not to be taken in so easily again.'

'What about your nephew, Bertrand?' Bodkin asked.

'What about him?'

'How did he get on with Effie? He was her own age. He's quite a handsome chap from a good family. Didn't she flutter her eyelashes at him at all?'

Granville bit his lip as he thought. 'They got on well enough. He has his own set of friends over at the Milton. I know he used to see her over there now and again, but I don't think they were too close. She was closer to that Foxley chap, I think.'

'Didn't he resent her for coming into your life?' Bodkin asked. 'I mean, he's your heir, isn't he?'

'He is. I have no children of my own, sadly. My first wife died in childbirth and my second wife just couldn't produce one, although she had two boys with the chap she took up with after our divorce. As for Bertrand... he never said anything to me about any concerns he might have.'

'He must have been worried, though,' Bodkin said. 'There he is, your heir apparent; everything you have will go to him. Then suddenly there's a problem. If you had ended up marrying Effie, he wouldn't have got anywhere near as much as he might have. He might even have been written out of the will altogether if you and Effie had produced a child.'

'He'd have been looked after, anyway. He's in my will, but you're right, of course. He wouldn't have got anything like as much if I had my own children. I can't say whether Effie would have hung around long enough to inherit, and I honestly don't think motherhood was something she had placed at the top of her to do list.'

'Bertrand spends a fair bit of time at the Boat Club, doesn't he? He's good on the water. He beat Joe in the speed boat race at the regatta.'

'He likes to mess about on the river.'

'Where were you on the Saturday before Effie's body was discovered?' Bodkin asked.

Granville scratched his head. 'I really can't... Ah, yes. I was at home. I'd got a bit of a chill, so I spent the day resting. I didn't go out at all.'

'Can anyone confirm that?'

'Yes, I have a housekeeper. She'll verify my story.'

'You remained at home all of Saturday? You're positive about that?'

'Absolutely.'

'Did anyone come to see you at all?'

'Bertrand came over in the afternoon. He was sorting something out for me. Then Katherine came over in the evening. We had an early dinner, then an early night.'

'What was it that Bertrand was sorting out for you?'

'I can't remember now. Something to do with some test samples.'

'Poison samples?'

'Most of the things we make here are toxic in one way or another, Inspector. We make insecticides, vermin poison, solvents...'

'Chloroform? Do you make that too?'

'We do. We make less of it than we used to, but there's still a good market for it.'

'Who do you sell to, Mr Cresswell? I can't remember seeing a Cresswell Chemicals label on anything I've ever bought.'

'We sell in bulk, both here and abroad. There are six major companies who sell on our products to the public. They put their own brand on the tins, of course, but the strychnine, arsenic and cyanide crystals all come from here.'

'How is security, Mr Cresswell? Have you ever had a problem with things going missing?'

'Security is tight, Mr Bodkin. It has to be with the products we deal with. As you must have noticed when you arrived, we have high fences and a security team on the gate. Believe me. No one could just walk out carrying a barrel of cyanide.'

'So, everything goes out in bulk? Even products like ether and chloroform?'

'Those containers have to be double sealed,' Granville said. 'Ether is particularly volatile. It's a highly flammable substance. We take the strictest care when handling things like that. One spill and the whole place could go up.'

'Do you have much in the way of spillage... leakage... do you have many accidents here?'

'We do get the odd burn when some worker or other isn't as careful as they ought to be. But no one has died on these premises for over ten years and that was down to an unfortunate incident with a faulty weld at the end of a steel drum. It wasn't our fault.'

'You're giving me a cast-iron guarantee that no one could take anything out of this facility without being caught?'

'I can happily give you that guarantee, Inspector. It just isn't possible.'

'Back to Effie Watkins for a moment. How did you feel when you heard she had been murdered?'

'I was shocked of course.'

'Just shocked? You didn't feel anything more emotional?'

'She was out of my life by her own volition. She made a fool of me. Why on earth should I feel emotional about it?'

'She had shared your bed, Mr Cresswell. Were you void of all emotion when she was in it?'

'I get emotional if I lose one of my dogs, Mr Bodkin. But they are loyal creatures. She walked out on me, so I don't honestly understand why you think I'd really care what happened to her. She probably made someone else look like a prize idiot. I'm not going to say she deserved what she got, but I won't lose any sleep over her.'

Bodkin got to his feet. 'Thank you, Mr Cresswell. That will be all for now.' He smiled at Amy as she got to her feet, then turned back to Granville. 'Where can I find Bertrand?'

Granville picked up the phone and dialled an internal number.

'He's in the test lab. It's at the top of the metal staircase. There's a small office up there. I'll just let him know you're coming.'

## CHAPTER
# THIRTY-EIGHT

THEY FOUND BERTRAND CRESWELL WAITING FOR THEM AT THE OPEN door as they got to the top of the iron staircase. After nodding to them, he offered his hand, first to Amy, then to Bodkin.

'Uncle Granville warned me you'd be coming up,' he said, brushing his thick brown hair away from his forehead. 'Come on through. There's an office just along here. We can talk in private.'

He led them past a row of benches that were laden with small canisters and glass bottles, with stoppers or rubber seals holding in the contents. At the far end of the room was another bench on which sat three large fume cabinets, a row of six Bunsen burners, and two pairs of elbow length rubber gloves. Protective clothing hung on hooks at the side of the bench.

'So this is where the testing is done,' Bodkin said as they walked towards the office. 'What do you actually test? The strength of the poison. How quickly it would knock a rat out?'

'Purity. We test the purity of the substance. Everything we produce has to meet a certain standard. Once we can prove that it does, we label the batches in the drums and send it on its way.'

Bodkin pointed to a small glass bottle that was waiting to be tested. 'What's in that one?'

Bertrand craned his neck to see what Bodkin was pointing at. 'Ether,' he said.

'Is chloroform tested in the same sized bottles?'

Bertrand nodded. 'All the liquids come up in small sample bottles. They have really good seals on them. It's a good job really, or we'd all be out like a light as soon as we stepped into the room.' He paused as he opened the office door to show them in. 'If you want to know anything technical, you'll have to ask the lab team. They're at lunch at the moment.'

Once Amy and Bodkin were inside, he closed the door and waved his hand towards a pair of foldaway wooden seats, similar to the ones they had seen in Granville's office. When they were seated, Bertrand offered them a choice of tea or coffee, but once again Bodkin declined.

'We have a few questions for you, Mr Cresswell,' Bodkin said as the young man took his seat behind the desk. 'I'll get straight to the point. How did you get on with Effie Watkins?'

'Pretty well,' Bertrand replied. 'We weren't best friends or anything like that.'

'But you got on well enough. I believe that you used to meet her at the Milton, or at the Boat Club?'

Bertrand nodded. 'Now and again.'

'Didn't you fancy her at all? She was a lovely young woman and about the same age as you. You were both single and available.'

'She wasn't available, Inspector. She was seeing my uncle. Anyway, she didn't like me that way. She had a thing about Quentin.'

'Ah, Mr Foxley-Walton. I was going to get round to him. Were they close?'

'She hoped to get close, I think, but Quentin liked to play the field. His parents thought he'd marry into a titled family one day and he didn't want to disappoint them by taking someone like Effie back home to meet them.'

'She was from a well-to-do family, though. She was hardly dragged up in the Spinton slums,' Bodkin pointed out.

'She wouldn't have been good enough for them even if she hadn't been the type of girl she was.'

'What type of girl would that be?' Amy cut in.

'Oh, you know, a good-time girl. A girl on the make.'

Bodkin nodded as if in understanding. 'Did she ever try it on with you? Did she ever try to tap you up for money?'

Bertrand laughed. 'I don't have any money. Not enough for her, at least. I used to buy a round now and then and I'd always include her in it.' He rubbed at his acne scars self-consciously. 'I don't think I was handsome enough for her, anyway. I couldn't compete with the likes of Quentin and Joe.'

'What about your uncle? Did you think you could compete with him?'

'I wouldn't have tried to. Not while he was seeing her. It wouldn't have been right.'

'Do you have a girlfriend, Bertrand?'

'No, not an official one.'

'So you play the field too?'

'Not really. I'm just waiting for the right person to come along.'

'Very laudable,' Bodkin said. 'Now, let's get down to the nitty gritty. When did you last see Effie?'

'It would have been the Friday night before she was found. I was at the Milton with Quentin. Effie, Joe and another girl came in... Jilly something. She's one of Joe's friends.'

'How were they all getting on together? Did there seem to be any friction between them?'

'No, it was just a normal night out. We danced a bit, had a few too many and went home.'

'Who did Effie leave with? Was it Quentin? We all know she had a thing for him.'

'No, Quentin left alone. He had a room at the George.'

'You're sure she didn't follow him?'

'Positive. She went home with Joe.'

'And this, Jilly person?'

'She got her own taxi. I was in the foyer of the Milton when it arrived.'

'What time was this?'

'Around a quarter to twelve.'

'What did you do?'

'I hung around for a bit, had a last drink, then went home in my own taxi.'

'Where do you live, Bertrand?'

'I have a flat in Highwater.'

'Near to Joe's flat?'

'On the same street, but at the other end.'

Bodkin looked puzzled. 'I find that a bit odd, Bertrand. You admit that you don't have a lot of money to throw about, then you get your own taxi to more or less follow Joe's car back to Highwater.'

'He was with Effie, so I didn't want to play gooseberry.'

'It's only a fifteen to twenty-minute ride, if that. I'm sure they'd have been okay about it. Did Joe offer you a lift?'

'No,' Betrand sighed. 'We haven't been getting on all that well since I put my name forward for the speed boat event. Jack Maplin dropped out to allow me to enter. We only have two boats, you see. Joe would have beaten Jack by a street, but he knew it would be a tight call racing against me.'

'I asked earlier if there was any friction in the group,' Bodkin reminded him.

'I thought you meant with Effie, and the answer to that is no. Everyone knew what she was.'

'So, you all left at more or less the same time?'

'Yes... no... Quentin left earlier. He had a meeting in the morning and he was staying at the George.'

'Ah yes, he left at around eleven-thirty, didn't he?'

'Something like that, yes.'

'Not eleven?'

'No, it was a bit later than that.'

'Which taxi firm did you use?'

'I'm sorry?' A panicked look came over Bertrand's face.

'It's a simple question. Did you ring for a taxi or walk out onto the High Street to hail one?'

'Oh, I hailed one. I'm not sure which company it was... Actually, I think it was a private hire.'

'I see, so not only did you miss out on a free lift from Joe, you spent extra on a private hire car?' Bodkin shook his head. 'You must be better off than you make out, Mr Cresswell.' He was silent for a moment. 'It doesn't matter, we can check anyway. All the private hire cars are licenced. We'll soon find out which one picked up a single young man on Spinton High Street and drove him to...' Bodkin pulled out his notebook and pen... 'What's your address?'

Bertrand grimaced. 'Flat two. Pullman House. West Street, Highwater.'

Bodkin jotted down the address. 'Thank you.' He put the notebook and pen on the desk, then scratched at the stubble on his chin. 'You say you didn't see Effie again after she got into Joe's car outside the Milton, is that correct?'

Bertrand nodded.

'You didn't go to the club on Saturday then?'

'No, I was here until one-ish. Then I met up with a couple of friends for a round of golf.'

'Which friends were they?' Bodkin picked up the notebook again.

'Norbert Hoskins... his dad runs the restaurant in Highwater, and Charles Darwin.'

'I bet he spent more time looking at the wildlife than hitting the ball,' Bodkin said.

Amy held back a laugh, but Bertrand missed the joke. He looked quizzically at the policeman. 'I'm sorry?'

'Never mind. Now, what about after the golf?'

'We had a quick drink in the clubhouse, then I went home.'

'By private hire?'

'No... hang on, I came back here. I had to pick up something for my uncle. He was at home with a bit of a cold, so I had to drop it off.'

'Where does he live?'

'Grafton Hall. It's on the Gillingham Road, just past the Braithwaite Hotel.'

'What was so important that you had to make a special trip over there?'

'He wanted to see a sheet of late test results and give me some instructions for Monday. One of the vats was due to be cleaned, and he wanted to make sure I put the right people on the job. He was going to be in London if he was well enough. Oh, I had to take him a sample container, too.'

'A container of?'

'Potassium cyanide. His gardener asked for some as they have both a rat and mole problem at the Hall.'

'So he asked you to bring him one of the sample containers?'

Bertrand nodded. 'I know it's not strictly the right thing to do, but you can see his point. Why pay for it when you make the blooming stuff?'

'I wouldn't think there's a law against it,' Bodkin said. 'I assume the container was sealed?'

'They are all sealed when the samples are taken, then the testers break the seal, run the test, then reseal.'

'Phew! You wouldn't want that stuff spilling all over the back seat of your car, would you?' Bodkin furrowed his brow as he asked his next question. 'What happens to the containers after testing has been done?'

'We have our own incinerator. It's all disposed of as directed by the government, Inspector.'

'And the samples of ether and chloroform?'

'They go in too.'

'I see.' Bodkin nodded to himself. 'How did you get to your uncle's house?'

'Katherine picked me up. She gets to drive one of my uncle's cars. I've been promised a company car for a while, but it hasn't materialised.'

'So how do you get to work every day?'

'David, the head lab technician, lives near me. He gives me a lift on his motorbike.'

'Did Katherine drive over from Grafton Hall to pick you up?'

'Yes... No... I'm not sure. She might have been out shopping. All I know is she turned up just after I got here.'

'Was security working on the gates?'

'They're here twenty-four hours a day. We run a night shift.'

'Where did she find you? In the lab?'

'No, I hadn't picked up the sample. I was in the office putting my golf clubs back in the cupboard over there.' He pointed to a single wooden door on the wall opposite. 'I have to leave them here. I've no way of getting them to the course if they're kept at the flat. It's too far to walk, and it's no fun catching the bus carrying a bag of clubs. My friends pick me up from here, so it isn't a problem.'

'Okay,' Bodkin said. 'Katherine finds you in the office, then you pick up the sample and away you go for the rest of the weekend. Is that right?'

'Sort of. I didn't pick the sample up, Katherine did. She'd

already got it when I came out of the office. She'd put it in a paper shopping bag.'

'How did you get home after you'd seen your uncle and received your instructions for the Monday morning?'

'Uncle rang for a cab and paid the driver in advance.'

'When you got home, what did you do?'

'I had a bath, listened to the radio, had something to eat, then got an early night. I intended to be up early to get out on the river. I wanted to practice my turns, ready for the big race, but I ended up sleeping in. I didn't get up until nine.'

'I'm glad you brought that up, Bertrand. What time did you arrive at the Boat Club?'

'Ten-ish.'

'Was there anyone else there, someone to open the boat sheds for you?'

'No, not that early on a Sunday. I have a key to the sheds.'

'Did you have to do any work on the boat before taking it out?'

'No, it just needed a bit of juice and there are always a few gallons knocking about.'

'How long were you there altogether?'

'Between picking the boat up and dropping it back off. I'd say three hours.'

'So you were gone by one?'

'Or just after.'

'Did you go into the club at all? Think carefully about this.'

'No, I just parked the boat up and left. I fancied a couple of pints, and it's cheaper up at the Riverboat pub than it is in the club.'

'Did you see anyone else about when you were parking up the boat?'

'No one.'

'Joe wasn't there?'

Bertrand shook his head. 'I didn't see anyone else.'

'One last thing while we're on the subject. You told Amy that you practiced your turns down by the reed beds, starting them before you got to the widest part of the river. Now, I want you to think hard about this. Did you notice that the reed beds had been disturbed in any way? Can you remember any damage? Was there a gap in the reeds, quite a large gap? Wide enough to get a motor boat in, say?'

Bertrand thought for a few seconds. 'I honestly can't remember. There could have been, I suppose. I was concentrating on my turns.'

Bodkin got to his feet, and Amy followed suit. 'Thank you, Mr Cresswell,' he said. 'I don't suppose Katherine is about today, is she?'

'You're in luck,' Bertrand said. He pointed through the window into the lab beyond. 'She's just walked in the door.'

# CHAPTER THIRTY-NINE

BODKIN GOT TO HIS FEET, TURNED AROUND AND TAPPED ON THE WINDOW to get Katherine's attention. Then he crooked his finger and made a beckoning motion.

'Miss Downey, do you think you could spare me a few moments?'

Katherine peered in through the half-glass door. Bodkin opened it and stood aside to allow Bertrand to leave. Katherine shot him a narrow-eyed look as he passed.

'I don't have a lot of time,' she said as she entered the room.

'It shouldn't take long, please, take a seat,' Bodkin said as he waved his hand towards the chair behind the desk.

Katherine stared long and hard at Amy before sitting down. 'I was right about you. I can always smell a rat.'

'Miss Rowlings is working with the police on this matter,' Bodkin said firmly, 'so I expect you to show her the same respect that you are about to show me.'

Katherine put her bag on the desk and gave Amy a more appreciative look. 'You certainly had the rest of them fooled, Mata Hari. They were all taken in.'

Amy treated her to a sweet smile. 'I was just being myself. Only a few details about my personal life were changed.'

Before Katherine had the chance to respond, Bodkin spoke again. 'How did you and Effie get on... before you found out that Granville was having a relationship with her?'

Katherine shrugged. 'All right, I suppose. I was one of the few that saw through her from the start, but as she was having a fling with Philby, I didn't see her as a particular threat. So we used to have the odd, girly chat.'

'And when you found out about her and your boyfriend?'

'The chat was less girly and more... advisory, shall we say?'

'But she didn't take your advice. She continued to see Granville, and you were suddenly out on your ear. That must have been hard to take.'

'I've had better days.'

'So, you just accepted it? I find that hard to believe, Miss Downey. You have a reputation for plain speaking. I can't see you giving up your hard-won prize just like that.'

'There wasn't a lot I could do. I was presented with a fait accompli. She'd played her hand very cleverly, and I didn't see it coming.' She paused for a moment, then took out a silver monogrammed cigarette case and lit a Craven A with a matching Ronson lighter. After taking a shallow draw, she blew smoke across the desk towards Bodkin. 'I cornered her in the powder room at the Boat Club a few days later. I told her in no uncertain terms that she was to drop Granville or it would be the worse for her.'

'You threatened her with violence if she didn't do as you asked?'

'I left the threat hanging in the air. I didn't actually mention what I might do. Not that it mattered. She didn't give a hoot. She just smiled that sickly smile of hers and told me that I'd had my turn and it was her turn now. Then the minx had the nerve to ask me what he liked to do between the sheets. She wanted me to give her a few tips.'

'That must have really got your back up,' Bodkin said.

'I was bloody livid. I think I actually pulled my hand back to slap her face, but then Nan Parkin came in and I had to step away from the conflict.'

'Did Effie keep out of your way after that?'

'Not that you'd notice. She used to have a dig at me every chance she got. Especially if Granville was with her.'

'You still went into the club when the two of them were together? There must have been a lot of sniggering and gossiping behind your back.'

'Some of the wives felt sorry for me. One of two of them had already fallen foul of Effie's ambition.'

'Was there anyone in particular who might have been angry enough to want to kill her?'

'HA! Put the names in a hat and pull one out. No one liked her, Inspector.' She took another draw of her cigarette. 'None of the women, at least. The men hung around her like flies around a steaming cow pat.'

Bodkin stretched out his legs and crossed his feet at the ankles. 'You seem to hand out verbal warnings on a regular basis, Miss Downey.' Bodkin looked across at Amy, then back to Katherine.

'Only when I feel under threat, Inspector. I thought that my future was secure for a long time. Then Effie stepped in and my castle walls came tumbling down. I don't intend to allow that to happen again.' She looked long and hard at Amy. 'I thought she might be another threat, but this time I was prepared for it.'

'You can't go through life looking over your shoulder all the time,' Amy said. 'I was no threat to you, but if you feel your relationship with Granville is so insecure that you're seeing rivals everywhere you look, then it might be time to just step away.'

'I worked hard to get to where I was, and now I'm back in pole position again. But he's a man, and men are fickle. Their heads can be easily turned. Women get accused of not knowing what we want or of changing our minds all the time, but at least we stick to our men when we land one.' She took a long draw from her cigarette then stubbed it into the ashtray, leaving a long curl of blue-grey smoke rising into the air in front of her. 'Haven't you landed one yet?' she asked Amy.

Amy and Bodkin exchanged a quick glance.

'Ah, I see. It's like that, is it?' Katherine grinned. 'Well, get him tied down as soon as you can, my dear. He looks to be a good catch from where I'm sitting.'

Bodkin shook his head slowly. 'Back to the matter in hand, Miss Downey. When did you last see Effie Watkins?'

'At the club on Saturday the twenty-second, it would have been mid-afternoon. I was over at Highwater dropping off a friend and we popped in for a drink.'

'Did you speak to Effie?'

'Oh yes, we rabbited away like old friends who'd met up accidentally for the first time in decades.' Katherine shook her head and rolled her eyes. 'No, we didn't speak... well, I didn't reply when she asked me how Granville was, at least.'

'She made a telephone call just before she left. Did you see her do that?'

'No. I was chatting with my friend and Lesley at the bar.'

'Did you see her leave?'

Katherine nodded. 'I saw her leave. The bi... she waved at me as she walked out.'

'Think carefully, Miss Downey. This would have been around a quarter to five. Did anyone follow her when she left the club?'

'No. Not that I remember. She seemed full of herself, though. As if she had landed another big catch.'

'Were you in the club on Saturday evening?'

'No. I left not long after Effie. Granville wasn't well. I'd rung him and he asked me to stop off at the works to pick Bertrand up. He had a few things to talk to him about... oh, and he wanted a tin of rat poison picking up.'

'Was Bertrand waiting for you outside when you arrived?'

'No, he was in here.' She waved her hand to the side.

'Did he remember to pick up the sample tin?'

'I picked it up for him. He was busy trying to stuff his golf clubs in the cupboard. They kept falling out.'

'So you picked up the poison? What did you do with it?'

Katherine shrugged. 'I slipped it into a brown paper bag and put it on the back seat of the car.'

'Did he take it in to Granville when you reached Grafton Hall?'

Katherine screwed up her face as she thought. 'Erm... No. I rather think I took it in.'

'What happened then? What did you do while Granville was giving Bertrand his instructions for the vat cleaning on the Monday? Were you there for the rest of the evening?'

'No. As I said, I'd met up with a friend to do a bit of shopping earlier and she'd left a pair of shoes on the back seat. She had told me that she was going out for the evening with her husband and was planning on wearing them. So I gave her a quick call, then nipped them over to her. When I came back, Bertrand was just climbing into a taxi. I'd have given him a lift when I drove over to deliver the shoes, but he was locked away with Granville and I didn't know how long he was going to be there. Granville doesn't like being disturbed when he's talking business.'

'Then you stayed the night?'

Katherine nodded.

'The housekeeper can verify this, I take it?' Bodkin asked.

'No, Granville gave her the night off. She wanted to go to the pictures or something with her sister.'

Bodkin nodded to himself. 'Now, let's move on to Sunday morning.'

'We had a long lie in, if you see what I mean,' she fluttered her eyelashes at the inspector. 'We didn't get up until well after eleven. Mrs Humphries was back by then. She got a bus back from Spinton. That's where her sister lives. Anyway, we had a bit of brunch in bed. Granville read the serious Sunday papers, and I worked my way through the scandal sheets.'

'And the rest of the day?'

'He had some work to do, so he was in his office most of the afternoon. I went for a drive. I got back about four and sat in the garden under a parasol sipping Pimm's. Granville joined me for a while about five-thirty, then we went in for dinner. I suggested going out, but he still wasn't feeling a hundred percent, so we read for a while, then had an early night. He had to be in London on Monday for a meeting in the City.'

'Where did you go? You said you went for a drive.'

'Just around the lanes? I took the Riley Kestrel for a spin.'

'Did you see anyone while you were out?'

'A farmer, a cow or two. No one I knew.'

'These lanes. Did they take you anywhere near Highwater?'

'Close, but not into the town.'

'And you didn't bump into Bertrand at all?'

'I told you. I didn't see anyone I knew.'

'One last question,' Bodkin said, leaning forward suddenly. 'Exactly how much did you hate Effie Watkins? Enough to want to kill her?'

Katherine stared hard at Bodkin, then she took a deep breath before she replied. 'I never got to find out, Inspector.'

Bodkin got to his feet. 'Thank you, Miss Downey. I'll be in touch if I need to speak to you again.'

Katherine stood up and walked towards the door. She stopped when she came alongside Amy's chair. Looking down at her, she winked and flicked her head towards Bodkin. 'Tie him down while you have him in your clutches, my dear. He's quite assertive in a grumpy sort of way.'

'What did you make of that?' Amy said when they were back in the car. 'She really is a piece of work, isn't she?'

Bodkin nodded, 'She's that, and more.'

'Do you think she would be capable of murder, though?'

'I'm not sure. I think she's capable of a lot of things.'

'What about Bertrand? Did you pick anything up from him?'

'He's a strange one. I was just about to ask you the same question, but before you answer, let's take a ride over to the George Hotel. There's something niggling away at me like a nasty itch and I need to scratch it before I can move on with the inquiry.'

Bodkin slipped the car into gear and pulled out of the parking space, then raised his hand to the security guard on the gate as he passed through. After driving through the narrow Victorian terraced streets that lined the edge of the town, he drove past the station, turned onto Main Street and stopped outside the George Hotel.

The George was an Edwardian structure that had been built at more or less the same time as the Town Hall and the library. Boasting twenty rooms on two floors, it attracted mostly company reps and travelling salesmen. The wealthier visitors to the town always stayed at the older and much grander Milton.

They were greeted at the desk by a brown-haired, twenty something woman wearing the company logo on the breast of her blazer, which looked to have seen better days and was at least one size too big.

'Welcome to The George,' she said with a well-rehearsed smile. 'Is it a double room you require? How many nights?'

Bodkin pulled out his warrant card and showed it to her. 'I'm Inspector Bodkin and this is Miss Rowlings. I'd like you to look at your register and tell me when a man named Foxley-Walton last booked a room here.'

'Ah, Mr Foxley-Walton. He's a regular. He keeps coming back. Never stays more than one night, but he told me he'd never dream of going anywhere else.'

'When was he last here, Miss...?'

'Mrs... Mrs Jean Surridge.' She flipped over a couple of pages. 'The last time was on Friday, the twenty-first of July. I actually booked him in. It was my turn for the night shift.'

'What time did he check in?'

'Let me see... Eleven thirty-five. He took room fourteen. It's at the back on the first floor.'

'And when did he check out?'

'Oh, I don't need to look for that. I was on the reception, filling in my nightly report for the manager. Mr Foxley-Walton came down at seven-fifty.'

'You have a very good memory, Mrs Surridge,' Bodkin said with a smile.

'Oh, I wouldn't forget him, sir. He always tips well. He gave me two bob.'

'Two shillings? That was very generous of him. What did you have to do for that?'

Mrs Surridge tapped the side of her nose. 'Keep quiet.'

'About what?'

'About his visitor,' she hissed, looking around the reception area to make sure she couldn't be overheard.

'This visitor?' Bodkin smiled at her. 'Tell me about that.'

'Mr Foxley-Walton always orders a bottle of wine to take up to his room when he stays... At least he has done whenever I've been on duty. He always says that an important business client will arrive shortly, and I'm to tell him which room he's in. It's all top secret, apparently. He said they discuss things that can't be spoken about openly in the office in case word gets out and the deal collapses.' Jean shook her head slowly. 'No one believes it. We all know what they're getting up to up there, but... well, he's a good tipper, so we keep his little secret.'

'This visitor is a man, then. Is it always the same one?'

Jean nodded. 'He doesn't stay all night. He always sneaks out about three-ish and there's always a taxi waiting for him on the kerb.'

'Can you describe this man... or have you ever learned his name?'

'I don't know his name, but he's been turning up late at night for about six months or so. Not every week. Just when Mr Foxley-Walton is in town.' She looked up at the ceiling for a moment as she thought. 'He's in his early twenties, I'd say. He's of average height and has a mop of thick, dark hair. Oh, yes, he has a few old acne scars on his face. He tries to cover them up when he arrives at reception, but you can't miss them, really.'

Bodkin thanked the woman and passed her a shilling over the counter. 'That's for you. Just to make sure your memory remains clear in case we need you as a witness in court.'

'Thank you, sir,' Jean said, pocketing the coin. 'It's serious then? I know it's an offence, what they get up to, but I thought the police turned a blind eye to it these days.'

'The inquiry is nothing to do with what he might or might not get up to in the privacy of his room,' Bodkin said. 'I'd like you to make a statement at some stage, though. I'll send a constable up later on. What time does your shift end?'

~

'Well, that's thrown the cat among the pigeons. I wasn't expecting that revelation,' Amy said, raising her eyebrows.

'It certainly adds to the complexity of the case,' Bodin replied, rubbing the stubble on his chin. He turned to face her across the front seats of the car. 'Now I'd like your thoughts on Bertrand Cresswell.'

Amy stuck her tongue into the side of her cheek as she gathered her thoughts. 'Okay, after listening to what he had to say earlier, I thought he might be a candidate, but that was for financial reasons. If he thought he was going to be left out of the will, or have his inheritance severely limited, then he might have a very good reason to want to see the back of her, but now, I think there's an extra motive. What if she had found out about him and Quentin and was attempting to blackmail them?'

'I like your thinking,' Bodkin said. 'What else?'

Amy thought again. She held up a hand and began to count on her fingers as she spoke. 'First, as I just said, he has a motive. Second, he had access to the chloroform and in a conveniently sized container. It would have been easy for him to slip one of the samples out in his pocket.' She pushed down another finger. 'Third, he was down at the reed beds on the Sunday morning. His alibi, that he was practicing his turns, puts him in the right place and at pretty much the right time that her body was dumped there.' She dropped another finger. 'Fourthly, he has no alibi for the time between leaving his uncle's house and ten o'clock the next morning. Effie made a phone call from the club. It might have been to him. Maybe he arranged to meet her somewhere, agreeing to pay her whatever she was demanding to keep quiet about him and Quentin. We only have Quentin's word that he was sleeping all afternoon. He had time to get up here, do the deed with Bertrand, then drive over to his mother's house. That meant there were two of them to subdue her. One to hold her, the other to tip the chloroform down her throat.' She paused for a moment as she put her hands on her lap. 'But what did they do with the body until it was dumped in the reeds the next day? I know... maybe they left it in the boathouse?'

'I like your reasoning,' Bodkin said. 'But Joe was seen in the boathouse on the Saturday afternoon. I can't really see them taking the chance of her body being discovered so quickly.' He started up the car and headed towards the High Street. 'Let's add Katherine into the mix. How does she fit into all this knowing what we now know about her?'

Amy bit her lip as she thought. 'Okay. We know she hated Effie. We know that she had access to the chloroform. HEY! She might even have stuffed a sample bottle of it into the bag at the same time she put the rat poison in. Bertrand never got to see the contents of the bag. She told us she took it into the house. She might well have had the chloroform in the car when she delivered the shoes to her friend... I now find that a very convenient excuse by the way. She had the motive, she had the means, and she had the opportunity.'

'All true,' Bodkin said. 'But I'm wondering if the motive was purely financial, and she and Bertrand hatched the plan together. Again, there would have been two people to overpower her. It still leaves us with the problem of what they did with the body, but it could just be that Katherine left it in the car overnight and she and Bertrand disposed of it the next morning.'

Bodkin chewed on his lip as he pulled up outside the chemist's shop on High Street. 'I want to know a bit more about where the local doctors, dentist and vets get their chloroform from. They can't possibly be buying it in bulk. They wouldn't get through a barrel full in a lifetime.' He got out of the car and stood on the kerb until Amy joined him. 'Let's ask the expert in all things medicinal. I believe our old friend Agatha Walker still runs this place.'

Bodkin pushed open the door to allow Amy to walk in first. Behind the counter stood a thin framed woman with pale skin and grey flecked hair. On her right lapel she wore an enamel badge with the single word, PHARMACIST, written on it. Around her neck was a thin silver chain attached to a pair of round-lens spectacles. She lifted them to her eyes as she turned towards her customers.

'Amy... and Sergeant Bodkin, what an unexpected pleasure.'

'It's Inspector Bodkin these days,' Bodkin said with a smile. He reached his hand across the counter and the woman shook it before giving Amy a beaming smile. Agatha had once been a suspect in a murder investigation but had since bought out the owner of the pharmacy and was now running the shop herself.

'Hello, Agatha,' Amy said brightly. 'It's so nice to see you. How's your sister? I didn't see her in church on Sunday.'

'She's down in Maidstone visiting our old Auntie Florrie,' Agatha replied. She'll be back on Saturday.' She focussed her attention on Bodkin again. 'How may I help you, Serg... I'm so sorry, Inspector?'

'I'd like to know how local doctors, dental surgeons and vets source their chloroform.'

'Local practices buy it through me. I buy it in from a distributer who can sell in the amounts I order.'

'So, you buy it in for them. None of them source it themselves?'

Agatha shook her head. 'It wouldn't make business sense for the distributer to sell in such small quantities. They only allow me to do it because there's a regular monthly order. I buy in ether too, as well as cyanide, arsenic and strychnine based poisons. But you know about that from the case involving poor Reverend Villiers.'

'I remember it well, Mrs Walker, which is why we came to you today. What sort of amounts are we talking about here?'

'No one needs gallons of it. The two local vets take more than the three dentists and the five doctors put together. The doctors use very little. The dentists use more, but the vets deal with large animals so they buy it in greater amounts.'

'So you've got the entire local market covered? That's handy to know.' He thought for a moment before going on. 'What sort of amount would say, a dentist order?'

'It depends how busy his practice is, but I wouldn't have thought more than half a pint at a time and that might last a month, depending on how many patients needed extractions.' She smiled at him. 'I can give you the exact measurement in CCs if you prefer?'

'No thank you,' Bodkin said with a quick shake of his head. 'Half pints and pints, I can understand. I can visualise it. I wouldn't know where to start with a cubic centimetre or whatever it represents.' The inspector grinned at the pharmacist. 'They use cocaine in dental surgery too, or is my memory playing tricks? It's been a while since I needed any work doing on my teeth.'

'They inject it into the gum and it does work well as an anaesthetic when they fill a cavity with amalgam.'

'You keep that in stock too, I take it?'

Agatha nodded. 'In some quantity. It's used in various ways in medicine.'

Bodkin thanked the pharmacist and turned towards the door. After promising to meet Agatha for a lunch date in the café around the corner, Amy followed the policeman out of the shop.

'Who knew cocaine was used so much in medicine? That was quite an eye opener for me,' she said with a surprised look on her face.

'It's been in use for a long time, Amy. You've probably got a bottle of cough linctus containing cocaine in your medicine cabinet at home.'

'Well, I'm blowed. You learn something new every day,' she said.

'What's next?' Amy asked as they sat in the car waiting for a bus to pass. 'We've had a very productive day, haven't we?'

Bodkin nodded. 'It's been extremely interesting, and the case has moved on a lot. What's next? We're going back to the station and I'd like you to arrange a date with that randy old goat, Angus.'

## CHAPTER
# FORTY

'Hello, Mr McIntosh. This is Amy Rowlings. I'm not sure if you remember me, but you gave me your card at the Highwater Boat Club ball on Saturday.'

'Of course I remember you. I'd never forget someone so ravishingly beautiful.'

Amy took the handset away from her ear and pulled a face at Bodkin. 'You erm, said that if I ever fancied going out to dinner, I was to give you a call.'

'Absolutely, my dear. When would you like to go? I'm tied up this evening, but for you, I'll make damn sure I'm free for any other evening you choose.'

'I was thinking more of an afternoon tea. Until we get to know each other better. Dinners are so formal, aren't they?'

'Anything for you, my dear. It rules out Hoskin's sadly, as the staff never arrive until six-thirty in the evening. You can't get as much as a biscuit until after seven. I know, how about the Café Blanc? It's just off the main Gillingham Road. They put on an acceptable afternoon tea. They do a nice cocktail too if you fancy one.'

'That sounds perfect,' Amy replied. 'How about tomorrow afternoon? About two-ish? There's somewhere I have to be in the morning and I'll need a little time to get ready afterwards. I don't want to turn up in my ordinary day clothes.'

'I'm sure you'd look wonderful wearing sackcloth,' Angus said. 'Where would you like me to pick you up?'

'I don't need a lift, thank you. I have something to sort out with my solicitor, Godfrey Wilson. His office is only just up the road from there. It's only a five-minute walk.'

'Spiffing! I'll see you at two then.'

'I'm so looking forward to it,' Amy said.

'Me too, my dear,' Angus almost purred. 'Me too.'

'All set,' Amy said when she put the handset back in its cradle. 'Two o'clock at the Café Blanc. They do a really posh afternoon tea, so I'd better wear something nice.'

'You won't actually be having afternoon tea with him,' Bodkin replied, stroking his chin.

'But I thought you wanted me to soften him up?'

'I do,' Bodkin replied. 'But only for a few minutes. You're the warm-up act. Wherever you sit, I'll be on the table behind.'

'Fair enough,' Amy replied. 'You'll have to take me for afternoon tea instead. It will cost you an arm and a leg and it will all be your own fault because you could have let Angus pay.'

'I doubt we'll be there long enough for a full on afternoon tea. I just want to catch him unawares. But I agree with you dressing up if you feel like it. I might even press my spare suit.'

Amy shook her head. 'Please do, Bodkin. But don't put it on until five minutes before we leave, or it will look like you've slept in it for a fortnight.'

Later that afternoon, Amy made a start on the dress repairs

for Brigden's. First, she took on the worst of the four. The dress was in beautiful condition, but the hem had a ragged five-inch tear which would need some very careful mending. In the end, she had to undo the stitching on the side seams and after carefully taking out a two-inch strip from each side of the wide skirt; she remade the seams and used the cut off material to stitch into the hem. By the time she had finished, there was hardly a trace of her workmanship.

The job took well over ninety minutes, so it wasn't until after tea that Amy was able to make a start on one of the easier repairs. She had just put her machine away and taken the dress into the bathroom to steam out the creases while she took a bath, when she heard a knock at the front door. Pulling on her dressing gown over her naked body, Amy hurried along the hall to open it. She found Bodkin standing on the doorstep with a pair of trousers in his hands.

'Long time no see,' he said.

Amy stepped aside to allow him to enter, then after closing the door, she followed him to the front room. 'Why are you carrying a pair of trousers, Bodkin? If they're a gift for me, I have to tell you that I prefer dresses.'

'The seam's gone. Right down the... The seams given way at the back. I was wondering if you could work your magic on them.'

Amy held the trousers up to the light and thrust her hand through the gaping hole at the back. 'It would take black magic to sort these out, Bodkin. They've had it. It's not the seam that's gone, it's the material at the side of the seam. It's so thin you could use it as a face veil.'

'Ah, I didn't know they were that bad. I just heard a rip when I bent over.'

'I'm amazed they lasted as long as they did. You need to get yourself round to Stan's Emporium first thing in the morning.'

'I don't want to buy another suit. The jacket is fine.'

'I'm sure they'll have a pair of navy trousers, Bodkin.' She tossed the torn pair back to him and went into the kitchen to put the kettle on. 'Take those with you and measure the legs of the new pair against them. The last ones you bought were three inches too long.'

'The slacks you chose the last time we went in fit nicely. I don't suppose you could come with me?'

Amy rolled her eyes heavenwards. 'All right, but you have to get me back here by ten. Sal is driving up don't forget.'

When she had made the tea, Amy carried a tray through to the living room and set it down on the table. 'I was just about to sneak an extra bath in. I'll be back to the once a week routine when Mum and Dad get home.' She pulled her dressing gown tighter around her. 'It's getting a bit nippy. I've got nothing on under this.'

Bodkin fiddled with his torn trousers as he looked quickly away from her.

'It's all right, Bodkin, this dressing gown isn't made of gossamer lace. I go naked underneath my clothes every day of the week, but you don't get embarrassed then.'

'I'm not embarrassed,' Bodkin said, still fiddling with the trousers. 'I'm just wondering what your mum and dad would think of you being...'

'With me wearing my dressing gown in the presence of a man? I don't think they'd lose any sleep over it.'

Bodkin got to his feet. 'I should go, Amy. I'm sorry for delaying your bath.'

'It's all right, Bodkin. I haven't run it yet. I've got plenty of time to have a soak before bed.'

Amy lifted the teapot and poured out two cups of tea. After adding milk and sugar, she passed one of them to Bodkin. 'While I was working on my machine, I was having a think about what we learned about Katherine and the Cresswells.'

Bodkin took a sip of his tea, then replaced the cup on his saucer. 'Oh yes?'

'Do you think all three of them could have hatched a plan to do away with Effie? They all had their different reasons, but they might have worked out a way to give each other an alibi. Granville is using this nasty chill he caught as his and the other two are using his illness as part of theirs.'

Bodkin thought about it. 'As a theory, it's a pretty good one. It might be that they are trying to protect Granville at all costs. He's the one with the money, after all.'

Amy sat at the table, crossed her bare legs, then pulled her dressing gown across her knees as Bodkin looked away. She placed one hand on her lap to hold the two sides of it together and picked up her cup with the other. 'Three of our prime suspects all in one place and all using each other as an alibi. But, let's just say for the sake of argument that they are telling the truth, where does that leave us, suspect wise?'

'We still have Joe at the scene. He lied about being at the Boat Club on the Sunday. He was the last one to be involved in a relationship with her... that we know of, at least. He's not off the hook yet by any means. Then there's old Angus. We can't rule him out until we've spoken to him, but we know how close he was to her. We've got his handwritten note to prove it.'

'Then there's Quentin Foxley-Walton. His alibi seems to revolve around taking forty winks at all hours of the day.' She giggled as she remembered their conversation with him. 'Did you really keep forgetting his name, or was it just a ruse?'

Bodkin winked at her. 'He wasn't happy about it, was he?'

'You really do like to get under the skin of the more well-heeled members of society, don't you?' Amy said before taking another sip of her tea.

'It's the only reason I get out of bed in the mornings,' Bodkin replied with a grin.

At nine forty-five the following morning, Bodkin, carrying a pair of new, freshly pressed navy trousers over his arm, answered the door of the cottage to find his sister standing on the porch. On seeing him, her mouth formed an O shape. She nodded to the trousers that lay over his forearm. 'There's a story here,' she said.

'I'm just leaving,' Bodkin said, landing a kiss on his sister's cheek. 'I'll see you on… when are you coming back? Saturday is it?'

Sal watched as Bodkin hurried through the gate and down towards his car. After opening the passenger door, he carefully laid the trousers over the back of the seat, then, after slamming the door shut, he hurried around to the driver's side.

'I bet your neighbours have been wondering what on earth you are getting up to,' Sal said as she walked into the living room. 'A ruggedly handsome man hurrying down your path carrying his trousers.'

'It's the second time in twelve hours, too,' Amy said. 'But the pair he carried out last night looked like they'd been torn from his body.' Amy picked up her bag and led Sal out into the hall. 'I do hope Kathleen hasn't changed her mind,' she said.

In the end, Amy need not have worried. Kathleen O'Toole was looking for them out of her grubby front window as they pulled up. The boys were dressed in their Sunday School clothes, dark short trousers and white short-sleeved shirts. They both carried brown paper bags stuffed with their meagre possessions as their mother ushered them out of the house.

'Where are we going, Mum?' Danny asked. 'Why isn't Marty coming?'

'Hush child. We're just going away for a little holiday. Come on now; get those bags into the boot of the lady's car.' Kathleen came out of the house carrying a large, battered suitcase that was held together with thin lengths of string. As she walked across the pavement, she cast nervous glances up and down the street.

'Have you got everything?' Sal asked as Kathleen carefully placed her case in the boot of the Ford.

'Everything I own is in that case. There's not much for a lifetime, is there?'

Sal smiled softly at her and walked her around to the open front door of the car. Amy stood back as Sal pulled a lever on the side of the front seat, then folded the back down, giving Kathleen room to clamber into the back seats with the boys.

Amy was just about to climb back into the car herself when she heard her name being called. She looked up the street to see Big Nose Beryl Hargreaves, her gossipy colleague, standing on the front doorstep of the house three doors along.

'Doing a daylight, moonlight flit are they?' she asked, craning her neck in an attempt to see past Amy and into the car.

'I don't know that it's any of your business, Beryl,' Amy said curtly. 'What are you doing here, anyway?'

'Can't a body visit their old mum now?' Beryl said. She craned her neck again. 'Where are they off to? They look like they're in a hurry wherever they're going.'

'As I said, Beryl and as I always seem to be telling you, it's none of your business. Now, get back to your mum. She'll be wondering where you've gone.'

'Mum's a good friend of Marty's,' Beryl said with a knowing smile. 'She knew his mother when she was alive.' She looked around Amy to the car again. 'He's at work. He won't be happy if he comes home to an empty house.'

'Just keep your nose out of it,' Amy said as she turned away from her fellow machinist. 'I suppose it will give you something to talk about at the Mill on Monday morning.'

'I don't know what you mean,' Beryl sniffed. 'I'd like to know how you got involved in this, though. Was it through your goody-goody church folk?'

'Goodbye, Beryl,' Amy said, then she turned away and hurried back to the car.

'I'm sure you'll have a lot of fun when you get there,' Amy said to the two worried looking boys sitting on the back seat. Sal pointed to the glove box and Amy pulled out a bag of minty humbugs. She held the bag over the back of her seat and the boys stuck their hands into it, each coming out with a large, stripey sweet.

'They're big enough to last you all the way to... wherever it is you're going,' Amy added quickly. She looked sideways to Sal as she drove off the Victorian estate and past the Dragon pub before turning onto Main Street. 'Is everything ready for them... down there?'

'They have a room in the hostel. It's clean, and it's got two beds, so they'll be comfortable enough for a few nights. I've got wind of a house we might be able to rent for them in a village a couple of miles out of town. You can see the sea from there.'

'The SEA!' Danny and his brother called out together. 'We've never been to the seaside.'

Sal dropped Amy at the Old Bull pub before making a turn at the telephone box. She wound down the window and pulled up alongside her as she crossed the road to the end of Long Lane.

'I'll see you on Saturday, Amy. I can't tell you how much I'm looking forward to spending a bit more time with you and Gee.'

'I'm really looking forward to it as well. I'd better nip down and tell Alice that we're skipping the movies this week. She brushed away a few stray hairs from her face. 'Have a safe journey.' She looked past Sal into the back of the car, where Kathleen was casting nervous glances out of the window. 'Good luck with your new life. I hope I'll see you again one day. Perhaps I'll come down to stay with Sal for a weekend.'

Sal took a quick look behind to make sure there was no traffic approaching, then she pulled out onto the Gillingham Road. Amy heard a faint voice call out as Sal pushed her hand into the air to wave. 'See you on Saturday.'

# CHAPTER
# FORTY-ONE

At exactly two o'clock that afternoon. Bodkin drove his little black Morris along a narrow, treelined, asphalt road that ran alongside the main Gillingham Road. At the end of the bumpy track was a large, white painted building, the front of which was partly covered by crimson climbing roses. White painted metal tables surrounded by wrought-iron chairs were set out on a forecourt. They pulled up in an almost empty car park at the back of the restaurant, and Bodkin gave Amy's hand a squeeze as she prepared to get out of the car.

'Do you think he's here yet? I don't want to be the first to arrive.'

'He's here,' Bodkin said, pointing out a man in a grey chauffeur's uniform who was standing at the side of a dark blue Bentley, as he puffed on a cigarette. He checked his watch, then opened the driver's door. 'Give me a few minutes to get settled, then make your big appearance.'

He leaned back in and gave Amy a peck on the lips. 'Don't forget. After a bit of small talk, I'll stick my size nine's in.'

Five minutes later, Amy got out of the car and, under the appreciative gaze of Angus's driver, smoothed down the lemon coloured dress that she had bought from Brigden's a couple of months before. The dress was cut in in a V at the bust, flared out from the waist and hung just below her knees. Her outfit was finished off with a pair of white, strappy sandals and two matching white clips holding her hair in place above her ears. Pulling a compact mirror from her bag, she checked her makeup, then made her way between the rows of flowering shrubs that lined the narrow path leading to the front of the restaurant.

She found Angus sitting at a table a few feet away from the main doors. A frowning Bodkin was seated at the table to the right of him. He was studying the drinks menu and was obviously perturbed by the prices.

'There you are, my dear,' Angus said as Amy approached. 'Fashionably late, but a picture of elegance.' He got to his feet and pulled out the chair next to his own, dragging it a little closer as he stood behind it, waiting for Amy to sit.

'I can't tell you how much I've been looking forward to this... Amy, isn't it? Do you know I thought I felt a little spark between us on Saturday night? You looked beautiful. That dress suited you down to the ground. If I'd been twenty years younger, I'd probably have dropped to one knee and begged you to marry me.'

*Only twenty years younger? He'd still be in his mid-fifties.* Amy thought. 'I'll be honest with you, Mr McIntosh. I hired the dress for the evening. I could never afford to own it.'

'Call me, Angus, please, my dear,' the old man said, patting her on the knee.

Amy tried hard not to flinch and just about succeeded.

'I'll buy you the dress. How about that?' Angus said eagerly. 'Just tell me where to find it and I'll send my man around to pick it up? I can't imagine anyone else looking half as good as you in it.' He placed his hand on her knee again. Over his shoulder, Amy saw Bodkin lean forward on his seat with a grim look on his face. She shook her head almost imperceptibly, and he relaxed again.

Amy took hold of Angus's hand, lifted it and placed it on the table, then she patted it. 'I hardly know you,' she said.

'I hope you'll get to know me really well,' Angus said, picking up the menu. 'Now, shall we have an apéritif?'

'Could I have a Pimm's Number One with lots of ice, please?' Amy said. Angus raised his hand and clicked his fingers. A few moments later, a waiter, wearing a short white jacket and black trousers, hurried towards them from his place next to the front door.

'A Singapore Sling and a Pimm's with plenty of ice,' Angus said, sending the young man scurrying towards the bar area.

'Do you know, I thought my days of romantic trysts with beautiful young women were over?' He held up his hands. 'Yet here I am in the company of one of the most beautiful young women in the town.'

Amy smiled. 'It's not that long since you had another pretty young girl on your arm, if what I heard at the ball was true.' She tapped him lightly on the back of his hand. 'I think you're being too modest.'

Angus pulled out a handkerchief and mopped his sweating brow, then, after smoothing his moustache with his fingers, he returned the handkerchief to his pocket. 'You're talking about young Effie. She was a friend of yours, wasn't she? Did she ever mention me at all?'

Amy nodded. 'I didn't believe her when she said she was seeing you, but she showed me a dress and a bracelet that you'd bought her. I still didn't believe a word of it until she showed me the note you wrote to her.'

Angus sighed. 'She was a lovely young thing. I miss her.' His expression saddened for a moment, then his eyes lit up again as he grabbed hold of Amy's hand. 'But now you have come into my life, so it's time to stop looking back.'

'How long were you together?' Amy asked. 'I don't mean to be rude, but there was quite an age difference between you.'

'She didn't care about that,' Angus replied. 'I'll be honest with you, my dear. Neither of us thought it would last for very long and that's how it turned out.' He sighed again. 'It was fun while it lasted, though I knew she wasn't in it for love.'

'Do you think she took advantage of you?'

'Good heavens no. I knew what she was from the first moment I saw her.' He reached out and took Amy's hand in his. 'I have a lot of money and not too many years left to enjoy the benefits of it. Effie was a pleasant distraction from my daily rounds of business meetings and my all too frequent trips to the doctor's surgery to get some relief for one ailment or another.' He squeezed Amy's hand. 'Never get old, my dear. It's a trap.'

'It's so sad what happened to her, though. She was only very young. She had her whole life ahead of her.'

'Let's not dwell in the past,' Angus said, looking directly at Amy's cleavage. 'Some might say she deserved what she got. If you play fast and loose with people's emotions, you might expect to be paying the piper before too long.'

'And some might say that the man leading the pipe band had a say in how she was paid,' Bodkin said, getting up from his seat just as the waiter arrived with the drinks.

'Who the devil are you, sir?' Angus's nostrils flared. 'This is a private conversation and you haven't been invited to join in.' He turned to Amy. 'I'm sorry for the intrusion, my dear.'

After the waiter had put the drinks on the table, Bodkin tapped him on the shoulder and asked for a whisky and ice. 'It's on his tab,' he whispered.

'I don't think you heard what I said, young man.' Angus shielded his eyes as he looked up at Bodkin. The policeman ignored him and, dragging out a chair, he flashed his warrant card before sitting down opposite the old businessman.

'Inspector Bodkin of Spinton police,' he said by way of introduction. 'Did you really mean what you said just then... about the young girl who was found dead? I think that's rather a harsh comment if so.'

'Policeman eh?' Angus blinked twice before giving Bodkin an odd look. 'Was this a planned meeting or did you just fancy a bit of company?'

'Oh, it was planned. I've been wanting to talk to you for a while, Mr McIntosh, and this seemed like a perfect opportunity.'

Angus stared hard at Amy. 'And you were the bait, I suppose.'

Amy put on a sad face. 'I'm sorry, but yes. I'm helping the inspector with the case.'

'I should have known lightning wouldn't strike twice,' Angus replied with a shrug. 'Never mind. The thought was nice while it lasted. I was sort of hoping you'd bring your lovely young friend with you. She reminded me of someone, but I can't think who. Stunning young woman, though. Absolutely stunning.'

Just then, the waiter appeared with Bodkin's whisky. He placed it on the table and began to write on his pad.

'Oh, put it on my tab, man,' Angus said. 'We can be civilised about this.'

'That's what I was doing, sir,' the waiter replied. 'He told me to.'

Amy put her hand to mouth to stifle the giggle that was about to come out. Angus gave Bodkin a glare, then told the waiter that would be all.

'One thing that I don't understand,' Angus said, taking a sip of his drink. 'Why didn't you just call at my home to interview me? Why bother with all this... theatre?'

'To be honest with you, if we'd called to arrange an interview with you at home, I suspect the first people we'd have met would be your legal representatives.' Bodkin picked up his own drink and swirled the whisky around, making the ice rattle against the glass. 'Your good health,' he said.

'You're damn right I'd have had the lawyers in,' Angus replied. 'I can still refuse to answer your questions until I can get one over here. There's a chap... Godfrey Wilson, who has an office only a couple of minutes' drive away. Do you think I need to nip into the reception and give him a call?' He looked at Amy suddenly. 'Weren't you at his office a few mi...? Ah, I see, forget I asked.'

'This is just a chat, Mr McIntosh,' Bodkin said smoothly. 'We're still looking into Effie's known associates. Unless you tell us here and now that you murdered her or ordered someone else to do it, I don't think I'll be bringing out the handcuffs this afternoon.'

Angus seemed to relax. He leaned back in his chair and looked up at the sky. 'Let's get on with it, then. What do you want to know?'

'When did you first meet Effie Watkins, Mr McIntosh?'

'Let's drop the formalities, shall we?' Call me Angus.' He gave Bodkin a friendly smile.

'Angus,' Bodkin said.

'As for Effie. I met her at a party at Grafton Hall. Granville Cresswell's place. We're partners in business. Anyway, Effie was there, looking as young and beautiful as she ever did. We got chatting and seemed to get on like a house on fire. The next thing I know, I'm inviting her to dinner and she's agreeing to come.'

'What did Granville have to say about that?'

'I don't think she told him, to be honest.'

'So, you took her to dinner? What then?'

'Oh, she gave me a lot of nonsense about always having found elderly men attractive. She never had a grandfather figure in her life, and she liked the idea of one. Anyway, one thing led to another. We had dinner a couple more times at Hoskins, then out of the blue, she turned up at my door with a suitcase in her hand.

She moved in that day. Granville was furious when he found out, but he wasn't about to get too upset with me. I've invested a lot of money with him, so he took all his anger out on Effie.'

'How do you mean? What did he do?'

'Oh, nothing extreme. He got her to meet him somewhere to talk things over, but when it didn't work out, he dumped her in the middle of nowhere. She had no money with her. She walked for miles to find a telephone to make a reverse charge call to me. The weather was foul that night, too. The poor girl looked like a drowned rat when Sinclair picked her up.'

'Sinclair?'

'My driver, come valet, come general dogsbody.' He held up his hands as Amy shook her head. 'I'm sorry, but he's not that good at any of the roles he's given. He's pranged the bloody Bentley twice.'

'Why don't you get rid of him, then?' Amy asked.

'He's cheap,' Angus replied. 'And I don't know what else he'd do if I gave him the old heave ho.'

'Did Effie enjoy her time with you? I know you bought clothes and gave her jewellery.'

'I bought her a couple of dresses when we spent a weekend in London. They were off the peg things, not cheap but hardly top drawer either. As for the jewellery. I can only remember giving her a bracelet. It was nothing more than a trinket. A former lady friend of mine had left it behind when she walked out on me. I had no other use for it.'

'Was that the little something you mentioned in the note you wrote to her?'

'It was. We had just come back from that London break. How did you know about that?'

'We found it in her flat,' Bodkin said. 'We find a lot of things during an investigation, Angus. It's amazing what turns up.'

'There's not a lot more to turn up regarding our relationship,'

Angus replied. 'Apart from the dresses and a few dinners, she got nothing else from me. I wasn't like Granville. He used to throw money at her. I think she expected the same from me, but I wasn't that stupid. I think that's when she realised she'd made a big mistake, leaving the Cresswell fortune behind.'

'How close were you, Angus? You said you hit it off right from the start. Did you continue to get on once she'd moved in?'

'To be fair, she was out with her friends as much as she was at home with me. We had a...' he shot Amy a quick glance... 'give and take sort of relationship.'

'You gave, she took?' Bodkin suggested.

'Not really, as I said. I didn't throw money at her. I gave her the odd ten shilling note to go out with when she met her friends at the Boat Club or, more often, the Milton, but that was about it. Granville gave her an allowance.' He laughed suddenly. 'That's one of the first things she asked me about after she moved in. How much will my allowance be?'

'That would have been a shock, when you told her she wouldn't be getting one?'

'I circled around the topic for a while. I wanted to know exactly what sort of girl she was before I gave her anything.'

'How long did it take you to find out?'

'Not long. Granville couldn't wait to tell me all about her little ways. I think he was desperate to get her back.'

'After sleeping with his business partner? After being dumped unceremoniously for... I'm sorry, it's not meant as an insult, but for someone old enough to be his father?'

'He knew I wasn't sleeping with her... All right, in the strictest sense, I was. But not in a sexual sense. I'm way past getting up to any of that nonsense. My old ticker would never have taken the strain.'

'So, if you didn't have sexual relations with her. What was the point of the relationship? Was she a trophy on your arm, a trinket to show off to your younger, jealous friends?' Bodkin took a gulp from his whisky glass.

'I liked to look at her, Inspector. She was a very beautiful and desirable young woman. Oh, I desired her. The flame might have gone out, but the embers still glow. No, I used to sit there and just look at her. Naked, of course. She'd pose for me on the bed or on the sofa. Sometimes in the garden. I'd get her to change position for me now and again while I sat with an artist's pad pretending to draw her.'

'Blimey!' Bodkin exclaimed. 'I think I've heard it all now.'

'You wait until you get into your dotage,' Angus said with a frown. 'You'd give anything to have someone like her lying naked in front of you.'

'So, you never touched her body? All you did was look?'

'No, I touched her now and then, but it was frustrating... for me, at least. I couldn't do anything more than touch, no matter how hard I tried. I had the desire but nothing to back it up with.'

'What did she think about it all? The lack of sex, I mean.' Bodkin downed the rest of his drink and rolled the remains of the ice around the bottom of his glass.

'I think she pitied me at first. Then she found it amusing. She was getting what she wanted, without having to go through having sex with a decrepit old so and so like me. I'm sure it would have been over long before it was if she had had to put up with that. I knew she was seeing other men behind my back, and I honestly couldn't blame her for that. She was a young woman and had her own unfulfilled needs, after all. I accepted it and we trundled along for a while.'

'So what happened to end it?'

'She started bringing men home when I was out.'

'Well, she had nowhere else to take them.'

'No, I suppose not, but I wasn't happy about it. I knew some of the men she was taking to my bed. She didn't use her own room.

She did it just to annoy me. I'd come home from a meeting or a night out to find my bedsheets needed a wash. She left a little present for me on my pillow one evening... A used French letter.' He grimaced as he looked towards Amy. 'I'm sorry, my dear, that was a little too much information.'

'How long did you let her get away with that?' Bodkin asked.

'The prophylactic was the final straw, Inspector. I threw her out that night. Well, I got Sinclair to throw her out.' She only had a short nightgown on and she was screaming the place down, threatening me with all sorts of acts of revenge. Eventually, I relented and got Sinclair to chuck some of her things into a suitcase and throw it out after her.'

'And that was it? Did you see her again?'

'I saw her quite a bit at the Boat Club. She had latched onto Joe, the club captain, by then... amongst others,' he added.

'Did you speak to her? Did she have anything to say to you?'

'I had nothing to say to her. It had all only lasted a few short weeks. I did hear from one of the girls at the club that she was going to try to get back in with Granville, but she never did as far as I know.'

'How long ago did you hear that, Angus?'

'Recently... it would have probably been the week before she died.'

Amy finished her Pimm's and put her glass carefully back on the table.

'Another?' Angus asked, raising his hand and clicking his fingers to get the waiter's attention.

'Not for us, Angus,' Bodkin said. 'I've only got a couple more questions for you.'

Angus held up his glass, pointed to it, then stuck up a single digit. The waiter nodded and disappeared into the bar to mix a new drink.

'I know you have a half share in the Boat Club, but how closely are you involved with Granville's chemical concern?'

'I own twenty-five percent of it.'

'Do you visit him on the premises or do you always see him at Grafton Hall?'

'Both. It depends. I was over at the plant a couple of weeks ago, as it happens. I'd met a chap who owned a distribution plant in the East End of London. He was shipping his bulk orders in from somewhere in Yorkshire. I wondered if we could sort him out with a better deal, so I got him up here and took him over to see Granville. We ended up with a new customer. He was really impressed with the way the works were run. Especially the purity results we could show him in the test lab.'

'When was this exactly, Angus?'

'It would have been Friday, the twenty-first. I didn't get involved in the technical talk. It makes my head spin. I left them to it in the upstairs office and waited for them in the lab. I had a nice chat with Katherine. She had hooked up with Granville again by then.'

'Did she ask after Effie at all?'

'Her name cropped up. I couldn't tell her much. Just that she was seeing Joe, but she already knew that.'

'One last question, Angus. Were you at the Boat Club on Saturday, the twenty-second or Sunday, the twenty-third?'

'No to both, Inspector. I had picked up a nasty bug from somewhere or other and I spent the entire weekend in bed.'

# CHAPTER FORTY-TWO

After arriving back home, Amy got to work on the second tricky repair of the Brigden's dresses, but this time she felt there was little she could do other than cut two inches from the bottom of the dress and to manufacture a new hem. Satisfied with the result and knowing that many prospective dress hirers would actually need to tack the hem up anyway, she pressed the new seam and hung the dress up in her bedroom before setting to work on the final dress which was the easiest of the four and just required her to unpick a bunched seam and rework it.

After a quick tea of sandwiches and a slice of the sponge cake Alice had left in the porch for her earlier in the day, Amy sat at the dining table sipping tea while she wrote a new suspect list, now they had interviewed what were probably the key players in Effie's murder. At the top of the page, she listed her fictional hero, Hercule Poirot's famous list of motives. Revenge. Gain. Jealousy and Fear.

1. Granville Cresswell. Motive. Revenge. Has a weak alibi regarding his illness with only his family to back him up. We now know that Effie was trying to get back

with him. Had motive and access to the chloroform, but no proof that he wasn't where he said he was on the day. Could have persuaded others to act on his behalf. I still feel there is more to discover.

2. Katherine Downey. Motive. Revenge. Gain. Jealousy. Fear. A full house of motives. Katherine had the most to lose out of all the suspects. She had worked hard to get Granville and almost lost everything to Effie. Had the motive, opportunity and means. Could have been working in cahoots with Bertrand and or Granville. Alibi is weak and requires further investigation.
3. Bertrand Cresswell. Motive. Gain. Fear. Bertrand is in a relationship with Quentin Foxley-Walton, which Effie may have found out about. Also, would have had concerns about his future inheritance. Had the motive and the means. His alibi is also weak and was in the vicinity of the reed beds a few hours before Effie's body was discovered.
4. Angus McIntosh. Motive. Angus doesn't quite fit in with any of the motives listed. Possibly revenge for the way Effie treated him towards the end. Could have had access to the chloroform and was maybe in league with Katherine. Requires a little more investigation as to his whereabouts. Like Granville, his alibi relies on his insistence that he had a chill.
5. Joe Lyndsay. Motive. Unsure. Possibly Jealousy or Revenge. Joe lied about being at the boat sheds on the Sunday. Not sure where he could have sourced the chloroform but was around when Effie was last seen. May have been working in league with the Cresswells, but it looks unlikely. He's hiding something. Had access to both speedboats.

6. Timothy Philby. Motive. Jealousy. Revenge. Timothy was made to look a fool in public and that gives him a definite motive for wanting to exact revenge. Close friend of both Granville and Angus. Had a source for the purchase of cocaine, so may have been able to get hold of chloroform, too. Was in the vicinity when Effie was last seen alive.
7. Lesley Philby. Motive. Jealousy. Had a big thing for Joe Lyndsay and was humiliated by her father's relationship with Effie. Can't see how she had access to the chloroform unless she was in league with another one of the suspects. Possibly Katherine and Bertrand. Hasn't been formally questioned as yet.
8. Quentin Foxley-Walton. Motive. Fear. Had access to chloroform via the lab he works in. Weak alibi for both the Saturday and Sunday. He was in a secret relationship with Bertrand that Effie may have uncovered. He lied to us in his interview. His movements need further investigation.
9. John Watkins. Motive. Unknown. Seems to have a cast-iron alibi as to his movements.

Amy had just finished writing out her notes when there was a knock on the front door. She opened it to find Bodkin standing on the porch.

'I wondered if you fancied a couple of port and lemons. I feel in need of a pint or two. My brain needs sustenance.'

'I'll just get changed, Bodkin. I can't go looking like this. I've been working on those Brigden dresses this afternoon.'

Ten minutes later, Amy came downstairs wearing the same lemon-coloured summer dress she had worn for their meeting with Angus. Bodkin nodded appreciatively as she stepped into the living room. 'I'm glad you chose that one. It really suits you.'

Amy curtseyed. 'Thank you, kind sir. I'll just grab my cardi and I'm ready.'

The snug of the Old Bull wasn't too busy, despite it being factory fortnight, and they found a table near an open window where a soft breeze filtered through. Bodkin took a big gulp of his pint, went to put it on the table, then decided to take another huge swallow.

'Flippin 'eck, Bodkin. You really are thirsty, aren't you? That's half your pint gone already.'

Bodkin wiped his mouth with the back of his hand. 'I was ready for that,' he said.

Amy opened her bag and produced the sheet of paper she had been working on at home. Bodkin read through it, then stuck up his thumb.

'Excellent work, Amy. This pretty much sums up where we are with the investigation and Lesley is on my list. I was thinking of dropping in on her tomorrow.' He picked up his pint again and, after raising it to his lips, he took another huge gulp. 'I'd better order another one before we discuss the case. This one won't last another five minutes.'

'Leave me out this time,' Amy said. 'I'll get the next ones in.'

By the time Bodkin had returned from the bar, two of Amy's colleagues from the Mill had sat down on the bench seats to the right of them. Bodkin nodded as they broke off a whispered conversation to acknowledge him. The inspector dragged his stool closer to the table, then leaned over it to speak in a lowered voice.

'I have a little bit of news about Effie's background. Ferris spent the afternoon on the telephone speaking to all the doctors and dentists in the area. There are eight in all. Effie was registered as a patient at Doctor Millington's practice in Spinton. She was also registered at the Golding Dental practice on the High Street. Neither of them has seen her this year.'

'So she didn't have anything to do with Ronald Parkin outside of the Boat Club, then?'

Bodkin shook his head. 'Ferris spoke to the receptionist at the practice in Highwater. She works for both Parkin's dentist and the medical practice. They are in the same building on Church Street.'

Amy brushed away a few strands of hair that the breeze blew across her face, then after picking up her notes and putting them back into her bag, she took a long sip of her drink. 'Ooh, that's hit the spot,' she said. She looked down at Bodkin's pint. 'Has your brain been suitably refreshed?'

'It's getting there,' Bodkin said, picking up his beer.

Amy took another glug of her own drink, then grabbing her bag, she got to her feet. 'I'm just nipping to the lavvy. I should have gone before I came out. I've been drinking tea all evening.' She patted Bodkin on the shoulder as she passed. 'Drink up, I'll get you another on the way back.'

At ten o'clock, a chatty, smiling Bodkin, downed the dregs of his fourth pint, then looked at it sadly. 'Time flies when you're having fun, doesn't it?' He sighed. 'I suppose that will have to be it for the night. I'd better get you home.'

'You're not thinking of driving home, are you?' Amy asked.

'No, I'll walk back.' He looked at his watch, then at his empty pint glass.

'Have another if you fancy one, Bodkin.'

He considered it, then shook his head. 'Much as the offer appeals to me, I'd better not. It will be late by the time I get home and I want an earlyish start in the morning.'

'You can stay at the cottage,' Amy hissed so that the two ear wigging friends couldn't hear. 'You can sleep in my bed.'

Bodkin's eyes were suddenly the size of saucers. Amy slapped the back of his hand and snorted.

'I didn't say I'd be in it with you. I'll sleep in Mum and Dad's bed.'

'I couldn't... could I? What would you parents say if they knew? What about the neighbours? They watch us like hawks. They'll be bound to know I didn't go home.'

'Don't worry about the neighbours. They're only keeping an eye on the place while my parents are away. I'll tell Mum and Dad you stayed over, anyway. It's not like we're going to get up to any mischief, is it?'

Bodkin looked at his empty glass again, then got quickly to his feet. 'There's an offer I can't refuse,' he said.

~

At eleven-thirty, Amy lay in her mum and dad's double bed feeling a little bit lost as she was unused to having so much room. As she lay on her back looking at the ceiling, she thought about Bodkin lying in her bed on the other side of the wall, so close in fact that if the wall hadn't been there, she could almost have reached out and touched him. Shaking her head to clear it of the thoughts that began to creep into her mind, she sat up, took hold of one of the fat, spare pillows, and after pummeling it with her hands for a few moments, she wrapped her arms around it and hugged it to her chest. Then, after sighing softly to herself, and snuggling up to her substitute Bodkin, she fell asleep.

## CHAPTER
# FORTY-THREE

At a quarter to seven the next morning, Amy woke up to the smell of frying bacon wafting up the stairs. After pulling on her slippers, she took her dressing gown from the hook on the door and pulled it on. As she walked into the living room, she found that Bodkin had already laid the table and made the tea.

'The toast is ready,' Bodkin said, passing the full rack to Amy as she licked her lips at the smell of the sizzling bacon. 'One fried egg or two?' he asked as she took a triangle of toast from the stainless steel rack and began to apply a liberal amount of butter to it.

'Two please, chef. I'm starving.' She lifted the toast to her mouth. 'Mum would be even more impressed if she could see you now. A man who doesn't mind cooking; I doubt she's ever come across one before.'

'I'm full of surprises,' Bodkin said.

'Did you sleep well?' Amy asked.

'Like a log. I woke up in the fireplace,' Bodkin replied with a grin. 'Your bed is much more comfortable than mine. I think I need a new mattress.' He took the fish slice and lifted the bacon out of the pan. 'You'll have to try it out one night... I'll sleep on the sofa, obviously.'

'You'll get some practice of that at the weekend. I presume you're letting Sal have your bed?'

Bodkin cracked two eggs into the pan and leaned back so he could look into the living room. 'Yep, but I'm not going to attempt to cook dinner. She had enough of my cooking when we were kids.'

After frying two more eggs, Bodkin cut a couple of tomatoes in half and dropped them into the pan. Two minutes later, with a tea towel draped over his arm like a waiter, he carried the breakfast plates through to the table, where he found Amy pouring the tea.

'What's the plan for today?' she asked as Bodkin cut a piece from a rasher of crispy bacon and dipped it into one of his eggs.

'I've got a briefing on the knicker nicker case first off. It might seem a trivial thing, but some of the people affected are friends with the chief super's wife and she's getting it in the earhole, which means he is too. After that, I'm going to catch up on the burglary inquiry. I think we're getting close to a result on that one. I should be free by about ten. If you'd like to meet me at the station, we'll have a drive over to Highwater to have a word with Lesley.'

~

At five to ten, Amy stepped off the bus opposite the chip shop on Middle Street and walked briskly down to the police station where she found Constable Parlour reading through a report.

'Hello,' Amy said breezily. 'Is Inspector Bodkin about?'

'He's had to go to the hospital, miss.'

Amy's jaw dropped. 'What for... what's wrong with him?'

'Oh, it's not him, miss. He was called out because someone's been shot. That's all I know.'

'Shot? My goodness. How long has he been up there?'

'An hour and a half, something like that.'

'Is Constable Ferris in?'

'He went with him, miss.'

'I see,' Amy replied. 'Do you mind if I wait?'

Parlour smiled and nodded to the bench behind her. 'Take a seat... oh you've got a pass, haven't you? Would you like to wait in the inspector's office? I can arrange a cup of tea if you'd like one. Trixie will sort it for you.'

Amy shook her head. The terms of her agreement had been laid out clearly, and she had been told that she wouldn't be allowed into the main part of the police station unless either Bodkin or Ferris were on the premises. She decided not to push her luck and settled down to wait on the green painted bench. As it turned out she didn't have to wait too long because fifteen minutes later she saw Bodkin and Ferris walk into the corridor behind the desk. As Amy stood up, Bodkin waved to her, then stepped smartly along the passage to open the door to allow her inside.

'Hello. I'm sorry I wasn't here to meet you, but something came up.' He turned to Ferris. 'Can you get Trixie to rustle up a pot of tea? I've neither fresh water nor milk in my office. Unless there's some clotted stuff in my filing cabinet.'

As Ferris walked off to find Trixie, Bodkin led Amy into his office. 'You could have waited in here. Sergeant Conway is about somewhere.'

'I wasn't sure if he counted as he wasn't here when Chief Inspector Laws told me the rules I had to stick to.'

Bodkin sat down behind the desk, and Amy took the seat facing him. 'I hear you had a busy morning?'

Bodkin shook his head slowly. 'That doesn't even come close.'

'I heard there was a shooting?'

'There was. We've finally caught up with the notorious night time knickers nicker. He's the one that was shot. He wants me to arrest the man that shot him.'

'Is he seriously hurt?'

'His backside was peppered by a man firing a shotgun. Luckily for him, his assailant was about thirty yards away or it might have been more serious.'

'Was he wearing trousers at the time?'

'Nope, he had just pulled on a pair of silk knickers and got them caught around his ankles. He tried to run, but he didn't get far. The funny thing was, he was hit by a cartridge of bird shot and the pants he'd just taken, had a pair of lovebirds embroidered on them. That's poetic justice if ever I saw it.'

Amy stifled a laugh. 'So he's going to be all right?'

Bodkin nodded. 'The nurse had a job on using just a pair of eyebrow tweezers, but she got it all out in the end.' Bodkin laughed to himself. 'You haven't heard the best bit.'

'Oh, do tell,' Amy said leaning forward in her seat.

'His name is Nick Botham.'

Amy put her hand in front of her mouth. 'No... really?'

'As Ferris was quick to say. We nicked Nick the knickers nicker.'

Amy laughed out loud. 'He's Knickerless Botham now.'

It took Bodkin a moment to catch on, then he began to roar with laughter. 'Ferris,' he shouted. 'Get in here. You've got to hear this one.'

~

Bodkin once again allowed Amy to drive along the two-mile stretch of Spinton Lane, but this time she remained behind the wheel until they reached the car park of the Boat Club.

'You're getting rather good at this,' he said as she pulled up perfectly into the space between two parked cars.

'When do you think I'll be ready for my driving test?' she asked as she let go of the hand brake.

'You've got a way to go yet, Amy. You haven't been out in traffic yet. Once you've done that and driven a few times through a busy town like Gillingham, then you might be ready. If you carry on as you are, you could be driving alone before the autumn is out.' He opened the passenger door, climbed out into the car park, and waited for her to join him. 'Just you wait until the ice and snow hits the streets. That's when you'll really learn how to drive.'

They found Lesley sitting at the bar, reading a copy of Woman's Own magazine. She sighed, closed it up and laid it on the counter as they approached.

'I didn't expect to see you here again,' she said to Amy. 'You had us for fools, didn't you?'

'That wasn't my intention,' Amy said. 'I really did want to come to the ball. I honestly enjoyed it and so did my friend Alice.'

'You had all the men eating out of your hand. I've never heard so many people asking questions about a new member. I include Effie in that and she really put herself about. You didn't have to. It was quite an act.'

Amy decided to take the compliment. 'Thank you,' she said.

'Miss Philby. We have one or two questions for you. We won't keep you long. I'm sure you're very busy,' Bodkin gave her a big smile.

Lesley looked at her watch. 'I've got a few minutes until the bar opens. What do you want to know?'

'What can you tell us about the afternoon of the twenty-second of July? It was a Saturday, and it was the last time anyone saw Effie Watkins alive. She made a telephone call from here not long before she walked out.'

Lesley nodded. 'She did. It would have been four forty-five, four-fifty, something like that.'

'She left alone?'

Lesley nodded again.

'No one followed her out?'

'Only me, but that was about ten minutes later.'

'You left the club? Where did you go?'

'We were completely out of milk. We have a few members who don't drink alcohol in the afternoon, and they tend to order coffee. I nipped up the shop on the green to pick some up while it was relatively quiet.'

'Did you see Effie while you were out?'

Lesley shook her head. 'No, I didn't see her at all after she left the club.'

'Did you see anyone on your way to the shop?'

'There was an old boy walking his dog and a couple of old ladies sat on one of the benches, but apart from that... Oh, wait... John Watkins was there. You know... Effie's stepbrother? The vet? I'd almost forgotten. He was sitting in his car opposite the church. It was odd, really. He pulled away as I walked across the road to say hello. He seemed to be in a bit of a hurry.'

# CHAPTER FORTY-FOUR

THE A2 WAS A BUSY ROAD AT THE BEST OF TIMES. ONCE KNOWN AS THE Great Dover Road, it had been an important connection between London and the ports of the southeast for centuries. Bodkin picked it up at Gillingham and from there it was a straight run through to Sittingbourne, a distance of some twelve miles.

The veterinary surgery wasn't the easiest place to find, and Bodkin had to stop at a telephone kiosk in the town and dial the number he had copied into his notebook to get directions. On asking of the whereabouts of John Watkins, he was told that he was out on his rounds but should be back by three o'clock at the latest.

The Fullerton Veterinary Practice was situated two miles outside of Sittingbourne in the village of Radfield. The building itself was a seventeenth century cottage that had been modernised to incorporate a window made up of thirty-two small panes, and a white painted front door.

Inside, they found themselves in a small waiting room along with a woman holding a wicker cat carrier and an old man with a Jack Russell dog on his lap whose sole purpose in life seemed to be to find a way to get at the cat.

Bodkin pulled out his warrant card and showed it to the young girl on the reception desk. 'I telephoned about fifteen minutes ago. I'm looking for John Watkins.'

'He's not in. Would you like to sit and wait? It could be an hour or so though.'

'We'll wait...' Bodkin said, but then had an idea. He leaned on the counter and lowered his voice as he spoke to the young girl. 'Would you happen to have the address of a local farmer that Mr Watkins paid a visit to? It would have been the late afternoon of the twenty-second of July. The call out was to do with a flock of sheep.'

'I'll have to get permission from Mr Fullerton,' the receptionist said as she got to her feet. 'What was your name again?'

Bodkin told her. 'Tell him it's a matter of the utmost urgency.'

The girl left her desk and pushed open a dark wooden door which had a white sign with the word Surgery painted on it in black. A couple of minutes later, she reappeared with a balding man of about fifty. He wasn't happy at being disturbed.

'What's all this about? I've got a very sick dog to care for.'

Bodkin held out his hand, and the vet reluctantly shook it. 'I'm Inspector Bodkin of the Spinton police. We spoke last week on the telephone.'

'I remember. I gave you the details you asked for then, didn't I?'

'There appear to be contradictory reports of Mr Watkins' whereabouts,' Bodkin replied.

'Contradictory reports? He was over at Mossley Farm. There is no ambiguity about it. I have his report in the filing cabinet. The farmer has been invoiced. He was at the farm on the day and at the time he said he was Mr Bodkin. I don't care what your contradictory account says.'

'It's probably a case of mistaken identity, but we need to check these things. His stepsister was murdered after all.'

'Shh, not so loud, man,' Fullerton hissed. He turned on his heel and walked back into the surgery, returning a couple of minutes later with the clinical report sheet that Watkins had filled out. 'Chronic Mastitis in two sheep.' He scanned the document. 'Both animals were euthanised. And a check of the rest of the flock carried out.'

'That must have taken a while. What time does he say he left the farm?'

'It isn't a very large flock, Inspector. Radley Giles only owns a couple of acres and about a dozen sheep. He had a rough time of it during the Great Depression and had to sell off most of his land.' He paused as he tapped the sheet. 'It's more of a hobby for him these days, to be honest. He isn't making any money out of his flock.'

'Where is this farm? I'd like a quick word with him while I'm waiting for Watkins to return.'

Fullerton showed Bodkin the address at the top of the form. 'Take the main road towards Sittingbourne. There's a big oak standing alone on the right-hand side of the road just before you reach the town. Turn right there. The farmhouse is a couple of hundred yards up the track. It's a bumpy ride.' The vet turned away from Bodkin and went back to his patient.

'Farmer Giles. Can you believe that?' Bodkin said as he turned the car around and headed back the way they had come. 'Farmer blooming Giles. I can picture him already.'

Mossley Farm was a ramshackle collection of ruined buildings, including a barn without a roof, a lean-to that had leaned too far and a large shed missing its double doors. The farmhouse itself was in poor repair, with sheets of corrugated iron nailed onto the roof in a patchwork pattern. They found the farmer sitting on a rickety chair on a wooden porch at the front of the building. He wore a dirty suit jacket, a shirt that hadn't seen a wash for many a day and a pair of torn, twill trousers. He woke noisily from his nap when Bodkin tapped him on the shoulder.

'Farmer Giles?' Bodkin didn't offer his hand.

'Who are you?' the man said, rubbing his eyes with the back of a grizzled hand that was almost the same rusty colour as his trousers.

'I'm Inspector Bodkin of the Spinton police.'

'Spinton? Did you get lost?' Giles sat up straight and yawned.

'I'd just like to ask you a couple of questions, then I'll let you get back counting sheep,' Bodkin said.

'It doesn't take long to count them these days. You couldn't drop off while you were doing it.'

'I heard you had a few problems with the health of your flock and you had to call the vet in?'

'I look after them myself normally. I can't afford the luxury of a vet, but it was an emergency. The ewes were suffering.'

'Chronis Mastitis wasn't it?'

Giles nodded. 'I should have got him in earlier, really, but I sort of hoped it would clear itself up. It has before now.'

'The vet was Mr Watkins?'

Giles shrugged. 'I dunno, if you say so.' He thought for a moment as he scratched meaningfully at his groin. Amy looked quickly away. 'He was a tall chap, going a bit thin on top. He knew his stuff, though.'

'You lost both sheep?'

'He had to put them down in the end. They were in a bit of a state and in a lot of pain. He had to chloroform them just to quieten them down enough to be able to examine them, but there was nothing he could do and he gave them both an injection while they were unconscious.'

'Then he examined the rest of the flock?'

'Not likely. I couldn't afford for him to hang around that long.

Anyway, the sheep were all over the bottom field. Although there's only a dozen of them, it would have taken hours to catch and check them over.'

'He wasn't here long, then?'

'About an hour. He was gone well before four o'clock.'

'Four? Are you sure about that?'

'Positive. I heard my old mantel clock mark the hour, and I'd dragged the carcasses into the shed and made myself a cup of tea by the time it chimed.'

'Thank you for your time,' Bodkin said and turned away from the house.

'Bodkin, if he left here before four, he could easily have made it to Highwater in time to catch Effie leaving the Boat Club. It's only twenty miles and half of it would have been spent on the A2. The Gillingham to Spinton road is hardly a farm track either.'

'We'll time it on the way home, Amy,' Bodkin said as they walked back to the car. 'First though, let's go back to the vets to see what sort of explanation John Watkins can provide. Remember, we were told he didn't have time to get up to see his mother because of that emergency with the sheep.'

~

John Watkins walked into the almost empty waiting room of the surgery with his tweed jacket hung over his shoulder. He smiled at the receptionist, then turned towards the door to the surgery. Before he could reach it, Bodkin and Amy got to their feet.

'Mr Watkins, I'm Inspector Bodkin of the Spinton police. We've been waiting for you.'

A puzzled look flashed across Watkins' face. 'Police? Is it to do with Effie?'

'Is there somewhere less public we can go?' Bodkin asked.

Watkins nodded. 'Through here,' he opened a door at the back of the waiting room and led them into a small kitchen. 'Now,' he said, as he hung his coat on the back of a chair. 'How can I help? Have you found out who killed my sister?'

'Not yet, but we're getting closer to apprehending the culprit,' Bodkin said. 'This is Miss Rowlings, by the way. She's assisting me on this case.'

Watkins smiled weakly as he nodded at her. 'Would you like a cup of tea while we talk?' He shook an electric kettle to check how much water was inside, then after topping it up at the sink, he plugged it into the wall and switched it on.

'We have received conflicting information regarding your whereabouts on the afternoon and evening of Saturday, the twenty-second of July,' Bodkin said as the vet spooned tea into the pot.

'I was here,' the vet looked up but didn't turn around.

'Here, as in the surgery?' Bodkin asked.

'I meant here, as in the area, I'll have to check, but I'm pretty sure I was over at Mossley Farm. Old Radley Giles had a couple of sick sheep.'

'Mastitis,' Bodkin said. 'You had to euthanise them.'

'You seem very well informed, Inspector.' Watkins poured boiling water into the pot and carried it over to the table. 'Milk? Sugar?'

'Both,' Bodkin said. The vet opened a cupboard and retrieved a milk bottle and a sugar bowl.

Watkins poured tea into three cups, then left Amy and Bodkin to add their own milk and sugar. 'So, what's this about old Giles? Has he been claiming I overcharged him?'

'Not at all. It's just that we have a witness who claims to have seen you on the green in Highwater at the time you were supposed to be checking out Old Farmer Giles's flock.'

'They must have been mistaken. I was here. I had to cancel a visit to my mother's because of the emergency.'

'That's what your mother told us,' Bodkin said. 'But Farmer Giles said you left his farm at about a quarter to four after putting two of his sheep to sleep. He claims that he asked you not to bother checking out the rest of the flock, as it would have cost him extra.'

Beads of sweat suddenly appeared on Watkins' brow. He slipped a finger inside his collar, then loosened his tie and undid the top button. 'It's a little warm in here,' he said with a quick smile.

Bodkin lifted his cup but didn't take a drink from it. 'So, Mr Watkins. It leaves us with a bit of a conundrum. One of you is lying and I don't think it's the farmer.'

The vet's cup and saucer began to rattle as his hands shook.

'All right. I was in Highwater that afternoon. Effie had asked me to meet her at the Boat Club. We had a few things to discuss. We hadn't parted on particularly good terms the last time we'd met.'

'Why did you lie about it? There's nothing wrong with driving up to see your sister.'

'I didn't want Mum to know I'd been up there after I'd told her I couldn't make it.'

'Ah, I see,' Bodkin said. 'You could have surprised her by popping in on the way home. You have to drive past her flat to pick up the A2.'

'I was too upset. My meeting with Effie didn't go as planned. I just needed to get as far away from her as I could.'

Bodkin took a sip of tea and leaned back in his chair. 'I think you'd better start at the beginning, Mr Watkins.'

The vet blew out his cheeks, then placed his forearms on the table. 'I've always had a difficult relationship with Effie, even before I qualified. Mum and I did our best to make her feel like family, but she never showed us that she wanted to be part of it. She used to flirt with me a lot when she was younger, but I put that down to her age. She blew hot and cold with me depending on whether she wanted something or not. I was away at university a lot of the time so Mum was left to deal with her on her own and she really was a handful.'

'How did you feel about her flirting with you, Mr Watkins?' Amy asked.

Watkins shrugged. 'What could I do about it? I ignored her most of the time, but if I did that she came on even stronger. She was an attention seeker, Miss Rowlings.'

'So you didn't respond at all to her flirting? Did your mother spot it?'

'She never did it in front of Mum. She wouldn't have dared.'

'So, she was an attention seeker. A lot of young girls are. What was so different about Effie?' Bodkin asked.

'Effie wanted everything. Not just the attention. I bought her some nice gifts for birthdays and Christmas, but it didn't matter how much I spent, it was never enough. She always wanted more.'

Amy held up a finger. 'You didn't reply when I asked you how you responded to her flirting? She was an attractive young woman. You were a young man. You must have been flattered at least.'

'I took it as a bit of fun to start with, but then it got a bit more serious. She climbed into bed with me one night, she was stark naked, and when I didn't respond in the way she thought I should have, she called me all sorts of names, then threatened to tell Mum it had been me that got into her bed.'

'Where was your mother at the time?'

'She was away for the weekend.'

'So she attempted to blackmail you? Did you pay up?'

'Unfortunately, I did, and it was the high end of a slippery slope. She knew she had me after that.'

'Why? You could have called her bluff, surely.'

'I... Not really because Mum caught me in her room with her one night when she came home unexpectedly.'

Bodkin and Amy exchanged glances.

'What were you doing in there?' the policeman asked.

'I'd gone in to try to persuade her to be reasonable. I didn't know she'd just got out of the bath. She had a towel wrapped around her which conveniently fell to the floor the moment Mum walked in.'

'How old was she at the time, Mr Watkins?'

'Sixteen. But she was ten years older, mentally. She knew exactly what she was doing.'

'How was all this resolved?'

'I moved out. Mum paid for a rented flat in Cambridge and she used to visit me up there.'

'So you didn't see Effie again after that?'

'She came up to the flat a few times when she was on the run from the trouble she was eager to leave behind.'

'And you let her stay, even after all she'd done?'

'Yes, despite everything. I liked her. She could be very good company when she was in the mood.'

Amy shook her head. Bodkin pursed his lips, then brought his hand up to his chin.

'And after university. Did you stay in touch?'

'I moved down here to Sittingbourne, so I didn't see a lot of her. Then I was invited up for a reunion at the Highwater Boat Club. I used to row for them when I was at Cambridge. Anyway, I turned up on the night to find that Effie was a member, and it wasn't long before she was rehashing all her old lies about me.

I'm not sure how many people believed her, but it was awkward, to say the least.'

'That can't have been pleasant, but back to the twenty-second. What did you want to see her about?'

'Effie called me at the practice and asked if I'd like to meet up. She said she was at a loose end that weekend and she wondered if I'd like to keep her company on Saturday night. She suggested we meet at the Boat Club but that we could possibly end up at the Milton and have a late night if I fancied staying over. She said there was something she'd like to discuss. I suspected that she had run out of money again or was between men.'

'You didn't mind giving her money after all she's done to you in the past?'

'It's not a problem. Dad left me some money in a trust. I'll never go short really and I earn a good salary as a vet.'

'Did she call you that afternoon, Mr Watkins?'

'No, she had called me in the week. Wednesday I think it was.'

'You didn't go to the Boat Club, though. You were seen in Highwater.'

'I was driving to the club, but I saw her coming out of the lane as I drove along the side of the green. I tooted her, and she stopped to talk to me.'

'What did you talk about, Mr Watkins?'

'She didn't look at all pleased to see me. I think she'd forgotten about the phone call in the week or something more important had come up. A new man maybe.'

'Did she say anything about why her plans had changed?'

'No, she just asked what I was doing there. I reminded her that she had asked me to come up, but she just shrugged and said she had other plans now.'

'And that was it?' Bodkin asked.

'Not really. I lost my temper a bit. I told her to get in the car, but she just laughed at that. Then she told me to go home and if I tried to ruin her evening, she'd go over to see Mum and tell her a few home truths. She was always threatening to do that, but usually when she needed money. I got out of the car and tried to remonstrate with her. I begged her to come with me. I offered to take her to the Milton to buy her dinner and make a night of it, but she wasn't interested. For some silly reason I grabbed hold of her arm, but she told me if I didn't let go she'd scream the place down. I did let go, but it didn't stop her from threatening me. She said she'd tell Mother that I had raped her when she was sixteen. It was all a pack of lies, but I couldn't risk her doing that. It would destroy Mum.'

'So what did you do, Mr Watkins?' Bodkin's mouth became a thin line.

'She demanded I give her some money. I had a six pounds in my wallet, so I gave her a five-pound note. She laughed when I told her that's all I could give her, as I would need money for petrol on the way home. She said she'd be back for more soon. Then she turned away and walked across the green. The last I saw of her, she was going into Hoskin's restaurant. Presumably to meet the man she'd stood me up for.'

'And you didn't see her again after that?'

'No, I sat there for a few minutes. I thought about following her but she would only have caused a scene, so I turned the car around and drove home.'

'Why didn't you stop off at your mother's flat on the way?'

'I just wanted to get home and think about things. Something had to be done about Effie. She had me on a chain and I had to find a way to break it.'

Bodkin and Amy exchanged glances again.

'How did you intend to do that?' the policeman asked.

'I don't know. I thought about trying to pay her off. Give her a decent amount of money to leave me alone, but that would only work for a while. I'd done it before. She always came back for more.'

'So, you decided to bump her off?'

'Don't be ridiculous. I would never have done that,' Watkins said firmly.

'Did you have a bottle of chloroform in your car when you drove up to Highwater?'

'I don't know... yes. I must I have. I used it on the sheep before I left. It would have been in the boot with all my other stuff.'

'You see the problem here, Mr Watkins? You had what was probably a large container of the liquid that was used to kill Effie. You were the last person we know of that saw her alive and we only have your word for it that you drove home after seeing her.' Bodkin stared hard at the vet. 'Or can you provide a witness that saw you back in Sittingbourne that evening?'

'No. I went straight back home. I can't remember seeing any... Hang on! I stopped for petrol on the way.' He got to his feet and pulled out his wallet from the pocket of the jacket he had hung over the chair. 'There!' he said triumphantly. 'My receipt. It's from a garage just outside Gillingham. It's timed at five forty-five. That proves I had left Highwater.'

Bodkin studied the handwritten receipt before passing it to Amy. 'That proves that you were in Gillingham, but you could have had Effie's body in your car, Mr Watkins.'

'But the attendant filled up for me. He'd have noticed if I'd had a body in the back seat.'

'He wouldn't have seen into the boot, though,' Bodkin replied coldly.

'The boot... HA! Come and have a look in my boot, Inspector. With all the junk I carry about, there isn't room to fit a cat, let alone a human body.'

Bodkin got to his feet and waved his hand towards the door.

'Don't bother bringing a cat with you to prove your point. A quick look will suffice.'

An hour and a half later, Bodkin and Amy were sitting around her dining table, discussing what they had heard from John Watkins.

'You're the body language expert, Amy. What did you make of him?'

'He told us a few lies. His eyes were flicking about all over the place, and he always hesitated slightly before trying to lead us off topic when he was getting too close to the truth regarding his relationship with Effie.'

'He's had a sexual relationship with her, in the past, at least. That was plain to see.'

Amy nodded. 'I wonder if the rape story was true. It might have been playing on his mind. I mean, why mention it at all? He could just have said she was accusing him of pestering her for sexual favours.'

Bodkin nodded as he picked up the ham sandwich that Amy had made for him. 'I don't think Effie would have gone to the police about the assault. She didn't trust them, not with the lifestyle she led. I think she used the assault to blackmail him instead.'

Amy bit into her sandwich and chewed for a while. After washing it down with a mouthful of tea, she put the sandwich down and began to count off points.

'They were in some form of sexual relationship. That's why he used to have her up at his flat in Cambridge and it had been going on for years. I don't believe a word of what he said about her teasing and leading him on. If I was someone who liked a bet, I'd put money on him being the one to make the first move. She was little more than a child. Okay, she might have been a bit flirty, but

I probably was too. Young girls are still learning what physical attraction is all about at that age.'

Amy dropped a second finger.

'He was paying her for sex. That much is clear, though I believe him when he says he was desperate to keep his mother out of it. I think he pestered her for sex regularly. He's not that bad looking, despite losing his hair. He has money behind him, a good job, so why isn't he in a relationship with a woman? I think he had a fixation on Effie. He just couldn't leave her alone.'

She dropped another finger.

'He could well be our killer. He had the means, the opportunity... if he had persuaded her to get into his car. And he had the motive. She was threatening to expose him for what he'd done to her in the past. His mother would have been devastated; Effie was his sister after all, even though they weren't blood relatives.'

'All true,' Bodkin replied. 'But what did he do with the body? He was, as he says in Gillingham, less than an hour after he says he saw her for the last time.'

'There's lots of woodland about the area, Bodkin. He could have killed her in the car. Left her body in the woods, then... Oh, I don't know. It doesn't fit with where she was found, does it? He is an expert on the water though, so he could have retrieved the body the next morning and hidden it in the reeds.'

Bodkin pulled a face. 'I'm not sure. It would have been easier to dump her somewhere on the way back to Sittingbourne. There are plenty of places along the way.'

Amy finished her sandwich, picked up their plates and carried them through to the kitchen. 'We can have a chat about it later; see if his evidence changes anything we know about the other suspects.' She put the plates in the sink, then walked back to stand in the doorframe. 'Just supposing he was telling the truth, who would she have been meeting in Hoskin's? It's a very exclusive restaurant.'

'My money would be on Angus or Granville,' Bodkin said.

'So would mine,' Amy replied. 'I suppose we can always go in and ask the staff.'

'It will have to be tomorrow,' Bodkin replied. 'I've got to catch up on the paperwork that Nick the knickers nicker left us with this evening, so I'll be at the station until late.'

Amy sighed. 'That's a shame. I was hoping to have another night on the sofa with you. We might not get another chance before Mum and Dad come home.'

# CHAPTER FORTY-FIVE

At ten o'clock the next morning, just as Amy had finished hanging out the freshly washed sheets on the line, she heard a click of the back gate and Bodkin stepped into the garden.

'I've been banging on the front door for ages,' he said.

'Sorry, Bodkin. I meant to get the sheets washed yesterday, but I forgot all about it. She looked up at the thickening clouds. I hope that lot stays off.'

Bodkin studied the grey mass of cloud overhead. 'Your garden could do with a drop, though. We haven't had any rain for ages.'

'If it doesn't tip down, I'll give everything a water this afternoon. Mum will never forgive me if I let her prize Dahlias die off.' She hooked the peg bag onto the line and lifted the wooden prop. 'How come you're here, anyway? I thought you were catching up on paperwork?'

'It's all done,' Bodkin said proudly. 'Most of it anyway and there'll be more when we catch Dick the Pick or whoever it is committing the burglaries.'

'Dick the Pick,' Amy snorted. 'I love the names you give to the criminals. I take it Dick is a lock picker?'

'Correct! Give the lady a coconut,' Bodkin said with a grin.

'You're in a good mood considering how early in the morning it is.' Amy looked suspiciously at the policeman. 'I'm not sure I like it.'

'How do you fancy driving me to Highwater again? I'd like to hear why Joe Lyndsay lied about his whereabouts on the day Effie went missing,' Bodkin said. 'You can take over when we get to Main Street. I'd let you drive all the way, but we have to pass the police station and Chief Inspector Laws is over here today. He has a meeting with the chief super.'

The wind had picked up somewhat by the time Amy pulled up in the centre of Highwater and the first few drops of rain had begun to appear on the windscreen of the car. On the green, an elderly man looked at the threatening sky as he urged his dog to hurry up and finish doing his business. A woman raised her umbrella and increased the length of her stride as she walked past the church gates heading towards the shops. Bodkin opened the passenger side door and looked down at the nine-inch gap between the car and the kerb.

'You're getting really good at this parking lark, Amy. We won't need to get a taxi ride to the pavement this time.'

Amy punched him playfully on the shoulder. 'What's got into you today? You never crack a joke before lunchtime.'

Bodkin shrugged. 'I've been spending too much time with Ferris.' He turned his head to look across the deserted green. The drops of rain had now become a thin drizzle. 'This is where John Watkins must have parked on the Saturday evening,' he said, looking across at the row of windows on the side of the restaurant. A black and white painted sign boasting the Hoskin's name was fixed above the shutters.

'I was thinking about him last night when I was adding to my notes. There's something that doesn't quite fit. The other day, you said you had an itch you couldn't scratch and I've got the same feeling myself, only the itch is right in the middle of my shoulder blades and I can't quite reach it no matter how much I stretch.'

'It's a horrible feeling, isn't it? Knowing something important is just out of the reach of your fingers.' He checked his watch against the church clock. 'I think Joe lives on the street behind the church. There's a little café on the corner. Shall we have a quick coffee before we disturb the skipper?'

'He might be down at the Boat Club,' Amy said. 'Shall we check there first?'

'The club is shut and won't open for an hour or so. Unless he's getting some training in on the river, I can't see him being there.'

Amy suddenly banged both hands hard on the steering wheel. 'Bodkin, that's it. Oh, you clever man. You've just scratched my itch.' Amy threw the door open and almost fell into the road in her haste to get out. After slamming the door shut, she scurried around the front of the car, shouting to the policeman as she stepped onto the green. 'Hurry, Bodkin. I think I know who Effie met on Saturday night.'

Bodkin got out of the car and began to follow Amy as she hurried across the grass.

'Where are you going?' he shouted as Amy quickened her pace.

'It's Hoskin's, Bodkin, don't you see?'

The restaurant was situated at the end of a short row of shops and offices. The entrance was hidden inside a small courtyard. Amy stepped into it then, standing in the middle of the cobbled square, she performed a three-sixty degree turn. 'You see, Bodkin,' she said, pointing to the dark, oak stained front door of the restaurant, where the opening times were displayed in a small glass fronted frame.

Bodkin shook his head. 'What am I looking at?'

Amy turned around to face a single door that was shared by the two separate businesses on the opposite side of the quadrangle. On the door were two brass plaques. The left-hand one listed Norton Medical Practice, followed by three lines of opening times. The right-hand plaque listed Ronald Parkin. Dental Surgeon. L.D.S. A light could be seen filtering through the curtained window of the doctor's surgery but the dentist's side was in darkness.

'I think she came to see Ronald Parkin, Bodkin,' Amy said excitedly. 'John Watkins just assumed she was going into Hoskin's.'

'How did you work that out?' Bodkin said, looking puzzled.

'Look at the opening times, Bodkin. It was only five o'clock. Hoskin's doesn't open until six-thirty.'

'The staff might well be there to prepare for the evening rush before they open the doors, though, Amy.'

Amy shook her head. 'That's what was niggling away at me. Angus told me that the staff never arrive before six-thirty. He said that you can't buy so much as a biscuit until well after seven. She didn't go to Hoskin's Bodkin. I know it.'

'I've learned to trust your instincts, Amy, and I'm not going to go against them now.' Bodkin pressed down on the handle and pushed on the door. It opened into a twelve-foot square reception area. A thirty something, fair-haired woman wearing a white blouse and a maroon coloured jacket looked up from her notes as they entered.

'Good morning,' she said. 'Are you registered with the practice?'

Bodkin took out his warrant card and showed it to the receptionist. 'Inspector Bodkin, Spinton police. We'd like a word with Ronald Parkin, if possible.'

The woman shook her head as she looked up at him. 'I'm afraid Mr Parkin isn't available today.'

'Why not?' bodkin asked.

'The dental surgery is closed. Mr Parkin is taking his annual holiday. There will be a replacement dentist, but he won't be here until Monday morning.'

'Where is Parkin going? Do you know?'

'Edinburgh I believe. His wife has relatives up there. They don't actually leave until tomorrow, but they've taken the day off to get their packing done.'

'What hours do the surgeries open on a normal week?'

The woman pointed to the two signs that hung behind her on the wall. 'The doctor's surgery is open nine to five on weekdays but is closed at the weekend. Mr Parkin's practice is also nine to five, but only opens for a half day on Wednesdays. He is here until one o'clock on Saturdays, though.'

'What if he gets an emergency patient at the weekend?'

'He is good enough to open up out of hours, but only for a select few patients.'

'Do you work on the weekends, Miss...?'

'Manson. Edith Manson. I work until one on Saturdays.'

'Does Mr Parkin have a patient list I could have a look at?'

'He does, but I don't think I can just hand it over without permission.'

'I'm conducting a murder inquiry,' Bodkin said firmly, fixing her with a stern look.

The woman gave in reluctantly. 'It's all rather irregular. I hope I don't get in trouble for this.' She opened a drawer in her desk and pulled out a half inch thick file. 'You can't take it off the premises,' she said quickly.

'Does Mr Parkin have an assistant?' Bodkin asked, as he took the file from Edith.

'Nan... Annette Parkin, his wife, assists him. He doesn't employ anyone.'

Bodkin flipped through the pages looking for Effie's name, but there were no Watkins listed in the file. He handed it back to Edith with a curt nod of appreciation. 'Do you have a spare set of keys for the surgery?' he asked.

'I have two sets at the moment. One is for the temporary dentist when he arrives on Monday, the other is a spare set for emergencies.'

Bodkin held out his hand.

'I can't... I mean, I'll have to ring and check with him first.'

'Call him if you must, but I want those keys now,' Bodkin growled.

Edith opened a second draw in her desk and pulled out a keyring that had four different sized keys attached to it. 'I want them back before you leave,' she insisted.

'You'll get them back when I've done with them,' Bodkin said as he turned towards the plate glass door. 'You've got a spare set if you need them.'

As they stepped through the doorway, they found themselves in a narrow corridor with a door facing them some twenty feet along the passage and a door leading off to either side. The door on the left was open and led to a waiting room which had four chairs arranged neatly around a beech coffee table. Bodkin pushed open the door on the right and stepped into the dental surgery. In the centre was a reclining dentist's chair. Along the opposite wall was a sink and draining board, which sat below a three-foot square window. To the right were two rows of cabinets. The floor mounted ones had solid, cedar doors, the wall mounted ones sported inlaid glass panels.

Bodkin opened a couple of the lower cabinets. One held a number of porcelain bowls. In another he found a stack of narrow drawers which when pulled out revealed the tools of the dentist's trade.

After closing the cupboard doors, Bodkin opened up one of the glass cabinets to find two rows of various sized glass containers, and a pile of cotton cloths. At the end of the front row were two half-pint bottles with heavy duty rubber seals around the stoppers. One was full, and the other had about half an inch of liquid in the bottom. The labels on both read chloroform CHCL.3 284 cc, and both had a handwritten date and an illegible signature underneath the printed chemist's name.

Amy, meanwhile, had gone through the open door at the end of the passage and discovered a ten by twelve foot cloakroom. Facing her was a tall cupboard which contained a couple of mops, a bucket and a variety of cleaning products, including bleach and Dettol. Further along the wall was a similar sized unit with a row of coat hooks across the back, on which hung two long white coats. At the bottom was a wooden chest that spanned the width of the cupboard. Amy lifted the lid, to find two more neatly folded laboratory coats, lying on top of a brown paper bag. Taking hold of the top of the bag, she pulled it out and opened it up. Inside, she could see the sheen of polished leather.

'Bodkin!' she shouted at the top of her voice. 'I've found Effie's bag.'

~

Amy handed the bag to Bodkin, and he sat on the dentist's chair to open it up. Inside, along with her lipstick, he found a brush, a comb and the plethora of other items that women carry in their bags. In a side compartment, he found a bunch of keys, an address book, and a purse. Inside the purse was a crisp five-pound note.

'It looks like John told us the truth about handing over a fiver when they met,' he said, dropping the purse back into the beautifully made leather bag. He picked up the address book and flicked through it. 'Quite a few numbers in here with a few names that you'll recognise. Here's Granville, Joe, Angus, Bertrand... and here's Ronald Parkin. There's an address too. Riverbank. Highwater. Kent.'

'We'll have to be quick, Bodkin. He might nip off early if the receptionist lets him know you're searching the premises.'

'Riverbank is our next port of call,' Bodkin said. 'I just want to make a quick telephone call first.' He walked across the room and read the number on the dial of the black phone that sat on the cabinet below the glass fronted units. 'That's not the number in Effie's book, so if it was Parkin she rang from the club that Saturday, she was calling him at home.'

'Are you ringing him now?' Amy asked.

Bodkin pointed to the two bottles of chloroform that were now sitting on the draining board next to the sink. 'Have a look at the dates on those two bottles.' Bodkin opened his own notebook and looked for the number of the Spinton chemist shop. 'Hello, Agatha? It's inspector Bodkin... yes, I'm fine, thank you. I'd just like you to check something for me. It's to do with a chloroform order made by the Highwater dentist, Ronald Parkin. Could you tell me when he put in the last two orders?'

The line went quiet for a full minute, then he heard Agatha's voice in his ear. 'He picked a two hundred and... a half pint bottle up on Thursday the twentieth of July. Then on Tuesday the twenty-fifth, his wife came in to order a replacement bottle. I wasn't the one who served her, but my assistant has left a note in the order book to say that Mrs Parkin had reported that Ronald had dropped the original bottle when he was carrying it from the car into the surgery. Customers usually bring the empty ones back to be sterilised and refilled.'

'Thank you, Agatha. You've been very helpful,' Bodkin said.

Back in reception, they found Edith talking on the telephone.

She put her hand over the mouthpiece as Bodkin, carrying Effie's bag in one hand, locked the door with the other.

'No one is to go into the dentist's surgery until further notice. I am designating it as the scene of a murder.' Bodkin slipped the bunch of keys into his pocket, then held out his hand to the receptionist. 'I'd like the spare set please, and if that's Ronald Parkin or his wife you're speaking to, tell them we're on our way.'

# CHAPTER FORTY-SIX

After getting directions from the receptionist, Bodkin drove past the church and took a turn-off along a narrow hedge-lined track, that only had room for one car to drive along at any time. The track forked twice, but Bodkin followed the river and eventually they came to a dead end with only a right turn available to them. Twenty yards further along, they pulled up alongside a blue Alvis and found Riverbank house directly in front of them. The house was old, almost certainly seventeenth century. Bits had been bolted on over the years, giving it a surreal sort of look with its overhanging eaves and three dormer windows protruding from the roof. Amy could easily imagine Boris Karloff stepping out of the front door into a pea souper of a fog.

Music blared out from an open window at the front of the house as they approached. When no one replied to Bodkin's knock on the front door, he led Amy around the side of the house and with the river gurgling along, only a few feet to their right they walked past a row of three leaded panel windows through which they could see a long galley-style kitchen. A few yards further on, they found a rickety-looking porch. Bodkin rapped on the back door and when no one responded to his third attempt, he twisted the knob and pushed the door open.

'Hello?'

There was no reply to his call.

'Hello,' he called again. Then, after waiting a full minute, he stepped into the kitchen with Amy hot on his heels.

The kitchen was some twenty feet long, but there was only a three-foot gap between the cupboards on either side. The recording of Enrico Caruso blared through the house, and Bodkin had to raise his voice so that Amy could hear what he was saying. 'You didn't tell me the Parkin's were stone deaf?'

On the worktop at the side of the sink, Amy saw a tray of sandwiches with a fine muslin cover over them, and at the side of that was a second tray that held an empty teapot and two cups and saucers. Alongside the teapot was a folded napkin with a long needle protruding from it.

Bodkin unwrapped the napkin to find a full hypodermic needle. 'Old Parkin might be into other things than cocaine,' he said to Amy.

'Maybe he's a diabetic?' she replied, but then she noticed the tin of rat poison on the windowsill. 'We've seen one of those before,' she said as she pointed it out to the policeman.

Bodkin suddenly became suspicious and, after wrapping a tea towel around his hand, he picked up the tin. The label contained a warning message, with the words Poison and Potassium cyanide printed in large letters. Placing the tin back on the windowsill, he carefully unwrapped the hypodermic, then holding the needle close to his nose, he took two quick sniffs before deciding he could just pick up the very faint scent of bitter almonds.

'I wonder if that's a welcome present for us?' Bodkin said. 'I think we'll skip any offer of lunch.'

Pointing the syringe into the sink, he pushed down the plunger until he had emptied it, then, after picking up a glass from the side, he ran fresh water into it from the tap. Dipping the needle into the glass, he filled and emptied the syringe five times before he was sure that it was free from poison. Then, after filling it one last time, he placed the hypodermic carefully on the napkin before wrapping it up again.

At last, Caruso stopped singing his aria and silence descended onto the house.

Bodkin pulled open the door to the lounge and called out hello again. This time, he got a response as Nan Parkin opened the door from the stairs and stepped into the room.

'It's good manners to wait until you're invited before you walk into someone's house,' she said.

'You have my sincere apologies,' Bodkin said, flashing his warrant card, but we're here on a matter of some importance. 'We tried both doors, but you didn't hear the knock over the sound of the record player.' He slipped the card back into his pocket. 'I'm Inspector Bodkin. You already know Miss Rowlings. Is Ronald about? I'd like a word.'

'I didn't hear because I was upstairs packing,' Nan replied. 'We're going away tomorrow.'

'So I understand. We'd just like a quick word before you go.'

'Ronald's in the boathouse. He's taking the engine off his motorboat. He doesn't want anyone messing with it while we're away. The doors on the boathouse are long gone.' She motioned them to sit on a comfortable-looking sofa. 'I'll just give him a shout.'

A few minutes later, a flustered-looking Ronald Parkin walked into the lounge, wiping his oily hands on a piece of rag. 'I won't offer to shake hands. Mine are a bit greasy,' he said with a forced smile.

Bodkin smiled in acknowledgment. 'We'd like a word with you both regarding Effie Watkins,' he said.

Parkin sat down on a grey-coloured armchair on the opposite

side of an oval-shaped coffee table and leaned forward, his hands clasping and unclasping continually. 'Nan will be here in a moment. She's just making tea. There are some cheese sandwiches if you fancy one, too.'

'I'll give her a hand,' Amy said, as she got quickly to her feet.

Out in the kitchen, Amy found Nan pouring water into the teapot. The folded napkin was still on the tray, along with two extra cups and saucers.

'Do you need a hand?' Amy asked brightly.

'You could pass me the milk, if you don't mind. It's in that top cupboard over there.' She pointed to a wall cabinet on the back wall of the kitchen. By the time Amy had taken the bottle out and turned back to her, the napkin was unfolded and Nan was slipping something into the drawer at the side of the sink.

As Nan put the top onto the teapot, Amy pointed to the tin of cyanide on the windowsill. 'That's something you don't see in a kitchen every day of the week,' she said.

'Oh, goodness,' Nan replied. 'I'd forgotten that was there. Ronald has been baiting traps. We have a big rat problem here being so close to the river.' She picked up the tin and slid it in onto the bottom shelf of a tall cupboard. 'He's always leaving things lying around.' She picked up the tray of sandwiches and passed it to Amy. 'If you could take that in, my dear, I'll bring the tea things.'

Amy carried the tray through to the lounge and set it down on the coffee table, giving Bodkin a wide-eyed look as she turned around to sit down on the sofa again.

Nan Parkin placed her tea tray next to it a few seconds later, then sat herself down on the arm of Ronald's chair. 'So, what's all this about?' she asked.

'As I was just explaining to your husband. We have a few questions to ask regarding Effie Watkins.'

'We hardly knew the girl,' Nan said, leaning forward to pick up a small plate from the tray. She picked up two of the sandwiches and put them on the plate before placing it on the table in front of her husband. 'Can I tempt you?' she asked, smiling thinly at Amy.

'No thanks, we had breakfast in the café in Highwater before we drove up,' Amy said.

'Tea then?'

'Not for us, thanks, but don't let us stop you,' Bodkin said.

'I'll just let it brew for a bit longer,' Nan said, putting a sandwich on a plate for herself.

'Effie Watkins?' Bodkin said, reminding them of his question.

Ronald was about to speak, but Nan cut in before he had the chance. 'As I said, we hardly knew the girl. We spoke now and then at some function or other, but we kept our distance in the main. It was obvious what kind of woman she was.'

'What kind of woman would that be?' Bodkin asked.

'Man mad, to put it bluntly. I don't know what she got up to before she moved up here, but it wouldn't surprise me if I learned that she spent most of her time on her back.'

Bodkin scratched the back of his head. 'You think she was a prostitute, then?'

'I don't like to speak ill of the dead, but I think the evidence was there. She used her charms to earn a living. I can't see what the difference is.'

'That's rather uncharitable, Nan,' Ronald said. He reached towards his plate, then decided to leave it and patted his wife on the knee instead.

'Have you been out in your speedboat recently, Mr Parkin?' Bodkin asked.

'Not recently. It's got a bit of a problem with the propeller.'

'What would you call, not recently? A few weeks? Months perhaps?'

'Oh, it must be months,' Nan said, answering for her husband.

She looked sideways at him. 'It would have been Easter time. Is that right?'

Ronald nodded but said nothing.

'So if I were to have a look, there wouldn't be any green stuff wrapped around the propellor? No torn reeds, for instance?'

Ronald cleared his throat. 'I don't think so... there shouldn't be... though I did fire it up and let it run for a while so I could try to figure out how bad the damage was before winching it out of the water.'

Bodkin nodded slowly. 'I understand. Now, changing the subject. When was the last time either of you saw Effie?'

Nan raised her eyebrows as she thought. 'It would have been the week before she was found. I can't recall seeing her after that, can you, Ronald?' She shot him a quick glance before concentrating on her sandwich plate.

Ronald merely shrugged. 'I honestly can't remember.'

'Did Effie Watkins make a telephone call to you on Saturday the twenty-second of July? It would have been around four forty-five in the afternoon?'

Nan shook her head. 'No. She didn't ring here. Most of our calls go to the surgery. We don't get many private calls at home, so I'd remember.'

'And, as Effie wasn't a patient of yours, you wouldn't have seen her at the surgery either?'

'No,' Ronald said quietly.

'Did Edith give you a call to warn you that we were on our way?' Bodkin asked.

'She did mention that you wanted to speak to us,' Nan said. 'We'll be having a word with your superior officer about the way you took it upon yourself to break into the surgery. You can count on that.'

Amy and Bodkin exchanged glances. 'We didn't break in, Mrs Parkin. We were provided with a key.'

'You didn't have our permission, so to me, that's still breaking in.'

Bodkin ignored her protestations. 'I believe you had an accident with a bottle of chloroform a couple of weeks ago?'

'How on earth did you know about that?'

'And you had to order up a fresh bottle a couple of days later?'

'So, what if I did?' Nan said. 'It needed replacing. We have to have a good stock of the stuff.'

'Indeed,' Bodkin said, smoothly. 'What happened to the original bottle?'

'Ronald dropped it. Luckily, it was outside, next to the car. It could have been nasty if it had happened inside.'

'Heaven forbid' Bodkin replied. He smiled at her. 'Did you manage to stick the broken bottle back together again? Only I found it on the shelf next to the replacement only an hour ago.'

Ronald stuck his head in his hands. 'Nan,' he said.

'That's an old bottle it's—'

'It's got the date it was issued written on the label,' Bodkin said. He was silent for a moment as he let it sink in. 'Amy found something else, too. Something that really can't be explained away so easily. She found Effie's handbag hidden away in a cupboard. Now, how did that get there if she's never been in your surgery?'

'I must have found... That's right. I found it on the green. I took it into the surgery to look after it until I could tell her where it was, but of course I never got that chance.'

'Nan,' Ronald said again. 'Don't. It's time the truth came out.'

Nan closed her eyes. 'Shut up, Ronald,' she hissed.

'I can't live with it, Nan. I'm sorry.'

Nan suddenly became very calm. She leaned forward and poured tea into two of the cups. After adding milk, she handed one to her husband, then picked up her own. She stared into the swirling liquid for a long moment, then, after taking a deep breath, she turned to her husband. 'Drink up, Ronald. It's getting cold.' She waited until he had taken a drink before downing hers in one long swig.

'They can't hurt us now, my darling,' she said, reaching down to put her hand on his thigh. 'Goodbye, Ronald. I love you.'

'What do you mean goodbye? Nan, what have you done?'

'She thinks she's just poisoned you with cyanide,' Bodkin said. 'But she's mistaken. I emptied the syringe and replaced the poison with water.' He pointed at the teapot. 'That might be why it became tepid so quickly.'

Nan suddenly leapt to her feet. Grabbing a knife from a pot of pickled spread on the sandwich tray, she waved it at Bodkin. 'Get away from us or I swear I'll kill you.'

Bodkin was unperturbed. 'That's a butter knife, Nan. What are you going to do with it? Spread us to death?'

The inspector got to his feet and held out his hand for the knife. Finally defeated, Nan meekly passed it to him, then sat down on the arm of the chair again. 'Will they hang us?' she asked.

# CHAPTER FORTY-SEVEN

'How did you catch us out?' Ronald asked after a long period of silence.

'Amy worked it out as she usually does. She's good at this sort of thing.'

'How? We didn't think we'd left any traces.'

'None of the evidence really pointed towards you, to be honest,' Amy said. 'It was all down to timing in the end.'

Bodkin clapped his hands together. 'Right, let's have the whole story.' He looked from Nan to Ronald. 'Who wants to tell it?'

Nan put her hands on her lap and studied them for a few seconds. 'I killed her. Ronald had nothing to do with it... the murder, that is.'

Amy opened her mouth to speak, but Bodkin put his hand on her knee to silence her.

'I'm the one to blame,' Ronald said, holding up his hand like a schoolboy ready to answer a question in class. 'Nan might have done it, but it was all my fault at the end of the day.'

'You were having an affair with Effie, I take it?' Bodkin said.

Ronald nodded. 'Affair is pushing it a bit. We only did it the once.'

'She led him on,' Nan spat. 'She was always leading men on. Ronald was never unfaithful to me until that... creature came along. Oh, he'd flirt with women. He'd feel them up on the dance floor just like he did with that trollop of a friend you brought with you to the ball, but that's as far as it went. He knew I was there, watching him. He just needed to feel that he could attract women... young women.' Nan patted Ronald's leg. 'He rescued me, you know? There's never been anyone else for me.'

'He rescued you? How did that happen?' Amy asked.

'I grew up in quite a well-to-do family down in Sevenoaks,' Nan said. 'My father was a businessman, but he was involved in some sort of financial scandal and we became pariahs. A lot of people lost money, and no one wanted to know us after that.' She smiled at her husband. 'But Ronald didn't care. He asked me to dance at a wedding when no one else would come near me. I fell in love with him there and then and we were married inside six months. Sadly, we weren't able to have children, but we had each other and that was enough for both of us. We moved up here when the practice became available and we've been here ever since. We joined the Boat Club just after we bought this house and we made some very good friends. My family scandal never came up, or if anyone did know, they kept it to themselves. We've been very happy here. As I said, Ronald needed an ego boost now and again and he got that through flirting with pretty women. They knew what he was all about and everyone put up with it with good grace.' Nan's face hardened. 'Until that... bloody woman turned up. She egged him on, encouraged him to go that bit further, then she'd ignore him for the next few weeks while she went gallivanting around with the wealthy. When she tired of them or ran out of money, she'd cosy up to Ronald again, but nothing happened between them.'

‘When did it get to the stage that something did happen?’ Bodkin asked.

Ronald sighed. ‘I was weak, so weak.’

Nan took a deep breath. ‘It was at the last dance before the ball. She was flirting with everyone, as usual. Ronald had had a few too many and when she whispered sweet nothings in his ear while they were dancing, he fell for it hook, line and sinker. She promised to meet him if he could find somewhere they wouldn’t be caught. Ronald suggested the surgery after hours. Providing it happened before Hoskin’s opened, no one would ever know. I think Ronald expected her to call him at the surgery, but she didn’t. She got our telephone number from someone and, true to her bitchy character, she rang him at home.’

Nan paused as she gathered her thoughts. ‘I thought it was a bit odd when Ronald said he’d had a call from a patient who needed urgent treatment. I offered to go with him. I’m his assistant after all, but he came out with some cock and bull story about someone having something stuck between their front teeth and they were in a lot of pain, but he could easily manage the job alone. Anyway, I watched him drive off in the Alvis, then I pulled on my boots and followed him on foot. I saw the car parked at the rear of the complex and let myself in the back door with the keys I keep for emergencies. We have a set on reception, but Ronald had lost his set twice before, so I got another set made just in case. The radio was blaring out when I arrived. I couldn’t see them anywhere. Then I saw her arm hanging over the side of the dentist’s chair. I edged up closer and that’s when I truly found out what sort of a woman she was.’

Nan closed her eyes as if reliving the experience.

‘Her underwear was strewn all over the floor. All she had on was her stockings, and they were round her knees. She was calling something out to him. Asking him to come back and service her again, I suppose. I’m not sure because the radio was so loud. Anyway, I suddenly felt anger raging inside me. Ronald was mine. What right had this harlot to try to take him away from me? I turned around and saw the chloroform bottle on top of the cabinet. I grabbed a thin cloth and turned back to the chair. She was lying there, the recliner pushed right back. She had her eyes closed as she pretended to conduct the radio orchestra. I just leaned over, put the cotton cloth over her face and poured the chloroform down her throat. She only struggled for thirty seconds. It was easy.'

'That explains why there was so much left in her system after she died,' Bodkin said. 'That was a bit of a puzzle, even for the experts.'

'Ronald come back in from the lavatory a few minutes later, fastening his trousers up. He was shocked when he saw what I had done to her, but then he showed his true colours and after we'd cried together for a while, he said he'd help me get rid of the body. I helped him get her dressed. That was the hardest part of all, but we managed to make her look decent after a few attempts. Honestly, you wouldn't have known anything was wrong with her, apart from the look of surprise she had on her face. Ronald wanted to close her eyes, so she looked more peaceful, but I was still angry with her and I wouldn't let him. I stood out by the car keeping watch and Ronald carried her down and put her in the back seat. Then we turned off the lights, locked up and drove home.'

'What did you do with her when you got back here?'

'We left her in the car while we thought about what to do with her,' Ronald said, adding something to the story for the first time. 'We couldn't leave her in the trees at the side of the track. We get a lot of dog walkers up here and one of the animals would have sniffed her out. In the end we decided to put her in the boat and dump her body somewhere downstream. There's a wood down towards Chatham and I was going to put her in there. I got up at dawn on the Sunday, carried her to the boat and laid her on the floor. Nan wanted to come with me, but I didn't want anyone to see two people in the boat if I was spotted. Someone might put two and two together and think the woman was Effie, alive and well, sitting in a boat with me. Anyway, what's the saying, the best laid plans and all that? When I got to the Silverstream, I could see a rowing boat on the water down by the park. There were two fishermen in it. I couldn't possibly risk passing them in case they saw what was in the bottom of the boat. I thought about just dumping her over the side, but the current might have taken her towards them, so I hit on the idea of leaving her in the reed beds. I thought she'd be safe. Possibly until winter, maybe forever. I had no idea that the local kids gather blooming bull-rushes in there.'

'What about the bag?'

'I found it under the chair on the Monday morning. It must have been kicked underneath in the struggle. Nan didn't feel up to going in to work after what had happened and I knew it was a very distinctive bag. So I hid it in the box in the cupboard. I figured that it would be safe in there. If her body wasn't discovered, and the bag wasn't found, I thought that everyone would just think that she'd moved on.'

Bodkin got to his feet. 'Thank you for being so candid. Could you both please stand up?' He turned first to Nan. 'Annette Parkin. I am arresting you for the murder of Effie Watkins.'

Nan's head dropped. 'I'm so sorry, Ronald. I did it for us.'

Bodkin turned to Ronald. 'Ronald Parkin. I am arresting you for aiding and abetting the murder of Effie Watkins and of illegally disposing of her body.' Finally, he turned to Amy. 'Could you use the Parkin's telephone to call the station? Tell them we need two empty cells.'

CHAPTER

# FORTY-EIGHT

'Hi Mum, hi Dad. I hope you had a lovely time.' Amy waved to her parents as they walked out from the station carrying their cases.

Bodkin opened the boot of the Morris and helped James Rowlings deposit them inside.

'It's very kind of you to give us a lift, Bodkin,' Elizabeth Rowlings said, patting him softly on the arm.

Bodkin grinned as he opened the back door to let her climb into the car. 'I'm not the one giving you a lift.' He nodded his head towards Amy. 'She is.'

Amy's father looked shocked as Amy climbed into the driver's seat, but her mother couldn't remove the look of pride from her face. 'Oh, look at our Amy, Dad. She's behind the wheel.'

Amy grinned as she pulled away from the kerb and turned onto Main Street so smoothly that anyone would have thought she'd been driving for years. Mr Rowlings pursed his lips and smiled to himself. 'Well done, Amy, but the answer to your next question will get the same reply I give you when you repeatedly ask me to go onto the telephone network. No, I am not going to buy a car.'

'Have you had a nice, quiet, restful holiday, Amy?' her mother asked as she watched Bodkin carry her case upstairs.

*Well, if you count finding a dead girl on the first day, having a bust up with the man you love, helping spirit away a troubled young family, paddling in the Silverstream with your skirt tucked into your knickers, being bundled into a car on a drunken night out, placing a man's hand on your bare breast, letting a man sleep in your bed while you are lying a few feet away with images in your head that would embarrass a street girl? Apart from all that?*

'Oh, you know, the usual,' Amy replied as she followed her into the living room. 'Have a sit down. You must be tired after your journey. I'll put the kettle on.'

Half an hour later, Amy's father was sat in his favourite chair with the evening newspaper in his hands and his cup and saucer on the small table at his side. He turned the paper around so that his wife could read the headline.

MURDERERS CAUGHT! MARRIED COUPLE ADMIT TO KILLING EFFIE

'Were you responsible for bringing the killers to justice, Bodkin?' he asked.

Bodkin nodded. 'I played a small part.' He looked across the table at Amy. 'But I had a lot of help.'

A short while later, after promising to introduce his sister to the Rowlings the next morning, Bodkin left the cottage and drove back to his apartment where he had agreed to meet Sal. Amy had told him that she'd get the seven o'clock bus and meet them before going over to the Bell, where they were due to meet Ferris and Lesley. After having a quick bath, she got dressed, applied a little makeup and her favourite Vermillion lipstick before going back downstairs to sit with her parents for a few minutes.

'Will Bodkin's sister be coming to church with us in the morning?' Mr Rowlings asked as he put down his paper and smiled fondly at his daughter. 'You look lovely, by the way.'

'Sal isn't really religious, Dad,' Amy replied. 'But don't hold that against her. She's a lovely woman and does so much to help poor families and abused children.'

'She takes after Bodkin in that regard, then,' her father said. 'I wish he'd give God a chance.'

'There are reasons behind their choice, Dad. I know what they are, but it's up to them to explain why they feel like they do; it's not my decision.' She got to her feet, brushed down her candy striped dress, picked up her bag and after giving her mum a hug and planting a kiss on her father's cheek, she walked to the living room door. 'Sal calls Bodkin, Gee by the way. Please don't ask why, it's a personal thing.'

At seven, Amy caught the bus to Middle Street, got off by the chip shop and walked back down the hill until she got to Bluecoat House, where Bodkin lived in his rented police flat. She rang the bell twice and stuck out her tongue at Trixie when the blonde bombshell opened the door of her own apartment and scowled at her through the plate-glass window. Thinking that she could hear faint voices, she turned away from the front of the building and made her way along the tarmacked path until she reached the waste ground on the far side of the parking bays. Bodkin and Sal were standing side by side as they watched a large brown armchair catch light in front of them. Amy opened the paling gate and stepped onto the grassy area that had been earmarked by the council for further building, but then stopped still as she watched the siblings whispering together. Turning around, she walked back through the gate and closed it behind her. As the latch clicked, Bodkin turned and looked towards her. Amy smiled and held up her hands as if to say she was sorry for disturbing them. Bodkin raised a hand and beckoned her towards him, but Amy shook her head and pointed down the road to where the Bell Inn was situated. Miming taking a drink, she smiled again and as Bodkin put his arm back around his sister's shoulders, she walked away, smiling to herself.

When she reached the Bell, Amy walked around the side of the building, opened a timber gate and let herself into the beer garden where they had arranged to meet up with Ferris and Lesley. There were a dozen tables in the yard, but only two of them were occupied. Amy picked a table near the back steps of the pub and sat down on the bench seat to wait.

Fifteen minutes later a thickset man with a few days of stubble on his chin, wearing a clean, but tatty looking striped shirt and baggy pair of black trousers held up by a wide, leather belt, walked down the steps from the pub and sauntered across towards her. He placed both broad-fingered hands on the table and glared at her.

'Amy Rowlings. Yes, I know who you are. I've been keeping my eye out for you.'

'Why?' Amy asked with a slight tremor in her voice.

'Why? Because you're responsible for breaking up my family.'

Amy groaned inwardly but said nothing.

'You aren't going to try to deny it, then? Beryl said that you would.'

'Beryl thinks she knows everything, but she knows nothing of any value,' Amy replied, with more strength in her voice than she was feeling.

'Well, that's where you are wrong. Her information was of the greatest value. Beryl is a family friend. She also knows which side her bread is buttered.' Marty stood up as a woman came out of the pub and walked past them on her way to the toilet block at the back end of the yard.

'Me and you are going to have a talk,' Marty said. 'And you are going to tell me where Kath and the kids have disappeared to.'

'I'm not telling you anything, so you're wasting your time,'

Amy said. 'And don't think you can threaten me here. There are witnesses.'

'Do you think I'm that stupid, Amy Rowlings?' He leaned towards her, getting so close that she could smell the stale beer and tobacco on his breath. 'I know where you live. I know where you work. I know exactly where to find you. And, the next time we meet, you'll tell me what I want to know or you'll get some of what Kathleen got.'

He straightened up as he heard the back gate click. 'I'll look forward to that,' he said, then, turning away, he headed for the gents.

'Who was that?' Bodkin asked an ashen faced Amy as he stepped towards her. 'Was he bothering you?'

Amy took a quick look towards the back of the yard, her hands still shaking. 'It was Marty, Bodkin, Kathleen O'Toole's boyfriend. He... he says he's going to hurt me if I don't tell him where she is.'

Bodkin's face turned to stone. Turning on his heel, he stormed across the toilet block and as Marty stepped out of the door; the policeman pushed him in the chest with so much force that it sent him flying back towards the urinals.

Sal sat down next to Amy and tried to comfort her. 'Don't fret, Amy. Gee will sort this out.'

There was the sound of an extended scuffle and a few loud cries of pain. Then, three minutes later, Bodkin walked out of the toilets, rubbing the knuckles of his right hand. A couple of minutes after that, Ferris walked into the yard.

'What's happening?' he asked as he saw Bodkin looking back towards the toilets.

'Nothing,' Bodkin said innocently as a doubled up Marty, one arm hanging limply at his side, the other clutching his ribs, staggered out of the lavatory. Holding his hand up as a mark of submission, he skirted the figure of Bodkin and shuffled towards the back gate.

Bodkin stepped forward and opened it for him. 'Remember me, Marty, and remember what just happened, because if I ever hear that you have so much as mentioned Amy's name, or if I hear that you've hurt another young child, the punishment you got tonight will seem like a playful slap compared to what will happen to you. Do I make myself clear?'

Marty mumbled something incoherently through his bloodied mouth and almost fell out of the yard.

An hour later, the music started as the band in the main bar started their routine. Ferris got to his feet and began to mime the song whilst moving his body in time to the rhythm.

'I'm so sorry that Lesley stood you up, Ferris,' Sal said as she picked up her half pint of beer.

'She must have found out that I'm a copper,' Ferris said. 'I can't think of any other reason she would have done it. She was mad keen when I first asked her and she was still the same when I called her yesterday.'

'Well, if she's that fickle, then you're better off without her,' Sal replied.

'It would have been nice to have someone to dance with, though,' Ferris said sadly.

Sal got quickly to her feet and, after taking a large gulp of her beer, she slipped her arm through Ferris's. 'I'll dance with you,' she said and, laughing together, the pair walked up the steps and through the open back door of the pub.

'Fer–' Bodkin's shout stuck in his throat as Amy scowled at him and slapped him on the back of his hand.

'You're doing it again, Bodkin,' she said. 'Don't you ever learn your lesson? Sal can make up her own mind about who she wants to dance with. It doesn't matter if it's Ferris or any other man in there.'

Bodkin sighed. 'You're right. Of course you're right. I can't protect her forever.'

'She doesn't need protecting, Bodkin. She's not a little girl anymore.'

'It's just habit,' Bodkin replied. 'We were discussing that very subject as we watched Dad's chair turn to ashes. We've put the past behind us. We're only looking forward now.'

Amy put her hand softly on his. 'You were there for me earlier. My Bodkin, my knight in shining armour is always there when I need him.' She reached out a hand and softly stroked his cheek. 'But I won't always be a damsel in distress. There will be times when I'm in a mess of my own making and I'll find my own way out of it. So will Sal. You don't always have to come galloping over the hill on your white charger.'

She pulled her hand away, and Bodkin nodded slowly. 'I'll cotton on, eventually,' he said.

Amy took a sip of her drink and smiled at him.

'Sal asked me a question tonight,' Bodkin said. 'She wanted to know why I hadn't asked you to marry me yet.'

'Sal can join the club set up by Alice and my mother,' Amy said, grinning. 'What did you say?'

'I told her I hadn't asked because I know you would turn me down. You aren't ready for marriage yet.' Bodkin reached out and took hold of both her hands. 'But...' He looked across the table and held her eyes with his. 'One day, you will be ready and I'll be here waiting.'

Amy's eyes shone as she lifted his hand to her lips and kissed his bruised knuckle.

'One day, Bodkin. One day, I will be ready, and there will only be one answer on my lips.'

# ALSO BY T. A. BELSHAW

## AMY ROWLINGS SERIES

***MURDER AT THE MILL***

***DEATH AT THE LYCHGATE***

***THE MURDER AWARDS***

Printed in Great Britain
by Amazon

42214664R00233